A Slippage in Time

A Novel by Michael Putzer

D1570210

© 2011 Michael Putzer
All Rights Reserved.

No part of this publication may be reproduced, stored in a retrieval system, or transmitted, in any form or by any means, electronic, mechanical, photocopying, recording, or otherwise, without the written permission of the author.

First published by Dog Ear Publishing
4010 W. 86th Street, Ste H
Indianapolis, IN 46268
www.dogearpublishing.net

ISBN: 978-145750-608-6

This book is printed on acid-free paper.

This book is a work of fiction. While, as in all fiction, the literary perceptions and insights are based on experience, all characters, places, names, events and incidents are the product of the author's imagination or are used fictitiously. Any resemblance to actual persons, living or dead, business, establishments, churches, events or similarities to actual event, locales or real persons living or dead are coincidental.

Printed in the United States of America

Also By Michael Putzer

A Winter's Rage
The Church

Prologue

February 1975

Carol Flood loved cross-country skiing. Her favorite place to ski was the Koskin Wilderness Ski Trail that wound its way through the hill country not far from Lake Superior on what used to be old Indian land.

On this day in 1975 the trail conditions were just right as she signed in at the warming shack just after one in the afternoon. Signing in was just a safety check. The sign-in book was checked each night around five and in all the years it had been in use, there had never been any serious problems. An occasional problem arose when people failed to sign out after completing the twenty-mile loop.

It was a partly cloudy twenty-degree day in February with a hint of possible lake effect snow showers, when Carol put on her skis preparing to make the twenty mile loop. For Carol there was no better way to unwind. The experience was always energizing. Here she was able to put aside all the cares of her busy world.

Like always, she was thrilled by the shear vastness of the unspoiled land. Her thoughts embrace the solitude of the openness of the cross-country ski trail. Light snowflakes from the Lake winds begin to speckle the sleeves of her Colombia ski jacket as she became one with the countryside. As she skis by a large granite outcropping, she was not aware of the young couple at the small wayside rest area.

After seeing the woman ski by they followed about a hundred yards behind her and they marvel at how smoothly she navigated the trail making it seem so effortless. Then suddenly the couple saw her vanish not more than a hundred yards ahead of them, right before their eyes on a level open area. The man cried out, "Where'd she go? It's as if she fell into a large snow drift."

The woman puzzled by the sudden disappearance said in reply. "Let's hurry she could be hurt and in trouble."

Upon reaching the spot where they saw her vanish there was nothing. They stare up and down the groomed trail as far as the eye could see and there were no signs of her. There were no indentations in the snowdrifts or on the trail. The trail was smooth and firm where they thought they had seen her vanish.

Letting their eyes search the distance ahead once more, they were positive that she could not have skied out of sight or off the trail. The trail here was flat and open with good visibility in all directions.

Alarmed the couple made a thorough search of the area one more time, finding nothing.

"Could she have skied off the trail?" said the man.

"There are no tracks anywhere. There is no sign of her. No, ski poles, nothing. She just vanished in front of our eyes. Let's go back and report what we saw. Maybe someone knows her name and can call her."

Once back at the warming shack they use the emergency phone to file a report with the local game warden and he immediately knew who she was. "Sounds like Carol Flood she's always skis this trail alone. I told her to be careful and ski with someone, but she usually is alone. She is very experienced and I doubt that anything happened to her. Perhaps she was faster than you thought and she just skied out of sight. I'll give her a call."

"The only problem is that as we continued on we did not see any ski tracks in the light new snow."

* * *

After repeated phone calls failed to locate Carol Flood, they searched until nightfall with no sign of her. The next day a more extensive search was made expanding the search area with the aid of snowmobiles and still there were no signs of her.

The searches continued for the next few weeks until a huge snowstorm dropped more than two feet of snow making any further searching impossible. The searches were called off until spring and Carol Flood was officially listed as missing.

When spring came, the search was renewed with cadaver dogs and still not a single trace of Carol Flood was ever found. In addition to not finding a body, no clothing, no skis or poles were found.

Year after year people continued to search the trail and the nearby area and nothing was ever found. To this day, her disappearance remains a mystery.

2009

Chapter One

November 25-27, 2009 (Thanksgiving Weekend)

Nancy Monroe impatiently stared out the windshield of her Subaru Outback waiting for her three girlfriends to finish loading their suitcases and skis. The late November sunshine made her shoulder length blonde hair shine. She was small: five-four, a hundred ten pounds, shapely, but not physically imposing. She was however, attractive enough that both men and women more than often gave her a second glance. While quite and unassuming by nature, she was not timid and in her high school classroom, all of her students knew that she was in charge.

She was anxious to get started on their four-day holiday weekend over the Thanksgiving recess. It was already four in the afternoon and it was at least a four-hour drive from Appleton, Wisconsin to Hurley which was still in Wisconsin, but right on the Michigan border. All four were teachers in Appleton and this was their first time away since the school year began back in August. They had booked a non-refundable cabin reservation months ago in Montreal, Wisconsin. It was an old company-mining town in the heart of the "Snow Belt" and at the time of the booking, the agent had assured them that all of the ski hills in Wisconsin and the Upper Peninsula of Michigan would be open. He said they always had snow by Thanksgiving. Now it did not seem like such a good idea because of the unseasonable warm weather. With the reservation made all planned to make the best of the situation, if nothing else it would be time away.

On the drive up highway 51 Joan, Nancy's best friend, shared some of the facts she was able to learn about the area from the internet. "Did you know that Hurley and the surrounding little settlements were established around mining and logging in the late 1880's? Hurley was named after Glen Hurley who had won a lawsuit and rather than take a fee he asked that the town be named after him. It was a wild town and almost anything went.

There was illegal gambling, prostitution and it was a hang out for some of the prohibition gangsters in the 1930's. Even now, it's known as a place to have a good time.

One thing of real interest was a large hotel built there in 1884 called the Burton House. The hotel was ultra modern for that time. It was four stories and had over 100 rooms. Even one of the presidents stayed there. It burned down in 1948.

Now listen to this, the annual snowfall is more than 200 inches a year. Fact is that while snow always used to arrive before Thanksgiving it has been arriving later over the past ten years and may not come at all this year because we are coming. Back in the late ninety's the area had frequently received over three hundred inches of snow. Now some of the locals are even beginning to believe in global warming."

Joan continued to babble on about the area even though the others had fallen asleep except of course for Nancy. Finally, just before nine they arrived at the four-way stop marking Hurley's main intersection. Joan informed Nancy that if she turned right that was where the city's nightlife was centered. Nancy—tired—paid no attention to Joan as she made the left-hand turn onto Highway 77 heading for Montreal. At the four-way stop just before leaving the city, Nancy's eyes were drawn to the small café on her right. Looking at the building she was suddenly struck by a feeling of dejavu. She knew she had never been to Hurley before, but she was sure she knew what the café looked like inside. Pictures of Elvis Presley flashed across her mind leaving her with a feeling of fear and apprehension. Pulling away from the four-way stop she quickly dismissed the thought. She was here to have a good time.

* * *

Nancy had never heard of a Montreal, Wisconsin until she booked the cabin. Even in the dark, she was surprise to find that nearly all the houses on the town's gently curving main street looked the same. Nearly all were painted white. Then she remembered that the agent told her that Montreal at one time was a company-mining town with over a hundred neat white frame two-story houses. He said it was the only planned mining company town in Wisconsin designed in 1921. Nancy wondered how Joan had forgotten to pass along that fact or perhaps she was just too tired to relay the information.

Upon arrival, all agreed that while there was no snow the house was well worth the price and they were not disappointed. There were four bedrooms and a spacious living room and dining room. All settled in to have a drink and talked for hours. Shortly after two in the morning, they went to bed.

Nancy had more than enough to drink and felt guilty leaving her boyfriend—soon to be fiancés—back in Appleton working this weekend at the hospital. Michael Niffen was a medical technologist and she was sure he was going to give her a ring for Christmas. In many respects she was about as happy as she could ever remember. Everything was going her way and all her dreams were soon to come true or so she thought.

* * *

Thanksgiving morning arrived cold and bright, but without a trace of snow. The region had received eight inches of snow the first week of November, but that had all melted with mild temperatures in the forties. After cooking breakfast for themselves, they called around and found a local golf course country clubhouse in Michigan serving a complete turkey dinner. On the way into Hurley, they passed the vast tailing piles that stood like pyramids as a testament to the area's iron mining days.

After dinner, they went to a few bars on Silver Street and watched the end of the Green Bay Packer football game. All four were Packer fans from the Fox River Valley area and Nancy's father had season tickets from the early beginning of the franchise. Now that her father had passed away, the tickets were hers. She used them whenever she could but had no problem selling them. Packer tickets were always in demand. One bar led to another and it was well after midnight when they arrive back at the miner's house in Montréal.

That night as Nancy went to bed, she thought about Michael. This time she had a funny feeling that something was going to happen to ruin her happiness. She quickly chastised herself saying, "It's not going to happen. Michael loves me." What bothered her the most was that in the past when she really wanted something so badly, it had a way of not coming true. Something always came up to change things. She admonished herself again and as she fell asleep, she whispered, "Nothing is going to stop me from having Michael. I know he loves me and this time nothing is going to stop me from being happy. I won't let it happen." She had no idea of what was to befall her on Friday.

* * *

Having had far too much to drink the night before they slept excessively late and all agreed that even without the snow, they were having a great time just happy to be away from the city and teaching. Nancy woke admitting to herself that she too was having a good time despite the fact that Michael was not here. She dismissed last night's negative thoughts.

Not wanting to cook, the group packed into the car to have breakfast in town. They were on vacation so why should they cook. Nancy suggested that they try that small café they passed on Wednesday night on the way out of Hurley. The one that Nancy was sure had pictures of Elvis Presley. She had no way of knowing that her perceived fears of the café were about to reoccur in a way she could never have imagined.

Chapter Two

November 26-27, 2009
(Thanksgiving Day and the Friday After)

Robert Rahn went to bed Thanksgiving night—after letting Albert his three-year-old Airedale outside—hopeful that perhaps tonight he would have a dream-free sleep. He purchased Albert after his release from the sanitarium. He needed a companion and Albert was all of that and more. Airedales have a great sense of humor and Albert had more than his share. It had been just what Robert had needed. The dog proved to be a unique and entertaining companion. Being in the country Albert was also free to use his hunting instincts.

For the past three years, Robert still had the same reoccurring dream or nightmare on and off. It was more like an unpleasant dream rather than a full-blown nightmare since it came to him so often. It was always the same.

His psychiatrist, Dr. Ruth Aspen, had warned him to expect dreams like this to reoccur and that perhaps he would always have them, but the frequency would dwindle with the passing of time. Now nearly three years after resigning his job as broker on Wall Street in New York City and moving to Northern Wisconsin he still had the dreams only they were dwindling in frequency.

The dream was always the same with a policeman coming to his New York apartment telling that him that his wife and six year old daughter had been murdered in a mass shooting at a local neighborhood pizza restaurant where his wife Debra had taken their daughter Jenny to a friend's birthday party. The police officer repeated the same thing in every dream. How they were sorry for his loss and I know this is a bad time, but could you please come down to the morgue and identify the bodies.

Robert would usually wake up remembering how he went to the morgue and how he saw the bodies and made the identification. That was in September of 2006. From there he was never sure of how he had managed to get through the funerals and everything that followed. Had it not been for his good friend and associate from the firm, Ken Olson, he would never have made it. Robert had very few relatives, as he was an only child. His wife had fewer relatives so arranging the funeral was not complicated.

Immediately after the funerals, he prayed for an answer to that unanswerable question, "Why did God allow unimaginable bad things like this to happen?" He was not the first man to ask this question. It was the question asked thousands and thousands of times—perhaps even millions—by people who lost love ones tragically.

No matter how much he searched, he could no find an answer. If only there had been a plausible explanation for the shooting perhaps that might have allowed him to rationalize what had happened.

Robert's local parish priest told him after the funerals that God never meant us to escape difficult times, but rather he gives his grace to persevere. The priest went on to say that while we are hard pressed, we are not crushed. We may be perplexed, but not in despair. We are persecuted, but not abandoned. We are struck down, but not destroyed. However, the reality for Robert was that he was crushed, he was in despair, he felt abandoned by God and he felt destroyed. None of the words that people spoke could change the way he felt. Debra and Jenny were still dead. He wanted to die. He just wanted the pain and the agony to end.

While politely listening to their council he could only ask himself the same question, why did God let this happen and where was He during all of this violence, killing and injustice. His wife and daughter were innocent that day. There was no evil or malice in their hearts and God allowed this gunman to take their lives.

Robert thought back to how by the end of September, he found himself sliding down into a black hole of despair and he knew there was nothing he could do to stop it. It just took him down further each day and he realized that before he could ever hope to recover he had to hit bottom. While suicide was a possibility, it was repulsive to him because of his Catholic faith. That did not stop him from hoping that someone would push him in front of a train on the subway platform or perhaps lightening would strike him dead. He did not care how he died, only that it would happen soon and end his misery. No drugs or amount of bourbon could diminish the memory of what had happened. A lone gunman had entered the restaurant and started shooting.

The total rampage lasted only fifteen minutes. The man was a fired postal worker who walked into the pizza restaurant and began shooting. Armed with two unregistered handguns he had purchased from a gun show he killed five people and wounded seven others before being killed by police. In all the death count was low at five compared to other similar shootings, but that was of little consolation to Robert. He only knew that two out of the five were the most important people in his world and nothing would ever be the same.

Finally, at the lowest point of despair Robert found his way to the office of a Psychiatrist friend he had known over the years and had used before when the stress of the New York financial industry had got to a point that he felt he could not handle it. The stress he felt back then seemed like nothing considering what he was going through now. Doctor Ruth Aspen was in her late fifties and was very good at what she did. After one initial session, she knew that Robert was in need of serious help. She thought of all the people she had seen over the years. Robert either was close to suicide or was just plain dying from depression, anxiety and stress. She could see that he did not care about living and truly wanted to die.

She checked him into a sanitarium in up state New York. After nearly three months of therapy, one night he had a dream where his daughter, Jenny, came to him saying, *"Daddy it was not your fault, you have to believe that. You had no way of knowing that bad man would be there that day. It's okay Daddy, don't be sad. Mommy and I are in heaven and you have to go on living your life so that you can join us someday. So please don't cry, Daddy.*

In the morning, he told Doctor Ruth that he was getting better and that he was sure that he wanted to live. In fact, he knew God wanted him to go on living. There are things that he still had to do, although he was not at all sure what God had in mind for him.

Thus after three months of treatment just before Christmas, Dr. Ruth released him. During the next few weeks of counseling, she told him that she thought he ought to get out of the financial business and think about relocating some where far away from the state of New York. It would be best if he could just forget about New York City. She knew money was not a problem.

He took her advice and setout to find a new place far away from New York City and anything that at all reminded him of what had happened here.

Shortly after that was when he contacted a large real state company and began researching different places to live and now here he was in Hurley, Wisconsin.

* * *

When he woke up on Friday morning, he was rested and pleased that he did not have the same reoccurring dream. Instead, he had a very different dream that was disturbing to him just the same. He dreamt of a young very attractive blonde woman who was in a state of panic and she appeared to be confined in a very unfamiliar place. She kept saying, "I don't belong here." The dream was so strange and befuddling that it disturbed and bothered him the rest of the day. He tried to figure out what had caused him to have such a dream and he could only think it was from all of the literature that he was reading about paranormal events.

Since early on in his life he had the ability to pick the winning side whether it was sports, politics or just local everyday issues. He was right most of the time. He had also learned to use this ability only when it mattered. There were times he even used it in the negative sense. He would bet against someone or something he knew was going to win. In this way, he was able to conceal his ability. This same ability made him millions. It started in grade school when he found out he could usually pick the winning team. He just knew which way things were going to go. After graduating from college with a degree in finance and marketing, he ventured out into the stock market to make his first million. Now at the age of 35 he was done with being a broker and banking. He had more money than he could ever spend. Since the death of Debra and Jenny he was trying to use his ability to see the future in ways that were not just about making money. That was what bothered him so about last night's dream. The woman in the dream appeared to be desperately in need of assistance. He felt that he had to find a way to help her, but he knew nothing about her. She was only a dream and perhaps she was not even real. Just someone he had read about in some of the paranormal research he was doing or someone he had seen on television.

Without knowing anything about her there was nothing he could do. He would just have to be vigilant in reading the newspapers and listening to the radio to see if there was any reference to a blond woman. He thought of it as a long shot and told himself that he was making too much out of the dream.

Chapter Three

November 27, 2009
(The Friday after Thanksgiving)

On the Friday after Thanksgiving, Michael Niffin had just finished his twelve-hour holiday weekend shift at the hospital where he was a medical technologist. He hated working the midnight to noon shift; it completely threw off his system. It was worse than jet lag. He was not one to sleep in the day and getting out of work at noon, sleeping was the last thing on his mind and today was no different. He had other things on his mind. He was soon going to be an engaged man. He had been single since college and had finally found the right girl. Nancy Monroe was everything he had been waiting for. He had met and dated other girls since leaving college but none seemed to measure up to his expectations until he met Nancy. She was attractive, intelligent and she knew what she wanted out of life. He admired the way she was dedicated to teaching high school. With the way teenagers were now days he felt you really had to be dedicated to the teaching profession with the lousy pay.

Leaving the Memorial Hospital parking lot, he had a feeling that something was not right, but he gave it no further thought and attributed it to being without Nancy. Now on his way to the jewelry store, where he was going to make his last payment on the ring, he felt sure that she knew he was planning to propose at Christmas. Then he was hoping they could get married over the summer vacation. He wanted to be her husband.

He hoped that she was having a good time up north in Hurley. It was good for her to get away. Having low seniority at the school, she did not always have a chance to get away on school recesses. It seemed she always had some sort of assignment—be it attendance at a basketball game or forensics—there was always something.

They had been dating for the past year and while he loved her dearly, he could not understand why she was reluctant to sleep with him. Now days everyone jumped into bed with one another. Hell, most of the teenagers she was teaching were no longer virgins and he was sure that her students would have been shocked if they had known that she was still a virgin. Even though she refused his advances, he admired her that she was willing to wait. In fact, he thought it was very unique that he was dating a virgin. Furthermore, they had their entire life ahead of them to get to know each other in intimate ways.

On the way home from the mall with the ring he once again found that he was uneasy. Could it be the fact that he was about to ask her to marry him and he was bothered by the fact that he would be loosing his freedom. Maybe he was getting cold feet or perhaps it was the thought of her saying no. He could not say why he felt this way, but he knew when she called that evening all those doubts would be dispelled. He knew that he loved her and she loved him, but he had no idea what awaited him when he got home.

Chapter Four

November 27, 2009
(The Friday after Thanksgiving)

Nancy Monroe never expected trouble as she entered Sally's Café on the Friday morning after Thanksgiving with her three girlfriends. It was cold under a low gray sky that perhaps promised snow after all, though it would be too late for them to ski. All were famished. The café was located on Hurley's Silver Street. It was small and quaint with six booths, two tables and a few counter stools. That, however, was not what you noticed. Upon entering, you could see that almost every inch of the wall space was covered with some sort of picture of Elvis Presley. It was a shrine to the King. The place was busy and as they waited to order, Nancy found that the smell of bacon frying mixed with excessive cigarette smoke was making her feel nauseous. The extra glass of wine the night before may have added to her discomfort. The no smoking ban in Wisconsin would not go into effect until July 5th of next year. As far as Nancy was concerned, July 5th could not come soon enough. She thought there was no reason that she had to have cigarette smoke served with her breakfast.

Feeling like she might throw-up, she headed to the bathroom. The restroom sign pointed to the rear. Following the sign, she found herself in the back storage room just off the kitchen. *Surely, the restrooms were not outside.* Turning to the left, she saw what appeared to be the basement door with a restroom sign with an arrow pointing down. Grease and dirt covered the door around the handle, which apparently had been there from years of use. After opening the door, she saw worn wooden stairs illuminated by a single bare 50-watt light bulb. Had it not been for a second wave of nausea she would have gone back. Now desperate she descended the stairs.

Once at the bottom of the stairs, she doubted that the restroom was down here. Looking towards the front of the basement, the light only showed out about the first fifty feet and from what she could see it looked like a storage room with old counter stools, a discarded water heater and other restaurant equipment. There must be fifty years of trash, she thought. It gave her the creeps. She looked to her right and found two doors, one marked Restroom and other marked Private. She tried the restroom door and found it occupied. Waiting she thought, *surely this bathroom can't be up to code, unless it's grandfathered in. It has to be at least seventy-five years old or more. There has to be a safety or health code against such a thing. Certainly, it's not handy-cap assessable.*

Still feeling sick, she tried the door again. Still finding it locked, she looked at the other door marked Private. She heard the sound of machinery running—perhaps the furnace. Feeling nausea build up once more she tried the door marked private thinking perhaps it might be a restroom for the employees. When she tried the door, she was surprised to find it unlocked. Once inside unable to see she searched for a light switch and finding it the door slipped from her hand and slammed shut. With inadequate light, she was unable to see a sink or toilet. Before she could search any further, she felt dizzy and sick again. The dizziness drove her to the floor where she sat trying to gain control of her equilibrium. Finally, the dizziness began to fade and she could feel the evaporation of the sweat beads on her forehead. She felt slightly better. She felt relieved only to find that she could not locate the entrance door. Becoming disoriented she frantically searched the room in panic, all the time telling herself to remain calm. *You know the door is here.*

Now she was sick, throwing up in an old waste paper basket—although there was nobody to see her—she immediately felt embarrassed. *How can this be happening to me?* One good thing was that she was no longer feeling the affects from her hangover. She reached into her purse for a Kleenex and she wiped her mouth. Now on the cold floor she brought her legs to her chest and sat there hugging herself. Telling herself aloud repeatedly, "this can't be happening." Then she passed out.

When she came to, she realized she must have fainted. Disoriented with an indefinable fear descending on her, she was unable to come to grips with where she was. While she did not understand the danger, she knew she had to get out of there. *This can't be happening to me. Could this be one of those things that were always happening to women on that show, CRIMINAL MINDS. Abduction of women took place on nearly every episode with very few happy endings.* After a few agonizing minutes, she was able to gain control of her emotions. Now more relaxed she continued to search for a way out no longer frantic.

Coming to grips with the reality that for whatever reason the door she entered was no longer there or at least she could not find it. Then just for a minute, she had an image of herself like those kids in that Narndia book by Robert Lewis and thought that perhaps she had entered a closet that opened into another world, but that was absurd. Searching in her purse, she found a key ring flashlight and was able to see further into the far end of the room. Now more in control she did a systematic search of the room. Finding nothing, she proceeded down towards the dark end. The basement seems much larger from what she could remember of the building from the outside.

At last, she felt a cold draft coming from outside. Moving to the cold breeze, she found a doorframe. There were stairs that led up to an old-fashioned cellar door that you had to lift up in order to go out like a storm cellar. Lifting with all her strength, she found herself peering out into what appeared to be the back alley of the café. Crawling up the stairs going from dark to light she was surprised to see the sun glaring off snow. It had been cloudy when she entered the café and there was no snow. Standing there, she thought, *this is impossible. Where did all this snow come from?* There had been no snow banks anywhere just a few minuets ago when they had entered the café and now here she was surrounded by snow banks. *Okay, maybe they did have a Lake Effect snowstorm and maybe I was out longer than I thought, but there is no way that much time passed that allowed then to plow all this snow into these large banks.* Squinting because of the sun glaring off the snow, she could see that she was still behind what looked to be the cafe.

Snow banks towered over everything and she was surrounded by mountains of snow. She'd never experienced so much snow. Cautiously she moved west towards the nearest street—Fifth Avenue. Nancy took two steps onto Fifth Avenue before she froze at the sight of what lay before her.

In front of her on the opposite corner of the street was an immense four story wooden framed building counting the upper roof dormers. The giant structure appeared to be a hotel with an outside porch that wrapped around both sides of the building. It had to be the hotel that Joan had read about when they came into the city. She remembered her saying that it burned to the ground in 1948. So how could she be looking at it now? There was no way she could have missed such a building on their way into town that morning.

That was when the real panic set in and she felt sick again and hurried to a near-by patch of dirt between snow banks throwing up for the second time that day. Feeling embarrassed again, she was hoping no one had seen her as she continued up Fifth Avenue with the huge hotel to her right. On the other corner was a hardware store. She was sure this morning the post office had been there and where the hotel now stood, there had been a two-story office building that housed a medical clinic. *Where am I*? Next, she stumbled up Silver Street finally seeing what she thought was the café that they had entered that morning only minutes ago. *Perhaps I'm sicker than I thought, nothing seems to be the same.* It was all like something out of another century. She stood there mesmerized.

Fortunately, she had not taken off her ski jacket when she had gone in search of the café's bathroom and she was not immediately cold. Realizing she was attracting attention from others passing by, she began to quicken her step. That was when she saw the streetcar coming two blocks away. *I must be hallucinating or having a mental breakdown.* Hearing the sound of metal wheels on steel track, she knew she was not dreaming. She stared in disbelief as the streetcar turned the corner and headed up the street. Still unsure what to do she followed Silver Street back to the café.

It was still there only older looking and she noticed the sign no longer said Sally's. Now it said Nuncio's Pasty Shop. She looked back down the street again and once more stared in disbelief at the massive hotel. "It's the hotel that Joan talked about on the ride up here and she said it burned down in 1948 and nothing about it being rebuilt. If it is the same building that would mean I'm back in time before 1948 and that can't be."

Standing there in shock, she saw strange looking cars like something out of a vintage antique auto show. There were names and models she had never heard of like Studebaker, Hudson, Nash and Packard. There were also familiar names like Ford, Chevrolet and Pontiac, but she did not see her Outback. She stared in disbelief.

The only explanation she could come up with was that there was a classic car show in town, but where were all the present day cars. Up and down the street there was nothing but old classic cars. There was no way that a classic car show would be taking place in the dead of winter. *This can't be. Where am I? God please help me.* More bewildered, confused and distraught she turned and started back for the café.

As she entered people she had never seen stared at her as if she were naked or from another planet. Her friends were nowhere to be seen. The entire appearance of the place was different. There were no Elvis Presley pictures. She approached the man behind the counter and could only assume that he must be Nuncio. She asked if he had seen her three friends—a question by now that she already knew the answerer to. He said nothing and only looked at her with a perplexed look on his face and when he did speak, it was not any English she had ever heard. He had an Italian accent, speaking in broken English with hand gestures that made her think the man was having a fit. Once the outrage was over, he just stared at her. *Where am I? Could this be a bad dream?* Dazed and confused she headed back out the door and onto the Silver Street. Large power poles ran down the main street on the sidewalk. The large hotel to her right was still there. Looking down into the next block, she searched again for her car. It was gone. Now in that instant she thought of something her boyfriend, Michael Niffin, had said one time about a parallel universe. At the time, she had dismissed what he had said as nothing more than his fascination with science fiction. Now she was on the verge of becoming a believer. Right now, it seemed like the only explanation or she had entered the Twilight Zone. A feeling of mass hysteria came over her and she just wanted it to stop. She had to get away.

Chapter Five

On Friday morning the day after Thanksgiving Robert Rahn was in his third floor study with Albert staring out over the land thinking how beautiful the land was in late Fall. As of yet, no cold air had dropped out of Canada to generate excessive amounts of Lake-Effect-Snow. Robert looked forward to the snow. He had moved here in the summer from New York City and while he was aware of the massive amounts of snow that the Great Lakes could produce he had never personally experienced it. He had seen pictures of Buffalo, New York.

In March of 2008, he had hired a private airplane to fly him into a small regional airport in Gogebic County Michigan, just outside of Ironwood to see the property that he had purchased. Marjorie Callahan, his real-estate agent, was there to meet him. After signing all the papers, they set out to see the property along with John Lafferty, a local construction contactor from Hurley to search out a building site. Marjorie recommended John as the best contractor in the area.

On that late March afternoon with the temperature in the low thirties and the sun shinning Robert saw his land for the first time. They stopped at the driveway that led into the property and there was no way they were going to go any further with snow still piled three feet high. Robert thought it was a "wow" property! It was sternly beautiful covered with a mixture of poplar, tamaracks, white pines and other deciduous trees. There were numerous granite outcroppings mixed into rolling hills and bluffs. Just like what he had seen in the aerial picture that Marjorie had sent. She also told him that the property abutted Indian Reservation land and there would be no development at least not in his lifetime.

The parcel also had over a mile of streams that meandered through beautiful rolling hills. The diverse habitat provides an abundance of wildlife. It was everything Robert wanted.

Snowshoeing in that day John and Robert searched for two hours before finding the ideal home site about a half mile in from the town road.

The elevation was right for the home to overlook the rest of the property and Lake Superior.

* * *

Construction started in the spring with the excavation of the road as soon as the frost was out of the ground. Everything was framed in before the first snowfall and work on the interior progressed through the winter. By the summer of 2009, it was complete and Robert made the move from New York. He was happy to be out of New York City away from all the things that reminded him daily of his wife and daughter and how they had been killed. Perhaps now he could put the tragedy behind him or at least minimize the hurt he felt inside.

* * *

It had not taken long for the community to hear about the stock broker from New York who purchased just over one square mile of land—640 acres—and had hired John Lafferty to build a customize home designed by some architectural firm from Boise, Idaho. Extra men were hired working double shifts to expedite the completion of the project. The extra cost was not a consideration. The extra employment was welcomed during these hard economic times, but people could not figure out why anyone from New York City would want to relocate and build here. The first thought was that this was just a vacation home, but when they heard that he would be living here permanently, they truly did not understand.

The rumor was that, Robert Rahn had been a highly successful Wall Street broker and had suffered a nervous break down after the death of his wife and daughter in a New York restaurant shooting. Some deranged postal worker had gone on a shooting rampage that killed in total five other people and wounded seven more. Rahn's wife and daughter had been among the unfortunate killed that day.

Knowing this people had at least some understanding of why he had left New York for this remote area, but all agreed that if he wanted seclusion he had come to the right place.

Those that worked on the construction were amazed at the size of the house and the rural setting. It was more than a half mile off the road on a small rolling hill that looked over most of the area. The house itself had a walk out full basement making the house look three stories high and had over 7,000 square feet of living space which included a separate guest quarters. The garage had 1,800 square feet and was bigger than most people's houses. In the center of the house, there was a room that some of the workers described as a study with a copula that was at least sixty feet high over looking Lake Superior.

Most could not figure out what a single man wanted with so much space and no one knew for sure what Rahn was going to do with all of his time.

John Lafferty never talked about the house or the cost, some of the workers put the cost at over three million dollars with landscaping and roads. The house was wired for everything imaginable. There was a complete security and surveillance system on the property with special satellite receivers for the internet and phone service. There was also a GPS locator; it was as if it was a part of the CIA.

Some people thought that perhaps if you lost your wife and daughter in a shooting you'd be paranoid too. Of course, if you lived your entire life in New York City you most likely did not trust anybody.

* * *

After Robert Rahn had moved in, he made arrangements for all delivers and all contacts with local merchant to be handled by Marjorie Callahan, his real-estate broker. He had very little contact with anyone else. There were times when some local people saw him at the Catholic Church on Sundays or at a local business place. The only people that really knew him were Marjorie Callahan and John Lafferty.

1941

Chapter Six

November 28, 1941 (Friday)

Running east down Silver Street away from the café Nancy now panicky stumbled on the snow-covered sidewalk and fell to her knees. Not wanting to be embarrassed and hoping no one saw her fall, she quickly got to her feet. Looking around all she could see was snow. The snow banks were everywhere. *Where am I?* Now she noticed people staring at her and it was then that she noticed how they were dressed. Their winter clothing was not at all, what she wore. Her yellow Columbia ski jacket made her standout. They in turn were wearing drab over coats made of what appeared to be wool.

Now noticing that she still had her purse, she reached inside pulled out her cell phone. When she opened it up it made its familiar welcoming sound, but read **No Service.** There were no bars, nothing. She closed it and said to herself, "so much for, can you hear me now!"

Now panic engulfed her as a man standing nearby approached her. He had seen her attempting to talk into a strange devise that she held up to her ear. He thought she must have been a little touched perhaps from the fall and from what he could see, she thought the gadget was a telephone. He asked, "Are you okay miss, can I help you?" When she said nothing and seemed confused he said, "Shall I call the police? Are you hurt? Do you want to me to take you to a doctor? There is one just across the street."

Seeing that she was very attractive it occurred to him that he might be able to take advantage of the situation. She was dressed so differently. He thought that perhaps she was from one of those eastern cities of New York, Philadelphia or Boston. Certainly, she was not from around here.

She just stared at him, as her breathing became short and quick. He was sure she was going to hyperventilate. Nancy's heart was racing and she felt like she was about to have a heart attack. She only knew that she had to get away, this was the most bizarre thing that had ever happened to her. She took off running. Where she was going she did not know only that she had to run. The people on the street just stared in awe.

"Hey, lady come back you need a doctor."

She ran. Dizzy, disoriented she knew she had to get away. This had to be a dream. It seemed very much like a re-run episode of the old Twilight Zone.

Her heartbeat, already fast became frantic. She almost collided with an elderly couple that appeared to be out Christmas shopping. She could not comprehend the foreign world around her. The cars were old like something out of an old movie. She saw no familiar names. They were all vintage antiques. *Where am I?*

She continued to run crossing a four-way-stop never bothering to look for on-coming traffic and that was when a 1939 Packard hit her knocking her to the pavement. The driver immediately got out to see if she was all right. Finding her incoherent, he hailed the first police officer that he saw. She was down on her knees and seemed to be ready to pass out. When she could not give him her name, the officer and several other men carried her up to Dr. John Frost's office, which was above the local department store. Had it not been for the careful driver who nearly avoided her, Nancy's ordeal may have ended right there.

When the men entered the office, Doctor Frost was annoyed by the disturbance. Next he heard, Nancy yelling out, "Where are you taking me? Put me down, who are you people. Get away from me."

He did not appreciate being disturbed when he was with a patient and called out to his Nurse, Martha Laine. "Martha, what's the ruckus out there?"

"Doctor it's a young lady, she was just hit by a car, but we don't think she broke any bones. What do you want me to do?"

Seeing the situation, his demeanor changed. "Give her a sedative, get her changed and put her in bed. I'll be right with her after I finish up with Mrs. Jarvis."

Even after the sedative, Nancy continued to rant on saying, "I don't belong here, take me back to Sally's café where my friends are. I was up here for the Thanksgiving weekend. Please you have to take me back. I'm begging you take me back to my own time."

Martha had no idea what she was talking about. There was no Sally's Café and Thanksgiving had been last week, eight days ago.

Once the sedative kicked in and she started to calm down Martha was able to attempt to undress her. "I need to take off your coat and your blouse and get you into a dressing gown so Doctor Frost can examine you. Do you feel all right to sit up?"

When Martha went to help her out of the yellow coat, the women loosen the sleeves for her and Martha heard a distinctive ripping sound. Looking she saw that two strips of material held the sleeve tight had come apart. The strange fastener puzzled her. The coat was like nothing Martha had ever seen. Just the yellow color made it stand out. Now with the coat, removed Martha went to hang it up she looked at the sleeves again. When she attached the two pieces of material together, they stuck to one another. When she pulled the strips of material apart they made that ripping noise and then she put them together again they stuck to one another. *I've never seen anything like this.*

With the Columbia ski jacket hung up Martha turned back to the patient. Nancy was already pulling a pink sweatshirt over her head that said Green Bay Packers on the front and on the back, she saw a number 12 with the name, Aaron Rogers. When she came back after folding up the sweatshirt, Nancy was already unbuttoning her blouse revealing a lacey nylon/spandex yellow bra. It was unlike anything Martha had ever seen at the corset shop or in the Sears catalog. Next, she helped Nancy remove her slacks and Martha was once again shocked to see matching yellow panties that were extremely small. There was no way that they could come up to her waist. She had never seen a garment like this. They were so small that for all practical purposes this woman was almost naked. Martha had never seen anyone wear anything this small in all of her years as a nurse. Next, while helping her into the hospital gown she notice what she thought had to be a sun tan line, but she thought she had to be mistaken—no one would ever go out in the sun dressed in something that skimpy. There had to another explanation.

* * *

Mrs. Laine was now in her late fifties and had been Dr. Frost nurse and bookkeeper for the past twenty years. She was a kind and motherly woman. Her husband had passed away some time ago leaving her financially well off. With her children gone this job was her life. While always concerned about her patient's welfare, she found herself deeply drawn to this girl in a way she could not explain. There was something so different about her. She was the prettiest petite thing she had ever seen. She could see she was young in her early twenties and she instantly saw that she was not from around here. Her clothes were so different that she didn't know what to think. Now alone with her, she took her purse and looked though it to see if she could determine who she was and who to call. Looking through her pocket book she found a substantial amount of cash. There were at least five one hundred dollar bills and a number of fifties, twenties and tens.

Some of the bills looked different as if they were monopoly money, but it was not the money that surprised her the most but rather her driver's license. She was startled to see a color picture of the woman in front of her on the license. Then she almost dropped the pocket book when she saw the date of birth was October 27, 1986 and the expatriation date was January 2012. Looking down at Nancy, she thought, *according to this you won't be born for another forty-five years.* She was perplexed, looked deeper into the pocket book, and found several plastic like cards that had the name Nancy Monroe on them that said Visa, American Express and Master Card. It was like nothing she had ever seen. She also had a checkbook with a starting date of the year 2009. Among other things in her purse, she found a small compact device that opened and which had numbers on it. If she had not known, better she would have said it was some kind of futuristic phone, but that was impossible. The only thing she could think of was Dick Tracy's two-way wristwatch phone in the comics.

There were two other odd devices. One looked like a camera and the other she had no idea what it could be. There was one other thing that caught her eye, a small box that said TAMPAX tampons on the outside. Martha knew about tampons, but did not know of anyone who used them. She did not recognize the brand. All the women she knew used KOTEX feminine napkins. She did not know what to make of it. Lastly, she looked at the coins in the purse and saw that they were different from any that she had ever seen. The quarter had a picture on it of a cowboy and said Wyoming. Now fearing that the Doctor was finishing up with Mrs. Jarvis, she slipped everything back into the purse and made a snap decision hiding the purse under her coat, which was on the desk chair near by. She would deal with this later, but for right now, she did not want to see this young thing in any more trouble than she appeared to be in already.

She returned to Nancy now changed and in bed. She could see that the sedative was working and that Nancy was almost asleep.

Ten minutes later Doctor Frost entered the room and Martha woke Nancy up for the examination. Nancy was surprised to find that she was in bed under a blanket. Next, she noticed how primitive the room appeared. It was like no doctor's office she had ever seen. The ceilings were high and the floor was tongue and grove hardwood that creaked when the nurse walked. Like something from the fifties or before.

Then it came back to her. *I was having breakfast with my girlfriends. Feeling sick I went to the rest room in the basement. Then the next thing I was outside and everything was different. I must have taken a wrong turn. I ran down the street and there were strange people every where and that was when a car hit me and that must be how I got here. I thought I saw a date on the newspaper that said November 27, 1941. I must have been dreaming. There was that big hotel too.*

Before she could cry out Martha spoke to her, "I'm a nurse and my name is Martha Laine. Please don't be afraid everything will be all right. I just want to help you. A car hit you and you're in Dr. Frost's office." The soft gentle voice of the nurse calmed her.

"How long have I been here? Where are my friends? They must be worried." As Nancy moved, her head began to spin and she fell back into bed knowing she was not going anywhere.

Then she saw the Doctor standing over her saying, "Well, Martha, do we know who she is, did you find her identification?"

"No, Doctor there was nothing in her purse other than the usual things women carry."

"Strange, she seems to be coming around. Let's give her five minutes and see if you can find out anything more. She will probably be more responsive to you than to me."

After the doctor left the room, Martha said, "I know you are confused, but please trust me. I'll take care of you until we can find where you belong. If you need to make up a story just tell the Doctor that you are staying at the Miller Hotel for a few days and that you felt sick and for a time didn't know where you were. Trust me. I'll take you home with me until we can sort things out. Here he comes, remember what I said."

Nancy trusted the woman for whatever reason. Perhaps it was the sedative but she felt she had to trust someone until she could figure out where she was and a way out of here. There had to a logical explanation.

Dr. Frost entered noticing for the first time that his patient was very attractive. "So how are you feeling? You certainly are a lot more in control then when they brought you in here."

"Well you gave us quite a scare, are you feeling any better?" said Martha.

"Yes, but I'm so dizzy and confused. What's the date?"

"It's November 27th Friday."

"No, I mean what year is it?"

"1941 of course!"

"That can't be right. It's 2009."

"No dear, it really is 1941."

Martha continues to look at the girl seeing bewilderment on her face. Then thinking back to the date on her driver's license she couldn't help but think that perhaps this girl was from the future, but that was impossible.

Then she considered her clothes. It was nothing she had ever seen around here. Perhaps it was fashionable in Paris, London or New York but surely not here in the backwoods of northern Wisconsin.

"Really I think I'll be alright other than a few black and blue marks," said Nancy.

"What's your name? I know you're not from around here," said Dr. Frost.

"My name is Nancy Monroe and I was on my way to Duluth when I stopped here for the night. I'm staying at the Miller Hotel. I'm sure I'll be just fine. I'm sorry if I caused you any problems. Just leave a bill and I will pay you once I've gone back to the hotel."

Doctor Frost continued with the examination and while he did not show any outward reaction he was stunned at the bra and panties she was wearing. When he finished he told her that she should rest and wait a couple of days in case she had a concussion. If she vomited or had sever headache she should call or come right back.

"My nurse will take care of everything once you have dressed."

"Thank-you Doctor, I'm sure that I will be fine."

Nancy met the nurse outside in the office area. Martha was busy filling out the paper work from Nancy's examination. "The doctor says you seem to be fine, nothing was broken when the car hit you, but you may have a few aches and pains. No concussion was suffered and because of that he does not need to see you again. Where are you staying?"

"Well I suppose I'll get a hotel. What are the charges?"

"Don't worry about the charges. They aren't much and I can take care of that for you. More important since you have no place to stay why don't you stay with me for a few days or at least for the weekend then we can see about getting you a place to stay."

"I can't impose on you. You must have things to do. Furthermore, I'm a complete stranger. You don't know me."

"Look, I know you're in some kind of trouble and I have no one home so please trust me, I just want to help. Why not stay with me until we can sort things out. If nothing else, you would be doing me a favor by providing an old lady with some company. So not another word, you're coming home with me."

"Really I can't impose, you know nothing about me."

"I said, not another word."

While Nancy thought to protest more, she knew Nurse Laine was right. This was the best for her right now. What other choice did she have? She had money, but would the hotel take it if. So she said, "Yes, I accept, but you have to let me help out around the house."

"That's a deal, I'm sure I can find something for you to do."

Since it was Friday and there were no other appointments, Nurse Laine took Nancy home. With that, Nancy was into the next phase of her ordeal. She had no way of knowing what was going to happen in the months ahead.

Chapter Seven

Friday Evening November 28, 1941

As Nurse Martha Laine left with the patient, Doctor Frost could not help but think that she was making a big mistake befriending that girl. There was just something strange about her that did not fit. The clothes she wore were enough to make him, suspicious. In fact, he could not remember anyone stranger in all his years of practice.

During the exam, when he glimpsed the underwear she was wearing, he was almost embarrassed. She wore a matching outfit like nothing he had ever seen in his married life unless of course it was at one of the lower end bars on Silver Street in his younger days. He wondered if he should have said something to the police.

Nevertheless, it was not his problem and furthermore he wanted to finish up, tonight was poker night. He could only hope that Martha knew what she was doing taking this woman home with her. Then he thought to himself that it must have been twenty years or maybe thirty years since a young woman had aroused him like this. Had he been younger he would not have minded taking her home himself. She was a real looker.

* * *

Upon leaving, Nancy felt she had no choice but to go with the nurse. She was both mentally and physically exhausted. She could not come to grips with what had happened to her. She refused to believe it. Things like this just did not happen. Bewildered and distraught she just needed a place to rest and think.

Considering all things, the nurse seemed like a real nice person and she looked like she could be trusted. Furthermore, what choice did she have? If the police were to get involved, things might only get worse. She would just have to play along and see how things went still hoping that some how she would find herself back at the café and all of this was just a hallucination. She was still hopeful that things would go back the way they were and that her three friends would find her.

As they walked down Silver Street to Fifth, Martha could not help but see how Nancy was looking at everything, like a child taking in her new surroundings. Martha thought perhaps if that date on her driver's license was true she would indeed be looking at everything differently. She couldn't help but image what she might be going through. Surely, she couldn't be from 2009. She couldn't wait to get home and hear her story.

Nancy was thinking that perhaps she had accidentally stumbled onto a movie set. She had never seen so much snow and up ahead on the corner was that huge wooden hotel again. Nothing was at all, as it was suppose to be. This was supposed to be a ski vacation. She caught Martha glancing at her.

"Is that really a hotel?" She said pointing straight ahead.

"Yes, it is a hotel. It's called the Burton House, but its reputation has gone down hill from the time it was build and now days it does not have a very good reputation."

"When was it built?"

"I believe it was completed in 1896 by a mining speculator, John Burton. It was the finest hotel in Northern Wisconsin and the pride of Hurley. People came from all over just to see it and I think Grover Cleveland, the president, stayed there. It's a shame that it was let go. Now people take it for granted and some wouldn't even mind if it burned down, I'd like to see it preserved as a historical landmark."

As they turned the corner and started up Fifth Avenue, Martha said to Nancy, "Don't worry, I'm sure things will work out."

"I'm sorry I didn't mean to be rude ignoring you and all. Nurse Laine you have been more than kind to me and I really don't know what I would have done without you."

"Please call me Martha and don't be silly. I could see that you needed a friend. Honey, I've been around the block a time or two and can tell when someone needs a little help. The white house on top of the hill to the right just up from the Catholic Church, that's mine."

Nancy stared up at a large two-story gingerbread house that really was three stories if you counted the dormers in the attic. The sidewalk leading to the back door had snow banks nearly as tall as she was. It was amazing to think that people had to shovel all of this snow.

Once inside Martha showed Nancy to a second floor bedroom. "This used to be my daughters, but now days she seldom comes home. She moved to California some ten years ago, said she was not going to live in all this cold and snow."

"It's beautiful. It looks like something from years gone by. Sorry, I didn't mean that the way it sounded. It truly is beautiful."

"Hush now I know what you meant. My daughter left a few night-clothes that you can sleep in tonight and then on Saturday I'll take you to buy some clothes so that you have something nice to wear to mass on Sunday. Hopefully some new clothes will make you fit in around here. So people won't stare. However, I think people might stare anyway. You are a very pretty girl in case no one ever told you that before."

"My boyfriend, Michael Niffen, told me that a time or two and I think he was going to give me a ring for Christmas and now I'm not sure of anything." She began to cry.

"Now here, here. Let's not think of that just now. You take a nice long hot bath and then we'll have some supper and then we can decide what to do next."

"I hate to put you out Martha. I could go to a hotel."

"I live alone and there is plenty of room and besides I really could use the company. Once settled in, you can tell me everything. I know you're not from here. It's as if you jumped out of a novel."

* * *

When Nancy came down, Martha had supper prepared in the large formal dinning room. In the parlor Nancy saw a grand piano and it cheered her up for the first time since being here. At least some things had not changed. Next, she noticed some Thanksgiving decorations. The house was immaculate.

"Martha, do you play piano?"

"I do a little, I took lessons in grade school and I'm not any good. Do you play?"

"Yes, I do. I love the piano, it so relaxing. Is it alright if I play it sometime?"

"You can play anytime you want. You can play right now. We have a few minutes before supper will be ready. I'm not sure the last time it was tuned, but I'll have the tuner come by next week."

Nancy began to play a number of old Neil Sedaka songs which she knew by heart like, Laughter in the Rain, That's Where the Music Takes Me, and Breaking Up Is Hard to Do.

When Martha heard Nancy, she stopped and was astounded. She had never heard any music like this and when she came back to say that dinner was ready she said, "Child where on earth did you learn to play songs like that? I don't believe I've heard anything like it."

Nancy blushed realizing she should have played some of the old classics instead of Rock and Roll.

"Oh these are just some songs that my teacher taught me years ago." Once again she thought, *I should have played the classics.*

"No, no, I like the music it was just so different. We can eat now."

"Martha you didn't have to set the dinning room, we could have used the kitchen."

"It's no bother and further more you are my guest."

"What did you do on Thursday for Thanksgiving? Did you have family over?"

"Thanksgiving wasn't yesterday; it was the Thursday before over a week ago."

"But I saw the decorations."

"Oh those, I just didn't get around to taking them down."

"But Martha Thanksgiving is always on the fourth Thursday of the month."

"No, it is whenever the President proclaims it. Most of the time it's the third Thursday of the month. Now to answer your question, I didn't have anyone over. Like I said before my daughter is in California and my son is in the navy. Both of them were unable to get off. As for my son he is worried that we might be going to war with Germany or Japan."

"The war, what war are you talking about? You must mean the one in Afghanistan?"

Martha was dumbfounded. "Afghanistan, what on earth are you talking about child. I never even heard of Afghanistan. Don't you know that just over two years ago the Germans attack Poland and have been beating the hell out of the rest of Europe except for the British Isle and they are not in good shape after all of the bombings. The only hope is that with Hitler attacking Russia he may have bitten off more than he can chew. You know it gets almost as cold in Russia as it does here."

Now it was Nancy's turn to be dumbfounded as she remembered what had happened.

"Is it really 1941?"

"Yes, dear it truly is."

"The Japanese will attack Pearl Harbor in Hawaii in ten days on December 7th." The words were out of her mouth before she realized what she had done.

"Child, why would you say such a thing. My son is stationed in Pearl Harbor and furthermore the U.S. and Japan are currently engaged in peace talks. From what I heard on the radio, it appears that there will not be a war. What war were you talking about, this Afghanistan thing."

"I shouldn't be talking so much. I guess I'm just sort of out of my head. I'm truly sorry for getting you involved and I wouldn't think at all ill of you if you called the authorities and had me taken away, so maybe I should just leave and you can pretend I was never here."

"Look Nancy, I'm an old lady and nothing you can say is really going to make a difference. We have no control over what happens in the future. I'm lonely and someone like you can only make my life interesting—you have already. I can tell that you are not a danger to me. You are a good person so now why don't you start at the beginning and tell me what happened to you before you got hit by that car."

With that, Nancy had another cup of coffee and made a decision to tell her everything. She was sure that Martha already knew more than she would admit to. Furthermore what did she have to loose. If this were something that would pass in the morning, there would be no harm. If this was permanent then she was going to have to trust someone. She would tell her most everything, but perhaps it was best to keep some things to herself.

* * *

"My name is Nancy Monroe and I'm 25 years old from Appleton, Wisconsin where I teach social studies and history at the local high school. I came up here with three of my girlfriends to go skiing. We rented a miner's cabin in Montreal and this morning went in for breakfast at Sally's Café, and that is when everything went wrong. I went to the restroom and could not find my way out. When I did, I was in the back of the café and that is when I saw that big hotel, the Burton House. It was not there that morning. I panic! I just could not believe where I was. The café was there but now was called Nuncio's. When I couldn't find my friends inside that is when I really freaked out and started to run down the street. After being hit by a car the police took me to Dr. Frost's office.

There, that's the short story. Now are you ready to call the insane asylum and have me put away?"

"No Nancy, I'm not going to call the police. While I am amazed, I have to say that I don't think you made it up. Maybe having that accident caused you to think this way, but I can see that you believe what you're saying. Why would anyone make something like that up. I have to tell you, that while you were sedated in the Doctor's office, I was told to look for some identification and in looking through your purse, I came upon your driver's license. The first thing I noticed was that it was in plastic and had your picture on it—my own license is paper—seeing your picture, I knew it was you, but what bothered me most was that the expiration dated was 2012. Looking further, I found some plastic cards that had your name on them. They too were like nothing I have ever seen. In addition, your clothes are not like anything that is being sold around here. That was when I made up my mine to protect you and see what you had to say. It was just too strange to bring up with the Doctor. He would have called the police. Therefore, while I am astonished by what you've said, I do want to believe you and I want to help you.

Does what you just told me explain the unusual songs you played on the Piano?"

"Yes, Martha. Those songs are from 1960's and 1970's."

"I think both you and I have had enough for one day. I think we should just leave everything right here and get a good night's sleep. You must be exhausted."

"That sounds good to me. My head still hurts. I can't thank you enough for your kindness."

As Nancy went upstairs to bed, she wondered if Martha had plans to call the police. There was no way she could blame her. She slept immediately upon putting her head on the pillow. Still thinking she could not possibly be back in the year 1941.

* * *

Martha too thought about calling the authorities, but she did not want to get Nancy into trouble with the law. Besides, it was the first time in a long time that Martha felt this alive. It put new meaning in her life and she no longer felt depressed like she usually did around the holidays.

Then Martha went back over what Nancy had blurted out about the Japanese attacking the Hawaiian Islands. While it was fantastic, Martha could only pray that it would not come true. Her son was stationed there and it worried her.

Sitting there, she thought she had to do something with this information and decided to call her daughter in California. Martha knew that her daughter worked with a number of Japanese Americans in Los Angeles and would have more information if a war seemed likely.

"Carrie, this is your mother, how are things in California?"

"Mom, what a surprise I was just thinking about you. I suppose you are up to your ears in snow?" She said with a chuckle.

"Let's just say we are going to have a white Christmas."

"Well, mother I will take 70 degree weather over snow. So why did you really call, I know it wasn't to discuss the weather."

"Well I was just wondering if you heard anything about a war with Japan. It has been on the news here and I figured with all of the Japanese that live out there maybe you would have heard more."

"Well yes we are worried about the war because we are so much closer to Japan and there is beginning to be a lot of distrust of the Japanese Americans. It is not a good situation, but why the interest?"

"The reason I'm asking is that I took in a young woman for the weekend and she was saying to me that Japan was going to attack Pearl Harbor in Hawaii on December 7th."

"Mother, that woman sounds a little crazy, why would you take in someone you don't even know? They could rob you or worse do you bodily harm."

"Carrie, it's Christmas and she had no place to go. Besides I was lonely."

"Well alright, but to answer your question, I don't know anything about an attack on Pearl Harbor other than to say relations are not good with the local Japanese. Should I call someone with this information? Maybe someone in civil defense would know?"

"Do what you feel is necessary, but please don't tell anyone where the information came from. I don't want to get this girl in trouble.

Carrie, there is one other thing you can do for me. Would you see if you could call or send a telegram to your brother warning him not to spend the weekend on his ship if possible? He's on the battleship U.S.S. Pennsylvania."

"I'll tell him, but what should I say if he wants to know why?"

"Just say that his mother had a premonition."

"Okay, mother I'll call him right after I'm done talking with you. Now back to that woman that is staying with you. Are you sure that you are going to be all right with her in your house. She really could be a danger."

"She's not a danger or a threat. She is just someone who needs my help and beside I'll have someone to spend Christmas with. Don't worry I'll be all right. I'll call you on Christmas."

As Martha hung up the phone, she was hoping that she had done the right thing by telling Carrie. In the end, she thought that Carrie would do what was best. Martha thought, *nevertheless this is going to be an interesting Christmas. If Nancy is from the future, life could be interesting around here for this old woman. I can't wait to know what else she has to say about the future.* She was happy looking forward to what was to come although still worried about her son, but most of all she was happy to have this lovely young lady in her company. This Christmas was not going to be as lonely as she thought after all.

Chapter Eight

Friday November 28, 1941

That same evening after examining Nancy Monroe, Doctor John Frost was hosting the usual Friday night poker game with his associates. The Friday night games were sacred except perhaps if Christmas happened to fall on Friday. The group had formed several years ago as a fraternal development group they called "The Alliance." There were six members in the group who were all wealthy businessmen. Doctor Frost thought that he was perhaps the poorest one of the six. Most of the members could be considered old money having inherited what they had. The group formed to look out for their own interest within the community and most of all they were about making money for one another and the group. He knew the group was not interested in the community, but rather in their own personal pocketbooks.

The Doctor's friends called him Jack. He was called "Jack Frost" all through school and now at fifty the name still stuck with him whether he liked it or not. Over the years, he had just learned to accept it.

He came to Hurley in 1918 just as the First World War was ending fresh out of medical school looking for a job in a small town. As luck would have it the current Doctor was near retirement and looking for a young assistant to take over the practice. That was twenty years ago and now at the age 50 he was well established and trusted in the community.

Oscar Kosken was the leader of the group. In addition to leading the group he was extremely influential within the community. While he had never held any elected office, the town's elected officials privately recognized him as having the final say in any important matter. He was a man who had spent most of his life giving orders and rarely did he if ever take orders. He was used to getting his own way.

Oscar ran the only local lumberyard and had his hands in the timber business. He was a wealthy man not of his own making but because of what he had inherited from his father and his grandfather before him. Now he spent most of his time maintaining and increasing what he had. The Alliance had been his idea. It was a way to control business activities within the community and to make sure that unwanted endeavors were eliminated before they could become a threat to the status quo. Thus if anyone wanted to start any kind of a business in Hurley they had to go through Oscar Kosken. The truth was that while the members of the Alliance benefited financially, you could bet that Oscar did much better personally.

Oscar's wife passed away in 1930 when their son, Eddie, was only ten. After her death, Oscar pampered and protected the child. Now at the age 21 Eddie was a spoiled brat who did whatever he wanted. Oscar took care of everything. When he fathered a child in high school, Oscar made sure that no one ever knew it was Eddie's child and paid for an illegal abortion. Eddie knew his father would protect him. Oscar had even kept him out of the draft with his influence with the local draft board.

* * *

Dr. Frost chastised himself for the way he always let Oscar dominate him. Around Oscar, he felt like he was six years old again. So while he was eager to tell the group about his incident with Nancy Monroe he was not looking forward to being derided by Oscar, but he knew he had to tell someone and it might as well be this group.

The other four members consisted of Leo Coppalo, Ralph Winslow, Peter Cadence and Fred Banister.

Leo Coppalo ran the town's only general store, the Mercantile, consisting of clothing, hardware and groceries. He really had a monopoly on business.

Peter Cadence was the owner of the Miner's State Bank. He was a shrewd businessman that never lost an opportunity to make money off of the misfortunes of others. With money from the Alliance members, he had invested in many homes and properties in the area.

Fred Banister made his early wealth in western mining ventures by leasing or owning a number of mines. The mining of iron ore brought him to Hurley where he speculated in various mining operations.

Ralph Winslow was a lawyer with his own law firm and well established in Hurley and the surrounding communities. He was an excellent trial lawyer.

* * *

Before the poker game got started, the conversation was about the war in Europe. Things were looking even worse and it looked like the U.S. was bound to get involved no matter how much the President said otherwise. Some thought the President was looking for a way to enter the war.

"It looks like the Germans are really taking it to the Russians. The newspaper said that they could be in Moscow by Christmas," said Dr. Frost.

Leo Coppalo said, "I hope we don't get involved. It's alright to give the Brits supplies, but I don't see us getting involved with the fighting."

"From what I read in the paper maybe we won't be fighting the Germans, we may end up fighting the Japs. Relations are not good with Japan right now," said Ralph Winslow.

Peter Cadence sat there patiently waiting for the game to begin.

Finally, Oscar Kosken said, "Enough of this war shit, let's play cards. I need to get my money back from last time."

"As if you need more money. You own half the town now," said Fred Banister smiling.

After getting the group another round of drinks, Doctor Frost thought now was his best opportunity to bring up his contact with Nancy Monroe. Oscar already had several drinks and he felt Oscar would not put him down or make fun of him.

"I've got to tell you guys about what happened to me today. Perhaps I shouldn't be saying this, but I'm confident that none of you will say anything." Smiling he went on. "Further more it really doesn't matter."

"Well are you going to tell us or not," said Oscar.

"Just before lunch the police brought in a young woman, very attractive. A car hit her. She wasn't hurt bad, but she was hysterical, saying things like, 'what am I doing here, where are my friends?' and just plain carrying on. I had to sedate her. After she came out of it, I had a chance to examine her and that was when I was able to see the underwear she had on. Not that I was looking, you know, but I had to examine her."

"Yea sure you weren't looking, you dirty old man," said Oscar.

Doing his best not to be intimidated by Oscar he continued. "Well anyway, what I saw was what I'd call a matching set—brassier and panty. They were both yellow and the bottoms were tiny. I mean tiny. I've never seen another patient wear anything that skimpy. They didn't come up to her waist at all. The brassier, well let's just say it accentuated her breast. Now in all the years I've been treating women, no one has ever worn anything like it. The material it was made out of was different. Stretchy, like no fabric, I've ever seen. Then later when she left the office with Martha, I notice her outer clothes were totally different. She was wearing pants—tight fitting—that showed her really attractive rear end and the jacket was like nothing I've ever seen. I know you don't carry anything like it your department store, Leo."

"So, do you know who she is and where she's from?" said Oscar impatiently.

"Martha said her name is Nancy Monroe, a school teacher from Appleton, Wisconsin just visiting, but from just the way she acted she didn't seem to be normal. The way she looked around at everything it was as if she was seeing things for the first time. It was just strange, but boy was she cute. I sure wouldn't kick her out of my bed."

"Do you know where she's staying? I'd like to have a look at her. Maybe I could introduce her to my son, it would be nice to see him date a nice girl for a change," said Oscar.

"Come on Oscar, you just want to get a look at her yourself, don't kid us and furthermore I said she was a nice girl nothing like what your son is used to dating."

"Come on guys, I know Eddie hasn't exactly lived up to my expectations, but he is not that bad of a kid. He just doesn't seem to know how to treat women is all. I think that is because his mother died when he was so young."

"When she left, Martha told me she was taking her home with her, because she didn't want her to be alone after what she'd been through. It was like she didn't have any place to stay. I'll have to talk with Martha on Monday and see how her weekend went."

"Was there a police report made on the accident?" said Fred.

"No, she was not really hurt, only minor cuts and burses. The police didn't think it was necessary. The only thing that bothered them was the fact that she didn't seem to know where she was or what day it was. She asked several times wanting to know what year it was. That was why they really brought her to me because they thought she might have a concussion."

"Jack, do you think we should do a little background check on her. You know, just so we know what's going on in the town. When you think about it if she is as strange as you say, I think we ought to check her out," said Ralph.

"Maybe you just want to meet her."

"Tell you what I'll be sure to find out what Martha has to say on Monday. So let's not jump to conclusions like she's a Nazi spy or something."

With that, they went back to playing cards and shortly after midnight the game broke up.

2009

Chapter Nine

November 27, 2009
(The Friday after Thanksgiving)

The other three girls at Sally's Café, Joan, Emily and Donna continued their non-stop conversation until Emily said, "What's keeping Nancy?"

"You're right she's been gone a long time. I know she wasn't feeling well. Do you suppose she could've passed out or is really sick?"

"I'll check on her."

Emily proceeded to the back and found the same perplexing restroom situation that Nancy must have faced. She quickly noticed the arrow pointing down and made her way downstairs. Being in a hurry she did not notice how creepy the basement was until after she wrapped on the rest room door.

"Nancy, are you Okay?"

When no one answered, she tried the door and found it unlocked. The restroom was empty. Next, she noticed the door marked private and decided to try it. Finding it firmly locked she turned to go upstairs and as she did she looked back at the rest of the unlighted basement that served as a storage room and called out Nancy's name. With no reply, she headed up the stairs thinking perhaps that she had missed Nancy. The only other thing she thought was that perhaps Nancy had come upstairs and gone out the back door for some fresh air, remembering how she complained about the cigarette smoke.

Scurrying up the stairs, she headed for the back door to have a look outside, expecting to find Nancy out in the cold, instead she found nothing. Going further into the alley, she found several people outside from a near by building grabbing a smoke. Saying to one, "Have you seen a girl in a yellow ski jacket come this way?" They all said no. Next, she ran to the corner and still did not see Nancy and it was then that she headed back to the café.

When they heard that Emily had not found Nancy all three hurried out searching up and down Silver Street. Nancy's Subaru Outback was still parked where they had left it and Nancy was not inside. After fifteen more minutes of futile searching, they went back into the café to talk with the owner and the waitress.

Finding the owner, Sally Millburn, they asked, "Our friend went to use your rest room about thirty minutes ago and now we can't find her. She wasn't feeling well and we've search everywhere. She was wearing a yellow ski jacket and navy blue slacks. Can you help us?"

Sally had been in the restaurant business now for twenty-five years. The last ten as owner of her own place and thought she had heard everything. Never before had she lost a customer. There had to be a reasonable explanation.

Then her waitress said, "I remember seeing her go down, she looked like she was about to be sick."

"Maybe she went outside for some fresh air or went to her car?"

"No, her car is still there and we looked everywhere outside. Is there another way out of the basement?"

"No, there used to be, but that was closed off before I bought the building. The only way out is up through the kitchen and the back door."

"If she came up and went outside I think we would have seen her. I know she did not go out the front door," said Donna.

"Well there are some other rooms downstairs, maybe she got lost. Let's take another look downstairs. That basement is perhaps a hundred years old."

Finding nothing in the basement, they searched the second floor apartment and still found nothing.

"I think we better call the police," as Sally moved to the phone.

* * *

Ten minutes later Office Stabler arrived and Emily explained the situation.

"So she's been missing for about 45 minutes, is that right?"

"Maybe closer to an hour, I'm not sure how long she was in the restroom if she was ever there. We rather lost track of the time."

"Did you ever consider the fact that she may have run away? Was there something bothering her? Was she depressed?"

"No, there is no way she would have run off. Why on earth would she have come up here to run off, if that was even a possibility?"

"Now, now, I know you're up set, but I have to take everything into consideration. Give me a description of her and I'll get it out to the rest of the force and we'll do a check of all the business up and down the street, we'll also check the hospitals, just in case your friend was in an accident or she fell and hit her head. She could be just wandering around. I'm sure we'll find her. This is not the big city."

Not having the keys to Nancy's car the police took the girls back to their miner's house in Montréal where they debated as to who was going to call Michael Niffin, Nancy's boyfriend.

* * *

Back at the miner's house, they drew straws to see who was going to call Michael. It was shortly after noon. If they were lucky they would catch him before he left the hospital.

"Michael, this is Emily, Nancy's friend. Remember me?"

"Sure Emily I remember you, where's Nancy. Isn't she with you?"

"That's why I'm calling. We were out for a late breakfast this morning around ten and well I don't know how else to say this, she wasn't feeling well and went to the bathroom and never came back, she just disappeared."

Michael did not speak right away and when he did, he was calm. "Is this a joke and what do you mean she disappeared. People don't just disappear, at least not in small out of the way place like Hurley. Now put her on the phone, enough is enough; the four of you have had your little joke."

"Michael, I know how this sounds, but it is true. You can call the Hurley police. We wouldn't kid you about something like this we all know what Nancy means to you."

Now Emily thought she could hear him holding back tears. "What happened? Maybe she just took a long walk. What should we do? Should I come up there?"

"The police are searching for her and told us that we should give them until this evening. They are thinking that they will find her. I don't think there is anything you can do by coming up here right now. We'll call you tonight and let you know if anything has turned up. I'm sure we'll find her. Why don't you call the Hurley police and see what they think you should do. Maybe you can give them more information about Nancy that will help them in their search. And Michael, I'm really sorry about all of this. We can't image how this could have happened if only one of us had gone to the bathroom with her."

"I don't blame you and I know you're doing everything you can. This is just such a big shock. I'll call the police, but I'm coming up. I'll get somebody to cover for me and I'll leave early in the morning. Look for me around ten, I'll meet you at the house, Nancy gave me the address and the phone number. Thanks for everything."

Chapter Ten

Saturday November 28, 2009

On Saturday morning, the front-page headline of the local Ironwood Gazette read, **Visiting Appleton Woman Missing.** Officially, the news was out, but rumors of the disappearance started on Friday morning when the police were called to Sally's Café. In a small town, the news spread quickly and everyone had his or her own version of just what had happened. A number of people remembered seeing the four young women enter the café that morning but no one remembered Nancy Monroe leaving .

The police were treating this as a missing person although it could not officially be considered a missing person for 48 hours. There was a good possibility that the victim may have just walked away. Rumor was that she was about to become engaged and perhaps this was just a case of cold feet. People still remembered the runaway bride from down south that ran away only to show up a few days later.

* * *

Before Michael arrived, the girls called the Gogebic County Airport just outside of Ironwood, Michigan and reserved a rental car. The police were kind enough to give them a ride to pick up the car. The girls went up and down every street and talked to everybody that was outside. They stopped at all businesses and late in the morning, they returned to the house to meet Michael. Michael looked like he had not slept and his eyes were red and swollen as he had been crying most of the time. After exchanging greetings they talked through once again what had happened and they decided to go through all the events that let up to the disappearance.

They started with Sally's café and Sally was more than willing to help. They went over the entire building again and found nothing. They searched the back alley and found nothing new. It was as if Nancy had never been there.

By now, the disappearance of Nancy was the talk of the town. As in all small towns, rumors and facts floated freely among the people. By late afternoon, the team was exhausted and was out of options. The only thing they could agree on was that they had to face reality and admit that Nancy had really disappeared. Fact was she had vanished. It was as if she had never existed. The police had no leads and nobody could remember seeing her. There were a few false leads that turned out to be nothing at all. Everything had come to a dead end. The police kept Nancy's car. A forensic team was due from Wausau next week to go over the car to see if they could uncover any evidence into her disappearance.

Sunday afternoon Joan, Emily and Donna left for Appleton. Classes at the high school were due to resume Monday morning and besides there was nothing more that they could do. Michael decided to stay a few more days just in case something turned up.

* * *

Michael thought the case was very similar to one that had happened in the Madison area some years back. A young women was last seen driving away from the local strip mall on a summer evening and no trace of her was every found other than her locked car at her boyfriend's apartment building. Eventually they notified police.

There were no other signs of her at the scene. No one saw her walk away from the parking lot or get into anyone's car. Her purse was still in her locked vehicle. There were no clues in her disappearance. Authorities believe she was taken by someone she knew. There was no indication that she was forcibly kidnapped. In the years since she has not been seen.

No arrests were ever made in the women's disappearance and her case remains unsolved. Foul play is suspected, but never proven.

Now alone in the miner's house, Michael could not help but think how eerily similar the two disappearances were. As his mind wondered, he even entertained thoughts that perhaps aliens had abducted her. It was a wild idea but it seems like the only thing that could explain the disappearance. In all the time, he had known Nancy he was sure that she kept no secrets from him and he could not image she would run away or God forbid think of sucide. She loved her job and teaching was something that she had always wanted to do. There had to be some other explanation.

Finally exhausted he cried himself to sleep determined to continue the search no matter how long it took. Like all the others in similar situations he had no idea just how long this nightmare would last.

On Tuesday, Michael decided to leave for home after the police told him that in cases like this where there was no physical evidence of foul play and no suspects or persons of interest there really was not much they could do. They would leave the case open until they were able to find some tangible evidence, they could go no further. They were at a dead end.

Eleven

November 29, 2009 (Sunday Morning)

On Sunday morning Robert Rahn made one of his infrequent trips into Hurley to pick up a copy of the Sunday Duluth News Tribune at the only grocery store. He usually attended Mass at our Lady of the Lake Church in Ashland on Saturday evening where people did not know him. A troubled look came over his face as he read the front-page headline while he waited to check out.

Visiting Appleton Women Missing in Hurley

Nancy Monroe, 25, was last seen at Sally's Café on Silver Street in Hurley, Wisconsin on Friday morning November 27, 2009. Monroe disappeared after failing to return from the café restroom. Police were called and a search of the café and the surrounding area businesses found no trace of Monroe.

It went on to say that, she was five-four, a hundred ten pounds, with blonde hair and blue eyes. She was a schoolteacher from Appleton, Wisconsin here on a holiday weekend with three other women. She was last seen wearing ski pants, an Aaron Rogers sweat shirt and a yellow Columbia ski jacket.

It had to be a coincidence. Could this really be the girl in his dream on Friday night? There was no picture in the paper, but the description did fit the girl that was in his dream.

After paying for the paper he rushed to his car where Albert, his three year old Airedale waited patiently in the restored 1979 Buick Estate wagon. "We've got some work to do," he said to the dog. They drove off in the direct of Silver Street.

Although he was not real familiar with the town, Sally's Café was not hard to find since the business street was really only four blocks long. Parking, he got out and went into the café. The locals at the "bullshit table" stopped talking about yesterday's playoff high school football game and turned to look at who had entered. He saw them whisper to one another as he walked by. Knowing that while most had never seen him they knew who he was. Word travels fast in a small town.

The café was small and inviting. All of the Elvis Presley memorabilia on the walls took him aback. He did not like the fact that smoking was still allowed, but all of that would change come July when the state went smokeless. There were still a few people at the counter finishing their coffee. The Sunday church breakfast rush was over and the help was preparing for the noon meal which most of the seniors came for because the center was closed on the weekend. Not to mention the fact that Sally accepted the local senior vouchers.

Robert sat down and immediately spotted Sally. She was a thin woman in her fifties who looked like she knew her way around a kitchen. Seeing him she came over with a menu saying, "You must be Robert Rahn; it's a pleasure to meet you."

"How'd you know who I was?"

"Well sir, I think just about everybody in town knows who you are, especially after the way you helped the police catch that child killer. What can I get you?"

"Just two eggs and toast, but what I'd really like, is some first hand information about what happened here on Friday. I just read about it in the Duluth paper this morning."

"All I can say is that it was a shock to me. You know our food may not be the best, but we never had anyone disappear before."

"Did you notice anything different about the woman, Nancy Monroe?"

"I was cooking so I only caught a glimpse of her, but a glimpse was all you had to have to see that she was very attractive. She was about the prettiest thing I'd ever seen. It was clear to everyone that she was not from around here. We were busy and the next thing I know maybe twenty minutes later my waitress tells me that the girls she was with say that they can't find her. After that we searched the restrooms and the basement and then we called the police."

"Where is you restroom?"

"Down stairs in the basement."

"Is there another way out of the basement?"

"No, there is a back door, but you have to come back upstairs. Why all the questions? You sound like a lawyer, are you?"

"Since you know about the boy back in October, then you already know I'm not a lawyer. I'm just interested, thought maybe I could help."

"Sorry to be rude. I was only thinking that the last thing I needed was for somebody to file a law suit against me."

"No I'm not going to sue you, but I'd like to have a look around downstairs after breakfast if I could."

"Sure anything you can do to help find that poor woman would be appreciated."

Robert finished his breakfast and watched as the "bullshit table" emptied with the guys leaving one by one but never saying a word to him as they left.

Next, he went to the basement. The restroom was off to his right as he came down the stairs and facing him was another door marked private. He could see this scene being used in a spooky movie or perhaps a Stephen King novel. Then he had a very peculiar feeling as if someone was watching him. When he looked back up the stairs, no one was there, but the feeling persisted. The feeling grew stronger when he entered the door marked Private and he noticed a familiar chemical smell. At first, he thought it smelled like ant-freeze, but that was too sweet. It was more like that cold weather ether starting fluid that came in an aerosol can. Was there a spiritual presence here like on that TV show Ghost Hunters? Going further into the room the feeling stayed with him and the smell grew stronger as he got to the outside wall. He noticed what once might have been steps and some different bricks in the wall as if a door had been there. He made a mental note to ask Sally. Moving away from the outline of different bricks the smell grew less and less and the feeling that someone was watching dissipated. Other than the weird feeling of not being alone and the chemical smell, there was nothing out of the ordinary.

Once up stairs he said to Sally, "I saw on the back wall what looked to a bricked over doorway, was there ever a door down there that went directly from the basement to the outside?"

"I think there was years ago, well before my time. I know there are stories as to why that door was bricked over and I know who could tell you about that, Karl Prosser. He knows a lot about the early history of Hurley and Ironwood. If you'd like to talk with him, I can give him a call."

"Yes, I'd like that."

With that, he left leaving a fifty-dollar bill on the table and thanking Sally for her help on his way out.

1941

Twelve

Saturday & Sunday November 29-30, 1941

Several times during the night, Martha thought she could hear Nancy crying and went to check on her to make sure she was all right. She found Nancy was indeed sobbing, but it was in her sleep. She wanted so much to comfort her but thought it was best not to wake her. She needed her sleep even if it seemed to be tormented.

Nancy woke just after eight and looked at her room through bloodshot eyes. It was still the same strange room and she realized it was not just a bad dream. Wiping her eyes, it all came back to her. She remembered Martha the nurse taking her home. It was real. Then she took in the room. It had a high ceiling—at least twelve feet—with decorative moldings and the floor was real tongue and grove hardwood with large mopboards, nothing at all like the rented house in Montreal or her apartment back in Appleton.

The windows were covered with three flounced curtain treatments. Two of the room's walls had wood paneling while the others were painted off white with a stenciled floral pattern of pink and green around the doorway and windows. There was a fireplace that looked like it was no longer used. The trim around it was painted a teal color.

As for furniture, there was a four-poster-bed and beside the bed was a striped red, white and blue chintz covered wingback chair. Behind the chair was a tin ware shaded floor lamp. There was a coffee table with a red lined duffle bag holding some knitting. Below the table was a hooked rug. On the side table, there were magazines and a steeple mantel clock. A brass lamp sat on the shelf above a desk, which had a Windsor style chair beside it.

Getting up she went to the window and gazed out at a world that was not familiar to her. There still was snow everywhere and down the street was the Catholic Church with the strangest collection of cars parked outside. Then it came back to her as her eyes continued to search the room.

Have I really gone back in time? That's impossible. Never the less there was no way she could reconcile what her eyes were seeing.

She turned from the window as the adrenaline that had surged through her subsided and threw herself on the bed crying. Lying there, she heard another strange sound that she had only heard in old movies. It was the sound of a streetcar. Racing back to the window there it was as big as life. Still wiping tears from her eyes, she finally had to admit that she was no longer in the year 2009. "This isn't Kansas Toto."

Putting on the robe that Martha had left for her, she headed down stairs to explore the rest of this strange world. There she found Martha in the kitchen smiling at her. "Did you sleep well child? You've been sleeping for more than twelve hours."

"Martha, what year is it really?"

"It is Saturday November 29th and it is still 1941."

"Thanks Martha, I guess I'll just have to get use to that, but it is going to take me some time. I'm sorry to be such a burden on you and you've been so kind."

"Nonsense, I have breakfast prepared and then we are going to go shopping for some proper clothes for you. You need to get with the style," she said laughing. Nancy smiled for the first time in the year of 1941.

* * *

After breakfast, Martha took Nancy shopping at the local department store owned by Leo Coppalo, who happened to be working although he had a splitting headache from too many drinks at last night's poker game.

When he saw Martha enter the store he knew immediately who was with her. She was every bit as attractive as Doc Frost had said and more. She was slender, but shapely just a wisp of a girl and petite did not really describe her. Leo wasn't sure exactly why, but he could feel himself becoming aroused and could not help but think about what the Doc had said about her underwear. He wondered if she was wearing it now as his eyes undressed her

He found himself rushing to meet Martha saying, "Martha, what brings you in here this morning? Oh, excuse me for being so rude, who is this with you? I'm Leo Coppalo the owner."

Martha had never known Leo to be this friendly and she knew it had to be Nancy's presences. "Leo, this is Nancy Monroe. She is staying with me through the holiday season. Her Mother and I were good friends before she died and Nancy is just on holiday. She may even stay longer if she likes the area. I know I like having her." Martha and Nancy had made up the story before going out.

"Well, I am pleased to meet you Nancy, if there is anything that you need please let me know." Then he called out to Lisa his clerk saying, "Would you please help Martha and Nancy here with anything they need."

The first order of the day was to pick out several dresses that Nancy could wear for every day and a couple for going out to dinner and church. They also picked out a couple of pairs of pants that were not stylish in the least. She also bought several blouse and some skirts and jackets. Then she bought Nancy an outer coat to replace the Columbia jacket that was more in the style than what she was wearing. Nancy ignored Lisa when asked where Nancy had purchased such a different coat.

Lastly, they went to the lingerie department where Nancy was out fitted with bras and underwear. Nancy could see that there was nothing risqué considering the bikini and thong panty styles of 2009. They did have some sheer panties, but they were still designed to sit high on the waist and low on the legs. Everything came up to the belly button. They were what Nancy referred to as "Granny Panties". Obviously French and high cut panties had yet to be invented. In the end she settled for several pairs of tap panties. They were more like shorts than underwear.

When they left Martha told Nancy that she was a good seamstress and could alter anything that did not fit properly. Nancy was amazed at how little everything cost until she realized that these were 1941 prices.

* * *

That evening after supper, Nancy and Martha listened to the radio. She was getting used to the idea that the only way to be informed or entertained was through the radio. There was only one evening newspaper and no morning paper. There was no CNN to watch. She liked the idea that there were no cameras every place that brought you instant footage of late breaking news. There were no camera phones. Going to bed, she told Martha that she was going to need an Ambient—without thinking—if she was going to sleep tonight. Martha had no idea what she meant, but let the subject go saying, "Have a good rest Nancy. Tomorrow, we'll go to mass if you feel up to it."

* * *

That Sunday Martha took Nancy to mass and of course, there were the usual people who wondered who she was. Martha explained that she was the daughter of an old friend who passed away. She was here to stay with her for a few months. Before they left for Mass Martha made sure that Nancy had something to wear on her head. Nancy did not ask why, but remembered that it was a requirement for women before Vatican I.

Martha told her the pastor of the church was Father Erich Schuster who had been a priest for nearly thirty years and was set in his ways. Newly ordained Father Jacob Unger assisted him. Nancy seemed to remember the name from somewhere, but could not place it.

She was surprised to find that a small church like this had two priests. Then she remembered that in the forties and fifties there was an abundance of priest—no shortage.

Next Nancy saw that the altar was against the back wall of the sanctuary, it was not facing the people. Then she saw that the rest of the church was separated from the sanctuary by a railing. When the mass started, the priest came out with two altar servers—both boys. He faced the altar with his back to the congregation. Nancy could not keep her mind on the mass with it all being in Latin. She had heard about such things, but never in her lifetime had she seen any church that still practiced the Latin mass. She could not understand anything except for the homily and even that seemed foreign to her. When it came time for communion the alter servers placed a cloth on the railing then the people knelt in front of it twenty at a time as the priest gave communion. When it was done, the cloth was removed. No one but the priest received the precious blood. When she went to communion, she was ready to place out her hand until she saw everyone else receiving on the tongue. The priest seeing this gave her a cross look that gave the impression that he was ready to excommunicate her. Finally, the mass ended and they left. She was relived. She knew this was going to take a lot of getting used to and she could only pray that she would not be here too long. She could not understand how some people back in 2009 had actually wanted to go back to Latin.

After mass, Nancy asked Martha if they could go to lunch at that pasty shop. She had to have another look at the place and the basement restroom in hopes of perhaps ending this nightmare, even if she had to admit that the nightmare was now more manageable because of Martha's kindness. Never the less she still did not want to stay. She wanted to get back to Michael and wondered if he was looking for her right now only years into the future.

Martha agreed and they went to lunch at Nuncios. As they entered Nancy could see that a great number of the people were smoking and thought it unusual until she remembered that smoking was a custom of the time and tolerated—no one had yet made the connection between lung cancer and smoking. The same Italian man that she had approached only yesterday was there and he seemed irritated as he saw Nancy enter the shop. When he saw Martha, his demeanor changed as he showed them to a table.

"Martha, I tried to speak to him yesterday and he ignored me and now here he is so friendly to you."

"I've known him for years. His English is terrible, but he understands more than you think. He just does not like strangers."

"I need to look at the bathroom."

"Nancy, there is no bathroom for customers here."

"There has to be. I know I used it or tried to use it two days ago. It was down stairs back through the kitchen. Can you ask him please? What happens if you really have to go or get sick?"

"What they have is just a toilet, no sink and it's just for the employees. If you really have to go they'll let you use it, but from what I know of it, you don't want to go down there. The smell alone will astound you. It is worse than an outdoor toilet in the middle of July. Believe me."

"I still want to see it. Martha, I've got to see it."

"Oh Nuncio, my friend has to go really bad. I would appreciate it if she could use your toilet down stairs?"

"The toilet is only for the workers and emergencies. I'm sorry."

"Please she has to go bad and she won't make it home, please."

"Alright I'll show you where, but remember I warned you. It's not suitable for a lady."

Nuncio led her into the back kitchen thinking, *maybe once she sees the toilet she'll stop coming here. On Friday, I lost customer because of the scene you made.*

Once in the kitchen he opened the stairway door and turned on the light saying, "At the bottom, you'll see it." *You'll smell it!*

As Nancy started down the steps, she heard the door slam behind her. Nearly scaring her out of her wits, but she continued down. Next, she felt strange and just barely made the last four steps. Dizzy she slid to the floor now engulfed by a strange pungent smell—it was not the toilet. The smell was chemical, like fingernail polish remover. She sat there on the cold floor for what seemed to be an eternity and then the dizziness subsided and the smell passed. She was suddenly all right, except for the dirt and cobwebs on her new dress.

Then she noticed that there were two doors just as it had been in 2009. The first door said **Toilet** and the other door was marked **Private.** The smell of the toilet even with the door shut made her feel sick and she did not bother to look inside. It was the other door that caught her attention. Opening the door marked private she was engulfed by a stench worse than the toilet and she throw up on the dirt-covered floor. Even though the smell was so bad, she pressed on. She had to explore the rest of the room. All the while, she felt as if someone else was in the room with her. Then looking forward she found it—the stairway to the outside. Lifting the door up she peered out at the back alley and just for a passing moment, she thought she'd gone back catching a glimpse of what she thought was a Silverado Chevy pick-up truck and then it vanished. For that split second, thinking she gone back she was in ecstasy and then when the truck vanished her feeling went to one of despondency. Looking further, she noticed all of the snow and the old parked cars. *I know that Silverado was there or was it just me wanting something too much. Damn it, It's still 1941.* Slowly she lowered the door and sat down on the last step sobbing, "I'm never getting out of here. Why God, how could you let this happen to me. What did I do to deserve this?"

Then worried about Martha she did her best to dry her eyes and wipe the dirt off her dress and headed back upstairs. She kept her head down not wanting anyone to see how she looked. When she got to the table Martha said, "Nancy what happened to you down there. You've been crying and look at your dress."

With every eye in the pasty shop on her, Martha took her arm and out they went.

Once home in the living room Martha made tea and they talked. "Child, what happened down there? I'm not sure I'll be able to get the dirt out of your dress. Tell me?"

"On the way down I got dizzy and had to sit down on the floor. I couldn't help it. There was this strange smell like finger nail polish remover and all the while I was there it was as if someone else was there in the room with me. I could feel him."

"Was it a man?"

"I never saw anyone, but I know it was a man and I got a feeling that he was concerned about me, no matter how strange that sounds. When everything subsided, I went into another room down there marked private and the smell in that room did make me throw up. After that, I found the outside door to the alley and as I opened it, I thought I saw a new 2009 truck. Martha I was so happy I thought that I had really made it back to 2009, but when I looked closer, there was still all that snow and the cars were old. After that, I just cried. That's what took me so long. Now I think I just want to lie down."

"You take a nap. We won't eat until six."

* * *

When Nancy woke up at four in the afternoon it was already turning dark and it had started to snow again. She lay there finally coming to grips with the situation. While still over whelmed by everything that had happened she felt lucky that she had found someone as understanding as Martha. She didn't want to think what else could have happened to her. She was sure if it had not been for Martha they would have institutionalized her. She could only imagine what a mental institution must have been like back in 1941. Now she found herself warming reluctantly to the fact that she was going to be here a long time or perhaps forever.

She had not given up on her God and she continued to pray that her personal nightmare would somehow be over and that someway she might be able just slip back through time and find herself back in 2009. Going back to Nuncio's Pasty Shop had not proved successful. There appeared to be no way back there, but then she thought of the feeling that she had of someone else in the basement. *Was someone looking for me—separated by 68 years? Perhaps it was Michael.*

What must Michael be going through wondering where I am? And what about Joan, Emily and Donna. Have they gone back to Appleton? What will they say to the high school staff? Will the Post Crescent carry the story that an Appleton West high school teacher had disappeared in Hurley, Wisconsin?

Who knows, perhaps I'm standing in the same space as they were this afternoon just separated by 68 years.

The idea blew her away.

Thirteen

Monday December 1, 1941

On Monday December 1st, Nancy woke and once again was disappointed that she was still in the same room and that her search for a doorway in time had failed. However, she was no longer startled by her new surroundings. She was actually finding the bedroom comforting. It was her safe place in this world turned upside down. Then remembering the strange feeling in Nuncio's basement, she felt slightly optimistic about her future. She was almost sure there was a spiritual presence watching her. Maybe there was still a glimmer of hope.

This was her fourth day in this strange new world of 1941 and now she laid thinking about this coming Sunday, December 7th. *Is there anything I can do about it? Hundreds of men and women are going to perish in this upcoming Japanese attack and maybe I can stop it. If I'm able to stop the attack or minimize the losses, what does that do to history? The people that died may live and what would that due to history. Kids would be born that never would have been and perhaps others would not have been born. This type of thinking was always coming up on shows like Star Trek and other science fiction movies all the time. Some books say time travel is impossible and even if you went back, you could not change history. It's the old paradox, if you went back in time would you be able to kill your own grandfather and at the same time eliminate yourself from ever being born. The thought is that you would not be able to do it. Something would stop you.*

After more thought Nancy decided that she had to try to contact the authorities no matter what the consequences were. She would only feel guilty if she did nothing and yet how was she going to tell people that she knew the Japanese were by now en route to the Hawaiian Islands to attack Pearl Harbor. Finally late that morning, she composed a letter to the State

Department in Washington D.C. hoping that by some chance someone might take the warning seriously and take a second look at what the Japanese were doing. She felt better that she was at least doing something rather than doing nothing at all. Since it was Monday and Martha was working, she would not know that she went to the post office by herself. She had already let it slip that the Japanese were going to attack and she was hoping that Martha had not taken her seriously. Martha already knew Nancy was from another time and did not want that to get out to the rest of the community.

She walked down Fifth Avenue, walking in the street because of all the snow. When she came to the corner of Fifth Avenue and Silver Street, she saw the Burton House on her left and on her right where the Post Office had been in 2009 was a hardware store. She did not panic, but remained calm knowing that in a town with only six blocks the post office should be easy to find. As she walked along, she found that people did not gawk at her as they did a few days ago now that she had new clothes. She found the post office two blocks up.

When she entered, she noticed that it was not much warmer inside. The clerk had his back to her busy with some paper work. When he turned around, she noticed his large head, which sat on an all too small neck for the size of his head. His hair was combed back in a pompadour making him look confrontational. He appeared to be cold when he said, "Hello, may I help you?" The look on his face said, *who are you and what are you doing here?*

"I'd like to mail a letter please."

Without making eye contact, he took the letter with a look of doubt on his face. Pausing he said, "Washington D.C." It was not a question.

"Yes, that's correct. How much will that cost and will it get there before Sunday?"

"We'll have to send it by airmail and that will cost more. Do you want to do that?"

"Yes, that will be fine."

"That will be eight cents?"

She tried not to let her astonishment show, but she could see that he noticed as he said, "is there something wrong, is that too expensive?"

"No, I was just thinking of something else I had on my mind."

Reaching into her pocket, she gave him a 1984 quarter that was worn and looked old. She regretted that she had not asked Martha for some money. It was too late now and she could only hope that the Washington quarter of 1984 was the same as the Washington quarter in 1941. It was a good thing it was not one of those new state quarters. She was glad that the clerk was more interested in looking at her than at her money. He gave her seventeen cents back and said nothing else to her as she left.

As she left she shivered not from the cold, but from the bad feeling she had about the clerk. Something about him made her feel uneasy. Dismissing the thought, she hurried along Silver Street to Fifth Avenue only pausing to glance at Nuncio's Pasty shop, wondering if that place would be the key to her return. Once home she wondered if anyone would look at the letter and if they did would they take it seriously? Never the less she felt good about the fact that she had sent the letter unaware that the postal clerk had not mailed it.

* * *

After Nancy left with no one around Bran Crowther slipped Nancy's letter in his coat pocket to take home. He knew that this was a violation of postal rules and he was putting his twenty-five years of employment at risk. He could be fired if caught, but he was sure this woman would never know one way or another if the letter was ever delivered. He wasn't sure why that woman had made him feel so ill at ease. Perhaps it was the fact that all his life attractive women had easily intimidated him. He felt that there was more to it than that. After seeing the address on the letter—the State Department—he felt certain that there was indeed something different about her and that was what made him determined to find out what was in the letter. He did not realize at the time that this impulse to take the letter would lead to something unimaginable.

That night he waited until after supper before excusing himself to the solitude of his den where he opened the letter and read it slowly to himself.

To Whom It May Concern:

I am writing you this letter because I believe it is my duty as a citizen of the United States. I know that you may think that this is a crank letter, but please even if you do, investigate my allegations. I am confident that if you proceed, you will find that what I am saying is correct.

This coming Sunday, December 7th, just before 8:00 AM Hawaiian time the Japanese will attack the Pearl Harbor Navel base by air from aircraft carriers. If you do some checking you will find the Japanese carriers are already at sea en route to Pearl Harbor. If you do nothing, the battleship Arizona will be blown up and nearly all of the crew killed or wounded. This attack will be devastating to the U.S.

Pacific Fleet not to mention that over 3000 men will be killed.

I realize that this maybe hard for you to believe, but please do some checking. If I'm wrong you have lost nothing, if I am right you may be able to save hundreds of lives.

Sincerely yours,
A Concerned Citizen

Dumbfounded he sat there not at all sure of what he had read. That lady must be insane to put something like that in a letter to Washington. Then he read it again. He still could not believe what she had written. She had to be a real nut job. How could she possibly know that the Arizona would be blown up? The paper that evening said that the U.S. was still conducting bilateral talks with the Japanese and they were confident that the Japanese would remove their troops from China. There was no mention of any threat to the Hawaiian Islands. Surely if war was eminent the U.S. Intelligence would have already known that the Japanese carriers were on the way. Even if they were on the way what could a few hundred planes from aircraft carriers expect to do to a well-armed navel base.

Next, he thought of turning her into the authorities. Wasn't she guilty of treason or something? Then he thought better of it as he would have to explain how he came into possession of the letter. It was so preposterous that he decided to put the letter in his underwear drawer and leave it there until December 7th. No way was he going to pass this on to the government with how busy they were. He told himself that he would just have a good laugh on Sunday afternoon when this turned out to be a hoax.

Fourteen

Sunday December 7, 1941

On Sunday December 7th, Nancy and Martha came home after the 10:30 AM mass and Nancy asked Martha if she could listen to the radio. Martha thought it strange, because she usually played the piano with any free time.

It was fifteen minutes before noon and Nancy knew the first attack would take place right at noon central time. She had no idea how long it would take for the news of the attack to be reported unlike in 2009, when it seemed that major events were reported almost instantly.

Martha had a floor model Zenith Radio that she had purchased in 1939. It was huge with a high gloss wooden finish. The radio took several minutes to come on and when Nancy asked Martha why it took so long, she explained that the tubes had to warm up first. Nancy had never seen anything that had tubes.

Nancy was still hoping that perhaps her warning letter to the State Department had been read and that the war had been averted or at least the attack on Pearl Harbor would be repelled. As she waited listening to music, Martha was busy making lunch.

When Martha called Nancy for lunch at 12:30 PM nothing had been reported on the radio and Nancy was beginning to think that perhaps her letter had made a difference. In 2009, news was almost instantaneous and most of the time you could count on CNN to have live video feed by satellite. If the attack was happening, it had been in progress now for more than thirty minutes.

When she ate quickly, Martha asked, "Why the hurry child, what's so important on that radio?"

"Oh nothing I was just listening to the Sammy Kaye's Sunday Serenade."

Nancy continued to stay by the radio and Martha sat with her. It was a tranquil Sunday afternoon. Then at 1:30 PM as NBC was finishing up with Sammy and his Orchestra came the words that Nancy had dreaded. **"We interrupt this program with a special bullentin:"** Even before the announcer started to speak, Nancy knew that her letter had failed to reach the proper people. Her heart sank and she thought she was going to be sick.

Before Martha could react to how pale Nancy was, she heard the announcer say:

> **Three separate waves of more than 150 Japanese bombers and torpedo-carrying planes were launched in a surprise attack on Pearl Harbor, the chief U.S. Navel base in the Pacific. The attacked occurred shortly before 8:00 AM Hawaiian time. Hits were scored on the battleships Oklahoma and the Arizona, both were sunk. The third wave destroyed much of Pearl Harbor's fuel, torpedo storage, maintenance and dry dock facilities. Casualties amounted to 5,500 of which 3,000 are fatal.**
>
> **At the time of the attack, Japanese representatives were in Washington under the pretext of negotiating peace. No formal declaration of war was issued by Japan before the attack.**

They both stared at each other in disbelief waiting for the radio to say that this was only a radio dramatization. Martha remembered back in the fall of 1938 when Orson Welles brought the country to a state of mass hysteria in response to his radio broadcast of an alien invasion by Mars. His broadcast of "War of the Worlds" had been so real that people believed the earth was really under an attack. For a fleeting moment, she was hoping this was the same thing until the live broadcaster said, **"This battle has been going on for nearly three hours... It's no joke, it's a real war."**

"Nancy, did they say anything about the U.S.S. Pennsylvania, the ship my son is on?"

"No, they only said that the Arizona and the Oklahoma were sunk. From what I can remember, the Pennsylvania only sustained minor damage. So, your son should be okay."

"Thank God for that. I feel so bad about those other sailors on the Arizona and the Oklahoma. The only thing we can do is pray."

"Martha the war has started. We are involved now whether we like it or not."

"I can't believe this, but didn't you say on that first Friday night, that war was coming with an attack on the Hawaiian Islands. Nancy you knew!

That was why you were glued to the radio. I'm not at all sure how people are going to react to the fact that you knew this would happen. If they find out they may come looking for you."

'"Martha, I'm scared. There are some things that are different from how I remember."

"What do you mean child. Perhaps you don't remember, after all it happened years before you were ever born."

"No, Martha, I'm a history teacher and I know this stuff. Besides that my father was a World War Two history buff and he was always talking about what happened at Pearl Harbor and about how the Japanese could have won."

"What ever do your mean?"

"He always said if the Japanese had sent a third wave and destroyed much of Pearl Harbor's fuel, torpedo storage, maintenance, and dry dock facilities, they may have hampered the U.S. Pacific Fleet far more seriously than loss of its battleships. It may have postponed Pacific operations for more than a year and perhaps prolonged the war another two years."

"So what you're saying is that in your history books there were only two attacks instead of three and that your history doesn't completely agree with the history we are living now."

"Yes, that's what I'm saying and it scares the hell out of me."

"Why didn't the Japanese send the third wave?"

"They were afraid the American anti-aircraft guns would have improved considerably and they did not want to risk loosing their pilots while suffering higher aircraft losses. Besides that, they did not know where the American carriers were. They just plain got cold feet. It was only after they were back in Japan that they realized that they had made a mistake. That is why six months later they attack Midway Island. Knowing what I know now, I'm no longer sure of that history and that's why I'm scared. This could be a much longer war and I have to wonder if we can win it."

"My God Nancy what are we going to do? We can't let on to people that you know anything about this."

"Martha, I'm sorry I got you into this, but let's just see how things go in the next few weeks. I'm not sure anyone would believe me if I told them what I think I know. You are the only one I can trust."

"Oh my God, Nancy do you think anyone else suspects that you are from the future?"

"The only ones that might are Dr. Frost and some of the people who saw me those first few days. I'm not sure what they think. Do you think Dr. Frost has any idea? Has he said anything to you about me?"

"He may have suspicions. He has asked me a number of things about you indirectly. He may have also told his poker buddies."

"We will just have to see what happens in the days and weeks ahead."

* * *

That same evening when Bran Crowther was visiting relatives and heard about the attack by the Japanese, it hit him like a ton of bricks. Although he had never passed out in his entire life, he thought he was going to now. His Uncle saw how pale he was and told him to lie down and he did not refuse. Lying there he thought, *What have I done, that woman was only trying to save American lives and perhaps stop this war and I didn't mail the letter. It's like I'm responsible for all of these deaths.*

After lying there for more than fifteen minutes, he began to feel better. Then he rationalized, *that letter would never have gotten there in time anyway and who was going to believe her?*

How did she know? That woman is different. Maybe she is a spy or something. I wonder what people really know about her other than she is supposed to be Martha's sister's daughter or something.

He made up his mind that he was going to find out more about her next week. The question on his mind was what else did she know?

Secretly he began to speculate that if she knew the future there was no end to what that could mean to him and some of his friends. What else might she know? Did she know if the stock market was going to go up in the years ahead? Did she know who was going to win at different sporting events; if she did the possibilities of winning gambling bets were endless? He thought of just how valuable she could be, if she could truly predict the future or if she was from the future.

Fifteen

Monday December 8, 1941

On Monday morning, Martha got Nancy up for morning mass at six in the morning. It was a holy day—the feast of the Immaculate Conception. After mass, they had breakfast and Martha went to work. Nancy stayed home and read the special edition of the newspaper that confirmed what they had heard on the radio. There really had been three waves of bombers.

After having the night to think things over, she was not as anxious as she had been the night before. Perhaps the third wave of bombers would not make that big a difference in the complete history. She could only hope.

Later that night before the President's radio address to the nation, she heard the reporter say again that there were three separate attacks on Peal Harbor by the Japanese carrier planes. He did not however elaborate concerning the Pacific fleet operations or the possibility of a prolonged war. That was good news. Only here in 1941 she thought they would not talk about that anyway. Not like in 2009 where every network reporter talks constantly, speculating as to what will happen next.

* * *

Later that evening less than 24 hours after the attack on Pearl Harbor President Franklin Roosevelt called a joint session of Congress to declare war on Japan. Nancy and Martha listened to his speech along with 80 million Americans—almost two-thirds of the population. He began with words that Nancy remembering hearing years back when Americans remembered Pearl Harbor day. She never in her wildest dream thought she would hear them spoken live.

"Yesterday," Roosevelt began, ''December 7, 1941—a date which will live in infamy—the United States of America was suddenly and deliberately attack by naval and air forces

of the Empire of Japan. With confidence in our armed forces, with the unbounding determination of our people, we will gain the inevitable triumph, so help us God."

The total speech was only six and a half minutes long and both Nancy and Martha had tears in their eyes when he finished.

Nancy saw Martha looking at her with a beleaguered look on her face. Then she said, "Nancy, I know we must win the war but what will it cost in lives? How long will it take?"

"Martha, in my world we did win and I think we will win here in this world. Let's just wait and see what happens and then maybe we can try to figure out what to do next. We need to keep all of this between you and me."

"I won't tell anyone, but Nancy just think about how hard this is for me with my son now in this war, I'll be worried about what is going to happen to him. Then I have to think about you living with me. I have so many questions and the very thought that you may know the answers scares me."

"Martha, I don't know anything personal about you, I don't know when you'll die or if you get sick or what happens to your son. In fact, I know very little about what will happen to the city of Hurley. With some of these changes, I'm not sure what I know about the future. I may know the big things in history like what you read in the history books. All I can say for certain, is that in my world, the Japanese loose the war but actually come out better by loosing. In the future, you will be surprised to know that Japanese cars will be sold in the U.S. and they will be the market leader. They will dominate the electronic industry with televisions, computers, video recorders and much more that you wouldn't understand. As for right now Martha, I'm worried about you and me and how we will get by in this time of trouble. I have no way of knowing if things will turn out the way I know. Who knows, perhaps my being here is enough to change history."

"I'm sorry Nancy, please forgive me. I'm just an old woman who is concerned about the near future, like what will happen to my son. There is one thing that I do know and that is that I love you Nancy and I thank God you came into my life. Without you, my life would not be very interesting and you have given me friendship and for that, I thank you. Please don't leave me."

"Martha, I won't leave and not because I have no where to go, but because I have become very fond of you. You have been most kind to me—like a mother. So let's stick together and see where this adventure will take us."

Sixteen

Tuesday December 9, 1941

On Tuesday December 9th, Bran Crowther was at the post office still undecided what to do about what he now called the Pearl Harbor letter. Now that the U.S. had declared war on Japan he mulled over in his mind what he should do with the information he had about that woman that lived with Martha Laine. How did she know about the attack and the sinking of the Arizona he could not help but wonder what else she knew? Was she some kind of soothsayer? He continued to think, if she was able to see into the future, how extremely useful that could be. Maybe he could make some money knowing the future. It had not entered his mind to use this information to help the war effort.

What perplexed him was how to proceed. He thought about telling his wife, but she would only dismiss it as one more of his get rich schemes. There was one friend he thought he could trust, Leo Coppalo, who owned the local department store. He called him saying he had something to talk over with him. They agreed to meet for a drink after work.

* * *

"Leo, it's good to see you. It sure was a surprise what happened last Sunday. I never saw it coming."

"The entire government never saw it coming. Those Japs knew what they were doing. Can you image negotiating with someone while an attack is imminent? So what did you have on your mind."

"Do you know that woman that is staying at Martha Laine's house?"

"Yes, I do. Doc Frost was talking about her last Friday night at the poker game. They brought her up to his place after she was hit by a car on Friday November 28th. Wasn't hurt bad, but he said she was a looker. Acted really strange though. Then on Saturday, she was into my store with Martha and they were buying all new clothes. It was like as if the woman had nothing to wear. She seemed strange like she had never been shopping before. Can you imagine a woman who did not look comfortable shopping? Why do you ask?"

"She was in to the post office last Monday wanting to mail a letter. The strange thing was that the letter was addressed to the State Department, in Washington. Now you have to keep this between you and me. I kept the letter and opened it that night. It said the Japanese were going to attack Pearl Harbor before eight in the morning on December 7th and that the Arizona battleship was going to be sunk. I thought it was just a prank letter and stuck it away and then Sunday when I heard the news well you could have knocked me over."

"Are you telling me that she knew this stuff in advance and was trying to warn the government?"

Reaching into his pocked he said, "Here read the letter for yourself."

After Leo had read it twice he said, "I don't believe it, but it sure sounds genuine. How could she know stuff like that?"

"I have no idea how she knew, but I think she was trying to warn the government."

"Do you think she's a spy?"

"I don't think so, she seems too naïve."

"What do you think I should do? I don't want to sound like an idiot going to the police. I don't think they'd believe me. Besides, I'd have to tell them how I got the letter."

"I agree, most likely they would not believe you, but I'm not sure there is anything for us to do."

"Here is an angle I want to run by you and maybe we can include a few of your poker friends if you think it has any merit. Let's just say she can predict the future. If we were to know certain things maybe we could make a few bucks. Like what if she knows that Wisconsin will win the NCAA basketball tournament again this year as they did last year or who is going to be the next heavy weight boxing champ. Then what if she knows how this war is going to end. Just think about it. The possibilities are unless."

"That's not a bad idea, but there is no way Wisconsin wins everything this year. That was a fluke last year. They may not win another championship in our lifetime. There is one little thing, how do we know she is for real?"

"Here's what I was thinking. At the next poker game maybe you could see what Doc thinks about this. You don't have to tell him about the letter just yet, but maybe you could see if he might talk to Martha and you know one thing could lead to another. If this turned out right, think of the money that could be made. There'd be enough for everyone."

"Our game is this Friday night. I'll feel him out and see if he can even meet with the girl. You know, maybe he could have her come in again for a follow-up. That would be a good excuse."

"That sounds like a plan."

"The game is at my house and you could sit in. You don't have to produce the letter, but you could just say you saw her at the post office.

"I'll be there. What time is the game?"

"Starts at eight, bring your money."

Seventeen

Friday Night December 12, 1941

Since Tuesday after talking with Bran Crowther, Leo Coppalo had time to think. He still found it hard to believe that anyone could predict the future, but he had seen the letter with his own eyes. Perhaps this Monroe girl was for real. Some sort of mystic. He knew when she came into the store last Saturday with Martha there was something different about her. Just the way she looked around the store, like she was seeing everything for the first time. It was as if she didn't belong here. It was not like she was from a foreign country, she just did not fit into society. The more he thought about it the more he believed that it was possible for her to be from a different time, no matter how fantastic that sounded. Now tonight he was going to propose to his friends, they do some investigating.

* * *

After everyone had arrived and had a drink, they sat around talking about how things had changed so much since they last met. Then Leo said, "before we get started I asked Bran Crowther to come over tonight not only to play cards, but he and I have something we'd like to discuss with the group. What Bran has to say may shock you just as it did me, but let him finish and then we can talk about it."

Bran related what he had told Leo on Tuesday night and when he finished he passed around the letter for all to read. The group was speechless. Oscar Kosken was the first to speak. "You say she tried to mail this letter, what made you keep it?"

"For one thing it was the way she acted. You know as if she'd never been in a post office before. She was looking all over and didn't seem to know what stamps cost. She was just strange. Damn pretty, but strange. When she left, I just had to see what was in that letter. I thought it was a crank letter until Sunday night when I heard the news about the attack on Pearl Harbor. Doc, you know her what do you think about her?"

"When they brought her in the afternoon of the accident I didn't really pay much attention to her other than she was in a state of panic and I thought that was normal for someone just hit by a car, but she did say some real strange stuff. She said, 'Take me back to Sally's. I have to get back to my friends.' I had no idea what she meant by Sally's. She also said, 'I don't belong here.' and then she asked, 'What's the date?' When I told her it was Friday, November 28th she got upset and said, 'No, I mean what year is it?' When I said 1941 she said, 'It can't be.' That was the last thing she said to me."

"Why would anyone ask what year it was?" remarked Fred Banister.

"I don't know, only that maybe she was out of her head due to the car hitting her."

"Bran and Leo both said when they saw her that she looked like she didn't belong. What if, let's say she didn't belong to this time. If I were from the past or the future, wouldn't one of the first things you'd ask, is what year is it?" said Ralph.

"Alright, that's more than I can take. How would someone travel through time? Aren't we going off the deep end," said Oscar.

"I have to agree, but it was the disbelief in her voice when I told it was 1941. Then she started to cry," said Doctor Frost.

"Did she ever say what year she thought it was?"

"No, but it seemed like Martha knew what she was talking about. When I asked Martha if she had identification she told me no, but she did have a purse. Now that I think back, it was very strange. I think I've got to have a talk with Martha."

"That's what Bran and I were thinking. You could also ask Martha to bring her back in for a follow-up exam. She really couldn't refuse and you could get a better idea of who she might be by talking directly to her."

"That's a good idea. I'll talk to Martha on Monday. And if we find she's from Mars then what are we going to do?"

"If we can determine who she is and her story checks out, then we just forget about this letter and chalk it up to a coincidence. And if things don't add up then I think we have to go slow and come up with a plan. There has to be an explanation for what she knew and why she was trying to contact Washington. I for one can't bring myself to believe she is from the future. That my friends, is pretty far out."

Ralph Winslow who was quite most of the night said, "I've been taking all this in and I think there has to be a reason for why she is here and I don't think she came from the future. I think there is plausible explanation for all of this. On the other hand, if she does have the ability to see into the future, think about what that could be worth. You know I'm a fan of boxing and if I'd have known that Max Schmeling, that German, was going to beat Joe Louis in the rematch fight, I'd have made a fortune. Therefore, I think we have to pursue this. Besides she may even be able to tell us who will win this damn war and how long it is going to last. I don't know about the rest of you, but I'd like to know that. I've got a kid that just turned nineteen and I'd like to know if he is going to have to go off to war."

"The next step, I think is for Doc to have another look at her and talk to Martha. The rest of us can ask around and see what others in the town know. Then let's meet back here next week and talk about what to do next."

"That sounds like a deal, now I think we've wasted too much time already and I'm ready to take your money."

2009

Eighteen

Sunday December 13, 2009

It had been two weeks since Robert Rahn had search Sally's café basement looking for any clues that would help him find Nancy Monroe. To date the police had turned up absolutely nothing. The only thing he had to go on was a feeling. It was the presence of someone else there with him in Sally's basement. Could it have been Nancy Monroe?

After the search of the basement, he ordered an EMF (Electro Magnetic Field) meter, an infrared thermometer and Geiger counter. He planned to use all three items to see if he could discover the presence of a ghost, like on that popular TV show, Ghost Hunters.

He planned to use the EMF meter to measure AC electromagnetic fields, which are usually emitted from man-made sources such as electrical wiring. EMF readings in a home are between 9.0 - 30.0. Anything that registers in the 2.0 to the 7.0 range has been attributed to spirit activity, since it is scientifically impossible for low-level fields to occur naturally.

The Geiger counter he planned to use to monitor for changes in the background radiation. In the literature, it stated that ambient radiation increased in the presents of a ghost.

With an **infrared thermometer** he would be able to detect cold spots in the middle of a room where as regular thermometers can only measure the surface temperature of objects. It was thought that spirits sometime emit cold spots.

* * *

While he waited for his equipment to arrive he spent most his waking hours working on background information for her case. He could not get her out of his mind and he told himself that it had nothing to do with the fact that she was the prettiest women he had every seen or the fact that he was lonely. He had been intrigued by the case and followed the progress of the investigation in the local Ironwood Gazette—what little there was. He had also spoken with the police and they welcomed any help he could give them.

How did this woman disappear? There was no viable explanation. She had no known enemies, was well liked and there were no witnesses. She simply vanished. The police investigation was starting its third week and had turned up nothing. The only thing known was that she had gone to the bathroom in the café where she was having breakfast and never came back. Robert had been all over the café and the restroom and he too found nothing.

He did an internet search of her and found only good things. She was 25 years old and had been employed in the Appleton School District four years and her performance reviews were commendable or outstanding. She was well received by parents and students alike. She was active in her church. There was nothing to lead him to say that she was depressed or unstable in anyway. There was no history of drug use and no known medical problems. He was amazed at what a person could find on the internet and most of it was free. There were other detailed sites for a small price, which would provide you with everything that you wanted to know. In today's world, there was no such thing as privacy.

He had several pictures of her and other information from her high school and college yearbooks. She was very attractive and he thought that had to be the only reason for her alleged abduction. He could come up with no reason why she herself would want to disappear. She had a steady boyfriend, Michael Niffen and it appeared that he was going to ask her to marry him this Christmas.

He could only think that it had to be some deranged person that had kidnapped her and transported her out of the state. By now, she was probably dead.

With no signs of a struggle and no physical evidence to go on, Robert turned his thoughts to the paranormal. He knew that the police, like most people were grounded in the here and now. They did not want to give credence to a paranormal solution. Since he and the police had exhausted all the other possibilities, he tried to see if there was a paranormal reason for what had happened. He had come to this conclusion that not all things could be explained by conventional thinking.

There were countless cases of how people had traveled back in time. Most of these people were stable and reliable. The problem was that in all of those cases the person had returned and was only gone a short time. There were no stories of anyone returning after a long period of time. He could only speculate about those. There were other cases where people just plain vanished and were never seen again. Their disappearances were never really explained. There were explanations like in that movie, Close Encounters of a Third Kind, where an alien spaceship returns bringing back people who had vanished. That was just Stephen Spielberg's idea of an explanation.

Next Robert considered the possibility of an alternative reality. There were all kinds of theories posted out on the internet and it was hard to sort out what was creditable and what was not. Much of it was from people who could be said to be mentally unstable.

Then there were time slippages, an event where it appeared that someone had gone back to another time. It was as if a past era briefly intruded on the present. Time slippages were spontaneous in nature and localized, but it was believed there were places on the planet that seem to be more prone to these events. As well as some people being more inclined to experience a time slippage than others. If time is really an unmovable force that physicists say it is, why do the experiences of some people seem to repudiate this concept?

There was one theory that suggests that if someone could go back into the past he or she might affect our present. Others argued that if someone were to be transported into the past, their mere presences might alter the history of our future from that point. It was thought that it might not be noticed because a new parallel world would be created. This was related to quantum mechanics physic, which claimed that there were many worlds similar to ours, but different. There was however, no analytical way to prove it.

His research next led him to an internet search of "Quantum Mechanics." There he found so much information it was overwhelming. Hugh Everett introduced the term "Many-Worlds Interpretation." As best as he could determine from quantum mechanics theorized that there were many other similar worlds, which exist in parallel.

It went on to explain that we move freely in three dimensions called space. There is a fourth dimension of time and in time; we are rooted to one place. It also said that the universe is more complicated than we could ever imagine. There is not just one universe, but an uncountable number of them. They are all roughly the same size and complexity. They affected each other, so when something went wrong on one it had an influence on all of them.

The more he read the more he thought he was reading from a copy of Fantastic Worlds. Quantum Mechanic made it possible that there really were alternate universes, not just a well-worn theme of science fiction. The "many worlds" interpretation of quantum mechanics allows a time traveler to alter the past without producing problems. You would just go into another universe. Thus the quantum theory did not forbid time travel.

It went on to say that suppose in this world you were driving and had a near miss, you might feel relieved and fortunate to have escaped. In another parallel universe, you may have been killed. Yet in another universe, you may have been in an accident, but recovered. The number of alternative scenarios is endless.

Therefore, if Nancy Monroe had gone back into the past—to a parallel world—she would find upon arrival the same history that we know in our history books. Going forward she would by her presence there be creating a new parallel world that may be very similar to ours or maybe not, depending upon the impact she made upon that world, however some things may change just because of her presence.

The article went on to say that it was possible that someone or a number of people may have arrived in our medieval past in Europe during the fourteenth century and may have altered our present world. During that time, the world was in chaos with famine, climate changes, economic collapse, social upheaval, endemic war and the physical and psychological devastation of the Black Death. In all of recorded history, there has never been such period utter disaster. Many died because of war, famine and the Black Death.

What made people believe that someone changed things is that there was a dramatic change from the fourteenth century to the fifteenth century from an intensely spiritual society to a secularism and materialism society that embraced technology and science. Why this profound shift? Was it because of one hundred years of strife or was it because of the presence of someone or a group of people that went back into the past and transformed society. There is no reason to believe that suddenly a people's intelligence would improve so dramatically in such a short period of time without help from an outside source.

So if Nancy had really crossed into a different time, where was she? What might it be like to find yourself in a different time? Perhaps you might go mad. If you were so different, people might think of you as a witch or mystic. Would you survive? The more he thought, what if Nostradamus had gone back in time from the twentieth century. Was he a time traveler rather than a clairvoyant? If he were from the twentieth century he surely would have been able to predict things like the rise of Hitler, Napoleon, both world wars and the fall of the twin towers. Just think about the things we know now and if we went back in time three hundred years, we would certainly be seen as a prophet but you have to be very careful to blend into society and how you put out the information. Perhaps that was why Nostradamus did his writing quatrains.

Considering all of this, he still did not know what to do with what he learned. Where would he start in his search for Nancy Monroe? If she slipped though time to another world, how could he ever hope to locate the site? If he found where she entered was it possible for him to follow her. Was there a way to pick the right time where she was. It was not like H.G. Wells, The Time Machine where you could set the machine for a specific time and go back.

If Nancy was truly in the past he did not have a clue as to how he was ever going to find her much less rescue her. Even if he found a time portal and was able to enter it, how would he locate Nancy? Then if some how he was lucky enough to locate her how would he be able to get her back. He felt hopeless and was ready to give up, but decided to do some more searching. Maybe he would run across something new on the internet no matter how fantastic it was.

Then he remembered that the Maya civilization predictioned that something was going to happen on the winter solstice of 2012, it made him remember that many places on the earth were sacred to the American Indian tribes. Perhaps somewhere on Indian lands near him there might be a time portal.

He remembered hearing a story about a woman who disappeared in 1975 while cross-country skiing. In fact, the cross-country trail was not far from his property. After an extensive search, no trace of the woman was ever found. She remains missing to this very day.

Then he recalled reading about people who had sighted a black panther in the area. The DNR had told people that it was impossible for a panther to exist in a cold climate. Could the black cat have come through a time portal? It would explain what people saw.

On the Sy Fi channel there was a show called, Monster Quest, where people had seen a pterodactyl, which was impossible, unless it came back through time.

Being at a dead end, he knew the nearby local Indian reservation had several interesting landmarks that were not far from his house that he could search, but first he would search his own land first and that would have to wait until April or May. In the meantime, he would ask Sally if he could have one more look around her café with his new instruments. Even if the time portal had moved, there should be some signs that it had been there.

With the day drawing to close, he sat down to have an evening cocktail with Albert. He had to admit that he thought finding Nancy Monroe was a long shot. When he leveled with himself, he had to admit that he really didn't put much faith in this time travel stuff. He thought the only reason he continued to pursue this was because he had nothing better to do. He never admitted to himself that he might be falling in love with a woman he had never met.

1941

Nineteen

Saturday/Sunday December 13/14, 1941

Martha went to work on the Monday after the Japanese attack knowing very well that nothing would ever be the same. She knew Nancy was different from that first evening when she took her home, but now with Nancy knowing about the attack on Pearl Harbor she was sure that Nancy either was able to know the future or she was from the future, no matter how outrageous that sounded. Martha thought that she should be scared having Nancy living with her, but other than that first night she felt at ease with Nancy. In fact, she trusted Nancy. Now her only two concerns were for Nancy's welfare and her safety. Martha thought, *what if someone else was to find out about Nancy.*

Nancy stayed home other than going out to mail her warning letter. She was still trying to come to grips with the fact that she was in the year 1941. Each night when Martha came home from work Nancy could see that Martha was tired. Nancy hated to disturb her with her questions, so she found herself looking forward to the weekend when they could finally have time to talk.

For Nancy it was the first time in five years that she could remember being idle. She read the newspaper and listened to the radio and everyday the news got worse. The Japanese attacked The Philippines and invaded several islands in the Pacific. They were on the offensive all over the Pacific and in Asia. On top of all of that, the U.S. declared war on Germany and Italy on December 11th. It was one thing to read about all of this in the history books, but it was another thing to be living it.

The war was going according to what Nancy could remember except for two things. The first was the third attack on Pearl Harbor by the Japanese carrier planes and the second was the fact that the radio said that the Germans had surrounded Moscow and that the Russian government had moved out of the city. She knew there were only two attacks and that the Germans had been stopped outside of Moscow. Other than that, things agreed with what Nancy knew of the history of the Second World War.

With these changes in history, Nancy had serious doubts about how this war was going to end. Before she had always thought that the price in lives was going to be high, but she had no doubts that the U.S. and its allies would win, now she was no longer sure. She wondered if it was her presence in this time that was changing things.

* * *

After visiting Nuncio's Pasty Shop and not finding any clues as to how she got here or how to get back, she had started to accept the fact that she was here to stay. The only thing that gave her hope was the fact that after the visit to Nuncio's she had experienced a feeling of dizziness and nausea. She also had a feeling that some sort of spirit or presences was in the room.

She still thought about Michael constantly and cried herself to sleep at night thinking of him. While she knew that Michael loved her she now found that she was having doubts about how much she really loved him. Perhaps it was just the fact that she was coming to terms with the idea that she was never going to get back to 2009 and she did not think that it was possible for Michael to come to her.

She thought, *he will in time move on and forget about me.* Each night when she went to bed, she still thought that perhaps she would wake up in her own apartment back in Appleton. When it didn't happen, she started to resign herself to being trapped here in 1941 and with each passing day, she spent less time feeling sorry for herself. On Friday, when she woke and found she had not cried herself to sleep, she knew she was resigning herself to being here and making the best of it.

* * *

Now that she finally had some time off, she didn't like it. The days went slowly and Nancy thought about everything. She constantly thought about Michael and her girl friends. What must they be thinking? She thought *it must be all over the papers that I'm missing. I wonder if the police are still looking for me. I can't imagine the cost. Maybe there was a manhunt like on TV, I'm too old for an Amber alert. Did the school replace me? How long would they leave my job open? Perhaps with Christmas coming, people have just forgotten about me. They are use to moving on.* Then she cried and felt sorry for herself for the first time since Wednesday. She was glad that her parents had died early. Although she missed then dearly she was thankful they did not have to go through all of this. The days passed slowly, she read more than she ever did.

By Saturday December 13th, she decided it was time to confront Martha about getting a job. She just could not take sitting home everyday with nothing to do. Since this was wartime and she was trapped here, she was determined to do her part.

When Martha came home, Nancy asked her to sit down and talk. Before they talked Martha poured each of them a glass of wine and left the bottle. "Martha I've been here two week now and I think I need to get out. I need to get a job. I want to contribute. But before we talk about a job I have a personal question."

"What kind of personal question?"

"I'm having my period and well…I've run out of protection. What do women use in 1941 and please don't tell me rags."

Martha laughed. "No, women don't use rags. They use KOTEX sanitary napkins with belts or pins."

"Are napkins the same as pads, because I don't use pads, I use tampons and for God's sake, what's a belt?"

"I suppose napkins are the same as pads and a belt is how you wear the napkin."

Nancy cringed, "I might have heard about belts, but I've never seen one, I don't think they even sell them anymore. If we use napkins or pads, they have adhesive on the back that sticks to you panties and they have panty liners for waning days, like KOTEX LIGHTDAYS."

"Adhesive! What in the world is panty liner?"

"There is adhesive on the back of the pad and you stick it to your panties and that is how it stays in place and a panty liner is a very a thin pad shaped to fit into the crotch of your panties."

"Sorry dear, no such thing like that today. Today you have to use a belt or pin it to your underwear when wearing a pad, but that adhesive idea sounds really interesting."

"Please tell me that they sell tampons. I really hate using pads and I'm not going to use a belt."

"Yes, they have tampons and you can buy them at the drug store, but most people don't use them. The very idea to most women is discussing. It's sort of …well like a violation of yourself."

"Martha you have to remember that times change. In 2009 they even have birth control pills that you can take so that you only have your period three or four times a year."

"What is a birth control pill?"

"It's a pill you take so you won't get pregnant."

"Maybe I need another glass of wine. When I was still having my period and you wanted to avoid pregnancy you used the rhythm method or you slept in separate rooms. Anyway many children were born by the rhythm method if you know what I mean."

"I've heard of the rhythm method. I don't know if many people use it anymore. Further more in my time abortion is legal since January 22, 1973. It is all about the woman having the right to choose."

"That's against God's law. No one has the right to take a life. Nancy, maybe there are things I was never meant to hear. In 1941, abortion is illegal and there is really no place to get one even illegally. You would really have to know someone. Women do not have the right to choose."

"I'm sorry Martha to bring all of this up. However, in the twenty-first century, women have many rights that they do not have here in 1941. In our elections, there are all kinds of debates over the right to choose and the right to life. The fundamentalist Christians are very powerful in our politics. The Catholics are very much against abortion and prayer services are held on the anniversary of Roe versus Wade every January. You have to be there, I guess to believe it."

"Nancy I have no idea about Roe versus Wade, but getting back to your question about your period, we'll go down to the Pharmacy tomorrow to get you what you need. It may not be what you are use to, but it will keep you protected.

Now what else did you have on your mind?"'

"I wanted to talk to you about getting a job. I've got to do something. I can't stay in this house all day. I'd like to be a teacher again."

"I'm not sure that you should teach, however, maybe there is a chance. You know now with the draft there are fewer men teachers, not that we had that many, but maybe you could get a job in one of the county townships. It would be teaching, as you have never seen before. It would be back to the one room schoolhouse way of teaching, but I'm sure you are qualified. Except you can't teach any of that modern stuff, if you know what I mean.

Let me see what I can do. The good thing for you is that they are looking for teachers so they wouldn't be too picky, I mean as far as wanting to know where you are from and where did you go to school."

"Martha you are a sweetheart, how can I ever thank-you."

"You have already thanked me, just your presences here with me has eliminated my loneliness. With you around my days have been anything, but dull. I'm not sure I want to hear any more about tampons, abortion or women's rights. Now let's have supper before I have another glass of wine."

Twenty

Monday December 15, 1941

When Martha arrived at work on Monday morning, Doctor Frost was waiting for her. She only hoped that he had not seen the look of dread that came over her face. She did not have to ask what he wanted to talk about, she knew. It was about Nancy. She had planned for this moment and now that it was upon her all of that planning seemed for naught.

"Martha, did you and Nancy have a good weekend?"

"Yes, Doctor. I caught up on my rest after the shock of last week."

"Just how is Miss Monroe? Is she feeling any side effects since the accident?"

"I think she is doing fine. Maybe a few black and blue marks, but nothing else to speak of. Why do you ask?"

"I thought I should see her again. You know just a follow-up to make sure that she is doing all right. Can you get her to come in with you tomorrow morning?"

"I suppose I can arrange it. I'll tell her tonight." Anxious to get away she said. "Well if that's all, I've got some work to do before the first patient arrives."

"No, that can wait; I have a few more things to ask. What have you been able to find out about Miss Monroe? Like why is she here and where is she from?"

Martha thought, *You mean like is she from another time?*

Taking a deep breath, she paused and said. "She's from Appleton, Wisconsin about 230 miles south of here where she was a school teacher for the last three years. That is until she was laid off. She came up here on vacation to get away. Her boyfriend broke up with her. Therefore, when I saw how frighten she was after the accident, I told her she could stay with me. She has no compelling reason to go back. And you know Doctor it was just what I needed I can't tell you how much it means to me to have someone in the house for company. She's like another daughter."

She was quite proud of herself and for the most part everything was true to a certain extent. She was sort of laid off and Michael sort of left her.

"Martha, do you find her different? I mean, you know, the clothes she was wearing and the way she was carrying on about going back to Sally's and her friends. She also seemed surprised when she found out that it was 1941. Did you find that strange?"

Now Martha had to lie or at least stretch the truth. Something she was not good at and she hoped it would not show on her face.

"Perhaps she is a little different. She comes from a much bigger town for one thing. As for what she said, when she was bought in here, I think that was just the shock of the trauma talking. I don't think it meant anything. Maybe there is a Sally's down in Appleton."

"I suppose you're right. I just can't get over the fact that someone would have to ask what year this was. That puzzles me. I would think that no matter what happened, you'd remember what year it was. Just make sure you have her in here tomorrow to be examinede.

* * *

That evening when Martha entered the house she told Nancy what had happened. "I didn't tell him anything about you other than you are an unemployed school teacher that broke up with your boyfriend and decided to stay on here for a short time after the accident. He asked me if I thought you were different and I told him it was because you were from a bigger city and the shock of being hit by a car. He seemed to accept everything I said. The bad thing is he wants to check you over tomorrow. We've got to go over your story. I think he may suspect something."

"Martha, slow down. We will get through this. What if I told him the truth?"

"He'd lock you up in the Iron Country nut house and believe me you don't want to go there. If you weren't nuts when you went in you would be when you came out."

"I was only kidding. I'll tell him exactly what you said."

"He was particularly intrigued by the fact that you had to ask what year it was. He could not get over the idea that someone would forget the year. So be careful tomorrow, he may ask you about it. Remember you can't let anything slip out like you did with me. Another thing it sounded to me like Doctor had been talking with others about you. He may be on to something. You have to be careful."

Twenty-one

Tuesday December 16, 1941

Nancy did not sleep well thinking about what she was going to say to Doctor Frost. She knew that others thought her attractive and had frequently told her so, she did not use that to her advantage when dealing with others. Seldom did she ever use her looks to beguile people, but tomorrow she planned to make an exception.

Sharply at nine, Nancy and Martha enter the Doctor's office. She was the first patient of the day. She was now wearing what Martha called a stylish housedress with anklets. Underneath she was wearing a full slip something she was not used too, but she liked the feel of the silky material. Martha told her that she looked more than acceptable. In fact, Martha told her that she made the clothes look great. She was sure that Doctor Frost would be distracted by her looks. They were both confident that her clothes belonged to the period.

* * *

The Doctor invited her into the exam room and told Martha that she was not needed. Nancy thought that apparently Doctor Frost was not worried about being reported for sexual harassments. In 2009, there would always be a nurse present.

"Miss Monroe, you are looking a lot better than the last time I saw you?"

She gave him a confident smile and she could see that he notice her. "Yes, Doctor. I'm feeling fine and Martha had a lot to do with that. She's been so kind."

"You look so different today. When they brought you in here, you were wearing some very different looking clothing. I couldn't help but notice how different they were. Where did you get them? "

"I have an uncle that travels and he brought the clothes back from Europe. I'm not sure what country he got them from. They are quite different, especially for around here."

Next, he proceeded to take her blood pressure and listen to her lungs and heart. "Everything seems to be normal. Do you take any medicines?"

"No, other than the pill for menstrual cramps when I get my period."

"The pill, what do you mean, the pill?"

She knew she had slipped up but reacted quickly. "Oh it's just the pill I take for the cramps. Midol I think is the name."

Had she made a second mistake. She could only hope that Midol had been around for the last seventy years or so.

"Midol, yes, I've heard of it. I don't recommend it, I prefer plain old aspirin."

She hoped that the relief she was feeling was not evident on her face. To think that Midol had been around that long.

"I'm glad your feeling well. I just have two more questions. When they brought you in the police said you were running down Silver Street when the car hit you at Second Street. It seems funny to me that anyone would be running on snow and ice covered sidewalks. Why were you running? Was somebody chasing you?"

Pausing she thought that Martha had not prepared her for this question. The only thing she could think to tell him was that she was a runner.

"I'm a runner. I run a lot, mostly in the summer. I try to run two or three marathons a year, so it is just in my blood. You have a marathon up here, don't you?"

It was another mistake. The Paavo Nurmi would not run its first race until 1969.

"We don't have anything up here like the Boston Marathon."

"I must have been thinking of some other place, just like I wasn't thinking about the conditions when I was running that night. I'll just have to be more careful in the future."

"You run races? What kind of races?"

How do I get out of this? I've already said too much.

"You know, just short races like three and five mile. Sort of like track just to stay fit."

"So where were you running to?"

"No place. I was just running. I appreciate you taking this time with me Doctor, but I can't see what these question have to do with my health."

"Oh, I'm sorry if I upset you. You're right. I was just trying to understand what you were doing when you got hit by that car. My curiosity got the better of me. Please forgive me."

"Just one more curiosity question, please. That night you asked me or Martha what the date was and when we told you it was the 27th, you got upset and said no, what year is it? I just found that odd that someone would have forgotten what year it was?"

"Doctor I really don't remember too much about that night. I think I was out of my head. I really don't remember what I said. Now I know you are busy, I think I better be going."

"Thanks for coming in and I'm sorry if I upset you with all of my questions."

Twenty-two

Friday December 19, 1941

As Doctor Frost was driving over to Leo Coppalo's house for the Friday night poker game, he had to admit to himself that he was anxious to share notes with the rest of the players. For the most part, she had answered his questions. However, he thought there were a few times when she may not have been telling the truth. All of the players were there when he arrived and as it turned out all were waiting for him. They all had drinks, but none of them were thinking about playing poker.

Oscar Kosken was first to speak, "So what did she say when you examined her?"

"First off when I talked with Martha on Monday she seemed very tense as if she knew what I wanted to talk about. She did however answer all of my questions as to why she took Monroe home with her and how long she was going to stay. I won't say she lied to me, but I don't think she told me everything. And when I asked her to bring Monroe in on Tuesday she seemed upset, but she covered it up."

"Well, what happened on Tuesday?"

"When I invited Miss Monroe into the exam room, she seemed disturbed when I wouldn't let Martha join us. Most of what she said agreed with Martha. She was up here on vacation and since she no longer had a job or a boyfriend in Appleton she decided to stay for a while after Martha invited her.

When I asked her about her clothes, she said they came from an uncle who traveled a lot and bought them in Europe."

"What did she say about her underwear? Did her uncle buy that too?" interrupted Fred.

"I didn't ask her about that, you idiot."

"Fred let him finish," said Leo.

"I asked if she was on any medications and she said, 'no, other than the pill.' It was the way she said, pill. It was as if it was a special medication. Then when I asked her what the pill was, she sounded fluster and said, 'it was Midol that she took for menstrual cramps.' She sounded relieved when I knew what Midol was.

Next, I asked her why she was running down the street when it was snow covered. She said it was because she was a runner. When I asked her more, she said she ran short races down in Appleton and some marathons. Running was just something she did, saying it was in her blood. Then she said something strange, 'there's a marathon up here, isn't there?' then I said you mean like the race they run in Boston. She said yes. Then I told her that there is no marathon race up here like that. Then she corrected herself saying she must have been thinking of another place. The funny thing is I think she knew something. As if there will be a marathon here someday. The other thing that was odd is I don't know any woman that runs marathons, only men. That seemed odd to me.

The last thing I asked about was why she wanted to know what year it was on the night she was brought in here? She just told me she didn't remember too much about that night. It was as if she just wanted to get away and we ended the conversation.

There really was nothing I could put my finger on just some of her answers were odd. Why would anyone be running down the street in November and asking what year it was?"

"Well Doc, I came up with something of my own. I was talking with Ed Yost the other day and he told me about this woman he saw running down the street a couple of weeks ago on a Friday night. When he saw her fall, she took a strange devise out of her purse, like as it were a telephone and held up to her ear. When asked, if he could help her, she said nothing. Just looked confused, got up, and continued to run, but he did noticed that she was wearing a pink sweatshirt that said, **Green Bay Packers** on it with the name Aaron Rogers. He said he never saw anything like it.

After talking to him, I went to the library and from what I could find out, there is not, nor has there ever been an Aaron Rogers on the team. So where to you suppose she got that sweatshirt?" said Leo.

"I think we should find some reason to get into Martha Laine's house and have a look around," said Oscar.

"What are you saying, we should just break in," said Leo.

"Yes, unless we can get invited in. Even if we were invited over we can't very well just go through Nancy Monroe's room."

"Here's what I'm thinking. I know Martha is a good Catholic and I would bet they both go to mass on Sunday. That would be a good time to do a little exploring. Both of them will be out of the house. It should be easy. Anytime I've been over to see Martha, I noticed that she doesn't bother to lock her doors," said Doctor Frost.

"So who is going to do it? said Leo.

"I don't think that any of us should be involved. We're well known in the community and if by an outside chance we were discovered it wouldn't look good. We need to find somebody else to do the actual dirty work. Here's what I'm thinking. Leo your kid Marvin and Doc your kid Henry could do the job. They both know their way around. All we'd have to do is pay them. What do you think?" said Oscar.

"Marvin isn't doing anything. I kind of hope they draft his ass maybe they can make a man out of him. All he does now is go out and raise hell. I don't know how many times I've had to buy his way out of trouble. I think I could get him to do it," said Leo.

"I'm sure I can get Henry to do it too. Besides they're close friends," said Doc.

"Here's what we will have them do. On Sunday, we'll have them break in. Masses are at nine and eleven and I'm pretty sure they go to nine. We'll just have them park up the hill and wait for whatever mass they go to. It shouldn't take long. We can get the boys together and tell them what we want. Is that agreeable with everyone?"

"Yes, but do you really think we are going to find something? Maybe we are taking this thing too far," said Ralph.

"Here's what, let Marvin and Henry have a look around, if they don't find anything out of the ordinary then we just forget about all of this and go on with our lives. And if they find something then we'll just have to formulate a new plan," said Oscar.

All agreed. No one had any idea what was going to happen from a little curiosity. They all started to play cards.

Twenty-three

Saturday December 20, 1941

On the Saturday before Christmas Nancy and Martha went to confession. Both were devote Catholics. Confessions were from 2:00 to 4:00 in the afternoon. It was not at all like Nancy's church back in Appleton, where confessions were perhaps for 30 minutes on Saturday morning and there would be no more than five or ten people. Some where along the line, people had gotten out of the habit of confessing their sins.

When they arrived shortly before two, people were already lining up even before the priest arrived and still more people were praying in the pews. Nancy thought that they would be lucky to get out of there by four until she remembered that back in the forties and fifties there was no priest shortage. There were two priests hearing confessions. St. Mary's, even though it was a small parish had a pastor and an assistant pastor. Of course, no one had yet to hear of the sexual abuse scandals in 1941. Thinking back, she remembered that many of the abuse cases that were brought forth in Nancy's time came from this time period, causing the Catholic Church to pay out millions of dollars. As she prayed before making her confession, she wondered whether one of the two priests here today could be involved. *Was it possible?* Then she dismissed the idea and went to stand in line.

As she entered the confessional, she could see there was no face-to-face confession. The confessional was dark giving her a claustrophobic feeling. For an instant, she felt like leaving. The panel opened and the priest started, "In the name of the Father and of the Son and of the Holy Ghost amen."

"Bless me Father for I have sinned, my last confession was four weeks ago." She paused, thinking it was really 68 years and four weeks ago.

"And what do you want to confess?" He said impatiently.

"Father I have sin against God, I find myself unable to always trust in him. Please forgive me for my lack of faith. It's just that things have happened to me that are hard to believe."

"What sort of things have happened to you?"

"I'd rather not say Father, but I have found myself in a difficult situation and it is hard for me to think that God would let this happen to me."

"You must always trust in God. Remember that Satan is always at work to undermine our faith in God. What other sins do you need to confess?"

"Other than my lack of faith at times, I'm not as charitable towards others as I should be. I should try to be more loving and kind. I am also sorry for the times I've blamed others. That's all I have. I really have no mortal sins to confess."

"You're not from around here are you?"

"No, I'm not, how did you know?"

"I recognized it in your voice and the way you speak. I know how the local people make their confessions and you are different, just the way you express yourself. What are you doing in town, not many people come here to live unless they work at one of the local mines."

"I'm really here for an extended visit living with Martha Laine. I am a school teacher and would like to find work."

"The parish has a Catholic School and we are in need of a teacher, why don't you stop by the office on Monday and we can talk."

"I'd like that Father, I will."

"Now as I give absolution, please make an Act of Contrition."

"O my God, I am heartily sorry for having offended you and I detest all my sins, because I dread the loss of heaven and the pains of hell. But most of all because I have offended you, my God, who are all good and deserving of all my love. I firmly resolve with the help of your grace, to confess my sins, to do penance and to amend my life. Amen."

"For your penance say five Our Fathers and five Hail Marys."

She left feeling the way she always did after confession, relieved knowing that she was in a state of grace and all things were right with her and her God. Therefore, whatever happened she was right with God. She also had renewed hope that perhaps she would be able to get out of this situation. No matter what happened, she had new faith in God.

Just after she finished saying her penance she thought again about the sex abuse scandal that the church would come to face in the eighties and nineties and perhaps even before that and she wondered if there might be a way she could help prevent what was going to happen now that she found herself in the past. Then she remembered where she had come across the name Jacob Unger. His name had come up in a job interview that she had as a newly graduated teacher. During that interview in 1975, someone told her that there was a priest who had to be moved because of alleged sexual misconduct. The priest had not been charged with a crime although it appeared that the local authorities had sufficient proof. As happened in similar cases it was easier to move the priest to another assignment outside the diocese.

She was sure that his name was Unger. Father Unger was only 26 years old now in 1941 and she wondered when the abuse started. In 1975, he would have been 60 years old. There was no way of knowing how many years he might have been an abuser.

Maybe God meant for me to be here to warn the church. She knew she had not been successful in warning the government about the attack by the Japanese on Pearl Harbor so what made her think she would be successful in this matter. She thought that the virtuous faithful in 1941 would not be willing to believe her and going to the church leaders would do no good. The fact was the leaders of the church were the ones that covered up the abuse by moving priest. No Bishop would want to hear about it. If she said something, she would only be ridiculed.

She felt her only option was to say something to Father Jacob in confession. Believing in the seal of confession, she was sure that he would not be able to say anything about it to others. By warning him, she might be able to change history and prevent the abuse. She might even be able to change Father Jacob's life. Then she wondered what the consequences might be. If this bit of history were altered, would it in turn alter other events? The only thing she knew was that if she could possible prevent an abuse from happening it had to be good, she would take her chances. Now she just had to wait to find the best time to confront Father Jacob Unger.

Twenty-four

Sunday morning December 21, 1941

Marvin Coppalo and Henry Frost sat in Doctor Frost's car watching Martha Laine's house just after eight in the morning. It was cold just slightly above zero and they left the car running to keep warm. Neither one wanted to be there after their usual Saturday night out on the town. Although they were under aged, Hurley was still a wide-open town, in contrast to Ironwood just across the river. They were only doing this for the money.

They both knew Martha Laine, but knew little about Nancy Monroe only that she was new to the town and their father's thought that perhaps she was a threat to the community. They did not know why. The only thing Marvin knew was that his dad had said she was the most attractive women he had ever seen. Marvin knew the old man had an eye for the ladies so she must be a knock out.

Their mission was to look for anything that was out of the ordinary and to get any identification as to who she was. They were not to take anything out of the house and they were to make sure that nothing was out of place when they left. If they were caught, they were on their own.

A light snow started just before the two women left for the church shortly before nine. Henry and Marvin waited until after nine making sure that the mass had started before they approached the house. It was just like Marvin's old man said, the rear door was open and they walked in.

"Mass should take at least an hour, but we want to be out of here long before that so let's make this fast. My dad said we should find what we're looking for in the girl's bedroom up stairs." said Marvin.

"Just what are we looking for?" said Henry.

Henry had already wonder off into the dinning room tacking snow onto the rug.

"Hey, dumb shit, look at what you're doing. If they see that dampness on the floor they'll know someone was in here."

"So who gives a shit. They'll think they brought in the snow."

"Take off your shoes and wipe up that snow. Let's get up stairs. I don't like being here."

Neither one had ever been in the house, but finding the upstairs was not hard. At the top of the stairs there was a central sitting room and around that were four bedrooms. The largest one had to be Martha Laine's. The one next to it looked like it had not been used. On the other side they found the largest of the three guest bedrooms and they were sure this was the room they were looking for. The bed was neatly made, but the room had the appearance of being used.

Henry was first to enter. Searching the dresser drawer he said, "Is this what we're looking for?" Holding a pair of very small yellow underpants. "I'd sure like to see her model these."

"Sort of, but put those back, what else is there?"

"How about this?" It was a strange device and when he pressed the button that said on words appear on what he thought was a screen. He had seen a prototype of television in a magazine and thought this looked like it. Only it was extremely small and thin. The screen read:

A Winter's Rage
A Novel by Michael Putzer
Copyright 2007 by Michael Putzer

"What do you make of this? I'd say this is out of the ordinary. Look at that date?"

"I'm not sure what it is, but I've never seen anything like this. It's like something out of a science fiction comic."

"This appears to be from a novel by Michael Putzer, whoever he is? You don't suppose this is the complete book do you?"

"That's impossible. There is no way you could get a whole book in there."

"What's that other thing right next to it?" Henry lifted out another object that was similar, but smaller. When he opened it, it played music and a light came on. It scared him so he almost dropped it.

"What the hell do you make of this? It has numbers on the front and some other symbols."

"I have no idea what it is, but our job is to just report what we've found. It's already twenty after, we better get moving. Mass is over by ten."

Looking in the second drawer, he came upon the pink sweatshirt that had Green Bay Packers written across it. "Look at this, it's a Green bay Packer sweatshirt like nothing I've ever seen and it's pink."

"Who's Number 12, Aaron Rogers? Look at this label. It says made in Pakistan. Where the hell is Pakistan? I never heard of it."

"Maybe that's why the material is so different. Come on, we've got to hurry."

Looking next in the closet, they found her yellow jacket that said Colombia. The label said made in Vietnam.

"So where the hell is Vietnam?"

"Beats the shit out of me. Everything I own is made in the United States."

"Where'd she get stuff like this?"

"I don't know, but I've never seen a jacket like this. Look at how the hood is held on with a kind of sticky stuff."

"We have to leave."

"We didn't find any identification, like a driver's license."

"She most likely has that in her purse and took it with her. Beside we've got enough. We've done our job. Time to go."

Putting on their shoes and wiping the floor, they left just as the mass was letting out.

Twenty-five

Sunday December 21, 1941

Martha started breakfast after mass and Nancy went up to her room to change clothes. While the room looked the same, she had the feeling that someone had been here. She had left the coverlet on the bed smooth and well made. Now she thought she could see where someone had sat. *Who would want to search my room?*

Just to be sure, she pulled out the top drawer of the dresser and immediacy saw that her lingerie had been rearranged. Out of place was the matching bra and panty set. Looking further, she could see that the KINDLE and the cell phone had been moved. There was no telling what else had been searched. She was thankful that she had taken her purse with her, which contained her driver's license, money, credit cards and her digital camera. She was sure that no one knew about the camera—not even Martha. She had taken a number of pictures since being here and thought if she ever got back, she could prove that she really had been here in 1941. On the camera were a number of other pictures that she had taken in 2009. If they'd seen those pictures they would have know for sure that she was from another time. Besides that, there was no way to down load the picture onto a computer that had yet to be invented, never thinking about the fact that the pictures could be viewed on the camera. She shivered just thinking of what they already must know. The question she could not answer was why someone would be so interested in her. She did not see herself as a threat to the community. *Was it because of the war that people were apprehensive?*

Coming down the stairs she wondered how much of this to tell Martha, but the question was answered for her when Martha said, "I think somebody was in the house when we were at mass?"

"What makes you think that?"

"The rug in the dinning room has damp spots and I know neither you nor I were in there. Then it looks like the floor was wiped up. On top of all that I thought, I saw footprints on the sidewalk when we came in. I just thought they were the paperboy's, but he hasn't been here yet."

"Martha, I think someone was in my room. My clothes were messed up and things have been moved. Why would someone do this? It scares me."

"I think we both know why?"

"Do you have any idea who is behind this?"

"I'd say it was Doctor Frost and friends. Perhaps that was why he was asking you all those questions. I sort of saw this coming, but I had hoped for better things from Doctor Frost."

"Martha, even if they knew everything what would they do with the information?"

"The people the Doctor is friends with are opportunistic, besides that they are greedy men. If they thought, you knew the future they'd be ready to cash in on what you know. It could be investments, sports bets, business deals and just think of how they would benefit if they knew how the war ended. They could become extremely rich and powerful people. We have to be careful Nancy."

"Martha, what can we do?"

"I don't know. We can only be alert and from now on lock our doors."

* * *

For the rest of the day the snow continued and by Sunday night there was more than a foot of new snow on the ground. Nancy loved the snow and it made her forget her problems for awhile. Nancy had to think that down in Appleton, twelve inches of snow would have paralyzed the city for several days.

Nancy and Martha spent the snowy day decorating the tree they had purchased on Saturday. Nancy thought it was great to have a real tree, not like all the artificial ones in 2009. She was also amazed at all the old ornaments that Martha had. Nothing like from her time where everything was made in China. In 1941, China was not an industrial power. In fact China had been at war with Japan now for four years or at least that was what she could remember. That was if her presence here had not changed things.

Twenty-six

Monday December 22, 1941

On Monday, Nancy went to see Father Eric Schuster concerning the job offer. She got the job and was to start in January when school resumed from Christmas break. She was happy to share the news with Martha that night.

When Martha came in the door that evening Nancy had a bottle of wine to celebrate. "Martha, I'm employed. I'm teaching at St. Mary's starting January 6th. I can hardly wait. Come let's sit down and have a glass of wine to celebrate the occasion."

As Martha took her wine she said, "I'm happy for you but you know you'll have to be very careful as to what you say. Remember your knowledge of history and social studies cannot go beyond 1942. If you make mistakes, kids have a way of telling their parents and that will start people talking. I don't want anything to happen to you."

"I know Martha, and I'll be really careful."

"How did you get by with Father Schuster? Did he ask you for references?"

"In all honesty he didn't seem to care, he asked me what school I went to and seemed satisfied. I think he just needs a teacher so bad he didn't want to go there. Plus the salary is not very good. He also thinks highly of you and I think that is the main reason I got the job. All because of you Martha Laine."

"What about a social security number, did he ask?"

"Yes, I told him I'd get back to him. He said not to worry. You know Martha living is a lot easier in 1941 when it comes to the government. There are no computers.

* * *

While Nancy was sharing her good news with Martha, another meeting was taking place at one of the local supper clubs. Doctor Frost and the Alliance men gathered to hear what Marvin and Henry found out on Sunday.

All had a first round of drinks when Leo said, "Well tell the guys what you found."

Marvin was first to speak. "We found two gadgets in her dresser drawers and that was not all we found. She has some pretty special underwear."

"Forget about the underwear and tell us about the gadgets," said Oscar Kosken.

"They were unbelievably small."

"I said to forget about her underwear, you perverts."

"No I was talking about the gadgets. The first one was very small and I don't know how to describe it, but it was like a cathode ray tube that I saw in science class once. It was sort of like those early television screens, but much smaller. There is nothing made that is that small. One device showed the name of a book, the author and a copyright date on the front of the tube. The name of the book was, A Winter's Rage by Michael Putzer. Now here is the interesting thing. The date of the copyright was 2007. How can that be?"

"Are you sure that you read it right. Could it have been 1937? You know in a novel it's possible to write into the future," said Leo.

"No, this was just the title page. I didn't look any further. If the rest of the book was there and I don't know how that's possible."

"Continue, we'll have to think about this, but finish, what about the other device?"

"The other gadget flipped open, played music, and had some symbols on it. It had ten numbers, a star and a pound sign on it. The only thing I could think of is that it was a telephone, but that too is impossible."

"What else did you find?"

"We found her pink sweatshirt and yellow jacket. When we looked at the labels, we found that the jacket was made in Viet Nam and the sweatshirt was made in Pakistan. Neither of us recognized those places and we could not find them in our school atlas. Why would anybody want something that was made in a foreign country? That was all we found, does that help?"

"Yes, it does. You have been most useful. Don't say anything about this to anyone," said Oscar.

"Do you still think she might be from the future now?" said Leo.

"I will say if she is not from the future that she sure the hell is not from around here. No way she was born and raised in Wisconsin."

"Where do you think she is from?" said Fred Banister.

"I think we should sit on this until after the holidays. Does everyone agree?"

All agreed and went home for the holidays.

Twenty-seven

December 24, 1941 – January 1, 1942

On Wednesday, Christmas Eve, Martha had to work until noon. To Nancy it seemed like something out of A Christmas Carol by Charles Dickens. Businesses were like Scrooge, not at all like in 2009, when people usually had two or three days off at Christmas time. Martha told her that Christmas time was different this year because of the war. Men were being drafted and families were being split up as never before. The war was going poorly. The Japanese had invaded the Philippines and U.S. troops were in retreat.

Martha and Nancy went to midnight mass at St. Mary's and Nancy found that she still was not used to the mass in Latin and the fact that the altar was on the back wall of the church and the priest did not face the people. She had to admit that the nativity scene was much nicer with all of the old hand carved figures.

After Nancy and Martha came home and exchanged presents. Nancy was in a melancholy mood. Tears came to her eyes when she thought about Michael and the ring she was sure she was going to get. They had even talked about a June wedding once school was out and now all that came crashing down. *What was Michael doing tonight? Is he thinking of me? There is no way he could ever guess where I am.*

Although she was adapting to her situation, it was times like this that made her break down and cry. She could not even imagine what her future was going to be. *Am I going to be here the rest of my life? Will I ever get married and have kids? What about Doctor Frost and his friends? I've just got to get out of here.*

On Christmas day came word over the radio that Hong Kong had fallen to the Japanese. Then on New Year's Eve, the word came that the U.S. had evacuated from Manila. Losing the Philippines was only a matter of time. The British fared no better. They were pushed into the navel base in Singapore and surrender there was only a matter of time. The Japanese appeared to be invincible. So far, she saw no changes in what she knew about the war. She was still worried that her presence could change history.

Although the news was bad, Martha had some short days and her and Nancy spent hours together talking. Martha continually asked about the future and what life was like in 2009. She was amazed when Nancy told her about how computers were used for everything.

Most amazing for Martha was that an African American was President and that a woman had run for President. She had a hard time accepting things even though she knew Nancy was telling the truth.

Nancy continued to keep some things secret when Maratha asked. Only saying, "Martha there are some things you really don't need to know."

With the extra time, Martha was able to teach Nancy how to knit as they listened to the radio in the evenings. They even had time to play cards. To Nancy, it all seemed better than watching television.

Twenty-eight

January 1, 1942 (New Year's Day)

New Years day 1942 came and while in years past most people were looking forward to a better year, 1942 did not carry with it any of that enthusiasm. The shock from the Japanese attack on Pearl Harbor had not fully registered on everyone. The Japanese were attacking all over the Pacific with the fall of Guam Island on December 10th, Wake Island on December 23rd, Hong Kong on Christmas day and The Philippines had been invaded and Manila bombed. Then on New Year 's Day, it was reported that they were fighting the battle for Bataan. It seemed like only a matter of time before The Philippines would fall. On top of all that, the United Sates was at war with Germany and Italy. Prospects did not look good.

Many of the young men from Hurley and the surrounding area had already enlisted in the service. This was only the beginning. While everyone thought it was a very patriotic thing to do everyone knew that in a war men died and were wounded. There was going to be a high price to pay to win this war and now Nancy was not so sure that we were going to win.

The football bowl games were still played on New Year's Day, but there were only four, not at all like in 2009 where there were bowl games from mid December to the first week in January. There was no BCS. She and Martha listened to the Rose Bowl although it was not played in Pasadena, California. It was moved from the west coast to Duke Stadium on the east coast. They were afraid of a Japanese attack. Oregon State won the game over heavily favored Duke. Nancy thought how things have changed. Duke was now only a basketball school and had not had a winning football season in years. It also made her think about Doctor Frost. If he had known who was going to win, he would have made a lot of money by betting on the underdog. She did not want to think about that problem today, but betting on future games was a way they could benefit. Her father had been a big sports fan and she remembered a lot of the big games and prize fights that took place in the forties and fifties. *I'll never tell them anything.*

As they sat listening to the game on the radio, she found it refreshing unlike television the radio allowed you to listen and do other things. It truly was a simpler time. There were no two hundred television channels to surf. There was no internet, no cell phones or text messages to answer. There was more labor-intensive work here, but when she thought about it, she felt that people had about the same amount of leisure time. In 2009, people were always busy having to do something and were no better off with all of the time saving gadgets.

2010

Twenty-nine

Monday January 11, 2010

Just before Christmas, Michael Niffen made another trip to Hurley to speak with the police. They told him that they did not have anything new and that while the case was active, it was unofficially closed unless they discovered new evidence. They did refer him to a local man, Douglas Petersen, a retired police officer who did investigative work privately. He was not a licensed Private Detective, but did this sort of work to stay in touch with police work. They assured Michael that, Big Doug, might be able to help him.

Big Doug was the type of guy who knew everybody's business and having spent forty years as a cop, he knew everything that went on around town.

He was the town's biggest gossip putting the closest woman in a distant second place. After retirement when people needed a favor, he was willing to help them out for a fee of course. Nothing is free in this world, he always said. Most of the jobs he got were referrals from some of his old police buddies. When someone needed some evidence to make a case in a messy divorce or to locate a missing spouse or child, he was there to help.

So, when Michael Niffen came to him on the Monday after Christmas, Doug was more than happy to help besides, he needed the extra money. He told Michael he would do everything he could to find Nancy Monroe. He also warned him that sometimes when he investigated he found out things that people did not really want to know. He told Michael that he needed a thousand dollar retainer and to give him three week. By that time, he should come back up to Hurley and he would have something for him.

* * *

Three weeks later Michael came back to Hurley on Monday January 11th to meet with Big Doug. They met that evening at the old Holiday Inn were Michael was staying.

"Doug come on in, I hope you have some good news for me."

"Well Michael, like I told you when we started that I can't always find out or give you the news you want. You already know that the police have found nothing new and the case is inactive. They do this when there is just nothing new, but with that said let me begin.

What I found out was that on Thanksgiving night your girlfriend and the others were out having a good time. They started out at a local bar on the upper end of Silver Street watching the Green Bay game and then later on the Dallas game. The bartender I spoke to said she was having a good time feeling no pain.

After that, they left and went to several other bars. The people that saw her said she was just having a good time. While she talked with a number of people both men and women she did not get involved with any of the men. She left around midnight with her three girlfriends. Nobody saw her leave with a man, so that's good news.

After that, we don't know anything until they all went to Sally's café on Friday morning for breakfast. Sally and the waitress said that when they saw her that morning she was not looking good—hung over. That was when she went to the bathroom downstairs and was never seen again.

I have to tell you there is nothing after that. I tracked down everyone that could have been around that building and no one saw her leave out the back door nor did anyone see her walking down a side street or anything. Zero, nothing. I've never come across anything like this in my entire life. There were two sightings, both turned out not to be her. The other one I followed up was a dead body of a woman the Sheriff of Ashland County found by the railroad tracks. The women turned out to be sixty years old suffering from Alzheimer. She wondered away from her home and was hit by the train.

Oh, I did a background check on her and she is so squeaky clean it makes me sick. Not even a speeding ticket. It looks like you were dating a saint. She was a regular at church, gave generously, and was a volunteer for everything.

Michael, I have to say it is as if the Rapture took place like in the Book of Revelation and she was just taken up into heaven. Removed by God. I have no other way to explain it. If she were kidnapped, there are no signs of it.

To be honest with you I am refunding half of the thousand-dollar retainer. Lord knows I've never done that before. I'm really sorry Michael I know you were going to be engaged on Christmas and I think you were going to marry a good one. I'll continue to keep an eye out, but I would have to say you should probably think about getting on with your life. If someone kidnapped her, they are no doubt miles from here and you'll never see her."

"Thanks Doug, I'm not giving up. I appreciate you being so honest with me. I'm not sure what I'm going to do next. I think I'll just go back to Appleton and will see what more I can do. Maybe the police will come up with something new."

Thirty

Tuesday January 12, 2010

On Tuesday January 12th, Michael Niffen got a surprise call from Big Doug. "Michael, this is Doug from Hurley."

"Doug, have you found something new?"

"No, but I have a contact for you that may help. There's this new guy who moved here from New York City in September and from what I know he is pretty weird. His name is Robert Rahn. He used to be a big shot stockbroker in New York on Wall Street. He moved here after his wife and kid were murdered in New York City, at a restaurant shooting back in 2006. After the deaths, he had a breakdown and was in a sanitarium for a period of time, near sucide so the story goes. After that, his psychiatrist recommended that he move out of New York and find some place far away from Wall Street. That is how he ended up here. Some say he's a clairvoyant, he has the ability to see the future. They say that ability was what helped him to earn all of his money. He was able to invest in all the right stock enabling him to come out smelling like a rose when all that sub-prime shit blew up. While everybody was making loans with little or no credit backing, Robert had actually bet against things going right and ended up making millions.

Now he is somewhat reclusive, but he did help the Hurley police locate the body of a missing boy—Patrick Lockhart—who was abducted three years ago. There were witness that saw the kid taken right off the street. They gave the police a description of the car and one of the men who took him. After a three-year investigation the police came up empty. They concluded that it was the act of someone from out of state passing through. For all they knew the boy was dead and buried some place in Arizona.

On the third anniversary of the abduction, the local paper ran an article. Two days later the police got a call from Robert Rahn telling them that if they were still looking for Patrick Lockhart's body they should search just off the North Country trail in the area of the abandon fire tower. There on the other side of the creek they'd find the ruins of an old farm house and his body would be buried in a low area away from the house.

When the police asked him to come in and make a formal statement, he refused and told them to start searching. Robert immediately became a person of interest. With nothing other than his statement they did not arrest him, but they did stake out his house while they started the search.

After two days of searching, Patrick Lockhart's body was found in a shallow grave in a low swampy area just as Rahn had said. The only reason they were able to find him was because of the recent drought that had dried up the wet area and uncovered the body. Now the police were sure that Robert Rahn had to be their man and they arrested him.

It wasn't until Robert Rahn was able to lead the police to the killer—a known sex offender—that the police released him. The whole ordeal had taken five days.

After finding that boy and his killer in October, people started asking him for help in finding missing loved ones. He was mobbed, but hasn't helped out. He remained in seclusion."

"So Doug, why do you think he'll help me? Sounds like the man won't even talk to me."

"Well maybe he won't, but here's why I think you should try. Nancy's disappearance has been in the papers, just like the Lockhart boy and I'd say that he's familiar with your case. He might just see that as a real case, not just people asking him to locate a runaway teenager or a wife that ran out on her husband."

"So what should I do, just go knock on his door?"

"Hold on I was getting to that. You have to call Marjorie Callahan; she handles all of his business. As I said this guy is a recluse. Seldom goes out of the house. That's another thing he lives out in the country on more than a square mile of land and his house has over seven thousand square feet. Marjorie's number is 715-561-5447."

"Doug, I'm willing to try anything to find her or at least bring this to a conclusion, but from what you said, do you think this guy is even stable?"

"Well there is one other thing I learned about Robert. Seems that after the death of his family he has taken a great interest in the paranormal, like unexplained disappearance. Things like the Bermuda Triangle and Parallel Universes. So I'm thinking from this information he may well be interested in the disappearance of Nancy. I know it sounds odd, but what have you got to loose."

"You're right, what have I got to loose. Thanks Doug, I will call Marjorie. Thanks again."

"Like I say, I'm not sure if this guy will even talk to you, but it is worth a shot."

1942

Thirty-one

Tuesday January 6, 1942

On Tuesday January 6th, Nancy started teaching at St. Mary's Catholic School. They still had eight grades and she was teaching fifth grade. She was more used to high school students, but she found it was teaching that she really enjoyed. What she had not anticipated was teaching all of the fifth grade subjects, not just one or two like in high school. She had to fit in english, math, science, reading, literature, geography and history. She had 22 students in her class and she wasn't sure how she was going to get everything done. There were seven classes time 22 students which meant that she would at times have 154 test papers to correct. In addition, she was asked to teach music because she played piano. This was going to be a challenge.

As she entered her classroom on her first day she saw the usual tongue and groove hardwood floors that creak as she walked. There too was the smell of the oil that the janitor used for cleaning. The room was heated by steam and she was going to have to get use to the constant hiss of the radiators.

As her students piled in, they all stared at her as if she were from another planet. Once settled in they began the day with the Pledge of Allegiance to the Flag and the Morning Prayer. Not at all like the public schools of 2009 where pray was forbidden. Next she introduced herself and went around the room getting to know everyone's name.

The day went by quickly and she was glad to have the first day complete. She knew her evenings would be busy with lesson plans, but she found she was happy. All day she had not made any mistakes. She did not speak of anything that took place beyond 1942. She did not talk about Iraq, Afghanistan, Vietnam, the Korean War, the moon landing, civil rights, gay and lesbian rights, nuclear weapons and there were so many other things.

Sports of any kind were off limits. She could not tell them that there were 32 teams in the NFL and that there was a Super Bowl. Baseball too had expanded from eight teams in each league to over thirty some teams with inter-league play.

She could not relate any personal experiences. She really had nothing of a personal nature to share with her students. She guarded against saying when I was your age. She thought to herself, *when I was your age most of you were most likely dead.*

She constantly reminded herself that she was 25 years old born in 1916. She could not talk about very fact that she was born in 1984. She told everybody that she was born on October 27, 1916.

Things went nicely the first week and she found she could keep up with all of the classes. She did however catch the students, both boys and girl constantly glancing at her as if to reassure themselves that she was real. Some told her that she talked funny and that they knew she was not from around here.

She dropped her guard only a few times during the first week. The first was when she referred to the President as Barack Obama and when everyone in the class wrinkled their noses, she realized her gross mistake and quickly covered it up by saying, "I was thinking of the leader of Egypt. Of course, we all know Franklin Delano Roosevelt is the President of the United States." That seemed to satisfy the class.

The next mistake came when, one of the students asked about the war and why the Japanese were so cruel. She explained that the Japanese had an emperor, Hiroito and that all of the people were loyal to him. They have very different religious ways of thinking. She went on to say that in the future Japan will be our ally.

"How do you know that?" said one of the boys.

Red faced she said, "I really don't know that. I guess I was only hoping that all nations could be friends and get along with one another like Jesus wants us to."

"Do you think we will win the war?"

"I'm sure we will. Our nation is founded under God and I'm sure we will prevail."

She could only hope that no one went home and told their parents what she had said. She thought she had handled the situation nicely.

She knew in the days ahead she had to be more diligent.

Thirty-two

Friday January 9, 1942

Oscar Kosken, Leo Coppalo, Ralph Winslow, Peter Cadence and Fred Banister gathered at Doctor Frost's home for the usual Friday night poker game, but tonight there was no poker. They had another subject to discuss—Nancy Monroe.

Oscar Kosken opened the meeting by saying, "I've been giving a lot of thought about what the boys found at Martha Laine's house. I thought the two gadgets they found were interesting for a better word, but what was on the book thing really made me believe that she is some how from the future. The copyright date on the book was 2007 and I don't think there is anyway to explain that away."

"You're telling me that you think she got here from the year 2007. Do you really expect us to believe that," said Leo Coppalo.

"Alright, I'll listen to anyone that has a better explanation."

"Just stop and think about this. We know that this woman is really different and not just beautiful and charming, but I mean really different. I think we can all agree that she does not seem to fit in around here or for that matter any other big city that I can think of. Then think about how she got here. Turns up on a Friday running madly down the street and is hit by a car. Doc you have to admit she acted strange asking what year it was and was surprised to find out it was 1941. The things we found in her room are not like any electrical devices that we know about. Let's forget about if she is from the future or not and just realize that she is extraordinarily different. The question for us is, what we are going to do about her," said Ralph Winslow.

"You know what bothers me, is that she tried to send that letter to Washington warning them about Pearl Harbor. How could anyone know about that?" said Peter Cadence.

"She could just be some kind of fortune teller, that got lucky," said Fred Banister.

"Here is what I suggest. I understand that she's working for St. Mary's school teaching fifth grade. Your Catholic Leo why don't you see Father Schuster and see what he can tell you about her. Maybe you can pick up something. You know ask him certain questions, like where she went to school, what year did she graduate, does she have any family in the area? Things like that," said Oscar.

Ralph Winslow said, "That may help us, but in the end why do we think she is a threat to us? I for one think we should just let this go."

"Let's go back to that idea that she's from the future for a second. If she is from 2007 think about what she knows. She'll know who wins this war. We know she knew about Pearl Harbor. She's what 26, 27 years old that would place her date of birth around 1983 or 1984. We might be able to learn from her about what stocks to buy and all kinds of other business trends. What will be the hot selling items? If she's a sports fan, just think about the possibilities. Knowing the winners in advance, just think of the money that could be made? Her knowledge could be worth millions of dollars.

"I for one would like to know about what might be coming in my field of medicine. I can't even begin to image what advances will be made," said Doctor Frost.

"Well doctor, you've got a point there. The possibilities seem endless. I'm all for making money. Leo you have been drafted to go see Father Schuster. Then let's meet back here in two weeks to plan our next move." said Oscar.

2010

Thirty-three

Thursday January 14, 2010

While Nancy was teaching fifth grade in January 1942, Michael Niffen had set up a meeting with Robert Rahn to see if he could help him find Nancy. The call to Marjorie Callahan on Tuesday was successful and now Michael Niffen was traveling west on US 2 to meet with Robert Rahn. Around eight miles out of Hurley, he saw the wayside where he expected to find Lake Forest town road that would lead him to Robert's house. He nearly missed the side road because of all the snow banks. January's cold had produced and inordinate amount of lake effect snow.

After two months of searching for his missing girlfriend, Michael was desperate enough to seek the help of a man who delved into the paranormal. One part of him told him this was a crazy idea and another told him he had nothing to loose. After all he and police had come up with nothing.

So when Marjorie Callaghan had set up the meeting, he was grateful for her help and understanding. Marjorie told Michael that since the tragic death of Robert's wife and daughter he had been studying various crimes regarding disappearances. Now as he turned his Ford Edge onto the unpaved road to Robert Rahn's house, he thought that perhaps this was a bad idea—a wild goose chase. Michael knew Robert was in his mid thirties and had been a successful banker or stockbroker in New York and had moved after the tragic deaths of his wife and daughter. The locals called him eccentric and that his house was more than just a house. After traveling three miles on the gravel road, he coasted to a stop, afraid that he had missed the driveway, but there ahead he saw that the land was fenced. It appeared to go back more than a mile. Going further, he came to a gated driveway with security cameras. Turning into the drive, he rolled down his window and pressed the speaker call button not at all sure what to expect.

An automated voice said, "Please state your name and a brief message for your visit. Expect a reply in two minutes or less."

He found it strange that someone would be so over concerned about his or her privacy and security, but then he thought if he had been from New York City, he too might be over concerned. With that he dismissed the thought and said, "My name is Michael Niffen and Marjorie Callahan set up this meeting she called you this morning regarding the disappearance of my girlfriend. She thought you might be able to help me."

After a two minute wait the gate rolled back and another automated voice told him to proceed.

More than half mile in nestled among several small rolling hills, Michael saw the house. He sat there amazed. The house itself had a walk out full basement making the house look three stories high. The house looked more like a lodge than house and Michael could not even imagine a guess as to how much living space there was. The garage was enormous. In the center of the house was a copula, which appeared to rise more that fifty feet or more above the surrounding land. He could only imagine how beautiful the view of Lake Superior was from there.

As he rang the doorbell, he thought the house was everything the town's people said and more. He could not comprehend what a single man would want with so much space.

When Robert answered the door, Michael was met by an over eager Airedale, Albert. Robert first ordered Albert to sit and then invited Michael inside. "He doesn't meet that many people out here and he thinks everyone comes to see him."

The house was even more impressive inside than out. Michael could not help himself from just standing there staring.

Robert, knowing his thoughts said, "Perhaps it is a little excessive and even more extravagant than I expected myself when I first saw it. Let me take your coat and then we can go into my study and talk."

"The house is just so beautiful and I'm not sure that is the right word."

With that, Robert led Michael to the second floor den where coffee was waiting. "Please sit down. I understand from Marjorie that you wanted to talk to me about the disappearance of your girlfriend, Nancy Monroe, back in November.

Since the death of my wife and daughter, I have done a lot of work on crime studies, particularly cases with bazaar circumstances like disappearances. I was able to help the police out in October with a case involving a missing local boy that was murdered.

I've been following the Nancy Monroe case since I first read about it in the newspaper, but I don't want to get your hopes up, I'm not sure that I can be of much assistance.

I do get the feeling that when it comes to a disappearance there is more to it than meets the eye. There may be some paranormal circumstances. Some would say that I'm crazy for thinking that way but sometimes there is no other way to explain it.

Oh please forgive my manors, when I start to talk, I tend to carry on. Before we get started perhaps you would like to see the view from the copula, it's really breath taking. I spend a lot of time up there. Then we can come down and have some coffee."

"I'd love to see the view."

When they reached the end of the spiral staircase and stepped out into what Robert called the viewing area Michael could not believe the panorama view that he saw. The landscape was covered with a fresh blanket of snow and you could see Lake Superior.

"It's breathtaking; I can see why you spend a lot of time up here."

Once back in the study having coffee Robert said, "Tell me about your girlfriend's disappearance. While I know the case I want to hear it from you."

"It was the Friday after Thanksgiving and Nancy and three other girlfriends went to breakfast in Hurley. They were up here for a four-day weekend. Nancy was not feeling well, went to the bathroom, and never came back. No trace of her was found after a search of the premises. The police searched for her and put out pictures, but no one claimed to have seen her. It was as if she vanished. Now after nearly two months, nothing has turned up and I'm at the end of my rope. I've been up here every weekend and have taken most of my vacation time looking for her. Now there seems to be nothing more I can do so when Doug Petersen told me about you, I called Marjorie and here I am."

"When she came to Hurley, why didn't you come with her?"

"I had to work; I'm an intern at the hospital and drew the holiday shift. I wanted her to have a good time. I was planning to give her a ring at Christmas."

"Have the police questioned you. Like a person of interest?"

"Yes, they did but when my alibi was good they gave up. At first they thought that it had to be someone like me, you know someone she was familiar with. They even thought that perhaps we wanted to fake her disappearance. Once they did background checks on Nancy, her girlfriends and me they gave up on that angle. After all that initial stuff, they have been helpful, but I always think by assuming it is the husband or the boyfriend they loose valuable time and may have lost evidence."

"There is a similar case that sounds like yours. A young woman—twenty years old—disappeared from a mall in Madison and has never been found. That was back in 1992 and the police have no leads. The case is still open. That woman would be 37 years old now."

"I remember that case, in fact the girls and I talked about it right after Nancy first disappeared. It's funny you should mention it," said Michael.

"As you may recall she was last seen driving from the mall on a late August night heading for her boyfriend's house. She arrived at her boyfriend's apartment complex apparently exited and locked her vehicle, then disappeared. She never entered her boyfriend's apartment and has not been seen again.

Her boyfriend thought he heard her arrive but never went to look. It was only after fifteen minutes when she did not buzz the apartment that he went to look and saw only her car. Unable to find her he called the police.

No one saw her walk away from the parking lot or get into anyone's car. Her purse was still in the car. There were virtually no clues. Some people were questioned, but nothing turned up. The police thought that perhaps she went with someone she knew. There were no indications of a struggle. No finger prints were found that could not be substantiated. To this day, no arrests have been made. The case remains unsolved.

My thought is that there has to be something more to this. This is very similar to the disappearance of your girlfriend, Nancy."

"Is there anything you can do to help me find her? Doug Petersen told me that you were into the paranormal trying to solve some of these things."

"Yes, I've looked into a number of things and like I said I did help the police find the body of a missing boy. We also apprehended his killer.

I'm sure some would say it's an obsession. When you look back through history, there have been any number of cases where people have just vanished. Sometimes, there is an explanation for the disappearances. The person was in an abusive relationship, owed an excessive amount of money or just wanted to start over. However, there are many other cases where people were happy, financially comfortable, good jobs and had family and there is no apparent reason for them to vanish. That is where I think your Nancy fits."

"If there is no explanation for these vanished people, do you have any kind of a theory? Like alien abductions?"

"There are people out there that believe unexplained disappearances have to have an explanation in the paranormal or supernatural. Some speculate that many alleged paranormal disappearances might be the result of tears in the fabric of reality, where people or objects somehow pass through a hole out of our known set of dimensions. This causes them to become out of step with our world in terms of time and space causing them to appear to vanish. Sort of like falling into a fourth dimension. Now this is where it gets interesting, some say that there are certain locations around the globe where the boundaries between our dimensions and the unknown dimensions are thin enough for people to pass through given the right conditions. An example would be the unexplained disappearances in the Bermuda Triangle.

There are cases where people have seen others disappear into thin air right before their eyes, while others have reported finding evidence related to a missing person, such as a trail of footprints that suddenly end inexplicably. There was a case in the 1920's where an area farm boy disappeared. His Father sent him ahead to the barn to do chores and when the father arrived all he saw was footsteps in the snow that came to an end twenty feet before the barn. The boy was never found. No trace of him.

History is littered with captivating tales of people who, for no reason inexplicably vanish from the face of the earth without a trace. Some of these stories are well-documented and some are mere legend and folklore. What they do however is force us to question how sure we are of our own existence. Where did these people go? Perhaps there are time portals, other dimension, time slippage or maybe UFO abductions?

There are all kinds of examples. There is a city in Missouri in the 1950's where a man vanished from a crowded bus. People testified seeing him on the bus, sleeping in his seat and when the bus reached its destination, he was gone. All of his belongings were still on the bus and the book he was reading lay open on his empty seat. The man was never found.

There is even a case that happened right around here. I think it was back in 1975, a lady disappeared while cross-country skiing. Two people behind her reported seeing her ahead of them on the trail when suddenly they saw her vanish right before their eyes.

They searched the spot where they saw her vanish and found nothing. A search was made that afternoon and the next day and still nothing was found. The searches continued the rest of the summer and in the spring and nothing was found. Not a trace. To this day, she is still listed as missing.

Then there is the case of the paralyzed 50-year-old man who was sitting outside his home in a wheel chair on a warm summer evening. He virtually could not move. With a storm approaching his sister went to wheel him in and he was gone. His wheel chair was there and his sweater, which he had around his shoulders remained. An investigation found no trace or clues.

So you can see that many of these cases are very similar to Nancy's. As with everything these phenomena of paranormal vanishing are debatable. Some are bogus and other incidents are open to interpretation. Of all these examples one would think that they all cannot be explained away as a hoax."

"So Robert, let's say these disappearances happen, has there ever been anybody who has come back?"

"In the cases I just talked about these people never came back. Nothing was ever verified. But there still maybe hope for Nancy. There are cases where people found themselves going back in time and came back. The bad thing is that they were never gone very long, not more than 2-3 hours. Sort of like blacking out.

In most cases, it happened quite unexpectedly where people visited another time briefly. They just slip back in time and they seem to occur randomly and spontaneously. Naturally, the skeptics say that these people were high on drugs and just hallucinating.

I don't mean to bore you with all of this stuff, but you can see I find it fascinating. So if you don't mind there is one more case I remember that is similar in a way to Nancy's disappearance."

"Please Robert, continue. I want to know everything no matter how far out it is."

"It happened back in 1963 at a small college in Lincoln, Nebraska where a secretary went to deliver a message to one of the professors and when she entered the room there was an overbearing musty odor. Standing there was a thin, black-haired woman dressed in a floor-length skirt. The woman did not appear to notice her and went about doing her filing. She seemed to be real, not a ghost. Then she simply faded away and was gone. It was then that the secretary looked out the window and saw that there were no modern buildings or streets. In fact, most of the campus was just an open farm field. It was than that she realized she was no longer on the college campus in the year 1963. Scared she fled the room. Once back in the hallway and sure she had returned to the present, she contacted her boss.

A later investigation of yearbooks found that the women in the room had been somebody who had worked there back in 1920. The thing about this, I wonder what would have happened if that women had decided to step outside. Would she have stepped into the 1920's and would she have been able to go back, we don't know. People did go back to the office but were never able to replicated the incident.

Therefore, you can see there are many unanswered questions. Perhaps something similar happened to Nancy when she went to the restroom in the basement and instead of turning back she went out some other door and found herself in a different time and was unable to step back through the portal where she entered."

"Let's just say that something like this did happen to Nancy. Is there anyway that she could get back to the present?"

"My thought would be that she would have to get back to the time portal or the place where two dimensions come together and then she might be able to get back. However, it is said that time portals are very fragile and tend to break down easily. They do not stay in the same place for any length of time. If they are constantly moving, she may never find the portal to get back. Since no one has come back, I'm not sure how people know this.

Do you remember on Star Trek, there was an episode when Spock and Kirk go after McCoy when he jumps into a time vortex? They had all they could do to locate the exact time that McCoy had entered and bring him back. While that's fiction I think Nancy may have been confronted by something similar."

"Do you think it might be possible to go in after her and bring her back like they did?"

"I suppose if you could locate the time portal where she went through, it might be possible. Then still there is no way to know what time period she entered.

Remember this is all conjecture. We don't know for sure that time portals exist. All we have are these unsubstantiated experts, like me and of course all of this is disputed by the scientific community as pure science fiction. However, if you're looking for an explanation as to what happened to Nancy and nothing else seems to explain it then it sort of makes sense."

"Seems to me, that gives me a reason for Nancy's disappearance even if it sounds like science fiction. There are two questions. One, will anyone believe me and two, even if she disappeared this way, what can we do about it?"

"You're right. First, I most likely would be the only one to believe you and second as of right now, I don't know of any way to cross over and bring her back. Would we be able to bring her back to the present time?"

"Robert I want to thank you for seeing me and the time you spent with me. You have given me a better understanding of what may have happened to Nancy, but I'm not completely sold. My thought is, if she disappeared in this manner and it pains me to say this, I think she is gone for good and there is nothing we can do about it. She is not coming back. What I have to do now is start coming to grips with this idea and start moving on with my life. That may not be easy. I'll be leaving this afternoon Robert. Please call me if anything comes up."

"Sorry I couldn't provide you with more help Michael, but I plan to keep on working on this case. I'll let you know if I'm able to find out anything more."

Thirty-four

Thursday January 14, 2010

After Michael Niffen left, Robert Rahn made himself a promise to renew his efforts to find Nancy Monroe. From all the information, he had gathered he was positive that there was not a typical explanation for her sudden disappearance. There was no blood at the scene and there were no signs of a struggle. There were no witnesses. No one had seen her after she went to the restroom down stairs in the cafe. Even the police had to admit, that it was as if she had vanished.

He felt sure that she was alive. *Why all this interest? I've never even met the woman. The only thing I know about her is what I read and what Michael told me. How ridiculous?*

Now when he was truly honest with himself, he knew the reason—he was falling in love with her. *How can this be? She's in love with Michael Niffen. She doesn't know I exist. Has it been that long since Debra died? Well it has been over three years and perhaps I am getting lonely. Maybe I need someone besides Albert.*

Next, he called Sally's Café. "Sally this is Robert Rahn, how are you today?"

"I'm find Robert, what can I do for you? I'm kind of busy."

"I'll be quick. I'd like to stop over and have another look around your restroom and the cellar, just to see if there is anything that I missed. Would that be okay with you?"

"Sure, why don't you come over after closing? I close at five that way there won't be curious customers looking on to spread rumors."

"Thanks Sally, see you at five."

* * *

He arrived at Sally's with a Geiger counter, EMF meter and an infrared thermometer just as she was locking the door. "Come on in, what's all that stuff?"

"These are devices that will measure differences in the earth's magnetic field. It may tell us if something is going on down in your basement."

"You mean like what they use in Ghost Hunters on TV?"

"Yes, I thought I'd try this, nothing else has worked."

"Go ahead, but let's keep this between you and me. I don't want people to think the place is haunted."

"Sure thing. I don't think it will amount to much anyway."

"I've got to sweep and clean the grill, so have at it."

"Thanks Sally, I won't take long."

With flashlight and equipment, he descended the stairs into the basement. There at the bottom of the stairs was the unisex restroom. He dutifully went around the door looking for any pry marks or just anything that he might have missed the first time that would give him a clue to her disappearance. There was nothing. Next, he sat down on the toilet as if he were using it. He let his eye float over the entire room. There was nothing out of place. After that he took out his EMF meter and scanned the area. The readings were all normal, 20-30.

Then he left and went into the room that was marked private. He had already gotten the key from Sally. This room went all the way back to the alley wall. With the light from the dirty cellar window, he once again saw where the wall had been bricked up. He spotted the remnants of what was once a stairway leading to the outside. All that was left was the first cement step. Standing there, he had the feeling that someone was watching him. Thinking Sally had come down he looked, but did not see her or anyone else. He was alone. Taking out the EMF meter again, he searched around where the outside door once was. The meter fluctuated between 3.0 and 6.0 in the dim light from the window. Not believing he turned on his flashlight and was astounded to see the reading remained the same. He knew that any reading in the 2.0 to the 7.0 range that could not be traced to another source was attributed to spirit activity. Going away from the door the readings returned to normal in the 20's. Next he moved to his right and took a reading, it was normal—no spirit activity. The same was true when he moved to the left. The low readings were only to be found where the door used to be. He held his breath. *What does this mean? Is there a ghost down here or could it be from someone passing through. Was that once the door to the outside or is that the door to another dimension? Could that door have opened letting Nancy walk through.*

He felt funny almost dizzy and for just a moment he thought he might loose his balance so he sat down on the dirty floor. Feeling better he took out his infrared thermometer. The temperature was 55 degrees where he sat. Getting up he went to where the door once was and the temperature read 37 degrees. Perhaps it was because it was an outside wall. Walking further away from the door the temperature returned to 52. Even by the window, it read 45 degrees. There was a cold spot in the room. Cold spots were an indication of spirit activity, but he was not at all sure what this meant. Tired he made his way back upstairs. He decided not to say anything about the readings to Sally. *What if that bricked up door had once acted like a time portal to another dimension—a gateway in time. Who sealed up that door and why? Could that doorway open again? Was that what happened to Nancy.*

He was perplexed. All of this was too fantastic. He just had to get home and think about what all this meant and he was extremely tired. He wanted to take a nap.

When Sally saw him she said, "Find anything, any ghost down there?"

"No, nothing has changed, but do you know when that back door was closed off?"

"That was long before my time. The only thing I know is Karl once told me it was used for outside deliveries. Then I think someone got hurt or something and they decided to close that door for good."

"Thanks for all of your help Sally. I'll keep looking."

Thirty-five

Sunday January 17, 2010

Sunday morning Robert sat in his upstairs study with Albert reviewing all of his facts and findings. Since Thursday, he had done nothing but eat, sleep and think about finding Nancy Monroe. He had to admit he was obsessed with her. The EMF and infrared temperature reading he got on Sally's café still bothered him. From the literature, he read those EMF readings were definite indications of spirit activity. He reconfirmed the fact that there was a cold spots in the same area, but he had no idea what that meant?

Do the readings mean that Nancy Monroe was now a spirit haunting Sally's basement? If that's the case then Nancy Monroe must have been killed in that basement? Yet there were no blood stains or signs of a struggle. There was nothing found on the dirt floor. Furthermore if someone had killed her down there how did they get rid of the body? You would've had to come up the stairs and out the back. Witnesses saw nothing.

He sat feeling dejected. Then he asked himself, *are you just chasing a dream? Just give it up and let this go. This woman means nothing to you. You don't even know her. She is most likely dead.*

Needing to get away, he asked Albert if he'd like to take a walk. Albert never refused a chance to go outside. The sky was blue with no clouds over the lake and the temperature was near thirty degrees. This was commonly called the January thaw. Since there were no skunks, porcupines or raccoons to chase he let Albert run loose.

With Albert running free, he was able to think. *What do I know so far? The place where I got the low EMF reading was where the old door to the outside had been. There were no abnormal readings on the rest of the wall. Was it possible that this was where two dimensions came together to form a time portal? Some believe that there are more than three dimensions. If there are indeed dimensions we have yet to discover or understand, is it possible to slip through one of these dimensions and if Nancy did pass through to this unknown dimension, what would become of her? I have no idea. If that sealed door in the basement was the gateway to another world how did Nancy go through? Maybe it opens under certain circumstance that I don't understand. There are cases where people just disappeared into thin air like that one in Tennessee where a wife and two children were watching their father walk across the field and they saw him disappear. One second he was there and the next he was not. In this instance the gateway was in the ground. A circle marked the spot and for years after that, nothing would grow there. Some even said you could hear voices coming from the ground.*

Is the doorway in Sally's basement a doorway to a parallel world? Perhaps the people on the other side in another dimension caused the low readings. If this truly was the doorway into another world or time, how did Nancy go through? There was no door there and what was the real reason that the door was taken out. Maybe some time ago the old owner of the building suspected strange things going on, so he removed the steps and sealed the door. He may have thought the place haunted.

Now more confused than ever, he called Albert and headed back to the house. A chilling north wind had started to blow off the lake, signaling the start of some more lake effect snow showers.

Once in the house, he made up his mind to see if he could find any old abstracts for Sally's property. Maybe he could learn why that door had been closed off. There had to be a reason and it did not appear to be for delivery reasons.

On Monday morning, he would stop by Sally's cafe, talk to her about doing further investigative work in her basement, and ask about the abstract. He was determined to get to the end of this even if it meant that he had to buy the building.

* * *

On Monday, he saw Sally and she was more than willing to help. She suggested that since she would be closing the place down the second week in February to make her yearly trip to Grace Land he could do all of his work that week. In that way, he would not have to put up with nosey customers who were sure to ask questions.

While she did not know why the doorway in the basement had been sealed off, she did have the old abstract for the property, which she gave him. She also talked to Karl Prosser and told him Robert Rahn would be coming to see him. Karl was in his mid eighties, but still had all of his facilities. He might remember what happened here years ago.

1942

Thirty-six

Friday January 23, 1942

Oscar Kosken, Leo Coppalo, Ralph Winslow, Peter Cadence, Fred Banister and Doctor Frost gathered over dinner at one of the local restaurants rather than play poker. For the time being Nancy Monroe was more important than any poker game.

No sooner had the group ordered drinks when Oscar asked, "So what did Father Schuster have to say. Tells us Leo."

"You all know how strict and stand offish Father can be, I must have been there half an hour before he would really say anything. It took that long for the brandy I brought to kick in. After that, he said a lot of interesting stuff.

First, I told him I was there to talk about Miss Monroe because a number of concerned parishioners had asked me if I knew much about her. Since she was teaching our children they thought they should know a little bit more about her background. He agreed with me on this and so I started asking questions. Like how old she was, years teaching, where she got her degree and if she had any references.

Next, he cautioned me that everything he said should remain confidential between the two of us, except for some general things that I could tell the parishioners. Then he went on to say, that she was the best teacher he'd ever seen. She has a thorough knowledge of all of her subjects and she is a gifted piano player. He went on to elaborate that the kids really love her for music class because she can play things that are so different. By that, he meant she plays things he'd never heard before. They are up-tempo and have a swing to them. He just liked the fact that she could teach music appreciation besides all of her other classes. That was a big plus.

Then he added that when she is teaching she seemed to have the ability to connect the past and the present with the future. She seems to know which way the world is going. I interrupted him and asked what he meant by that. He told me he was sitting in one of her history classes when one of the student asked a question about the war. He was worried that the United States would loose and that maybe the Japanese and Germans would invade America. He was amazed at how she handled the question. First, she told the student that she was sure that good would prevail over evil and that God was on our side and that while things were not going our way right now she was sure that things would turn around. She told them she thought that by the end of June things would be turning around in the war with Japan. She went on to say the United States was like a sleeping giant on the day the Japanese attack Pearl Harbor. And you know once you awake a sleeping giant, he will become very angry. Perhaps by now the Japanese have already learned that they should have just let the United States go on sleeping. He went on to say that it was a great answer and how it reassured the children, but it bothered him that she seemed so sure that the war would turn around. Even the fact that she said June would be a turning point. He wondered if she could see the future. Did she have a gift and if she did he prayed to God that it was divine."

"What else did he have to say about her?"

"He said that besides being a beautiful woman she never let it get in the way. He was surprised at how well mannered she was and how she was friendly and out going to everyone. The thing that bothered him most was that he could not understand really what she was doing here. With the way she could teach he was certain that she could have been making a lot more money teaching some where else down state, but then he added that he was very glad to have her for how ever long she wanted to stay.

He went on to say that, he had concerns about the fact that she did not have a social security number or a copy of her teaching certificate. She told him that she had sent for copies and he would have them soon. He said she graduated from a teacher's college in Oshkosh.

He also said that he had a strange feeling about her. When he interviewed her he felt like she was from some other time. She just did not seem to belong here. Sometimes he observed that she had a far away look about her, as if she was thinking of somewhere else that she should be. But he noticed that each day that was becoming less and less noticeable. She appeared to be adjusting.

He summed it all up by saying that he didn't care where she was from. He saw her almost every day at mass and he could tell that she was a good Catholic. He added that at mass sometimes she seemed troubled. For now, she was an answer to his prayers. If she had not applied for the job he would have had to increase class sizes and perhaps even eliminate the seventh and eighth grades. There was no way that he was going to let her go even if that teaching certificate didn't show up. Come September and the start of the new school year he would deal with it then.

That was pretty much everything he had to say. So what's next?"

"I think for now we just have to take a wait and see attitude. Then after, say a couple of months I think we have to make another raid and this time take all of the strange electrical things she has and anything else," said Oscar.

"Won't that tip her off?"

"It won't matter. After that we'll have to make a decision whether or not to let her be or take her in and interrogate her."

"When you say interrogate her, what do you mean?"

"We asked her to come see us and if she refused we'll have to take her by force. It's much too early to talk about that now. We'll just observe. Agreed?"

All said yes in agreement.

Thirty-seven

Mid February 1942

Ash Wednesday was on February 18th and Nancy received ashes at mass that morning along with the entire school. All the grades attend mass every morning and starting on Ash Wednesday all participated in the Stations of the Cross after mass. Nancy thought that it was particularly hard on the lower grades. The Stations were much longer than she remembered when she went to Catholic School in the 1990's. Then they only went to mass every Friday, not everyday like now. They had Stations only once a week at the Friday mass. She thought if Stations were hard on her now what must the younger children be going through. Even now, she counted the Stations knowing that once they nailed Jesus to the cross they were nearing the end. Other than the Stations, she actually enjoyed the Lenten season. It was time to get closer to God and this year she was praying that God would show her the way in this new world. She was hoping he would tell her what he wanted of her.

* * *

Nancy had school on Thursday, but would have Friday off because Thursday night she had parent teacher meetings. She was happy that Thursday was her last school day for the week. Nancy had now completed six weeks at school. While she enjoyed the work, she was thankful for this time off. She found having to teach all the different classes kept her busy with all of the papers to correct and class preparation. While sometimes she was tired, she found being busy was good because it kept her mind off of Michael. She still thought of her relatives and friends back in Appleton. She wondered if they missed her and if anybody was still looking for her, after all it had been nine weeks since she disappeared. She still thought about Michael everyday, but that too was subsiding. After the visit to Nuncio's she was coming to grips with reality that she was not going to find her way back. What ever it was that opened the door that day in the basement of the café was no longer there. If the doorway home had moved, she had no way of knowing where it was. Each day she thought less and less about the world that she left behind. She could see no way out and when she was alone with her thoughts at night she came to believe that she was here to stay. She truly lived one day at a time, never dwelling on the future. Things like marriage and children seemed far off. Further more if she met someone here, married, and had a family she was not sure, how that would alter history. The other thing that came into her mind was what if she was like the man in the movie, The Time Traveler's Wife. In the movie, he just kept moving onto a new time. If she had a life here with a husband and children what would happen to them if someday she suddenly slipped back in time and was gone. She could not even contemplate the very idea of leaving loved ones behind. As of now, she did not know of anyone who had the least bit of interest in her.

Still she had to wonder how her presence here would continue to change things. By teaching these children she was having an influence on them and she had no idea how that would change the future. She already thought that her being here had changed the attack on Pearl Harbor from two waves of bomber attacks to three and that the radio had said the Germans had taken Moscow. Both had not happened in her world of 2009. Did these things happen because she was here or was this just a different world from the one she knew? Now she wished she had paid more attention to quantum physic and the concept of many-world put forth by physicist Hugh Everett.

The war in the meantime was not going good for the United States. In the Pacific the Japanese were invading everywhere and there seemed to be no way to stop them. In Europe Hitler's armies were in control. All the U.S. could do was ship arms and goods to Great Brittan and Russia. Many ships were being lost because of the German U-boats.

Still Nancy was confident. She knew from history that 1942 was the turning point in the war with both Germany and Japan. The Japanese would be turned back in the battle of Midway Island and the Germans would be stopped in North Africa and in Russia. After 1942, both Germany and Japan would be fighting a loosing battle. She could only hope that this was true in this world and that she would not do anything to alter that future.

Later that night as Nancy and Martha listened to the news, they heard that President **Franklin Delano Roosevelt** had authorized the internment of all Japanese American on the west coast. All people of Japanese ancestry were excluded from the entire Pacific coast although they were American citizens and many were second or third generation.

Nancy was shocked and said, "Martha I never understood how they could do that to American citizens just like you and me."

"I don't think there is anything wrong with it, after all they did attack Pearl Harbor. Think of all those people that died at the hands of the Japanese on that day and are still dying."

Nancy replied, "Martha the interment will be declared unconstitutional in 1944 by the Supreme Court and in 1988 **President Ronald Reagan** will sign legislation apologizing for the internment. You know the whole action was based on race, war hysteria, and a leadership failure. Also the U.S. would later pay out billions of dollars in r**eparations** to Japanese Americans and their heirs."

"Did you say Ronald Reagan was president? The same man that's the actor?"

"Yes, he is but in the 1970's he got into politics."

"I saw him in that movie **Santa Fe Trail** in 1940 and later in the movie about that Notre Dame coach, I forget the name. How in the world did he ever become president?"

"Well Martha, there are still people who wonder the same thing in my time. He served for eight years and the Republicans thought he was the greatest thing since sliced bread. They still think of him as the great conservative. He certainly wasn't conservative when it came to spending. There he was fiscally irresponsible. During his eight years in office, he burdened the country with over 1.3 trillion dollars of debt, nearly tripling the federal deficit. My definition of a true conservative is one who lives within his means. A true conservative borrows only what he can pay back."

"Nancy there is so much I don't know and wouldn't know if it were not for you. I didn't think it was wrong to intern the Japanese, now that I think about it I suppose it was wrong to take people away from there homes and put them in camps."

"You know that there are many Japanese Americans signing up right now to fight for America against the Germans."

"Thanks Nancy for setting me straight. You know it is still hard getting used to the fact that you know what is going to happen."

"While this is a bad thing, I'm glad that this part of history has not changed because of my being here."

'What else should I know about Nancy?"

"You know Martha, I don't want to tell you anymore than I already have. It is not good for you to know too much. There are things about this war that it is best that you don't know right now. I'll tell you those things that you really need to know. For now all you have to know is that the war will be won by us, that is unless my being here changes things. And I pray that if things change they will be minor."

In bed that evening Nancy thought about all the hardships to come and she was now resigned to the idea that she was going to be part of it. There did not appear to be anyway out.

Thirty-eight

Friday February 20, 1942

On Friday February 20th at a meeting of the Hurley high school coin club, Kevin Cadence who was the president met with members to sort out rolls of coins looking for different dates and mints to complete the club's collection.

All the members were busy looking at coins when George Mathews stood and let out a high shrill scream better than any girl, all were shocked by the outburst. They had no idea what had happened. When at first he could not talk they thought it was some kind of seizure and were ready the go find the nearest teacher.

Then finally, he calmed down and said, "You've got to see this! You won't believe it! This can't be for real."

Quickly gathering around George, he showed them the quarter he was looking at with a magnifying glass. At first, Sue Ann Reynolds could not see anything out of the ordinary, but soon she too began shrieking saying, "Look, look, I don't believe this, It can't be true. It can't be true."

By now, the others saw it too and were amazed. The year on the Quarter was 1984. "This has to be fake," said Sue Ann.

"Maybe the mint made a mistake. They have in the past," said George.

"No matter, there isn't anyway that we can have a quarter from 42 years into the future. What are we going to do?" said Kevin Cadence.

"Why don't you take it to your father, he's a banker. He'll be able to tell if it's a fake or not?" said Sue Ann.

"But guys, it can't be real, just think about it. How would a coin from the future end up here unless that guy, H.G. Wells truly has invented a time machine. Furthermore, the date appears to be part of the minting operation. There appears to be no evidence of tampering. There are no scratches. You have to ask your father what he thinks," said Ron Cornell.

* * *

That evening Kevin showed his dad, the coin. "Dad we found this quarter in a roll of coins at our coin club meeting this afternoon and we wanted you to have a look at it."

His father took the coin and said, "What so special about this quarter?"

"Just look and you tell me."

At first his father saw nothing out of the ordinary. Then an astonished look came over his face. "Kevin, is this some kind of joke?"

"No, Dad! We really found it in a roll of quarters and we can't believe it either and that's why we wanted you to see it."

"There is no way this can be real, but it does not look altered in anyway. The area around the date is smooth and there are no scratches. There are no signs of tampering. I'll take it into the bank tomorrow and have someone look at it."

* * *

The next day a man from the Federal Reserve was at the bank doing an audit and Peter Cadence asked him to examine the coin. "With a date of 1984, it has to be counterfeit. Genuine coins are struck or stamped out by special machinery. Most counterfeit coins are made by pouring liquid metal into a die or mold. This procedure often leaves die marks, like a crack in the metal, however, there are no cracks on this coin. Next a quarter should have corrugated outer edges, referred to as "reeding" and on a genuine coin, they are even and distinct. This coin has that too. It appears to be real except for the fact that it looks to be an alloy not all silver. Notice it looks like it has a copper core. I've never seen anything like this. This is the best counterfeit coin I have ever seen. Whoever made this was damn good."

Lastly, he compared it to a 1941 quarter. They looked the same except for the date and the composition of the coin. The 1941 coin visually appeared to be 100 percent silver. Making the 1984 coin look more real was the fact that it was worn as if it had been in circulation for a number of years. It was not freshly counterfeited or minted.

"Peter, I'll be happy to send the coin off to be analyzed. They will be able to tell us the composition. From what I've seen it is the best counterfeit job I've ever seen."

* * *

Three weeks later on March 14th, Kevin's dad received a letter from the Federal Reserve saying that the 1984 coin appeared to be genuine in appearance except for the date and the composition. It was however made of a different metal composition. The 1984 quarter was made of approximately 9.0% Ni**ckel** and 91% Copper. The copper appeared to be sandwiched between the two layers of Nickel. The current 1941 quarter contains 90% **silver** and 10% **copper**.

In a conversation with the Philadelphia mint, they said that there was no way that their mint could have made this coin. The idea of the copper core was not possible for them to make at the present. Though it appeared to be genuine in every other way, they concluded that it had to be counterfeit. With the 1984 date, there was no other explanation.

2010

Thirty-nine

Monday February 8, 2010

On Monday February 8th, Robert Rahn picked up Sally at her house and drove her to the Rhinelander Airport so that she could catch a flight to Chicago and from there onto Nashville, Tennessee. It was the least he could do. She was after all letting him use the café to continue his search for Nancy Monroe who had now been missing over ten weeks. The police were still working on the case but there was nothing new. No witness had come forth and no sightings of Nancy were reported. They were at a dead end. Even her boyfriend, Michael Niffen, had not been around since Robert had last seen him on January 14th.

Robert was back from the airport around ten and before going to the café he went to see Karl Prosser. Sally had called Karl to set up the visit.

Karl lived about ten miles south of Hurley on County Trunk C on the original homestead. Moderate lake effect snow was falling as a cold front moved down out of Canada. Visibility was not good and he almost missed Karl's driveway had it not been for a rusted crooked mailbox with the name Prosser written on it. He could not see the house as he headed down the driveway, which had not been plowed in sometime and he was thankful for all wheel drive. The driveway opened into a field and there through the snow was the house.

The house was made of stone with a wood front in places. It was badly in need of paint, but Robert thought that perhaps when you were in your eighties it really did not matter.

He climbed the cement stairs onto the porch and wrapped. Sally had told him that Karl was expecting him. He waited and just as he was about to head back to his car, Karl appeared at the door. Karl wasn't just old he was ancient. He was stooped over with gnarled hands from years of arthritis. "I was about ready to leave thinking you weren't home."

"I'm home just about all the time unless I have to go to the doctor. Trouble is I don't exactly sprint to the door anymore and most of the time I don't hear anybody knocking. At eighty-five, I'm just damn happy that I can get around at all. My plan is to die right here. One thing I don't want is to be locked up in no damn nursing home were they charge you $300 dollars a day for a second rate hotel room with poor service. Those guys really know how to take your money."

Karl led him to a room that he called the library. There were thousands of book crammed into floor-to-ceiling shelves. There was a roaring fire coming from an enormous real wood fireplace on the only open wall. There were windows on both sides, which provided the only light for the room. Even with the clutter, the room had a warm cozy feel. Robert found that he immediately enjoyed Karl and the room.

"Here let me pour you a brandy and don't say no. We need something to keep us warm." With the brandy poured, he asked, "Now what is it I can help you with? Sally said it was something to do with that missing girl sometime back."

"Yes sir it is. You see I'm an investigator of sorts. I look into cases where people seem to disappear for no apparent reason."

"Sally said you were some kind of ghost hunter like those guys on TV."

"You could say that I suppose. When there is no obvious evidence then I think of the paranormal. Nancy Monroe disappeared with no signs of a struggle, no witness and there is no apparent reason for her to want to vanish. That is when I think there has to be another explanation. On the day she vanished she went down to use the bathroom at Sally's and never came back. Then when I investigated I found some strange readings with my EMF recorder. After talking with Sally she suggested that you might be able to provide me with some background history."

"Lord knows I've been around long enough. I was born in 1925, right here on this farm delivered by a mid-wife and I've lived here all my life. As a kid, I lived through the depression and let me tell you that was a real depression. When you lost your job there were no unemployment benefits. There was nothing and there was no place to turn. My folks made it through by scraping a living off this land. We took a deer out of season when needed and made a little moon shine to sell during those prohibition days. Those were real hard times. Not like now. I've seen the mining boom days and the wild side of Hurley. I served my country in World War II. My wife and I raised a family here and now that she's dead the kids don't come around much. They say I've got a negative attitude. Living as long as I have I guess that could be true. Anyway, they have moved away and have their own lives.

I'm here by myself. I suppose the kids will all come home once I die to collect what's left. So yes, I think I've seen it all and would be happy to help you. It makes me feel more alive just talking about it. There is not much use for a man my age."

"Let's start with the block of Hurley where Sally's building is. Sally gave me the old land abstract. The land was originally deeded to a mining company, from there it was divided into a number of lots over the years, and was bought and sold numerous times. What can you tell me about the building?"

"Sally's building from what I can remember was a Pasty Shop run by Nuncio DeMitri an Italian who hardly spoke any English."

"Do you remember what the building was like? Did it have an outside entrance to the basement from the back alley?"

"Yes, there was. I worked there one summer right before the war started. I think it was 1939. I was nineteen and couldn't find a full time job so I went to work there helping out for the summer. We used to unload all the supplies into the basement. He used the basement to keep food supplies cool. Only ice boxes in those days."

"This may sound strange, but was there ever a time when you felt funny working down there? Like someone was watching you? Do you know what I mean?"

"You mean was there a ghost down there?"

"Sort of. Did you feel anything out of the ordinary?"

"There was one time when I knew that I was alone and I sensed a funny odor. Not really unpleasant, It had the smell of an organic solvent from chemistry class. As it got stronger, I thought I was going to pass out, but before that could happen I ran up the stairs into the bright sunshine and was better immediately. Not wanting to tell anyone what had happened I just went back down and finished the job and never felt or smelled anything again. It was a onetime thing. I never told anybody about it until today."

"Do you know when that outside door was taken out and sealed over?"

"It was right after I got back from the army in 1946. There was a weird story about that. It seems that Nuncio's wife, Marietta, was down in the basement sweeping on a rainy summer day when she thought she heard someone calling her from outside the cellar door. Opening the door she found no one there, but she felt compelled to step out into the back alley to investigate.

The next thing she knew, she was standing in a paved alley street on a sunny day. First, she thought the rain had stopped while she was inside, but then she noticed that there were no puddles and the alley which had been dirt was now pavement and dry. Looking to her right there was a large green container with Waste Management printed on the side. It was like nothing she had ever seen, but she thought it must be for garbage, but it had not been there before. A printed piece of paper caught her eye and as she picked it up, she noticed it said, St. Mary's Bazaar, Sunday July 26, 2009. Without thinking, she placed it in her pocket. Next, peeking around the container, she noticed the vehicles were like nothing she had ever seen. The name on one said "Toyota." Going further, she saw two young women walking down Fifth Avenue who were scantly clad. It was as if they were in their underwear, but less. No woman of the time would have ever been seen on the street like that. Next, she saw a large warehouse behind her that had a Budweiser sign on it. Now scared more than ever, she hurried to the rear door of the pasty shop. Once inside she quickly ran upstairs. There she saw that it was cloudy and raining. When she told Nuncio what had happened, he did not believe her and immediately took her down in the basement and they both opened the outside door to the alley only to find a rainy summer afternoon and the same muddy alley that had always been there. She was emphatic about what she saw and kept to that story until the day she died."

"So no one believed her?"

"You have to remember that Marietta was known to have a drink or two. In fact, now days she would have been considered an alcoholic. So no one was ready to take her word for what she had seen. Besides, it was too fantastic. For months after she talked about what she had seen. Said there was another world right outside her door. No one really gave it much thought and she died a few years after that. It was only after her death that they discovered in her dresser drawer the advertisement for the St. Mary's Bazaar that was dated July 2009. My guess is that after no one believed her, she just forgot about having the advertisement or perhaps she thought people would think she made it up."

"After her death didn't anyone question the advertisement?"

"There were a few people that thought maybe she really did see something. But they had a hard time convincing themselves that she actually went into the future. You have to remember that was 1946 and people didn't believe or know of quantum physics or other world theories. That was purely science fiction back then. Even now, most people don't believe in time travel or other world dimensions.

Anyway, it was shortly after that, Nuncio had the cellar door closed off and as far as I know there was nothing more made of it until now.

Now let's have some lunch. It's not very often that I have someone to eat with and I am not going to let you run off. So don't say a word."

For lunch, Karl had a variety of luncheon meats and pasta salad and he opened a bottle of white wine.

"A bottle of wine is always best when it's shared."

Robert was surprised by the lunch. He thought that an old man in his eighties would be having "meals on wheels" by now.

"So what brought you up here? You seem to be too young to be retired?"

"I used to live in New York City with my wife and daughter, but they were shot and killed in a restaurant shooting about four years ago."

"Gee, I'm sorry to hear that. I still miss my wife and we had fifty-five years together. But why come to northern Wisconsin?"

"After I almost went insane, it took me several months to recover. It was then that my psychiatrist said I should look for some place far away from New York and Wall Street. So I did a search and well here I am. Meeting people like you Karl, makes me believe that I came to the right place.

Now I have to be going before the snow gets any deeper and I have to spend the night. Thanks for all of your knowledge and the great lunch."

"I hope you'll come back. I don't get many visitors."

"I will be back."

After bushing off six inches of snow, he decided to go home rather than go to the café. He had a lot to think about and tomorrow he would get a fresh start.

Forty

Tuesday February 9, 2010

As Robert drove to the café early Tuesday morning, he was still amazed at what he'd learned from Karl on Monday. It was obvious to him that Marietta DeMitri must have walked through a doorway in time and come back. The paper flyer that they had found among her possessions after she died was dated 2009 and that was all the proof he needed. What bothered him was how she was able to come back to her own present time. *If Marietta had gone into the future why was she able to come back? Perhaps it was the fact that she went into the future and that Nancy went back into the past. It could also be the fact that the physical door was present. That could have given her a way back that Nancy did not have. When Nancy went down to the basement there was no visible doorway, it had been bricked over. One thing I know for sure, that the portal between dimensions is located in Sally's basement. The place where the two worlds meet has to be there. The timing must have been right to slide through to the other side.*

He put all of the possibilities and the unanswered questions aside pulling into the alley behind the café. He entered discreetly not wanting others to know he was in the closed café. Today he would take measurements all over the basement.

The sun was up so there was no need for lights. On the basement wall facing the alley he could see the outline of the bricked over door, he started at the right hand corner taking EMF measurements every two feet. For the first fourteen feet the readings were normal. Then at sixteen feet, the meter read 3.5 consistent with his earlier readings. He moved two more feet and the reading remained the same and so for the next two feet. Two feet further the reading went back to normal. Were the readings indicating a spiritual presence corresponding to the door opening? He was sure this had to be the opening to another dimension. Then he backed away from the door three feet and took a measurement, it was a low reading. Then he moved another three feet and the reading remained the same. Moving another three feet the reading went back to normal.

Robert concluded that there was a spiritual space that was six feet wide on the wall were the door used to be and it went back six feet from the wall. This had to be the opening to the time portal that would open into the other world. *How does it open? What triggers it?*

Next, he took out his infrared thermometer. The room temperature away from the door was 56 degrees, but in the six-foot area, the temperature was 37 degrees. *This has to be the opening.*

He thought of that story of the disappearing farmer where there was this circular area on the ground where nothing would grow. People thought they could hear voices coming from the other side. With that, he placed his ear on the ground and heard only the sounds of the outside traffic and the furnace running on the other side of the basement. Still he was sure that he had isolated the opening where the two worlds met. *What's next. I can't just sit here waiting for it to open. Might as well go home and do some more research.*

He packed up his gear and moved everything to the ground floor and loaded everything in his car and left. On the way home he wondered if ley lines had anything to do with this opening. He knew very little about ley lines other than they were the alleged alignments of a number of geographical places of interest, such as ancient monuments that were thought to have spiritual powers. Their existence was suggested in 1921 by the amateur archaeologist Alfred Watkins. Believers in ley lines thought that the lines and their intersecting points resonated a special **psychic** or **mystical energy**. Robert thought that maybe this opening was on a ley line although he thought of himself as a skeptic when it came to ley lines. Never the less he would dig deeper into the subject once he got home.

Forty-one

Monday February 22, 2010

For the last two weeks, since taking the readings at Sally's Café, Robert virtually did nothing but work on Nancy's case. Nothing else mattered. Even Albert had to beg to be fed and walked.

Robert was positive that the opening into the past or another dimension was located in Sally's café basement. It was definitely where Nancy disappeared. Now more than ever he was convinced that time travel was possible even though no one—as far as he knew—had devised a sure-fire way to make it happen, but there were people that had reported traveling back through time. Some said it was quite unexpected, they just found themselves in another time and sometimes in another place—if only briefly. These events were referred to as time slippages. The big problem he had was that these time slippages were only for a brief period of time and they always returned like Marietta did in 1946. Afterward the people were at a complete loss to explain what had happened.

He had never come across an instance where a person was able to go back in time for an extended length of time and return. He found no references where a person went more than once to the same place in time and returned nor was there any reference of being able to come and go at will.

Then there were cases like Nancy's, where someone disappeared and never returned. Time travel and/or disappearance fit into two categories; one where the visit was brief and you returned and the other was where the person vanished and was never heard from again. No one knew for sure where he or she went. Nancy's case fit the latter. The odds were against ever seeing Nancy Monroe again.

* * *

Related to time travel and other worlds was the subject of time portals. When it came to the subject of disappearances some assumed that they had to have a connection with the paranormal. Many cases were shown to be bogus and others were open to interpretation. The theory that most intrigued Robert was the idea of parallel worlds. Quantum Physics states that there are many other world out there that run parallel to ours. There is the theory that there are certain locations around the globe that are linked magnetically where the boundaries between our set of dimensions and unknown dimensions are thin enough for people to pass through given the right conditions. Thus making it appear that someone had vanished. These time portals or doorways in **time** however seemed to be only something that was used by **science fiction** writers to transport characters instantaneously to the **past** or **future**. Yet he thought they existed and that these portals could appear to be ordinary like the doorway in Sally's basement. He just did not know how to open it or even if it could be opened. This was the only thing that Robert thought was meaningful. He thought he had certainly found one in Sally's basement, but for whatever reason it appeared to be inactive. Perhaps this time portal shifted. All he had to do was locate another portal in the area. The question was where to look. Sometime ago he had read an article titled, Finding your own Time Portal.

It said that time portals are everywhere but are more likely to be located in areas of deep gorges, rock outcroppings, and mineral deposits, especially copper, gold and sliver. In addition, if you can find an oak forest in the area you will have a better chance of finding a time portal. The Ancients believed that forests of oak held great power and magic. Finding a large oak tree might lead you to a time portal because the tree was said to have its top in the sky and its roots in the ground.

Once you located a likely spot you just have allow your mind to become quiet and in touch with the world around you. When your mind is clear, you will be able to know that you are near to another world in time. If there is a time portal there, you will feel the energy from the other world. You may feel sadness or a feeling of depression. Colors may become more vibrant and objects more detailed. You will feel the earth's energy rise into you from below, opening your mind and you into another time. Next, you may just find that you have crossed over or slipped into another time. It may take a moment before you realize that you are in another time.

Robert thought that perhaps this was just somebody writing down his or her fantasies. However, he would at least see if he could locate an ideal spot similar to the recommended criteria on his land. There had to be a place where there were rock outcroppings, ravines and perhaps mineral deposits on his land. He doubted that he would find any copper, gold or silver in the area.

Next, he thought that perhaps the time of the year or day had something to do when one could pass through a portal. There were articles that said the best time to find a time portal would be at dusk or dawn. The separation between worlds is blurred at transition times, or when it is foggy or on solstices/equinoxes. The phase of the moon could also be a factor.

When Nancy disappeared it was not during the solstices or the equinoxes nor was it foggy or at dusk or dawn. None of those factors fit. The only thing that was left was the phase of the moon and it proved, not be a factor unless there was something special about disappearing five days before the full moon, which was on December 2nd.

He put all of the possibilities and the unanswered questions aside and drove to the café. He decided to take more measurements all over the basement. The doorway to the past had been there once and he was determined to find it again although he really did not have a well thought out plan if he found it. Would he go through the time portal and perhaps never to come back. He didn't know. If he found Nancy would she believe him and would she come back with him. These were all unanswered questions. First, he had to find the time portal.

1942

Forty-two

Tuesday February 17, 1942

On Tuesday afternoon, Father Schuster stopped by Nancy's classroom and asked if she could stop and see him after class. He had some things to talk over with her. While he reassured her that it was nothing to worry about immediately all kinds of thoughts went through her head. *Is it about not having a social security number? Does he know about me? Did he write some letters asking for references and found that I don't exist.*

By four in the afternoon she was frenzied. Walking to the rectory, she was able to gain some semblance of control. She rang the bell and Father Schuster answered the door. He was a very stern looking priest around the school and at mass. She knew him as a no nonsense person. He was a strict believer in the rules. Everything was black or white. She wondered if he ever laughed.

"Nancy, thanks for stopping. Mondays can be very hectic. Let's go into my study."

The study was immaculate, not a thing out of place, not so much as a loose folder on his desk. He sat behind his desk and motioned her to a seat directly across from him in an authoritarian position. Now she was intimidated, expecting the worse.

"First I want to tell you that you are doing a great job. Comments I have received from the staff and parents are very good. And all the children like you."

"Thank you Father, I'm glad to hear that." She said feeling slightly more comfortable.

"Last week I got a call from a Mr. Bran Crowther. He has a son in your class—David Crowther. He wanted me to set up a meeting so that he could talk with you about his son's progress and he has some concerns."

"David is a real nice boy, polite and well mannered. He is doing very well in all of his classes. Did he tell you what his concerns were?"

"What he said was that he had concerns about your teaching style. His son told him that there were times when his teacher—you—would speak about things to come, like she could predict the future. He mentioned one-time where you said that you thought the Japanese would be our friends in the future and would become a world industrial power. He also said one day in music class that you played some music on the piano that none of the class had ever heard before. Now he was wondering if you were giving the children the wrong idea. He was concerned that you might be a fortuneteller, is the way he put it."

"I may have speculated on the future, but in no way did I predict the future. As for the piano, I play a lot of my own arrangements. That may be why they sound so different." She remembered playing some of the old Neil Sedaka songs that she loved when she was taking lessons. Now she regretted playing those songs. *I should have known better.*

"His real concern was that you might be turning the children away from God. You know the Bible and the Church condemn any kind of fortunetelling! Astrology and the Psychics are the work of Satan. I too find this very serious."

"Father I can assure you in no way am I a fortuneteller. I'm a teacher that may have some ideas on what the future will be, but I cannot predict it." *Only what I can remember.*

"You understand that I have to take these accusations very seriously."

"Yes, Father, I can meet with Mr. Crowther if you like."

"I think that is a good idea, but I must be present. Is that agreeable?"

"Yes of course, I would want you there, so there are no misunderstandings."

"Remember, I am taking this very seriously. There is no way that I want Satan to have a foothold in our school. Believe me when I say that I will fire you and I will make sure that you are no longer a member of this church if I ever determine you are misleading our children. You will remember that our Lord Jesus Christ was particularly protective of children. I don't think I have to say more. Are we clear on my position?"

Now she was angry. He had no right to imply that she would lead the children astray. "Father, I do take this seriously, but please I'm innocent. Why are you prejudging me?"

"I'm not. I just want you to know how serious this matter is."

"When would he like to meet?"

"I asked him to stop by tonight at six. I trust that will work for you."

"Yes. I'll be back here at six."

She was still so angry that without thinking she blurted out, "Father what would you say if I told you that someday I think the mass and all services will be in English. Would you call that predicting the future or just speculating about what may happen?"

"What in heaven's name are you talking about?"

"Just making a point Father, you don't have to be a fortuneteller to make a statement about the future. I could have said, we'll have a man on the moon before the end of the twentieth century. Those are just opinions. That's my point." *Only my opinions will come true.*

With that she walked out not bothering to say goodbye. She had all she could do to hold back the tears until she was back in her classroom. Then for five minutes she sobbed at the thought that someone would accuse her of being in partnership with the devil.

* * *

At six the housekeeper let her into the rectory and led her to Father Schuster's study. Bran Crowther was already there and she wondered if the two of them had mapped out a strategy. She felt she was part of the Salem Witch trials and perhaps there was no way she was going to get a fair trial.

Father introduced Bran Crowther and it was then that Nancy remembered him from back in December at the Post Office. She did not like him then and she did not like him now.

"Please to meet you, I remember you from the Post Office."

"Yes, I remember."

"Mr. Crowther and I have talked and from our conversations this afternoon you know why we are having this meeting."

"Before we get started let me say that I don't like what is being implied. I am not a fortuneteller, psychic, astrologer, clairvoyant or a witch. I am a faithful Catholic and have always been a practicing Catholic."

"We are not saying any of that, we just want to address the concerns that Mr. Crowther has from the information that his son told him. I'm sure that this is a misunderstanding. Let's get started. Nancy why don't you tell us about yourself and how you came to be here."

"My name is Nancy Monroe and I'm from Appleton, Wisconsin. I'm 25 years old and have been teaching for four years at Appleton West High School. I came up here with friends and just decide to stay here. My job was going to be terminated at the end of the semester and my boyfriend broke up with me, so when Martha Laine asked me to stay I thought it was a good idea. I like the area. That's how I came to be here."

"Weren't you involved in a car accident that caused you to stay?" asked Bran.

"Yes, that is how I met Martha Laine."

"It just seems strange to me that after an accident that you would decide to stay in an unfamiliar area. Am I right to say that you have no relative here and that this was your first visit to Hurley?"

"After the accident, which was minor I just made a snap decision. I'm not married and have no family responsibilities. Yes to the last two questions."

This was beginning to sound a lot like the questions she got from Doctor Frost during her check-up visit.

"What school did you get your teaching degree from? said Father Schuster. "

"The University of Wisconsin-Oshkosh."

"I don't think it's a university. Isn't it called the Oshkosh State Teachers College?"

I made a mistake, why didn't I say Lawrence University in Appleton?

"Yes, you are correct. Just made a mistake."

"You know we can check all of this? In fact you promised to get us a copy of your teaching certificate, which I might add that we have yet to receive," said Father Schuster.

"I know I sent for it. It should be coming. You know how slow the mail can be Mr. Crowther." *I'm going to be found out, maybe I should just resign now.*

Forty-three

Friday March 6, 1942

Peter Cadence did not tell the rest of his staff about the quarter coin his son had found until he had received the report from the Federal Reserve. A week later on March 6th when the guys gathered for the poker game Peter told them about his findings. Oscar Kosken as usual spoke first. "So what's so important that we had to have a special meeting?"

"I have something of interest that may just prove that our Nancy Monroe might indeed truly be from the future."

"And what might that be?"

"Two weeks ago, my son was having a meeting of his high school coin club. They look over coins that are in circulation that they get from the bank. They are looking for coins that will fit into their collection. You know, different dates and mints. Well anyway they were looking at quarters when they discovered one with a date of 1984. You can imagine what a surprise that was. The quarter looked to be real and they asked Kevin if I would have a look at it. When I saw the quarter it appeared to be real in every way except for the date and what appeared to be a copper center. It did not have any of the usual counterfeit makings. Therefore, I sent it on to a friend of mine at the Federal Reserve for him to analyze."

"So what does this coin have to do with Nancy Monroe?" said Leo Coppalo.

"I'll get to that, but first here is what I found out. The composition of the coin is indeed different. Rather than being made of nearly 100% silver it is made of 9.0% Ni**ckel** and 91% Copper with copper in the middle of the coin. Then in talking with the mint they said it was not possible at the present for them to mint a quarter or any other coin with copper sandwiched in the middle. They too were perplexed because in every other way the coin appears to be genuine. Their only conclusion was that it had to be counterfeit."

"Did you get the coin back?" said Fred Banister.

"No, they kept it because it was counterfeit."

"So in other words we do not have any physical proof."

"Your right, but we have a number of eye witnesses and here is what I did next. You remember Bran showed us that letter that Monroe sent."

"Yes, so what?"

"Well I called him and asked him how she paid for the stamp? And he told me she gave him a quarter."

"So you're thinking that the quarter she gave him is that quarter."

"Yes, it makes since. Furthermore, let me tell you again, that quarter was real. It was worn like it had been in circulation. I for one am sure it was real."

"So where do we go from here?" asked Oscar.

"I propose that we take another look around Martha Laine's house and this time we make it look like a break-in where stuff is taken and not just Monroe's stuff."

"I'm not sure I like the idea of really breaking in. Before when we just had a look around that was different, nothing was taken. Furthermore Martha is a friend as well as an employee," said Doctor Frost.

"You know Peter is right. There does not seem to be any other way. If we do this we will know for sure just who she is," said Ralph Winslow.

"Gentlemen, I agree that a break-in may be necessary, but before we do I think that there is another way to confirm who this women is and I'm surprised that we haven't though of it before," said Fred Banister.

"And what might that be?"

"We should be making inquires of all the local government departments. Let's do a search of birth records, she's a teacher so she has to have a teaching certificate on record, church records like baptismal records, social security number and there might be others. If we can't find any of these records than I say, we should go ahead and stage a break-in."

"He's right. We should have thought of this before. Remember, Leo, when you talked with Father Schuster and he said he still did not have her teaching certificate nor a social security number. We should have thought to check then. So who is going to do the checking?"

"I'll have someone in the legal department of the bank write the letter and make some phone calls," said Peter.

"This may take sometime, maybe a month or more. You know how long it takes to get replies from the government. And now with the war it could take even longer."

"When you get something just call another meeting."

With that they all left without playing any poker.

Forty-four

Late March 1942

It had now been four months since Nancy had arrived unexpectedly in late November of 1941. It was now 1942 and while she still thought of Michael Niffen, she could tell that her love for him was beginning to fade, although she would never admit that to anyone. With each passing day it was becoming clear that she was, here to stay. She was beginning to fit into the community and she loved her teaching job. The biggest problem facing her was how to fit into society legally. She had no birth certificate on record nor was there any record that she was a certified teacher. She did not have any records of having parents. If Father Schuster had not been so desperate to have a teacher she was sure she would have been found out by now. He was willing to look the other way because he needed her. Now he too was beginning to get suspicious. There were also others like Martha's boss Doctor Frost and some of his associates. They all were beginning to talk. Then there was the January break-in. What did people really know? How long would she be able to conceal her identity before someone would come forth wanting to know who she really was and how did she get here. She felt like the Great Imposter. She thought that perhaps she could last until the end of the school year and then in the summer she would have to consider moving to a bigger city. She knew that in the year 2009 she could easily obtained false documents. The reverse of that it was also true. It would have been easy to find out that she was an imposter. She wondered if it was possible to obtain a false identity in 1942. There had to be someway.

Putting aside, all of these thoughts she prepared to meet one of the parents to talk about their child's performance. She hoped this would not be an irate parent or another like Ban Crowther who thought that she was some kind of fortuneteller.

The student's name was Elisabeth Kershaw. Her father was Gerald Kershaw. He was a widower raising a ten-year-old girl by himself and she knew that could not be easy. Girls of ten would soon need a woman to explain the facts of life. That was the same here in 1942.

* * *

Gerald Kershaw arrived promptly at seven and the instant he entered the room Nancy experienced an unexpected attraction to him. He was well dressed. He wore a blue shirt and a tie with a blue blazer. She guessed that he was around five seven. His hair was brown and wavy with blue eyes that looked directly at her as he introduced himself.

"I'm Gerald Kershaw, my daughter is Elisabeth."

Her attraction to him was not something she had experienced in her four months here. She quickly dismissed the feeling and introduced herself, "Hello, I'm Nancy Monroe, your daughter's teacher."

"It's so good to meet you in person. Beth has told me so much about you. She says that you're the best teacher ever."

"Well thank you very much Mr. Kershaw, I do try to do my best and I hope I can continue to live up to your daughter's high expectations. Now how can I help you?"

He stood there for a moment just looking at her. Beth had said she was very pretty, but she was much more than that. He thought she was exquisite. She had such delicate features. Then he caught himself and said, "Like I said, Beth told me so much about you I just had to meet you. She's particularly taken with the songs you play for the class on the piano. She's been taking lessons for two years and she is now more determined than ever. She says all the time that she wants to play like you."

Nancy found that she liked him. She liked the interest that he was showing in his daughter. She did not see that in all of her student's parents.

"I'm faltered, Mr. Kershaw. I too took piano lessons when I was Elisabeth's age. It was only after I got to high school that I really started to appreciate music."

"Beth tells me that your music is so different. Why does she think that, I'm curious."

"Like I told others some of the things I play I write myself and others I have just made different arrangements. So I suppose that's why it sounds so different."

"Well that explains it. How is Beth doing in her other subjects? She says she is doing great."

"All of her grades are A's or B's. You have nothing to worry about. She is a very well mannered child and she has a great love for her religion. She is one of my most prayerful students at morning mass."

"While I'd like to take credit for that, I think her mother taught her to be that way and since her mother past she has been even more respectful and interested in Jesus. It was really hard on Beth loosing her mother three years ago."

"I'm so sorry for your loss and I know how hard it can be on a child. I lost both of my parents just after getting out of college and I thought that was hard. I can't image how hard it must be on a seven year old. You have done a very good job raising her."

"Thanks for saying that. I do the best although it is not easy. This war has not made things any easier. So far I have a deferment because I'm a single parent. If it gets worse, I'm not sure what will happen. But enough of my problems. Thanks for seeing me. You must want to get home."

"It is not a problem. I'm single so there is no one waiting for me." *Why did I say that? I hope he doesn't think I'm being forward.*

"Thanks for your time. Beth is waiting for me at home."

* * *

Later that night Nancy looked up Gerald Kershaw on the admission records and found that he was an accountant for one of the big mining companies. As she went to bed, she could not help thinking about him. He was a very nice man and she liked him. She admitted to herself that she was attracted to him and she found herself thinking of how she might see him again. Then she chastised herself, *whatever are you thinking. Why would he be interested in me? Even if he were, what would become of it? Me being from another tim*e. What would I tell him?

Suppose he asked me to marry him. What would I tell him when he discovered that there is no record of me ever existing? I could just tell him; oh, I'm from the year 2009. That would really put a damper on any relationship. Marriage, now you are being ridiculous Nancy Monroe. Just mind your own business.

After that, she fell asleep.

2010

Forty-five

April 2010

The week before Easter Robert found that he was making very little progress in his quest to solve Nancy's disappearance. He decided to explore some of his back acreage that was near the Indian Reservation for what he called sacred sites. He thought that these sacred sites just might be linked to a time portal based on some of the weird animal sightings people had reported like seeing a black panther. It was a long shot but since the ground was still frozen, it was a good time to go besides he needed to get out of the house.

The sites he was interested in exploring were just off one of his hiking paths on the northwest corner of his property. Some of the paths were old logging roads and others were narrow game trails meandering though out the area.

Robert remembered snowshoeing back here in February and having a funny feeling that he ignored at the time. Once again, when he came near a large oak tree he could feel that the air was different. Somewhat heavy and there was an ozone smell like just before a thunderstorm. The feeling past as quickly as it had started. He made a mental note of this place and decided to come back when the frost was out of the ground and explore further.

As he went back home he thought that the hike was worthwhile. He felt like it might lead to something. He wasn't sure what he wanted to do next, but he thought he was Nancy's only hope. Unofficially the case was closed.

* * *

Other than this site on his land that he would explore further in May, he had made very little progress in his quest to solve Nancy's disappearance. He continued to work with Sally Millburn working out a schedule to spend time in her basement monitoring the sealed doorway. He did this three times a week for a few hours each day at different times. So far he observed nothing new or magical, the doorway had not opened up to show him a way into the past. The only thing Sally asked was that he keep what he was doing quite. In a way, she was concerned more about Robert than herself and her business; she did not want people to think he was crazy. She had thoughts, that perhaps he was carrying things too far, but he wasn't hurting anybody.

On Holy Thursday evening before going to mass, Robert reviewed his finding in his study over looking the Lake. The lake ice showed signs of melting; perhaps spring was on its way. Most of the snow had melted, but people in the area knew that you seldom got away without at least one major snowstorm in April.

During the last two weeks of taking EMF readings in Sally's basement, nothing had changed. There were still low readings around the sealed door indicating the presence of spirit activity, but nothing outwardly was happening. To make matters worse he no longer detected the presents of someone being there nor was there any strange chemical smells. There were no new signs in all the hours he spent in observation. Had he expected to feel cold air or something touch his hands or face? Did he expect to see a portal open like that movie, Star-gate, so he could just walk through into another world? When he was honest with himself, he had to admit that with each passing day he expected less and less. If the sealed door was truly the portal, he thought it could have moved but he was sure that the doorway had to be there based on what Karl told him about Marietta's story and the fact that Nancy Monroe had disappeared without a trace. Then he finally started to agree with the voice in his head, *Perhaps I've carried this thing too far.*

* * *

Later that night at the Holy Thursday mass, he prayed for Nancy Monroe. First, he prayed that she was still alive and secondly that if she was still alive that God would keep her safe. *If she's in another world and she has survived all this time, I can't begin to image what she must be going through. How would one survive? How would one deal with the mental shock. Some would just go insane when they realized that they could not get back? How would they adapt.*

I can only hope that she met someone who was kind and understanding enough to take her in and keep her safe. If not she is most likely in some mental institution. I don't even want to think what that could be like in some alternative world.

Then he prayed that God would guide him. "Lord, please look after my wife and my daughter who are now with you in heaven. Please forgive the man that took their lives and help me to forgive him. Please look after me. Grant me the wisdom through your grace that I may see the way to go. Don't let me waste my time and energy in pursuit of things that cannot be accomplished. Show me the way."

That night as he drove home, he felt better. He was sure that God had heard his prayer. He made up his mind that he would continue to pursue Nancy Monroe's disappearance until Memorial Day. If there was no progress by that time, he would stop and find some meaningful charitable work to do.

1942

Forty-six

Sunday April 5, 1942 (Easter Sunday)

There was always something special about Easter for Nancy and it did not matter that she was in the year 1942. As far as she could tell, nothing had change concerning her God. She knew that all things were possible for God so it was within God's power to transport her back to the year 2010 and if it was God's will that she remain here she would except that too.

Now in 1942, Easter services started with Holy Thursday. It had not changed. The only thing different was that the bulk of the mass was in Latin. The mass started at 7:00 PM and she was getting use to the priest making the sign of the cross and saying in Latin, "In Nomine Patris, et Filii. Et Spiritus Sancti. Amen." She was also getting use to what she knew as the Rite of Reconciliation now called the Confiteor being in Latin. The same was true for the "Lord have mercy" which was now the "Kyrie eleison." She was now familiar with the "Lord be with you" in Latin as "Dominus vobiscum" and her reply, "And also with you" as "Et cum spiritu tuo."

What made it easier for her was that Martha had given her a copy of the Saint Joseph Daily Missal, which had all the Latin and the English translation. In reading it over, she found the mass was much more complete back in 1942 than it was in 2009. The prayers were fuller. She found that in 2009 most of the prayers had been shortened. In fact, her priest back in 2009 was able to say the entire mass in 45 minutes. Now in 1942 the mass was considered short if it lasted just over an hour. Even daily mass was at least 45 minutes. She found she did not mind the longer mass. There was more meaning and it made her feel closer to her God.

When it came to the Good Friday service there was no mass and there was no communion in 1942 and the service lasted from noon until 3:00 PM. In 2009, the service was one hour and you were allowed to receive communion but no mass took place. While the 1942 service was a long three hours, it had lots of meaning for her.

The only thing she did not like was the Holy Saturday Service. The vigil rituals were condensed into 45 minutes or so after the 8:00 AM morning mass. The priest recited all the Bible passages and blessings almost silently in Latin. A simple mass, much like any other weekday mass of the year followed. Few people were present. The service ended at noon and Lent was officially over. On Saturday in the afternoon and evening, there were long lines for confession.

She thought the Saturday evening vigil service in 2009 was much better. It started just after sundown with Service of Light, the Blessing of the Fire and the Preparation of the Paschal Candle .Then came all of the readings and she liked how the church was partially dark until after all of the readings and the light came on with the start of the resurrection mass. During the mass, there was the induction of the newly baptized and the new members were introduced to the congregation. The mass ended with communion celebrating the resurrection of Jesus Christ. She loved all of it.

The 1942 Easter Sunday Celebration was joyous and very similar to the 2009 celebration, but it seemed anticlimactic. For her the Saturday evening mass in 2009 was the best way—she thought—to celebrate the resurrection of her Lord and Savior. The only difference she noticed was that in 1942 there were fewer people compared to the huge crowds when you got the people who only came twice a year at Easter and Christmas.

While the mass was in progress, she noticed her fifth grade class all sitting together and seeing Elisabeth Kershaw, Gerald Kershaw's face came up in her mind and she wondered if he were here. Not wanting to draw any attention, she scanned the church with her eyes only and slightly turning her head to the left and the right. He was not in front of her or to the sides.

What on earth are you doing? My God Nancy, here it is Easter Sunday and you are looking around for a man you don't really even know, instead of worshiping your Lord.

Still when she thought about him she liked the way it made her feel, all warm and fuzzy inside. This feeling almost made her give in to her compulsion to turn and look in the back of the church. Even Martha noticed Nancy fidgeting. "Nancy, are you all right?" You're not sick?

"No, it is just very warm in here with all the people. I'll be alright."

She refocused her attention back on the mass. *I'll just have to wait until we go up for communion.* This was so unlike her. She was rarely attracted to men.

After Nancy came back from communion, her eyes searched the center aisle for a glimpse of him. She was rewarded and she felt flush. It took a lot to fluster Nancy but she realized her pulse had increased and she thought for sure that she was blushing. *What's come over me?* There he was and now feeling embarrassed she was hoping that he had not seen her looking, but he had. He smiled at her as their eyes met and she thought that he was genuinely interested in her.

After mass, she looked for him hoping to talk with him, but he was gone and so was Elisabeth. *Maybe I scared him off.*

* * *

Gerald Kershaw had spied her when he first came into the church. In fact, he had been looking for her. Even from the back, she was easy to find with her distinct long blonde hair draping over her shoulders. Finally seeing her face coming back from communion was a dream come true. He thought she too was looking his way and when their eyes met he felt a connection—or that was what he wanted to think—as they passed each other an aisle away.

It was only for a fleeting moment, but he was sure that he had to see this woman again, but her beauty scared him and his self-esteem faltered. *Why in the world would someone like her ever be interest in me?*

The courage he had mustered up to talk to her after mass faded and he quickly found Beth and hurried out of church.

Forty-seven

Thursday April 9, 1942

On April 9th came word that American troops had surrender Bataan in the Philippines to the Japanese.

With this news, Nancy could not help but think what was ahead for those poor men. While she had read articles of the cruelty that took place on the Bataan Death March, now she was faced with the living reality. From what she remembered, the march involved about 75,000 American and Filipino prisoners who were marched from the Bataan peninsula to prison camps some 25 miles away. Of that number only 54,000 survived the march. Beheadings, cutting of throats and casual shootings were common actions. Falling down or your inability to continue moving was tantamount to a death sentence.

Thousands died en route from disease, starvation, dehydration, heat prostration, untreated wounds, and wanton execution. Many more died in the internment camps from delayed effects of the march.

* * *

Ever since seeing her again at the Easter Sunday mass Gerald Kershaw could not get her out of his head. She was an indelible image etched in his brain. He had not been looking for romance the day he met Nancy Monroe at the parent teacher meeting and although he tried to deny his feelings for her, he knew he was romantically attracted to her. She was extremely beautiful and his first impression was that he did not stand a chance. Besides, he was still in love with his first wife and always would be. What he was feeling was merely a moment of sexual attraction that would pass, but it did not. The feeling although dormant remained and when he saw her at the Easter Mass, he knew that it was real. It was not going away. Now he needed a reason to see her again, if only he had the nerve to ask her out. He was sure that she was not seeing anyone or at least that was his great hope.

That night he asked Beth, "Are you having any problems at school?"

"No Daddy, everything is fine, why are you asking. It's not because you'd like to see my teacher again, is it? I noticed how you looked at her at mass on Sunday."

"What do you mean? I wasn't looking at her. Was she there?"

"You knew she was there because I saw you looking. And you know what?"

"No, what?"

"She was looking back for you too."

"Was she really, I don't think so."

"Yes, she was. Do you want me to ask her tomorrow at school?"

"Absolutely not! I was just curious is all. Besides your mother has only been dead three years and I still love her."

"I know you love Mom, but Dad I think she would want you to move on. So if you're waiting for my approval, you have it. Miss Monroe would make a great Mom."

"Now, now, where did that come from? I haven't even had a date with the woman."

"Well why don't you call her tomorrow and see if she'd like to come over for supper. You could always say you wanted to talk to her about me. You know growing up without a mother and all. You're good at making things up. What do you say, Dad. Give it a try."

"Perhaps your right oh wise daughter of mine."

* * *

On Friday morning, he took Beth to school early so that he could see Nancy. He had barely slept all night and now as he entered the school he was terrified. He thought he might bolt out of the building at any moment. He wondered why he was putting himself through all of this. *Just leave everything alone. There's nothing wrong with the way Beth and I are living.*

Then suddenly he was at the doorway of her classroom and there she was looking up at him. She was like something out of a McCall's or Red Book magazine wearing a black dress with a rounded neckline and cap sleeves. It was fitted at the waistline with a gathered skirt that flattered her figure. He thought she was the picture of femininity. He had never seen anyone look so stunning and he could do nothing but stare at her. He did not move until she said, "Mr. Kershaw how good to see you, come in."

At first, he was unable to speak and he knew that his face must have been as red as the apple on her desk. Then tripping over his well rehearsed words he managed to say, "I'm sorry to intrude, I just stopped by on my way to work and wanted to talk to you about Beth."

In the meantime, Beth went to hang up her coat giggling. She found her father's embarrassment funny. How could a gown man like my father have such a hard time talking to another woman?

"Beth is doing fine and like I said before, she is very polite and well mannered. You should be very proud of her. You've done a wonderful job raising her in the absence of a mother. I'm sorry I should've said that."

"No, that's fine, I know what you meant. Before I run out of nerve and time, I was wondering if you like to have dinner with us on Sunday evening at our house. I know it is short notice but both Beth and I would like to have you. I hope I'm not out of line."

"How nice of you to ask me, Mr. Kershaw, I'm flattered." Then he waited for the big, no I have another engagement, but it never came. "I'd be delighted, what time?"

For a moment he said nothing still too stunned to realize that she had said yes. "Please call me Gerald. Would six be too early." he finally managed to say. "

"That will be just fine. I'm looking forward to it."

"We'll see you on Sunday evening"

"Mr. Kershaw, I mean Gerald, I don't know where you live?"

"Please forgive me again. I'll pick you up at six. My house is on Maple Street. Not far from here, two blocks off Silver Street."

"See you on Sunday night at six."

As he walked out to his car, he said out loud, "Thanks God!"

Forty-eight

Sunday Night April 12, 1942

The dinner was delightful and she enjoyed his company. It was the first time she had been out on a date with a man since going out with Michael back in November of 2009. Gerald was a very good cook and she was not allowed to help with the dinner preparations. Nancy could see that Beth knew her way around the kitchen too. Nancy thought that her mother had taught her well at a young age. Then she remembered that in the 1940's homemaking skills were considered more important than in 2009. Women back then did not always work outside the house or have careers. Their career was being a mother and a homemaker, not like 2009.

After dinner they talked while Beth went to make sure that her homework was in order for Monday. Nancy thought that Gerald had worked that out with Beth before hand so he could have some time alone. Truth was that she was happy for the time alone with him.

In talking with him, she found that he was concerned about how the war was going. It bothered him a great deal that the Philippines were about to fall to the Japanese with the surrender of the Americans on the Bataan peninsula. In Europe, the Germans were still in control and he thought that with the coming of spring the Germans would finish off the Russians. They had nearly occupied Moscow at the end of 1941. He was doubtful if the United Stated could stand alone against Germany with the war in the Pacific.

She wanted to tell him that things were going to work out, but she too had her doubts how the war was going to end. History had changed in some small ways since she had been here. In the end she was still hopeful the United States and its Allies would prevail. She wanted to tell him that in early June the United States would gain control of the Pacific after the Battle of Midway. Then it would just be another three years before the war would be over. That was unless her very presence here changed things.

She knew this was not something that would be good for him to know. She just had to leave things alone and hope that history would continue to be played out. Yet she could appreciate the apprehension that people living in this time were going through. She had always thought that people living during this time had always thought that they were going to win. She did not realize they had doubts and even considered the idea that the United States could lose the war. She wanted to tell him that by the end of the summer the war would turn in the favor of the Allies and not to worry.

He was also very concerned about what would happen to Beth if he were to be drafted. Right now, he had a deferment as a single father, but if the war got worse, he was sure that he would be called. With no close relatives, this bothered him a great deal. She could see he truly was a good man.

She thought they shared a lot in common, although it was hard to take the time difference into account. When Gerald went to take her home, he was a complete gentleman. How different things were in 1942. In 2010, many men weren't so concerned if she kissed on the first date but whether or not she would put out on the first date, but Gerald made no advances though she secretly was hoping that he would a least attempt to kiss her.

* * *

When she arrived home, Martha was waiting for her. It reminded her of her own parents who always waited up for her to make sure that she got home safely.

Martha immediately said, "How did it go. Did he try to kiss you?"

"Martha, I'll never tell. No, he didn't even try. I had a great time and I really like him. The only thing is Martha, what happens if I really like him…you know."

"I know what you're saying. For now, just live in the moment. Don't try to think too far ahead. Enjoy what you have. None of us knows for sure what the future holds, not even you. Who knows maybe someone will come from the future to take you back or someday you will find your own way back."

"You're right; this was just a dinner I had at someone's house I shouldn't make too much out of it, but I did have a good time and I do like him, but Martha am I being fair with him? What if I really fell in love with him and he asked me to marry him. What would I do?"

"Don't think of all of those things. Just take it one step at a time."

"What if I let something slip out when we are talking, like what my world is like with air travel, nuclear bombs, homosexuality and other social issues? I haven't even told you everything about my world. If he were to find out he may not love me or want to marry me."

"Now, now Nancy just let this play out. You may know the future, but you can't know where this relationship is going to go. If it gets serious then you will have to decide what you are going to do. Even then if Gerald really loves you these things won't stand in the way."

"I suppose you are right. Love does conquer all. There is nothing I can do about my future here. I'll just have to wait and see what happens."

As she went up to her room she thought to herself, *I think I might be falling in love.*

Forty-nine

Sunday April 19, 1942

On Sunday April 19th came the only bright spot in the war for the United States since the start, when it was reported that U.S. carrier based B-25 bombers bombed Tokyo and three other major Japanese cities. In a winter where nearly everything had gone wrong for the United States, Americans were happy to hear the news of the raid on the Japanese home islands. It was America's first retaliatory air strike against Japan four months after the Japanese attack on Pearl Harbor. It boosted the morale of the American people when they needed it the most. While the raid did little damage, it demonstrated that the Japan's home islands were vulnerable. America and its Allies celebrated.

Nancy remembered seeing the old movie, "Thirty Seconds Over Tokyo" on Tuner Movie Classics. It was the story of James Doolittle who organized the raid on the Japanese homeland. The bombers took off from the aircraft carrier Hornet four hundred miles from the Japanese main island. The only actor she remembered was Van Johnson.

Nancy too enjoyed the jubilant feeling, but she was also happy for anther reason, the war was going according to the history books. Nothing had changed. She knew however that the good news would be short lived. Soon on May 5th, Corregidor was going to fall to the Japanese. Today she was not going to spoil Martha's good mood by saying anything.

* * *

While the country was celebrating the success of the Doolittle raid, Doctor Frost and his associates had been making plans for their own kind of raid. They had come to believe that they had to have more information on Nancy Monroe and the only way to confirm their belief that she could tell the future or was from the future was to break-in to Martha's house again. Doctor Frost had learned from listening to Martha talk that Nancy seemed to know a lot about the war before it really happened. Martha said that Nancy was sure the United States was going to surrender the Philippines and it happened. Martha also said the Nancy thought the war would turn around after June. That was when Doctor Frost called a meeting of the others. If she could tell the future, the investments they could make would make them all rich.

The group agreed that the next break-in of Martha's house would be on Sunday night, April 26th and this time they would do the break-in themselves. Martha had given Doctor Frost a key to the house when he was house sitting for her years ago when she went to see family in California. Doctor Frost knew that Martha and Nancy went to the movies almost every Sunday night and Martha had said they were going to see "High Sierra" with Humphrey Bogart and Ida Lupino this Sunday.

* * *

It had been warm for April nearly fifty degrees. Most of the snow had melted except for the huge piles of plowed snow. Doctor Frost selected Leo Coppalo to help with what he called a scavenger hunt. Ralph Winslow, Peter Cadence, Fred Banister and Oscar Kosken were waiting at the Office Bar, for the two to get back.

Once Leo and the Doctor saw Martha and Nancy leave they made their move. Martha left a number of lights on to make it look as if they were home. They had no way of knowing that this made the break-in that much easier. Once inside they went directly upstairs to what they knew to be Nancy's room. They went straight to the chest of drawers.

"This is where Marvin and Henry found everything last time," said Leo.

In the top draw, they found the strange reading device and the telephone thing just as before along with the yellow brassiere and panties. Doctor Frost paused, picturing Nancy. They took only the devices, putting them into a shopping bag, and continued to search the rest of the drawers. There in the second drawer was the pink Green Bay Packer sweatshirt, which they did not take. Lastly, they checked the other two drawers and in the bottom drawer under a set of sheets they found what looked to be a camera and very thin object no more than two inches wide by four inches long. It had buttons with numbers, zero to nine along with a plus, minus, times and divide. There were several other buttons. Their only conclusion was that it had to be an adding machine but neither of them had ever seen anything like it. They put both items in the bag. On the way out of the room they checked the closet and there was the yellow Columbia jacket. They did not take any of the clothing.

Knowing that Nancy would surely miss these things, they went about making this look like a real break-in. They took a number of jewelry items out of Martha's bedroom and a number of decorative things from the living room. Then Leo broke the glass in the backdoor on the way out. Then it was back to the bar to look at what they had found.

* * *

When Nancy and Martha arrived home from the movies, the first thing they saw was the broken glass on the back door. "Nancy someone has broken into our house. Do you think they are still inside?"

"We shouldn't take any chances, I'll call the police." Nancy reached into her purse still thinking she had her cell phone and then said, "I'll duck in quick and use the phone in the kitchen." Before Martha could say no, Nancy was already inside making the call.

Coming back out she said, "The police are on the way."

"Did you see any other damage? I can't think of why someone would want to rob me?"

"I don't think they came to rob you Martha, I think they came to rob me. Remember back before Christmas we thought someone was in the house, but nothing was missing. Well I think whoever it was came back to finish the job tonight."

Just then, the police pulled up outside the house. Hurley had its problems, but breaking and entering was not really one of them. Most of the calls the police got were for bar fights or domestic fights.

Recognizing Martha, the young office, Roy Dunlap said, "Martha what seems to be the problem. Said it was a break-in."

"There over by the door, see the broken glass. We called you right away, only went into the kitchen to make the call. Thought perhaps they might still be in there, but I think they are gone now. Nobody left here by the back door."

"We'll take a look inside. This won't take long."

After a few minutes they returned, "You can come in now. There's nobody here. It appears they didn't damage anything. Would you look around and see if you can tell what's missing."

Both Martha and Nancy immediately went upstairs. After looking around Martha knew some of her jewelry was missing and some statues were taken.

"Nancy did they take anything from your room?"

Nancy motioned for Martha to come over. "Martha they took all of my stuff, you know the things I had from the future. I can't tell them about that. Oh, they took my cell phone, KINDLE, calculator and my digital camera. I'm sure they would think I was nuts. We best not say anything."

When they were downstairs Roy Dunlap said, "Martha why don't you make a list of what was taken and bring it down to the station tomorrow. We looked around when you were upstairs and we noticed that most of the broken glass from the door is outside rather than on the inside. If they broke the glass to get in, the glass would be all over the kitchen floor and it's not. Dose anyone have a key for your place Martha."

"I think Doctor Frost has a key I gave him years back, but surly he would not have broken in here? Why do you ask?"

"Well it looks like someone wanted us to believe that there was a break-in with that glass on the outside. We'll make out a report and if you see or think of anything else give us a call. Do you have something to put over that broken window?"

"I've got a sheet to put over it for tonight. I'll call the hardware store on Monday."

"If you hear anything more tonight, don't hesitate to call us. By the way how was the movie?"

"We saw "High Sierra" with **Humphrey Bogart** and. It was good."

"I've been meaning to take the wife."

* * *

Alone after the police left, Nancy said to Martha, "What am I going to do now. Who ever took all of my stuff will know that I'm from another time. It may take them some time but they will figure it out. The things they took tonight won't be available for another fifty or sixty years. Then what will they do next? Expose me and have me committed?"

"I don't think they will expose you. My guess is that they may be after something else. They want to know the future and I think my good doctor has something to do with it. He and his friends would like nothing better than to know the future. Think of the money they could make if they knew how the war was going to end and when. They could invest accordingly. They'd make millions."

"So you think Doctor Frost is behind it?"

"Yes, it all starts to add up when I think of all the questions he has been asking me. I also think there are others that maybe on to you."

"What am I going to do? Will I have to move?"

"Let's not do anything rash, let's wait and see what their next move will be. But after tonight I am going to be sleeping with my pistol under my pillow."

Neither one slept well that night or any of the nights there after.

Fifty

Sunday Night April 19, 1942

Tommy Franks ran the Office Bar. Besides the bar, he was into a number of other things that he considered hobbies, but they all made him money. He could set you up with a girl if you needed one or if you wanted in on a high stakes poker game he could do that too. His real love was the buying and selling of guns—any kind of gun, rifle or shotgun. Not all of it was on the legal side. If you needed a weapon of any kind, Tommy could get it for you and he didn't ask any questions.

That Sunday night at the bar, Oscar Kosken, Ralph Winslow, Peter Cadence and Fred Banister waited for the return of the Doc and Leo. They couldn't wait to see what the pair had found. Now it was more than curiosity that drove them, it was an obsession. Could this mysterious good-looking woman truly be from the future or was she just able to predict the future. They all wanted to know.

Tommy was a good friend and he let the Alliance meet frequently in his private backroom for business meetings or just to play cards. Tonight it was for Alliance business.

When Doc and Leo arrive just after eight in the evening, hardly anyone was at the bar. They had the place to themselves.

As usual Oscar was the first to speak out, "Well what'd you find?"

Leo laid out the contents of the bag on the table and all stared in disbelief.

"So what is all this stuff?' said Fred.

Leo held up what looked to be a small camera saying, "This is what I believe to be a camera. The name on it says Cannon made in Japan. Next to that it says 6.0 meg pixels. There is no way that I can see that this camera was made in Japan. God help us if the Japanese are that far advanced we will have a hell of a time winning this war."

"So where did it come from?" said Fred.

"I have no idea. However, here is what I know. From looking at it on the way over here, it does not appear to have any film. When I press this power button here the camera lens opens up and there is a picture of what ever the camera is pointed at." He pointed the camera at Oscar, "I hope you don't break it?" The camera flashed and a picture of Oscar appeared and then was gone. "I haven't figured it out yet, but there must be a place where the pictures are stored. Behind this little door are the batteries that power the thing. We have similar batteries of this size that I think will fit. There is also this little blue card that I think is the film, but I have no idea how you develop the pictures. What I thought we could do is take it over to a friend of mine in Superior, Ethan Lynch. He runs a card and camera store. He knows everything about cameras and other gadgets. Anyway it's like nothing I've ever seen, maybe he can help us."

"Where in the world would she get such a thing?" said Fred.

"I have no idea, but wait there's more, than we can talk about what we should do next."

Then he held up another device. It was about five inches wide by eight inches long with a thickness of no more than a lead pencil. "On the top it says "**amasonkindle**." I think that is the brand name. I have never heard of it and could not find it anywhere. On the front is a flat screen with what appears to be a complete typewriter keyboard at the bottom. On the sides was printed **PREV PAGE**, **NEXT PAGE** and **HOME**. On the bottom is a button that says **MENU** and **BACK**. Remember what Marvin said last time, that this is a book like nothing we've ever seen. Well he's right, when you press the on button, the screen comes up with what I can only assume are book titles. None of which I have ever heard of." Here look at this one." He held it up, it read, A Winter's Rage a novel by Michael Putzer. "The copy right date is 2007 and from what I read in the prologue, it starts out in 1978 with a man and a woman buying land. The book is not science fiction. I can't explain it?"

"There is no way to explain it unless that woman is from the future and how the hell is that possible. Just who is this woman?" said Ralph Winslow.

"Is she even human? Could she be an alien from outer space?" said Peter Cadence.

"Believe me she's human. From my examination after her car accident, she's beautiful and she's got the nicest body I've ever seen. If I was younger I'd sure be in pursuit of her. She is definitely human," said Doctor Frost.

Now Leo held up what was a cell phone, "wait there's more. This I think is a phone. It no longer works because I think it runs on batteries, but

I can't for the life of me imagine anyone that makes a battery that small. There are no batteries made like this in the U.S."

"Do you think the Germans could have made something like this?" said Peter.

"If the Germans and the Japanese have stuff like this then I think this war is going to be lost. There is one more item you've got to see to believe.

This appears to be an adding machine, but look how small it is, not even a quarter of an inch thick. It has buttons for multiplying, dividing, adding, subtracting, percent and a square root sign. When I press the "ON" button it comes on and works," he said while demonstrating.

"That's amazing. We have mechanical adding machines and they are big and nothing that will do square roots. The only thing we have is a slide rule," said Oscar.

"This technology is way ahead of anything we've got. I hate to say it again, but do you suppose she's some kind of secret agent from Germany?" said Peter.

"I find that hard to believe. Even if she were a German spy, why would she be here? It's not as if Hurley is the technology capital of the United States. If she were a secret agent wouldn't she be on the East Coast in Washington. What's in Hurley?" said Leo.

"Here's an idea, what if she came here from the future on a time machine from say Germany to change the out come of the war?" said Peter.

"I'll say it again. What would she be doing here in Hurley? If she were a German spy she'd be in Washington D.C. Plus I talked with her and she doesn't have a German accent. I'll admit that she's different, like no one around here, but she is not a foreigner," said Frost.

"Remember that coin that your kid found Peter from 1984. Isn't that proof enough that she's from the future. Everything we've discovered points to the fact that she is from the future, it all makes sense, but I have no idea what she's doing here teaching school," said Ralph.

"Wait a minute, we're not sure where that coin came from," said Oscar.

"No listen Oscar, I think Ralph could be on to something. If she's not from the future—which is hard to comprehend—and only a fortuneteller, where did she get all of these things? There seems to be no reasonable explanation.

While I know this is far out stuff, do you remember a few years back when that Peterson boy was said to have vanished. Some said they thought he may have gone back through time, so it might be possible. She could be from the future."

"No he didn't vanish, he just ran away from home. You know his old man, he's a real bastard. If that were my old man, I'd have run away from home a along time ago."

"So where does all of this talk leave us and what are we going to do next?" said Leo.

"Here's what I say we should do," said Oscar. "Let's have Leo take all of this stuff over to his friend's camera shop in Superior and see what he can make of it. Then let's meet back here when Leo gets back with more information. How does that sound?"

"That sounds good to me," said Leo. "The only hold up is that Ethan is out of town next week. Is that a problem?"

"No we can wait another week. Right?" said Oscar.

All shook their heads in agreement. "Now let's have one more drink for the road and then go home and get a good night's sleep. I don't know about the rest of you, but my brain is spinning after seeing all of this stuff."

With that they headed for the bar and the meeting adjourned.

Fifty-one

Tuesday April 28, 1942

Ethan Lynch ran a high-end camera store in Superior. From early childhood, he had always been interested in cameras and taking pictures. Besides the camera shop he made a good living on the side taking what were called risky picture. If someone needed proof that a spouse or mistress was cheating on him, Ethan was the man who could get you indisputable evidence. There were sometimes when he found the business dangerous. There was one time that he was shot at by an estranged wife in an ugly divorce case. Otherwise, the money was good. Ethan was always interested in making money.

So when his good friend Leo Coppalo called him wanting him to looked at a camera and some other interesting devices that had come into his possession in what he said was a less than legal transaction, he willingly agreed. Ethan was curious as to what Leo had.

When Leo arrived on Tuesday afternoon, he made it clear to Ethan that before he would show him anything he had to keep all of this confidential. He also added that if he bought into this, he would be nicely compensated. Ethan was intrigued and readily agreed. In no way could he have imagined what he was about to see and examine.

* * *

As Ethan watched Leo leave he still could not fully comprehend what it was he had really seen or just what the impact of these things would be on the world. The camera was so advanced that he had no idea who could have made it although on the side of the camera it said, made in Japan. From what he knew, no one on the globe had that kind of technology, certainly not the Japanese or the Germans. He was sure from everything he read that the Japanese were not that advanced. He thought that was the same for the Germans.

Since he did not believe in people from outer space, he knew someone must have made it. He thought that maybe it was a private inventor, but the quality was too good.

When he asked Leo where he got these things, he would not say. The only thing he let slip in the course of their talks was that there was this strange attractive woman in town and then he went no further. When Leo asked if she were involved with this he said no and would say no more. Never the less who ever made it was at least thirty years ahead of their time. If they patented this, they would control the camera market not just in the United States but worldwide. Something like this would be worth millions.

The camera was at least four times smaller than anything on the market. The technology for taking and storing the picture was advanced beyond his imagination. He couldn't even understand how the pictures were developed. He could only think that there had to be another pieced of equipment for that.

Had the camera been the only thing that Leo brought that would have been unbelievable in it self, but when he showed him a telephone, book reader and an adding machine, he was speechless. The other three items were just as advanced and the technology was beyond anything that he knew of. It was as if the camera, book reader, calculator and telephone were from a distant future.

Leo wouldn't say where he got all these things only that he and his associates were involved in a situation and they needed his technical opinion.

Ethan was thinking, if only he could get his hands on this stuff he was sure he could sell it to a technology company that would pay thousands of dollars to be first in the market. With something like this, the competition would be left behind. He thought too about selling these items to the Germans, but that would be risky, besides he was an American.

These items were so futuristic he had a hard time containing his enthusiasm and keeping it from Leo. He never let on to Leo just how impressed he was. Although he had agreed to keep everything confidential, he knew he would never be able to keep that part of the bargain. This was in deed the chance of a lifetime.

Ethan made plans to get the items back. There was no way he was going to lose this opportunity. While he did not have any of the articles, he was able to take detailed photographs of each object while Leo was out of the room. With these pictures, he could at least start to approach potential buyers. He also remembered Leo talking about a blonde woman, maybe he could track her down. He knew a number of people that could do that for him. First, he had to have an interested buyer.

Fifty-two

Thomas Appleton worked for the FBI's Minneapolis Bureau for the last seven years. It was not what he had imagined when he joined the Bureau in 1935 at the age 32 searching for excitement and glamour. Now divorced because of his job, here he was stuck in one of the FBI's most remote outposts in the back woods of northern Minnesota and Wisconsin. His area was vast and his assignments were boring. The most excitement came when tracking down backwoods locals making moonshine.

In 1937 Thomas was assigned to the task force investigating supervise elements within the German communities. A number of German Americans were joining organizations that believed in Adolph Hitler and the Third Reich. Many were waiting for the day when Nazism would triumphant in the United States.

The best-known group was the German American Bund an American Nazi organization established in 1936 to promote a favorable view of Nazi Germany. The Bund, however, suffered a major setback in May 1939 when the leader was arrested for embezzling funds from his own organization.

After the arrest of Kuhn, Thomas Appleton obtained information that a Minneapolis entrepreneur by the name of Henrik Dahl was a major contributor to the organization. Upon further investigation, Appleton learned that Henrik Dahl had also been attending meetings of the Midwestern German American Bund in Milwaukee.

Because Henrik Dahl was well educated and wealthy, he was a man of interest. It was Thomas Appleton's job to keep track of all of his activities.

Appleton learned that Henrik Dahl immigrated to the United States from Germany in 1914 with his family just before the start of World War I when he was just a teenager. He learned that Dahl and his family were mistreated during the war years when the United States was experiencing a wave of anti-German hysteria. In some communities, there was a ban on German music and teaching the German language. Books in German were burned in the street. Many German Americans hid their ethnic identity.

While all of this made a lasting impression on the young Henrik Dahl, the matter was compounded when Henrik attended the University of Wisconsin after the First World War. He could not understand the terms of surrender that the Allies imposed on Germany in the Versailles Treaty. With the signed treaty, the Allies confiscated territory and forced Germany to accept sole responsibility for causing the war.

Even with all of these anti-American feelings, he still became an American citizen in 1921 mainly because he had no choice. With the state of affairs in Germany, going back to the mother country was out of the question.

Three years later Henrik graduated with a PhD in physics and electrical engineering in 1924. After graduation, he worked menial jobs as a waiter and a construction worker before eventually being hired by a technology company in Minneapolis.

By 1932 Henrik was an entrenched American capitalist with his own business. He now was a very wealthy entrepreneur running his own consultant company providing support to other industrial and technical corporations. His company had acquired a number of patents over the years and had made thousands of dollars from royalties from licensee agreements.

During these years, Appleton's investigation showed that while Henrik Dahl saw himself as an American citizen he still had a fondness for his German heritage. When Adolph Hitler came to power in 1933, Henrik took notice and believed this might be a way for the German people to regain their self-esteem in the world.

Although Dahl had given money to the German-American Bund at no time could Appleton find that he had done anything illegal nor had he done anything to endanger the security of the United States. By 1942 it was plain to Appleton that Dahl was not a threat to national security and the Bureau reduced Appleton's assignment to just monitoring Dahl's activities.

During all of this time, Appleton was fascinated by how Dahl was able to make money. It seemed that he was able to pull off business deals in which he was able to reap huge sums of money without having to invest a great deal of time and money. While Appleton was only to monitor the man's activities, he took a greater interest. He was determined to see if he could find some sort of angle in a way to extort money from Dahl. He thought there might be a way to leverage his FBI information and use that against Dahl to extort money. He wanted part of Dahl's success.

Fifty-three

Thursday, April 30, 1942

Two days after Leo Coppalo brought Ethan the camera, phone, adding machine and the reader, Ethan contacted his roommate from the University of Wisconsin who he had graduated with back in 1924, Henrik Dahl. After graduation Dahl had gone on to be a very successful and wealthy entrepreneur running a consultant company to advice other technical corporations. Ethan knew he was always looking for new ideas.

"Henrik, this is Ethan."

"Ethan, I haven't heard from you since Christmas, how is everything with you?"

"I'm doing fine. The reason I called is that I stumbled across some devices that I think you will find very interesting and they could make both you and me lots of money."

"I'm listening. Who brought you these devices?"

"I'd rather not say."

"Tell me! Otherwise, I'm not going to listen to anything you have to say. I've got to have a name if I'm going to get involved. I need to protect my ass."

"Alright, his name is Leo Coppalo. I've done business with him over the years. He is a legitimate businessman and I think he is part the group known as the Alliance. Believe me these guys are on the up and up."

"Good, now just what are these devices?"

"To make it simple I'm talking about a camera, telephone, adding machine and what I call a book reader."

"What is special about a camera, telephone and adding machine and what the hell is a book reader?

"Henrik, you have got to see these things to believe them. Words don't really explain what I'm talking about. It is as if these things came from the future, they are so advanced. I've never seen anything like this."

"You do know that the camera, telephone and adding machine have already been invented, don't you? Do you have these things in your possession?"

"I had them. Leo brought them to me and took them back with him, but I was able to take pictures of everything. You've got to see these picture. Is there a time we can meet?"

"Yes, of course we can meet, but if you don't own the devices what good will that do me. I can't patent something that has already been invented."

"That's just it. I don't think these things have been patented. I think they came from some secret facility and fell into the wrong hands. I think we can take advantage of this situation and I already have a plan to steal back the articles. Anyway when can we meet?"

"I'll be up in Duluth next week on Friday May 8th for some other meetings. We can have dinner at the Spaulding Hotel restaurant. Ethan this had better be good, otherwise you're paying for dinner."

"Believe me, you will not be disappointed."

Chapter Fifty-four

May 1, 1942

In May of 1942, Thomas Appleton was still assigned by the FBI to monitor Henrik Dahl activities, but Dahl was no longer thought to be an imitate threat to the United Sates. Thomas was disappointed that the Bureau had down graded his role. He had found Dahl to be his most interesting assignment since being assigned to this God forsaken outpost.

Appleton had no intention of not monitoring Dahl, because he was fascinated by Dahl's business activities. He decided to make this a personal matter and besides he had little else do. He was still hoping to extort some money from Dahl.

* * *

On Friday night May 1st, Thomas Appleton sat down to review his wiretap conversations of Henrik Dahl from the last few days. Since he was only to monitor Dahl's activities, he was behind in listening to the tapes. Tonight, however he finally heard something that made him perk up and listen. Most of the time Dahl's conversations were nothing but boring dribble, but today was different.

The call was from an Ethan Lynch in Superior. At first, there was nothing out of the ordinary, just usual pleasantries. Then Ethan said, "The reason I called is that I stumbled across some devices that I think you will find very interesting and they could make both you and me lots of money."

As Thomas listened, he was surprised when Dahl refused to listen any further unless Lynch told him who had brought the items to him. He made a note of the name, Leo Coppalo. He would check it out later.

Next Ethan told him what the devices were and Thomas had the same reaction as Dahl, what could be so interesting about a camera, telephone and an adding machine. It was the last item mentioned that intrigued him—a book reader. *What on earth was a book reader?*

Then Thomas really perked up when Ethan Lynch said, "Henrik, you have got to see these things to believe them. Words don't really explain what I'm talking about. It is as if these things came from the future, they are so advanced. I've never seen anything like this."

The conversation went on and Thomas Appleton was disappointed that Ethan Lynch no longer had possession of the items, only pictures. He had to give them back to Leo Coppalo. From what he heard, the items must have been beyond belief. Finally, he heard the two men say they would meet in Duluth at the Spaulding Hotel restaurant on Friday May 8th.

* * *

After listening to the wiretap, Thomas Appleton investigated Ethan Lynch and found that he ran a high-end camera store in Superior. He also learned that Henrik Dahl was his roommate from the University of Wisconsin. They graduated back in 1924.

Next Appleton set out to find out what the FBI had on Leo Coppalo and his group of associates called the Alliance. Things were looking up. He just might get rich after all.

* * *

Thomas Appleton found out that the Alliance had six members and that Oscar Kosken was the leader of the group. He ran the one and only local lumberyard and had his hands in the timber business. The other five members consisted of Dr. John Frost, Leo Coppalo, Ralph Winslow, Peter Cadence and Fred Banister. Leo Coppalo was in general retail sales, Peter Cadence was the owner of the Miner's State Bank, Fred Banister was into mining and Ralph Winslow was a lawyer. All of the members were extremely influential within the community although none of them had ever held an elected office.

What Thomas could not find out was how the Alliance members came to be in possession of these futuristic gadgets? He knew that Leo Coppalo had been the one to contact Ethan Lynch, but he did not know where the gadgets came from. He might just have to crash that dinner meeting that Lynch and Dahl had planned for next Friday at the Spaulding Hotel.

Fifty-five

Friday Night May 1, 1942

In place of the Friday night poker game, the Alliance met at the Office Bar just shortly after eight. It was cold for the first of May, but then May was never a very good month in Hurley. There really wasn't any spring, summer just started in June or maybe July.

The evening started with drinks all around as the team seemed to be procrastinating not wanting to get to the real business at hand. As usual Oscar was the first to speak saying, "Well guys let's get started. Leo what did your guy from the camera shop have to say."

"I took everything over to Ethan's on Tuesday and I stayed with him all afternoon. We started with the camera first and we were able to put in new batteries and took pictures until a message came up on the screen that said, **memory card full.** That we assumed was the blue tiny card. It seems that the blue card is the film, but Ethan had no idea how you would develop it. Then playing with the other buttons we figured out that we could look at all the pictures we took and that is where we found something really interested. There was over a hundred pictures that must have been taken by Nancy Monroe that were still on the camera. There were picture of Nancy and some of her girlfriends in what appeared to look like Hurley only it could not have been Hurley. Some of the buildings were too new and other buildings were missing. Next, we found one of Nancy and friends outside what looked to a high school. There was a sign and we could only make out the word Appleton and a date on the school that said 1962. That would mean the school was not built for another twenty years. There were several other pictures in what looked to be a school parking lot and you cannot believe what the cars looked like. They are like nothing I've ever seen. All are futuristic and that's not all."

"Hey can you show us the pictures, I'd like to see them," said Ralph.

"Sure just let me tell you about these other pictures, they must have been from the summer when these same girls were at a beach somewhere. Well you've got to see the swimsuits they're wearing. They are all two-piece suits and there is barley anything there. Believe me you won't see anything like this on any beach in the United States, at least not in 1942. They'd be arrested if they were on any beach here."

"Come on! Let's see!"

Leo held out the camera for all to see as he flipped through the pictures. "Do you see what I'm talking about?"

"She could be a pin-up girl in an outfit like that."

"Alright, settle down. So she's a very good looking woman. From what I've seen I have no doubt any longer that she is not from 1942. She has to be from the future. What about the other things? The phone, book reader and the adding machine."

"Just like the camera; he's never seen anything like it. The adding machine just blew his mind. There is nothing out there like this, at least nothing even close to this size. He did say that he read somewhere where a professor and a graduate student at Iowa State University built an electronic computer. It could do binary system of arithmetic, parallel processing and had a regenerative memory. The problem was that the computer was the size of a desk and weighed 700 pounds. It could calculate about one operation every 15 seconds. Just look at what this little thing can do."

"What about the phone and the reader?"

"The same thing. The phone did not have any power so we were unable to get it to work. He did say that it does not appear in anyway to have to be attached to a wire of any kind, but he had no idea how it could possibly work.

As for the reader we were only able to look at that one book A Winter's Rage and it had a copy right date of 2007 and the story is set in a time period from the year 2002-2004. We looked up the author in the list of published authors at the library and this person, Michael Putzer does not exist.

You know there are authors that write about the future, but I think this person had to be alive at that time to write about the things in his book or else he has the most futuristic imagination in the world. There are snowmobiles around but nothing that is sold in mass production like the author has in this book."

"Leo, can your friend in Superior be trusted to keep his mouth shut?" said Oscar.

"Yes, he told me he'd keep all of this to himself. The only thing he said he would want is to be cut in on any profit we were to make off these things. He said we should consider the idea of finding a small technology company that could study this stuff and turn it into products. He thought this was a great opportunity to make some big money and I have to agree with him. Just think of the money we could make selling a small hand adding machine."

"What did he think about the rest of the things?"

"He thought our best chance was with the adding machine. Then perhaps the camera, but we'd have to figure out how to develop the pictures. The phone and the reader seemed the hardest, but he thought there was a possibility of a company that might be able to make these into commercial inventions. He also said we'd have to be very careful who we worked with. Someone could steal this technology and get all the profit or worse still the government could get involved and then we'd have a lot of explaining to do."

"So where do we go from here? It sounds to me like our girl is from the future and I for one think she could be dangerous. Do you think we should turn all of this stuff over to the authorities and let them handle it?" said Fred.

"No, I don't think we should do that." Then Oscar paused. "I think we should keep all this to ourselves for the time being and just see how all of this works out. By now, Nancy Monroe must know that her things are missing, but I don't think she told the police. She would not want to draw too much attention to herself. I'm in favor of keeping an eye on her and see what she does next. What about the rest of you, what do you think?"

"I agree with you, but I'm concerned that if she's from the future that she just might decide to leave. What's she doing here in the first place? I don't think she traveled through time just to teach school in Hurley?" said Doc.

"Let's just think about this for a moment. What if she was part of an experiment sent back through time to the past and the experiment failed and now she can't get back. That might explain what she's doing in a place like Hurley. My guess is if she knows she's trapped here, she is just trying to make the best of it," said Leo.

"What if they send a rescue mission to bring her back? If that were to happen we'd loose her and a shit load of money," said Ralph Winslow.

"If that were the case I think they would have already sent a rescue team, after all she has been here since November. I think she's here to stay and we don't have to do anything hastily. Let's just keep tabs on her and see what she does next," said Peter Cadence.

"There is one other thing that I think we all need to agree up. If she's here to stay we need to figure out a plan to take advantage of all that she knows. The possibilities are endless and not just pursuing the gadgets that we stole. What do you think?" said Leo.

"That's all good, but I think we have to slow down. We are getting way ahead of ourselves. I agree we should keep all of these things in mind but in the meantime let's just keep an eye on Miss Monroe. We can get Marvin and Henry to do this for us. They didn't have a problem with the break-in and we can trust them. Is that all right with you Doc and Leo?"

"Yes, that'll work. I'll talk with Marvin tonight."

"Same goes for me," said Doc.

Everyone agreed to have the kids start on Monday. All the group wanted was to make sure that Nancy Monroe was still working and living with Martha. They didn't want to be surprised to find out that she had left town, disappeared, or had any suspicious visitors.

Fifty-six

Sunday May 3, 1942

Ever since dinner two weeks ago, Gerald tried to think of another reason to see Nancy. Had Beth not been such a good student he would have used that as an excuse. Finally on Friday he got up the courage to call Nancy and asked her if she would like to have breakfast with him and Beth after the early mass on Sunday. He told Nancy that it was Beth who had been urging him to call, but Nancy thought she knew better.

She said yes and tried not to let her enthusiasm show. Ever since the dinner at his house, she too had been looking for a way to meet without being obvious. The one thing she knew for sure was that in 1942 it was not proper for the woman to ask out the man.

* * *

Gerald had to confess that he had a hard time keeping his mind on the mass and it seemed extra long today. He thought Father Schuster would never quit talking. Finally, when it ended Beth went to find Nancy. When he saw the two of them walking hand in hand to meet him he knew he had to make this woman his wife. She was so good with Beth that he knew she would be a wonderful mother and what a great family they would make. Then doubt crept into his mind, *why would anyone so beautiful be interested in me, much less marry me.*

"Nancy, you look really nice to day. I'm so glad you could join us for breakfast."

"Thanks for asking me, it truly is a nice day."

"My car is over here. There is a nice place in Ironwood I want to take you to."

He thought just how wonderful it would be to be married to her, but then he thought about how little he knew about her. She had come into town unexpectedly. It was as if she had just shown up one day and decided to stay. Folks around town said she had a car accident and had gone to stay with Martha Laine for a few days and just decided to stay. In January when the teaching job opened up, she took it. No one seemed to know her family or anything about her background. Everyone did say that she was a very good teacher. Beth had told him that much.

* * *

Nancy enjoyed being with Gerald and Beth, but she thought perhaps she was not being fair to Beth or to Gerald. What if Doctor Frost said something to Gerald and exposed her? Would Gerald still like her as much as she thought he did?

She was sure that this could turn into a meaningful relationship. Now the only thing she had to do was decide if she wanted to let that happen. For now, she was just going to enjoy his company. She still had time to decide.

* * *

When Gerald brought her home after breakfast and was about to leave, she took his hand pulling him to her and kissed him. He seemed surprised but delighted. Then she said something she had not intended, "I'd like to see you again. I really enjoy your company."

There was an uneasy silence before he answered,. "I'd like that too. I thought you might think I was being too forward if I asked you. I'd be pleased to see you again Nancy. I really like you. I'll call you on Monday."

As Gerald got in to the car and drove away, Beth said, "Dad you have such a funny look on your face what happen. You look happy. What did Miss Monroe say?"

"I am happy because she said that she would like to see me again."

"Dad that's great. Are you falling in love with her?"

"Not so fast young miss. This only means that we like each other's company. Don't go planning a wedding just yet."

"I won't Dad, but I can dream a little bit, can't I?"

* * *

When Nancy arrived home, she rushed into the front sitting room where Martha was reading and nearly scared Martha to death.

"What on earth is the matter child? Did something terrible happen when you were out with Gerald?"

'No, no, everything is wonderful. He's in love with me."

"That's great news!"

"Yes it is, but what am I going to do if he proposes? You know, like we talked before. Do I just say Gerald there is just one small thing you ought to know about me, I'm not really from here I'm from the future."

"We've had this conversation before Nancy and you know we'll just have to take it one step at a time. If Gerald really loves you, then the two of you will be able work things out."

"What about the paper work? I don't have a birth certificate, baptism certificate or any other legal or church records. It was one thing to fool Father Schuster but I don't know how we are going to fool the state when it comes time to get married."

"Nancy, you let me worry about that. I've been around the block once or twice and there are a few people I know that maybe able to help us. The good thing is that we have some time. Let me worry about this. You just enjoy the fact that you are in love."

Fifty-seven

Friday May 8, 1942

Friday night at seven, Ethan Lynch met Henrik Dahl at the Spaulding Hotel restaurant in Duluth where Henrik was staying. They ordered drinks and neither one of them noticed the gentleman seated at the other end of the bar. He looked like an ordinary businessman. While they were at the bar waiting to be seated, Henrik asked, "Where are the pictures? After you hung up and the more I thought about it, the more I had to see what you stumbled across."

Opening his brief case Ethan brought out the pictures of the camera. "So other than it is a very small camera, what makes it so special?" said Henrik.

"For one thing it has no film." Then he showed him a picture of a small blue card. "This I think is the film, but I have no idea how you develop the pictures. We discovered how to take pictures and they showed up on the screen. We took picture until a message came on that said, **memory card full**. The memory card must be the blue card that acts like the film and I'm thinking you need some other piece of equipment to develop the pictures. Oh one other thing on the camera it said made in Japan. What do you make of that?"

"I'm not sure, but from all of my studies there is no way the Japanese have this kind of technology."

"There's something else, we found out how to look at all of the picture in the camera. There were all kinds of pictures with this blonde woman on them. I think, this woman is the one Leo was mentioning, but when I asked him about her, he would not say anything more. I'm not sure how she is involved, but I believe she fits into all of this somehow.

Anyway, I have to tell you that some of the pictures were what I'd call pretty risky of her in a two piece bathing suit. It was something you would not see here in the U.S. They were of her on a beach with friends. There were other pictures and one that really intrigued me. It was of a building with a corner stone that read 1962. I have no idea how that could be? That's twenty years in the future."

"The camera is advance alright and I'm not sure what to make of the picture. You've got to get me the camera. What else have you got? Let me see the picture of that reader thing."

"Here they are. It really is very thin and not very big."

"This looks like a typewriter keyboard on the bottom. You said that when you turned it on a book came up?"

"The name of the novel appeared. It was by a Michael Putzer and the name of it was A Winter's Rage. What was strange, the copyright date on it was 2007. My friend Leo thought that this stuff came from the future."

"And I supposed you believed him, Ethan. Pretty soon you'll be telling me Martians brought you all of these things. What else is there?"

"Here look at this. It's sort of an adding machine. Like nothing I've ever seen. We don't have anything like this. It adds, subtracts, multiplies and divides. Then on top of all that it can calculate square root. The adding machines we have are big and mechanical."

"Your right about that. As far as I know there is nothing this small that can do all of these functions. I read that somewhere at a Midwestern university some guy invented a computer, but it took up a whole room and weighed more than 700 pounds. This is really something. Let me see the pictures of the phone?"

Henrik was amazed by the phone, but had no idea how it could work unless some sort of wireless technology had been invented.

"Ethan, these things are fantastic, but if we are going to make any money, you've got to get the real things back, then maybe I can sell it to some government contractor or someone in commercial industry. Can you get the items back?"

"I think I can, but I'll have to steal them."

"Do you have any idea where your friend Leo got this stuff?"

"He really didn't come right out and say, but I think they stole this stuff from the woman he mentioned and I think it is the woman that we saw in the pictures."

"I believe that woman is the key to all of this. My thought is that she must know how all of this works. But, how did she get these things."

"I have no idea. It could be that she is the inventor, but she had to have help. How were they manufactured? Any chance your friends would go along with cutting us in on this?"

"Let me see what I can do. Maybe I can work out something where we won't have to include them. You know they live in Hurley and from what I remember of that woman in the picture if she is there she should not be hard to find."

"Why's that?"

"Well let me tell you if you ever saw her you would agree with me when I tell you she is the most attractive thing I've ever seen. Everyone in Hurley must know of her. I'm going back to Superior tonight and I'll get started on this first thing in the morning. I'll be in touch with you next week."

* * *

Thomas Appleton could not believe his good luck when Ethan Lynch and Henrik Dahl decided to eat their meals at the bar. The more they had to drink the louder they got and he was able to hear just about everything they were saying. When he left that evening, he felt he had everything he needed. Now he needed an action plan. He was either going to try to get the items first or force Leo Coppalo and the Alliance into a partnership.

* * *

After Ethan left, Henrik could not stop thinking about the picture he had seen or of the woman that had been in the pictures. She was more than beautiful and he had no idea how anyone might be dresses that way on a beach around here. It was unheard of. It was beyond comprehension. He knew of no institution of higher learning that was capable of making these things and yet he had seen the pictures.

Then just for a moment, he entertained the thought that perhaps it had to be someone from the future, but that was impossible. Time travel was just in someone's imagination.

More than any money, that could be made, he just wanted to see the real items and learn about the technology. Even better, he wanted to meet that woman.

* * *

After what Thomas Appleton had learned from the conversation between Ethan Lynch and Henrik Dahl, Appleton decided, it was time to take a trip over to Hurley and see what he could learn about Leo Coppalo and his Alliance friends. Perhaps he could even locate the mysterious blonde woman. He knew his director was very busy and that he would not miss him if he took a side trip over to Hurley Wisconsin.

Fifty-eight

Tuesday May 12, 1942

Ever since the break-in, both Nancy and Martha did their best to keep busy trying to put the ordeal behind them. Martha had new locks installed on the house and the police drove by the house more frequently. Nancy was still very worried. She felt sure that if her items from 2009 were examined closely she would soon be exposed and she had no idea what the consequences would be. She most likely would loose her job and perhaps legal action would be taken against her. What she really did not want to think about was being institutionalized.

Martha was sure that Doctor Frost and his associates were behind the robbery and it only increased Nancy's anxiety. Now with school ending early it only gave Nancy more time to think. She was determined to find a war volunteer job to keep her mind off her troubles.

* * *

Last week there was some good news and some bad news on the war front. First came bad news, General Wainwright had surrender the United States forces defending Corregidor in the Philippines to the Japanese. Without the prospect of any relief, Wainwright had no other choice. This meant that the Japanese were in full control of the Philippines.

Later that week came some good news. The United States was victorious over Japan in the battle of the Coral Sea. It was the first real victory for the United States Navy in the Pacific although it came at a great cost with loss of the aircraft carrier Lexington.

The Japanese had sought to extend their control by taking all of New Guinea and occupying the Solomon Islands. It was their objective to draw the United States aircraft carriers into battle so that they could be destroyed, thus providing them with air superiority in future battles.

The United States sank one Japanese aircraft carrier and one destroyer. In all over one thousand Japanese were killed, but the most important thing was that for the first time in the war the United States had stopped the southern expansion of the Japanese in the Pacific.

Nancy was glad to see that she had not changed any more history by her presence here. She did not want to be responsible for leaving these people with a different history where both the Germans and Japanese were potential winners. For just a passing moment, she had a vision of the German concentration camps from pictures she had seen in war books. *What might the world be like if the Germans had been victorious?* The thought vanished because as for now the war was going according to the history books.

Fifty-nine

Thursday May 14, 1942

On Thursday morning, Ethan Lynch called Leo Coppalo to arrange a face-to-face meeting. Ethan had contacted an interested buyer for the items who was willing to put down a substantial amount of money just to see them. Then if they were as good as he had seen in the pictures, he would be willing to work out a deal on how to proceed, but first he had the to see the real thing.

Ethan assured Leo that the buyer could be trusted and that he had known him for years. They had both gone to the University of Wisconsin together and had been friends and business associates for years.

* * *

When Ethan met Leo on Thursday for Lunch in Hurley his first question was, "So who is this buyer and just because he is your friend why should we trust him?"

"I went to school with him and he runs a company that buys and sells inventions. His name is Henrik Dahl, you can check him out, but for him to complete the deal he would have to see the actual items."

"If we agree to show him these things what's he planning after that?"

"He would start to look for an interested buyer and at the same time he'd apply for patents on all of the items."

"You know, we would have to be sure that we are the owners of any patents."

"Yes, you would be listed as the inventor/owner and he would have his name on the patent as a co-inventor. In that way all would share, equally in the profits from any sales or licensee agreement."

"I'd have to meet with the rest of the group and get their approval."

"That's fine. Do you think you can do that while I'm still here?"

"I'm sure I can. We usually get together for poker on Friday night. We could cancel that and talk out the details of this deal instead."

"Leo, remember back when you first came to me you talked about some woman that was mixed up with all of this, do you think I could meet her."

"I never said she had anything to do with this? I only said that she was new in town and came here around the same time we acquired these things. It is just a coincidence."

"I never heard you talk about a woman before. I'm curious, is she as pretty as you say she is? I'd like to get a look at her just to see what has you so animated."

"Let's stick to business. Here's what we can do. I'll pick you up tomorrow night and we'll meet with the group at the Office Bar. If that doesn't work I'll call you. Where are you staying?"

"I'm staying at the American House over in Ironwood."

* * *

After Leo left, Ethan had sometime on his hands and decided to see if he could track down the mysterious woman that Leo found so fascinating. He was sure she played a role in all of this intrigue. If she was as beautiful as Leo had said she would not be that hard to find.

He started with the hotel front desk. "I'm looking for a woman who works in Hurley. She is blonde, very attractive around 25-30 years old. Do you know of anyone like that?"

"No, sir I don't know of anyone like that. Just think about it, with a general description like that there could be a number of women like that. Do you have a name?"

"No, that's all I have. Thanks for your time."

Then Ethan thought, *if she is new in town, perhaps the police might know who she is.*

Stopping at the Hurley Police Department, he spoke with the officer at the desk and he immediately knew her.

"You're talking about Nancy Monroe, a real looker. Teaches grade school at St. Mary's up on the hill on Fifth Avenue, lives with Martha Laine. Why are you looking for her?"

"I met her a few days ago and well I just wanted to get to know her better if you know what I mean. Thought I would stop by and see if I could take her out for dinner. Like you said she's a real beauty."

All Ethan wanted to do now was leave before the desk office asked him any more questions, but before he could the officer asked, "What'd you say your names was again. You know for the records."

Before he knew it, he had blurted out his real name, "Ethan Lynch."

* * *

Since it was around three in the afternoon, he went to the school and waited for school to be dismissed. Just after three thirty, the kids came pouring out. Waiting ten minutes he made his way into the school building. Walking by each of the rooms, he passed by one and saw a blonde teacher and he knew immediately that it had to be her. She was petite with a nice figure even though she wore a very loose fitting blouse. She had a cute face, blue eyes, and high cheekbones and was very wholesome looking. He guessed she was maybe five feet three and 100-pound max. Even though he could not see her legs, he knew they had to be perfect too. What people had said about her being attractive was an under statement. She was beautiful.

Then he wrapped gently on the open door, not wanting to startle her. She looked up and said, "Come in, can I help you?"

"I hope you can. My name is Ethan Lynch and I was in town for a couple of days and I thought I'd look you up."

At that instance, she tensed thinking, *have I been found out? What's going to happen to me? Will I be arrested?*

"Are you sure you're looking for me. I'm new here and really don't know many people."

"Oh yes, I'm sure. They said you were blonde, petite and attractive."

"You'll forgive me, but I find this very strange. Please tell me what this is all about."

"Can we sit down some where and talk?"

Had this been 2009 she would have been alarmed with all of the school violence, but in 1942, she thought that was not the case as she led him to a table in the back of the classroom.

"I was contacted by Leo Coppalo sometime ago concerning some rather different items that he wanted me to look at." When he saw her face go flush and her body tense he knew she was involved. What he did not know was how. "In our talks he mentioned a blonde woman that was new in town, but did not say anymore. So I was curious and set out to find you."

"I know Mr. Coppalo only from shopping at his store. Otherwise I have had no contact with him. I'm not sure how this concerns me, sir?"

"I think you know exactly what I'm talking about. I believe what Leo showed me he stole from you. Two things bother me. First, the things he showed me are very advanced and secondly I can't figure out where they came from or should I say where you got them."

"Sir, I don't think I can help you. As I said, I don't really know Mr. Coppalo very well and I have no idea what he gave you. Now I'm going to have to ask you to leave."

"I'll leave, but I think you know what I'm talking about. Here's my card, if you ever need to talk to me, please give me a call. It was very nice meeting you."

* * *

Ethan left knowing that he was not going to tell Leo or anyone else that he had located Nancy Monroe. He knew she had to be the one who originally had the items and that Leo or someone else had taken them. What he could not figure out was how she came to have these things in the first place. Where would she have gotten such things? The only thing he could think of sounded fantastic, but it was the only explanation—she was from the future. She was new here and had no connection with the area. In the end, he decided to just tuck all this information away for use later at the right time.

* * *

After Ethan left, Nancy just sat there thinking, *my God he knows that those things are mine and now I know that Leo Coppalo and his friends are behind all of this. Martha was right. But what am I going to do. I've got to talk with Martha.*

* * *

Nancy left school early taking her test papers with her. When she got home, she was surprised to see Martha.

"Martha I'm so glad you're home."

"What on earth is wrong child, you look like you've seen a ghost?"

"A man came to see me at school after classes were out. His name was Ethan Lynch and he's connected with Leo Coppalo. Seems Leo showed him some of my things they took. He didn't say what the things were but I knew they were my things taken during the robbery. He said Leo had mentioned me in talking and he had to see who I was. When I asked how he found me, he just said he went looking for the most attractive woman in the area. Martha do you think I'm that attractive that someone could find me that way?"

"Maybe I never told you dear, but you are a very pretty woman. I can see why he knew it was you. But what did you say to him?"

"I told him that I only knew Leo from shopping at his store and that I did not know what he was talking about. Then I asked him to leave and he did. Now we know that Leo was involved in the robbery. You were right Martha. Dr. Frost and his group are involved in this. What are we going to do?"

"I don't think there is much we can do. The police are not going to believe us. We just have to wait and be vigilant."

"What do you think the Alliance will do to me?"

"I'm not sure Nancy, but I'll do everything I can to keep you safe. We'll just have to pray harder."

"Martha there is so much I haven't even told you about where I'm from and the future. What if these men came after me and tried to make me talk. What would I do? Maybe I should just leave."

"Nonsense, I won't let them take you and what about Gerald and Beth. Could you leave them? I know how fond you are of them."

"You're right Martha, I don't want to leave, but what other choice do I have."

"I'll talk to the chief of police; he is a friend of mine. I'm sure he can look into matters and find out just who this man is and what he wants. So don't run off on me, you know I love you and I don't want to loose you."

"I won't leave Martha. Maybe I don't always tell you, but I do love you. You're not just a friend, you have been like a mother to me. I don't know what I would have done had it not been for you."

Sixty

Friday May 15, 1942

On Friday night, the members of the Alliance met at the Office Bar to play cards. Before the game began, Peter Cadence asked, "How's the surveillance going on Nancy Monroe? It has been two weeks."

"Both Marvin and Henry said there was nothing out of the ordinary when I talked with them last night. There were no visitors," said Doc.

As they were about to start the card game Leo asked, "Before we start I've got a new development I'd like to discuss."

"Well what is it? I remember when we used to play cards," said Oscar.

"Yesterday I had lunch with Ethan Lynch, the camera man from Superior. He has a potential buyer for all of our items and I told him I'd talk with you guys."

"So who is this buyer and how much did your friend tell him. I don't like getting so many people involved," said Oscar.

"I know, but we can trust Ethan. The buyer is a friend of his that he went to school with. His name is Henrik Dahl, he runs a technology company that buys and sells inventions. He thinks he can patent our items and then sell them to a prospective buyer. They would either buy the patents from us out right or pay us an upfront fee plus royalties."

"How does he know what we've got to sell? You didn't show him everything, did you Leo?" said Fred Winnslow.

"No, I didn't show him the actual items, but Ethan must have taken pictures and shown them to the buyer. Guys, Ethan is only trying to help us out."

"Sure, and I suppose if he had the real things instead of just pictures we'd be out and he'd be rich. I don't like this Leo," said Fred.

"Look there is nothing we can do about it now, I know I made a mistake, but what choice do we have. I think we should listen to what this Henrik has to say."

"So what's his proposal?"

"The first one is obvious. He has to see the real things, if there is going to be deal. Then after he has had a chance to look over the items, he would file patents. We'd be the owners and he would be the inventor. We'd all share equally in the profits from any sales or licensee agreement. I think it is a good deal. There is no way we could do this on our own."

"I think there should be some up front money on his part," said Oscar. "Like $5,000."

"I think he'll agree to that if everything is what he thinks it should be."

"So where is Ethan Lynch in all of this?"

"He also wants a share of the profits."

"Holy shit! Pretty soon, we'll be including the bartender in all of this. What's next? Maybe we should just include Martha and Nancy in all of this while we're at it," said Oscar.

"Alright, alright, I have heard enough. Let's take a vote."

The vote was 4 to 2 with Leo Coppalo, Fred Banister, Fred Winslow and Oscar Kosken voting for and Doctor Frost and Peter Cadence voting against the proposal.

"The proposal passes. What's next Leo?" said Oscar.

"I'll let Ethan know and he can tell Henrik to move ahead. We'll have to give him access to the items. How do we want to do that?"

"One thing is for sure we are not going to give him access to all four items at once. I say we give him one item at a time. After he has completed his work on that item, we give him another and we have to have someone checking on him regularly to audit his progress. We've got to make sure that he just doesn't run off with our stuff and leave us holding the bag," said Peter Cadence.

"I agree. I think we should have a meeting with both Ethan and Henrik Dahl and make sure we all know the rules. We need to have a contract with him. Leo can you set up the meeting?" said Oscar.

"I'll take care of it."

"One thing before we adjourn. We need to think about what happens to Nancy Monroe and Martha Laine. Martha is a pretty perceptive woman and by now she must have a pretty good idea that we are the ones who took Nancy Monroe's things. If these things should go on the market in a few years, they will know. Then what are we going to do?" said Peter.

"I understand what you're saying, but I think we've got a lot of time to consider what our options are. If all else fails I suppose they could be eliminated. I could always contact my friend, an x-cop from Milwaukee, Stan Offenbach. He can be very persuasive," said Leo.

"What the hell are you talking about? There's no way that I want to be involved with murder. Martha Laine is a dear friend of mine," said Doc Frost

"Calm down Doc. It would only be our last resort, that is, if everything else fails. Further more Doc, you knew what you were getting into when you joined the Alliance," said Leo.

"Alright, let's take it easy. I think that this is a subject for another meeting. We'll keep watching Nancy Monroe. Let's have a drink. I'm buying."

Sixty-one

Monday May 18, 1942

On Monday morning, Leo Coppalo placed a call to Ethan Lynch telling him what had transpired at Friday's night Alliance meeting.

"Ethan I was able to talk the guys into having a face-to-face meeting to talk about all the different devices. The one stipulation is that they are only willing to part with one device at a time. After Dahl has had a chance to examine the device, they want him to write up a report before they are willing to move ahead with the other items. They also want to have someone—most likely me, checking on you to audit your progress. Their concern is that they don't really know your friend and are afraid they might get stiffed and be left holding the bag. They also said something about having some up front money as a guarantee. Can Dahl live with that?"

"The only thing that I think he will agree to now is to have this meeting as soon as possible. No way I can say he will agree to all that other stuff until after we have talked and he has had a chance to look over all the merchandize. Then perhaps we can come to some kind of written contract and the possibility of some up front money. Tell them we both have to trust one another. There is no way I want the law on my ass having to explain where I got these items."

"I understand where you are coming from and I agree that we have to have a face-to-face meeting to iron out all of these details. I think I can get them to agree to the meeting today. Are you going to be available the rest of the day?"

"Yes, I'll be in the lab all day. Tell them that the sooner we set up the meeting the better it will be. From what you showed me I think there is big money to be made."

* * *

That afternoon Ethan called Henrik back with the meeting information.

"Henrik, good news, they have agreed to a meeting on Tuesday June 9th a week after Memorial Day in Ashland at the Chequamegon Hotel. They were not happy about you wanting to see everything, but after a long conversation, they did agree that the best way to resolve all of this was at a meeting. Therefore, everything is set. The meeting will be at noon and they have reserved a special conference room."

"I appreciate all of your help. I'm looking forward to the meeting. See you on Tuesday the ninth."

* * *

During all of these meetings between Ethan Lynch and the members of the Alliance, they had no idea that FBI agent Thomas Appleton was observing them.

Appleton followed Ethan Lynch to Hurley on Thursday morning after hearing about the meeting with Leo Coppalo on his wiretap. He wanted to know how things were going to be arranged with Henrik Dahl and was hoping to find the blonde woman.

When Ethan met Leo for Lunch in Hurley, Appleton was there too. Once again, he noticed that Leo Coppalo took little precaution to hide what he was saying. It was easy for Appleton to hear.

Appleton learned that the Alliance was not a trusting group and he had to agree with them, he too did not trust Dahl. Leo did his best to convince the Alliance members that Dahl would be able to turn these things into money for them. Lots of money.

With all of the talk between Lynch and Coppalo about how to deal with Dahl, Appleton had to say he was pleased to hear them talk about the blonde woman. He was disappointed when Coppalo refused to tell him any more about her. He actually denied that she had anything to do with this.

After the meeting, Appleton followed Lynch back to his hotel and continued to watch him. About mid afternoon he saw Lynch leave and he followed. His first stop was at the Hurley Police Department.

When he came out Appleton followed him to the Catholic School on Third Street. There Lynch waited until school was out before entering just after three thirty. Once Lynch entered the building Appleton followed, careful not to be seen.

Next, he saw Lynch enter a classroom. The name on the door said, Nancy Monroe and there was this blonde, petite and attractive.

When Ethan left, Appleton came back and just stared at the women thinking, *how are you involved with all of this?*

As Nancy left school, Appleton followed and found she lived not even a block away. The name on the mailbox was Martha Laine.

* * *

On Friday night, Appleton was at the Office Bar early hoping to pick up some more information, but tonight he was not so lucky. The Alliance met in a private room and he was unable to hear what transpired. After the meeting he watched as the group left, he decided to drive back to Duluth rather than confront the blonde woman.

He was disappointed, but on Monday night when he listened to his wiretaps, he was rewarded with a wealth of information. The Alliance had set up a face-to-face meeting with Dahl to talk about all the different devices. The meeting was scheduled for Tuesday June 9 in Ashland at the Chequamegon Hotel. The meeting was at noon in a special reserved conference room, which did not please Appleton, but he had time to work on that.

2010

Sixty-two

Sunday May 23, 2010

The sun had not been out for days and so on this Sunday when the sunshine started to stream in Robert's bedroom window Albert knew it was time to get up. Whining he nudged Robert awake. The clock said half past six and even though it was early, Robert knew Albert would not leave him alone and besides it was too nice of a day to waste sleeping. Great spring days were hard to come by in Northern Wisconsin.

After breakfast, it was time for Albert's walk. Ever since Robert had purchased the land and even before building, he had developed a series of hiking paths that ran throughout the six hundred plus acres. Some of the routes were old logging trails long since reclaimed by the forest. Others were narrow game trails that went on for miles meandering though out the area. In the time that he owned the land, he was sure that he had seen all of it.

To make the paths permanent and more accessible Robert personally supervised a crew he hired through his builder to gravel the paths and build wooded bridges and walking paths where needed. When it was complete it looked like a wild life nature preserve.

Today they started out taking a route that followed one of the past farmer's fence lines on the northwestern corner of his property. All that was left of the old fence line path was an occasional strand of barbed wire sticking out of the ground and some rotten remnants of old fence posts. Two miles back at the corner of another forty; there was a large old oak tree, which had been split by a lightening strike sometime back. Embedded into the tree were strings of barbed wire running out in all four directions marking it as the corner of yet another forty. The tree stood proud with its intertwine branches and gnarled roots looking out over a small meadow.

Standing there looking up at the giant oak tree, Robert remembered what he had read about time portals. Time portals were everywhere but were more likely to be found around large oak trees or near an oak forest. Ancient people believed that oak trees held great power and magic. Finding a large oak tree might lead you to a time portal or a ley line. He also remembered that time portals were also in the areas of deep gorges, rock outcroppings, and mineral deposits, especially copper, gold and sliver.

From the oak tree, he could see the land tending upward and then slanting down to a ravine. At the bottom of the ravine was a small steam. Along the way were several rock piles grown over with weeds and grass. The place up ahead had all the prerequisites for the location of a time portal although he had no way of knowing if there were any copper, gold or sliver deposits. He had heard that at one time this area was thought to have copper deposits.

The place he was now looking at was isolated and away from people. Next he allowed his mind to become quiet and in touch with the world around him. Closing his eyes, he thought he could feel the earth's energy.

Suddenly Robert felt a change in the air. Even Albert came to attention lifting his head into the air as if smelling something new for the first time. Robert felt a shift in the atmosphere like just before a storm. It was not really colder, but the air felt denser. Except there was no noticeable change in the sky—it remained clear and sunny. Next came, the chemical smell of ether. This was what Albert must have smelled earlier.

Now what he saw up ahead was unfamiliar although he had walked this path with Albert a hundred times before. Instead of a rolling meadow leading down to a small creek at the bottom of a ravine there were piles of waste rock and mining tailings. The rock piles had a metallic luster while the tailing piles were reddish-brown in color at the surface. There were two small orange-reddish brown drainage streams running from the tailings down to the creek in the ravine. Robert knew the area was not like this a week ago when he and Albert had last walked and now Robert could no longer see the graveled path.

Still staring out he could see remnants of stone works and minimal vegetation in the areas of the waste rock and tailing piles. The rest of the area was in woodland much denser than before. Slowly he moved forward approaching the base of the first rock pile. Here Robert began to feel a marked sense of silence, deeper than he normally experienced. The spring insects were silent and the wind had stopped. A strange heavy mood was oppressing his spirit—a feelings of depression, eeriness.

Then he saw people as if in a vision. There were three men and two children. There was a girl of about eight standing in the bottom of a shallow pit. She was wearing a pinafore dress that came down past her ankles. Her hair was in two long pigtails. To her right on the top of a protruding rock sat what Robert thought to be her brother of about twelve and on his head he wore a tam hat. Further off were three other men wearing pants with suspenders and old fashion straw hats. One was gesturing to the other with his corncob pipe. Robert could tell it was not a workday—it appeared to be a Sunday. He thought they were having a Sunday afternoon picnic at what looked to be an abandon mine site.

Am I hallucinating? This can't be happening? After blinking his eyes several times the people began to shimmer and they became see-through gossamer images and floated away. Just before they faded away, he thought he could see their skeletal fames. They were gone but the rock and tailing piles remained. He was not hallucinating they had really been there.

Then unexpectedly the ether smell came back overwhelming him and he felt like he was being transported upward. Nauseous and dizzy at the same time he silently begged the feeling to stop and just when he thought he was about to be sick he passed out. The last thing he remembered was a feeling of tumbling hopelessly out of control.

When Robert came to Albert was by his side licking his face and they were both at the bottom of the shallow alder-choked ravine that bottomed out by the small creek no more than three feet wide. Now looking back he could see the graveled path again leading up the rolling hill where there were no rock or tailing piles only a few small granite outcroppings and some small mounds. It all appeared to have gone back to the way he knew it. For one moment, he thought he must have had a vision. *I know I saw the rock piles before I passed out. They were there. And how did I get here?* Getting up he called Albert and they headed back to the house. Walking back to where the rugged rock and tailing piles had been in his vision, he saw a number of small mounds that could have been crushed rock or tailing piles that had been flattened from years of weathering and were now over grown. *Could these be the remnants of a mining operation?* He had never noticed them before. *Could the area have been blasted in a search for iron ore or copper? Was copper once searched for in this area? Perhaps this area had once been a mine and that is what I saw in my vision.* He would have to ask Karl if there had ever been a working mine in this area, but for now he just wanted to get back to the house. He was fatigued.

* * *

After taking a shower and a nap, he woke just after one in the afternoon and decided to call Karl. He could not get the strange happening out of his mind. *Could this have been a mild case of a time slippage? Did that ancient dying oak act as time trigger?* He read that some places could bring on a time slippage. If you found what triggered the time slippage it was possible to reproduce it.

Perhaps under the right conditions and location I can produce a doorway to another time and place. I think that is what happened to Albert and me today. For just a brief instant we saw the land in another time, when there was a mine. I know if I told someone they'd say I was being outrageous to think that there are places where one could travel back in time. They'd have me locked up. Perhaps the past and the future are closer than we think. Maybe under the right natural conditions like today the barriers of time and space can be broken. I know I'm going to have to find out. Maybe I'll go back tomorrow and see if I can reproduce the same effect. First, I have to talk with Karl.

* * *

Karl answered after the twentieth ring. "This is Karl, what can I do for you?"

"Karl this is Robert Rahn, remember we talked sometime back."

"Sure I remember you. You said you'd be back to see me, where the hell have you been?"

"I'm sorry Karl I was busy, if you're not busy this afternoon I'll drive out. I've got a few things I'd like to ask you."

"Well let me check my social calendar." After two seconds Karl said, "Your in luck, I can squeeze you in around two. Will that work for you?" Then he laughed.

"I'll see you at two. I'll bring a bottle of bourbon, just in case we get thirsty while we talk."

* * *

When Robert arrived, Karl was waiting outside. Albert ran to the old man as if he was a long lost friend. "What a beautiful day. Don't get many days like this in May, we could sit on the porch. If that's alright with you?"

Producing the bottle Robert said, "That's just fine with me. Do you want me to get some glasses?"

"Already ahead of you there, ice and everything."

The old porch slanted to the front and Karl had already blocked the table to level it. After Karl filled both glasses and gave Albert an old bone to chew, he said, "What's on your mind this time. Did you ever find any ghost in Sally's basement?"

"No, I didn't. But this morning I was walking Albert and I came across what I thought to be an old mine and I was wondering if you remember any old mining history in the area?"

"Well you already know that just about all the major commercial copper mining was in the Upper Peninsula of Michigan. Way back, the Upper

Peninsula of Michigan supplied most of the copper for the entire nation well after World War II. Now the last mine closed sometime in the eighties. That mine over by Ontonagon was the last to go and it was not really an underground mining operation anymore, it was more of a chemical operation at the end."

"Was there any history of copper mining in Wisconsin?"

"Hold on I was getting to that, take it easy and besides we still have most of this bourbon to drink so don't be in such a big hurry. There was an early explorer, Jonathan Carver, in 1767 around these parts in northwest Wisconsin who wrote in his journal that while traveling down the Namekagon River he came across a branch that descended to a fork, and then ascended yet to another source and that is where he discovered several veins of pure virgin copper. Carver wrote about native copper, but without proof, copper men in Upper Michigan scoffed at his claim of early copper in Wisconsin.

There were some believers in Carver's assertion. Around the year 1900 copper men from Superior identified what they thought to be Carver's virgin copper with the start up of the Weyerhaeuser mine in the extreme southeast corner of Douglas County.

There are stories of finding copper nuggets weighing up to 175 pounds. In fact at the Weyerhaeuser Mine a copper masses weighing up to 500 pounds were taken out and metallic copper were extracted up until the start of the First World War.

Anyway, to shorten the story there were many ancient pits found around the area and some right here in Iron County. Those acquainted with prehistoric diggings on Keweenaw claimed the Wisconsin pits were also made by ancient miners. It was common knowledge that in Michigan ancient pits had led to the discovery of rich copper lodes. Small finds of native copper near the ancient pits drove the excitement still higher. So yes, just as you see in the western gold mining areas people started to poke holes here and there hoping to find that vein of pure copper. Yes, I suppose you could have an old copper mine on your property.

So you see there was lots of activity in the area. Some of this prospecting went on during the Second World War and right into the fifties. So why all this talk about mines? What brought this on?"

"Well if I tell you the whole story you have to promise not to laugh. You may think what I'm going to tell you is crazy."

"Go ahead, you'd be surprised at the stories I've heard over the years, but you'll have to forgive me if I chuckle."

"Early this morning Albert wanted to go for his walk. It being such a nice day there was no way I could say no. So we headed down one of the many paths that I had installed. We were about a mile out when the trail I was on, was not at all familiar to me. Up ahead were piles of rock and tailings that I had never seen before. You have to remember that I've walked these paths about a hundred times and I know every one. While I was standing there staring ahead, I saw four people—two men, a girl and a boy. It looked as if they were having a picnic on a Sunday afternoon. If I had to say they were dressed as if there were from around the turn of the century. After I rub my eyes, they vanished like they were ghost. They just floated away. Then I felt strange like the air had changed and there was the smell of ether in the air making me dizzy and sick. Then I must have passed out, because I have no idea what happened after that. When I came to, Albert and I were on the other side of the path and I had no idea how I got there. I don't know for sure how Albert got there. I don't think he passed out.

On our way back to the house, the rock piles were gone. All that was left were the small mounds that have always been there. When I looked closer I was able to see pieces of crushed rock that were covered over with dirt and grass. My thought was that some how I went back in time for just a brief moment and for that time I was at the site of an old mine. I have no other way to explain it."

"Did you notice how much time had passed from when you passed out and when you came to?"

"No, I never looked at my watch, but it would not have made any difference because I had no idea what time it was before I passed out."

"Did you see any mining equipment around the rock piles?"

"No I'm pretty sure there wasn't any. On the way back to the house it looked like it could have been a dig site and over the years the land had just reclaimed it. But believe me the rock piles were not there and the grass covered mounds were small compared to what I saw."

"Well I wish I could help you more. I don't know what happened to you, but I'm pretty sure there were a number of old mine sites in that area. Around 1900 there were number of people out of work who were hoping to get rich prospecting. You said the people in your vision were from around that time. Maybe they were just ghost from the past, you know like on that Ghost Hunters show. I sure don't know how else to explain what you saw."

"What are you going to do next?"

"I think I'm going to go back there again. I've got to know?"

"Did you ever consider that if you did go back in time, how are you going to get back? You could be trapped back there. Then what would you do? Just some advice from an old man that likes you, be very careful."

"I won't do anything rash, I like these visits too." With that, Robert thanked Karl.

"Come back sooner next time. I can't wait to hear more about the adventures of Robert Rahn. And Robert remember to be careful. I really do look forward to your visits"

* * *

On Sunday night, Robert lay in bed with Albert on the floor beside him unable to sleep. Robert could not help thinking about what had happened this morning. *Is it possible that I slipped back in time when there was an old mining operation on my land?* Based on what he had read on the inter-net he had all of the classic symptoms of a time slippage with a change in the weather, strange chemical smell and his mood change before he passed out. Just before sleep came, he made up his mind to investigate further.

Sixty-three

Monday/Tuesday May 24/25, 2010

Monday arrived overcast and cloudy. While it was still warm, the smell of rain was in the air. After eating breakfast, Robert procrastinated over a second cup of coffee as to whether or not he should go back to where he had blacked out. He was thinking he should be better prepared just in case he went back in time and did not return in a short time. *What if there was no way back.* He spent the rest of the day making calls and preparing.

He had to make sure that Albert would be okay if something happened. His first call was to Karl. "Karl, this is Robert, I need a favor."

"Sure Robert, what is it?"

"I need you to take care of Albert for maybe a couple days."

"Robert I have a Doctor's appointment tomorrow at Marquette and won't be home until three. I could take him after that. You're not planning anything crazy, are you, like time travel?"

"Don't worry Karl I'll be careful, but as a precaution I need someone to watch Albert."

"Sure I'll take him if you can have someone bring him over around three."

"I'll have my vet, Barb bring him over after three. I think he can stay there for the day."

"You be careful now. Don't do something foolish and stick me with this dog."

Next, he placed a call to his vet, "Barbara, I need a favor. Could you kennel Albert tomorrow and I need you to take him to Karl Prosser's place after three if I don't get back."

"Sure we can keep him for the day. I'll have Rob drop him off at Karl's if you're not back. Planning a little trip?"

"Just for the day, I'll drop him off tomorrow around eight. Thanks Barbara."

At least he knew Albert would be safe and if he never came back, he knew Karl would take good care of him.

The next order of business was what to take along on such a journey. In his backpack, he put in his digital camera, a first aid kit, a drug kit, some energy bars, some clean underwear, socks, and shirt and reluctantly he put in a small 32-hand gun. Ever since his wife and daughter had been killed by gun violence, he had stayed away from guns, but something told him that having a gun might just be necessary. For good measure, he also went back and put in a roll of duct tape, a knife and some rope. Now he thought he'd be set for tomorrow. Later he thought about money. He could take some with him but would it be accepted, if people notice the dates on the bills? That afternoon he went to the Gogebic Range bank and asked for the oldest money they had in fives, tens and twenties. He knew that none of the dates would be that old and that back then they had still had silver and maybe even gold certificates. He made sure none of the bill were the newly redesigned bills. If he had to use the money, he would just have to take his chances that people did not examine the money. Not like now when everybody checked the bill for counterfeit with a marker pin.

With five hundred dollars in cash, he thought he was all set. By the time he went to bed that night he was sure that he was doing the right thing. It was the only option right now if he was going to continue looking for Nancy Monroe. There was the real possibility that tomorrow when he went in search of the time portal there would be nothing there. He slept well that night with his mind made up. If there was something else, he always had tomorrow.

* * *

On Tuesday, Robert dropped off Albert at the veterinary clinic and immediately felt guilty at the thought that he might not see him again. On the way home, he began to doubt himself; *maybe I should just turn around and go get Albert and forget this foolishness. But, if I don't do this I'll always wonder if I could have found Nancy. Besides, I'm in love with her. I've got to do this and Albert will be okay.*

When he got home, he remembered one more thing, a picture of Nancy Monroe. Finally, at ten he left the house, setting out on the same path as on Sunday. The air was humid with a hint of rain. When he was just about at the spot where everything had happened on Sunday, he stopped and cautiously scanned the path ahead. Then came the ether smell overwhelming him and suddenly he felt a change in the air and this time he felt like he was being sucked into a vortex. The air felt denser somehow as the air rushed against his face. When the swirling air stopped, he found himself standing at the site of the abandon mine he'd seen on Sunday. He was back at the large rock piles and the mounds of tailings, but this time he did not see anyone else at the site. *I'm back, but in what time and where are the people? Could it be that the people were here only on Sunday because it was their day off? Now they're back at work.* Then he noticed that the sun was out with only a few cumulus clouds in the sky the rain was gone. The graveled path too was gone and he felt sure that if he tried to go back to his house it would not be there.

1942

Sixty-four

Tuesday May 26, 1942

Robert thought that his mind was playing tricks on him. *Am I really here or just succumbing to the loss of my sanity or a fantasy or just wishful thinking.* He felt trapped in a dream that he was unable to will away. Despite all these doubts and what seemed to be impossible, there was no question about what he was going to do. He was going to find Nancy Monroe even if it meant that he might never return.

The strange thing this time was that he remained in whatever dimension or time he had entered and he didn't feel any different. It was as if he were fitting in. Searching further, he went down towards the ravine and there he heard the sound of rushing wind. Looking closer he found the opening to the old mine. It did not have timber supports. It was just dug into the ground and then into the bedrock. It went back only fifteen feet.

Suddenly it set in; he had really traveled back in time and had no idea of how to get back. The last time the portal or new dimension had not kept him but pushed him out. In all the cases he'd read about that was the way it was—in and out—people did not stay. "What am I going to do now? What about Albert? What are my options?" he said aloud.

After ten minutes the only option he could think of was to start back to the house that he was sure would not be there. Starting in that direction he saw large ferns covering what was once a graveled walking path. The path was choked with black berry bushes with thorns that torn at his clothes scratching his arms and legs. Finally out of the berry bushes his way was blocked by alder brush that appeared to have grown unchecked for years. Halfway up the hill to his house, the forest of birch and aspen ended and he stopped to look around.

Everything looked so different. Walking further to the top where the ground leveled out he saw a dull gray barn that looked like it was ready to fall down. He was sure this was where his house had been and then he remembered that someone had told him that years back there had been an old homestead here. This had to be the last building standing. Once at the barn, he could see what was once an old log cabin in the back and to his right there was the old fieldstone foundation where once the house had been. Standing there a feeling of despair came over him. *What have I done? I've lost everything. What if I'm trapped here forever.* He had no way of knowing for sure what year it was, but seeing this old barn he thought that it had to be at least fifty years ago.

Before moving on he collapsed to the ground and cried. After what he called—a feel sorry for yourself cry—he remembered that the town road was only a mile away if it was still there. If he could find the town road he could make his way into Hurley. From there he would decided what to do next. To his surprise the town road was there and was not in any worse shape than it had been in 2010, in fact it was in better condition.

Walking along the road it was not long before he heard a car coming. He stopped and waved and the car stopped. It was a 1937 Chevrolet. The driver rolled down his window and said, "Hey buddy, do you need a ride?"

At first, Robert couldn't believe what he was seeing. Then he said the only thing that came to his mind, "Yes."

"Where you headed," said the driver.

"Into Hurley."

"My names Art Chester, I sell insurance. It's not easy these days with the war and all. What's your name?"

Robert hesitated trying to decide if he should use his real name. "I'm Robert Rahn."

"What are you doing out here?"

"Just looking a round, I collect rocks and mineral specimens. It's a hobby of mine. A friend of mine gave me a ride out here on his way to Ashland. I told him it was such a nice day that I would walk back. Usually I don't walk so far"

"I think you might be looking in the right spot. Not that many years ago people were prospecting for copper out here. There is suppose to be one of those early Chippewa Indian mines around here, they were still hoping to find large quantities like in the Upper Peninsula. With the war, I suppose it still pays to look, the price of copper is going up."

"Do you know what day it is?

"Sure it's Monday, May 17th."

"What year is it?"

"Are you telling me you don't know what year it is, come-on mister you have to be kidding me? Were you out in the sun too long, it's 1942 and we're at war with both the damn Japs and the Germans as if you didn't know."

"I've been working kind of hard lately and just for a moment the year slipped my mind. Sorry. Are you sure it's Monday. I thought it was Tuesday."

"Believe me, it's Monday."

Robert noticed the population sign as they entered the city. It read population 3,264. He was sure that in 2010 there were only about 1800 people in Hurley.

"Well we're almost there. Where should I let you out?"

"Just leave me off by the pharmacy. I need some aspirin."

Robert thanked the man and for the first time he notice how different the city was. It appeared bigger with more buildings. He thought, *perhaps this is because of all the mines that are still open. Hurley 1942. I wonder if Nancy Monroe is here.*

* * *

It was just after eleven in the morning and Robert could still not believe that he was really in Hurley 1942. He expected to wake up any minute and find that it was all a dream. He really did have a headache. Stepping into the pharmacy, he was again amazed at what he saw. To his right was an old fashion soda fountain with six stools. To the left there was a counter with an assortment of candies and shelves stocked with all kinds of things from feminine products to bandages. The prescription pharmacy counter was in the back of the store. Along the entire back wall there were oak cabinets with glass doors that housed all sorts of chemical bottles. Robert had no idea what was in all of them. A display counter to the left had a collection of mortars and pestles. Robert wondered where he'd find aspirin when the pharmacist asked, "Can I help you young man?"

"Yes, I'd like some aspirins."

"Sure, my names Al Hidde, are you new in town? You don't seem to be from here."

"Just passing through."

Then he reached onto one of the back shelves and produced a bottle of 100 Spartan Brand aspirins. "That'll be 39 cents."

"Do you have anything smaller?"

"Yes we do." He handed him a small tin of 24 aspirins. "That will be 15 cents."

Robert gave him a quarter and got back a dime. Al never glanced at the date on the quarter. There was no sales tax.

"Thanks."

"You have a good day. I hope you enjoy your stay in Hurley."

On the way out Robert stopped at the soda fountain and asked for a glass of water and took two aspirins. The sun was warm on his face as he looked up and down the street trying to decide where to go next. He had no idea if Nancy Monroe was here and he could only hope that they had entered around the same time. If Nancy Monroe had gone back to another time, he might never find her.

Dressed in jeans and a gray sweatshirt he thought that he really didn't stick out although several people gave him some odd looks. To his left was a department store on the corner called Leo's. He thought if he were here long enough and needed to buy clothes that would be the place. *If I have to stay long enough to buy clothes, I'm in real trouble.*

That was when he remembered his camera. Taking it out he made sure there were no people close and took several pictures up and down the street. Further down the street to his right in the middle of the next block he spotted a pasty sign and knew that it had to be Sally's building. He could see that it was that same building that one day would be Sally's café. Karl had told him that the building was built in the twenties. Now being hungry, he decided to eat and have a look around, but before he entered the café, he took a picture of the most impressive hotel he had ever seen which was cattycorner from what was to be Sally's in the future. It had to be the Burton House. He could see that it was not in the best shape. He also remembered that it would burn to the ground in 1948. On the other corner across from the Burton House was an old fashion hardware store where in the future the Post Office would be. Then he entered the pasty shop, *I'd love to have a look around in the basement.*

Nuncio's Pasty Shop was not busy and he was thankful that no one gave him a second look. The pasty shop occupied the same space, but Sally's arrangement was different. The kitchen was on the right and there stood an Italian looking man that had to be Nuncio. When the waitress came, he ordered a coffee and pasty. When she came back with the coffee, he showed her a picture of Nancy asking, "Do you know this woman?"

She appeared stunned but said, "Yea I know her she teaches up at the Catholic grade school on top the hill on Fifth Avenue. Why has she done something wrong? You're not a cop are you?"

"No, I'm just a friend."

"You look so different that I thought for sure you were a cop or something. You know, maybe the FBI with the war and all. If you're a friend, why are you asking around?"

"I wasn't sure what city she said, I only remember that she said it was right across the river from Ironwood, Michigan but in Wisconsin. It had to be Hurley. Does she come in here?"

"Well sometimes with Martha Laine, she lives with her. To me she always looks like she doesn't belong here, out of place sort of like you. I do remember one time when she first came here she went down to the bathroom, which is not really for the public, and when she came back, her face was a mess and her dress was dirty. She was just strange.

Although, I do have to say that she is most attractive woman I've ever seen here—like she stepped out of Hollywood movie. She's a real head turner. I thought it was possible that she was running away from somebody, you know hiding out here. You're not some old boy friend are you?"

"No, we went to school together and I was passing through and remembered that she said she was moving here and thought I'd stop in and say hi."

"What's you name. So if I see her I can tell her you were here."

"The name Is Robert Rahn, but I'm pretty sure I'll find her up at the school. Do you have a bathroom I can use?"

"We do, but only in emergencies. But I suppose it will be alright. It's in the back down the stairs in the basement."

"Thanks." Almost saying I know where it is.

As Robert started down the steps with his backpack, he had the crazy feeling that he was going to see the ghost of Marietta DeMitri. At the bottom, relief washed over him when he found the door to the bathroom—that he could already smell—and the door that led into the rest of the basement. Opening the basement door, he went directly to the back looking for the outside door. There in the back were the steps leading up to the outside alley doors. Standing there he felt dizzy and queasy as if he were about to throw up. Then the smell of ether engulfed him and he thought he was going to suffocate if he did not get some fresh air. Quickly he moved up the steps and with both arms he pushed up on the doors and watched as one flew to the left and the other to the right. Then he was outside breathing in the fresh air and it took him several moments to realize that it was raining. Then taking a deep breath his vision cleared and he noticed the cars. They were all newer models. Rubbing his eyes, he saw a Honda, a Mustang and Silverado truck. "This can't be," he shouted.

Sixty-five

Thursday May 28, 1942

On Thursday, Doctor Frost had no morning appointments after eleven so he asked Martha if she would like to have a light lunch with him at Nuncio's. He really had wanted to get Martha alone and see if he could glean any more information from her concerning Miss Monroe. He wondered if she'd say something more about the break-in.

When the waitress came to the table she said to Martha, "There was a man in here two days ago looking for that woman, Nancy, that's staying at your house. He had a picture of her and wanted to know if I'd seen her. Said he was a friend just passing through. I never saw him in here before."

"What did he look like, was he young, did he give you his name?"

"Yes, he said his name was Robert Rahn. He was good looking, in his thirties. The funny thing was the way he was dressed. He had slacks with big pockets on the side and a gray sweatshirt that said NIKE on the front. I had no idea what that meant. He also carried a backpack like the ones you see in the army. He was just different."

"What did you tell him?"

"I said I knew her and that she was teaching school at the Catholic grade school just up the hill on Fifth Avenue."

"What happened after that? Did he go up to the school?" Martha was pretty sure that if he had, Nancy would have told her.

"No, that's what is so weird. He said he had to use the restroom and since Nuncio left I said it would be alright. Before I could tell him it was in the basement, he seemed to know where it was. Then the weirdest thing happened. He never came back up from the basement. He just disappeared. I suppose he could have slipped out the back, but when I asked the cook if she had seen him, she said no."

"Did Nancy say anything about meeting someone Tuesday night," said the Doctor.

"No, I'm sure she would have said something. I wonder who it could have been. As far as I know she doesn't have any friends from around here."

"Maybe it was somebody from Appleton. Didn't you say she was dating someone down there? Maybe he came looking for her?" said the Doctor.

Then the waitress asked, "Would you like to order? If he comes back I'll let you know, He sure was good looking."

After they had finished eating Dr. Frost asked the waitress, "Did you happen to see from which direction he came? Did he say where he'd been or where he was going?"

"No, I assumed he was going up to the Catholic school to see her."

Doctor Frost paid the bill and left with Martha and said, "Martha I've got some errands to run before the next appointment. You go back and I'll be there shortly."

He headed east towards the Pharmacy. He could not help but think that perhaps if this man stuck out as Nancy Monroe did, he was sure someone else had noticed him.

* * *

Doctor Frost went down the street stopping at all the businesses on the north side of Sliver Street. It wasn't until he came to the Pharmacy and talked with Al Hidde, that he had any luck in finding someone that had seen the stranger.

"Sure I remember him. I happened to be in the front of the store when Art Chester left him off. I didn't think anything of it until he came in asking for aspirins. I thought he looked different. You could tell he was not from here and he had a backpack like nothing I ever seen."

"What do you mean different. In what way?"

"His clothes were not from around here. His sweatshirt said, Nike, on the front. Then the backpack had snaps on it that made a ripping sound when he opened it to get his wallet."

"Did he buy something?"

"Yes, he bought a small tin of aspirins."

"How did he pay?"

"He gave me a quarter, why?"

"Do you still have the quarter?"

Al opened the register and said, "Here it is," giving it to Doc Frost.

When Doc Frost looked at the quarter, the date was 1967.

"Look at the date on this coin, 1967. How can you explain that?"

"I can't," said Al. Unless, he's from the future and there is no way that's possible."

"Here's another quarter, I'm going to show this to Peter Cadence."

"Did he say anything more?

"No, other than he was new in town and was just passing through. But it was the way the guy looked around that really bothered me. It was like he was seeing things for the first time and was trying to drink in everything. I'm telling you it was weird."

"You said Art Chester left him off? The insurance guy?"

"Yes, I'm sure it was Art."

"Thanks Al."

* * *

After leaving the Pharmacy, he went back to his office and called Art Chester.

"Art, this is Doc Frost. I understand you picked up a man this morning and left him off at the pharmacy."

"Yes I did. Said his name was Robert Rahn and that he was out prospecting. This was about eight miles west of Hurley on the old Lake Forest town road. Why do you ask?"

"Well he was into Nuncios later that day and when we were in for lunch today the waitress told me he was looking for Nancy Monroe. Since he never saw her I was wondering what he said to you."

"He didn't say much, but it was the way he acted. When I stopped and asked him if he needed a ride he just looked at me, it was as if it was the first time he'd seen a car. Then there was the fact that he was out there all alone and had no car. Said he got a ride out there and was walking back, but he was a long way from town. I sure couldn't figure him out. Did you ever find out where he went?"

"No I never met him. The waitress said he went to the rest room and never came back. He just disappeared. Thanks for your help Art."

* * *

On Thursday night when Martha came home, she found Nancy in the sitting room looking dejected. "What's wrong?"

"It's just one of those long days. Martha sometimes I get real lonesome. You've been so kind to me, but there are times when I really miss being back in my own time. I was even thinking about Michael and that hasn't happened to me in weeks."

"Is that because of Gerald?"

"No, I like Gerald, but I'm afraid. What if I really liked him? You know loved him. Then what would I do. Just say Gerald you know I love you but before this goes any further there is something I think you should know about me. You see … I'm from the future. Then he'll say, 'Oh that's all right I still love you.' Yea I can see that happening. So Martha what am I ever going to do. Worst of all I don't think I'll ever be able to go back. "

"Just stay here and I'll get us a glass of white wine. I think you need it. I think I have some good news that may cheer you up."

Coming back with the wine she said, "Today Doctor Frost took me to lunch at Nuncio's and the waitress there said there was a man in yesterday looking for you. Said his name was Robert Rahn. Does that mean anything?"

"No, I never heard of him before."

"He knew you. The waitress said he had a picture of you. She told him that you were teaching at the Catholic School. Then he went to the bathroom and never came back."

"Did you say he went downstairs in Nuncio's and never came back?"

"Yes."

"Martha, this is going to sound crazy, but do you suppose he came from the future?"

"Darling, since you came into my life I am apt to believe just about anything. It could be possible. It certainly is a way to explain why he appeared to be so different."

"Martha if this is true that would mean that there is someone looking for me even if I don't know who this Robert is. But why would he leave without coming to see me, he was so close. Could he have gone back to the future though the doorway in Nuncio's basement?"

"It would explain why he never came back from the basement, but Nancy you were down there and found nothing."

"I know I couldn't find anything, but Martha this is good news. At least there is slim hope that maybe I could get back someday. I worry about what Leo or Doctor Frost may know. Maybe it would be best if I went back, if that's even possible."

"What about Gerald and Beth?"

"I think I'm falling in love with Gerald and I really love Beth, but right now, I guess I can't worry about that. I just have to be careful and see how all of this plays out. After all, this Robert Rahn may never show up again. I certainly don't want to hurt Gerald or Beth. There is just too much to think about, why not pour us some more wine, I'll deal with all of this later."

Sixty-six

Friday May 29, 1942

It was suppose to be just a regular Alliance Friday night poker game. Only tonight, Doctor Frost couldn't wait to tell them what he had found out after having lunch with Martha and about the 1967 quarter.

"I have a couple of things I'd like to discuss before we start playing cards. First, there is nothing new to report on the surveillance of Nancy Monroe. Secondly, you'll never guess what happened at lunch on Thursday."

"What now?" said Leo, less than enthused.

"I was having lunch with Martha and the waitress told us that there was a guy in on Wednesday asking about Nancy Monroe. He gave his name as Robert Rahn. He even had a picture of her. Said he was an old friend just passing though. The waitress told him that she was teaching up at the Catholic Church grade school and after that he went done stairs to the restroom and never came back. She said he just disappeared."

"So what are we suppose to take away from this," said Oscar.

"Now wait there's more. This is really going to floor you. I did some checking to see if anybody else had seen this Robert Rahn. Turns out, he was down at the Pharmacy and Al sold him some aspirin, said that Art Chester gave a ride in from outside of town. He paid Al with a quarter. I asked Al if he still had the quarter and he gave it to me. Look, it's a 1967 quarter. This Robert Rahn has to be from the future too."

Doc passed the quarter to Peter Cadence. "It looks real to me just like that 1984 quarter from Nancy Monroe. Perhaps this guy was here looking for her. It's what we feared, that someone would come to take her back before we were done with her."

The rest of the Alliance members passed around the quarter and all were amazed.

"What else did Al say about him?"

"Al said that he was just passing through, but said that Art told him that he was out prospecting."

"Prospecting? Prospecting for what?" said Leo.

"I don't know, Art didn't ask him. Said the man was about ten miles west of Hurley on the old Lake Forest town road. He saw him and asked him if he wanted a ride.

Then I told him about what I'd heard at Nuncio's and asked Art if he said anything about Nancy Monroe. Said he didn't say much at all, but it was the way he acted. When Art asked him if he needed a ride, it was as if it was the first time he'd seen a car. Art couldn't figure out why he was alone and no car. Well I was thinking he was from the future and with this coin. I'm sure he's from the future looking for Nancy Monroe."

"I know we think Monroe has to be from the future, but do you believe that people can really come and go just like that from the future to the past?" said Leo.

"Well I think it's possible. All three witnesses said he acted funny."

"So he acted funny. Now I suppose we're to believe that every stranger that comes into town and acts funny is a time traveler?" said Ralph Winslow.

Then Peter Cadence who had been taking all of this in said, "Just hear me out. The 1967 coin sure makes it seem that he is from the future. Let's just say all of this is possible and this man can come and go from the past to the future and back. What if we could somehow follow him back to the future? Think of the first hand knowledge we could get. We would not have to rely on what Nancy Monroe tells us. That is if we can make her talk. Think of the money we could make just knowing the future. Imagine knowing the out come of the war, what investments to make and better yet we might be able to change our future."

"Now wait a minute. This has gone too far. For one thing, did you think about how you were going to get back? You're talking crazy like something out of a science fiction magazine. If this guy is from the future, that doesn't mean we can follow him back to the future. I for one am not going to volunteer to follow him back. I'm happy right here in my time and maybe I don't want to know the future no matter how much money I could make," said Oscar.

"Alright, alright maybe I took this too far. Furthermore, now that I think of it, I'm not sure I'd want to go to the future either and then find that I couldn't get back. So what should we do next?"

"I'm not against making money. I'm just saying I'm not going off on some tangent. I was thinking that maybe we should take some action with regards to Nancy Monroe," said Oscar.

"What do you mean, what kind of action?" said Peter.

"Let's abduct her before this guy comes back and takes her away before we have a chance to find out what she knows?" said Oscar.

"Are you serious?" said Doc.

"Yes, I think we should act now. Doc you could come up with something to drug her and make her talk, you know, a truth serum," said Oscar adamantly.

"You mean use Pentothal on her to make her talk? Do you have any idea how dangerous that can be? It's an anesthesia used in surgery. Besides while Pentothal make the subject chatty and cooperative some are still capable of sticking to a falsehoods making the results dubious at best and I for one am not going to give it to someone without having a valid medical reason. "

"Don't tell me you haven't done some unethical things in your time. So don't sound so high minded. Besides think of what's at stake and all the money, we would stand to make. If you want a better reason, think of it as your patriotic duty, you know she could be a Nazi Spy. What do the rest of you think?"

"I'm not against talking to her, but do we have to use a drug?" said Peter.

"Oscar, what you are proposing is kidnapping and that is a serious crime. You could get the death penalty. Remember what happened to that guy who took the Lindbergh baby back in 1932, what was his name?" said Leo Coppalo.

"You mean Bruno Hauptmann," said Ralph Winnslow.

"Yea that's the guy. He got the electric chair in 1936 and I for one don't want that to happen to me," said Leo Coppalo.

"It won't, because Wisconsin doesn't have the death penalty," said Oscar laughing.

"Very funny! What we are talking about is serious. I think if we do something to this woman we have to let someone else do it for us so that we are not directly involve."

"What did you have in mind Leo?"

"Remember I told you guys about my retired ex-cop friend. He's from Milwaukee and hunts up here every fall, Stan Offenbach. Last fall he told me that he'd run out of retirement funds. He said that after his wife died of cancer he just sort of pissed his money away on gambling and women. Now he's hard up and he told me if there was anything I wanted taken care of he would be available for a price. So if you guys all agree, I could give him a call and see if he would like to help us out. I'm sure he could take care of this for us."

"What exactly are we going to have him do?" said Fred.

"Interrogate her and have him ask all our questions and if necessary use truth serum."

"And just what are we going to do with this information once we have it?" said Fred.

"What we do with it depends on what she gives us. Let us say she can predict the future or if you want suppose she is from the future. If that is true, we will want all the information we can get. Think of the benefits, mostly the financial ones. Doesn't that make sense?"

"If we get nothing, what then?"

"As long as she can't implicate us in anything we let her go and she is free to do what ever she wants."

"And what if she puts the finger on us, then what?"

"Well that is another story and we would have to reconsider our options"

"And would one of those options be murder?"

"Fred, it is much too early to even think about such a thing. Nothing is going to go wrong. Trust me."

"Let's give ourselves a little time to think this through. There is no reason we have to act now. Besides we still have to have our meeting with Ethan Lynch and Henrik Dahl." said Doctor Frost.

"Leo, when is that meeting again?" said Oscar.

"The meeting is on June 9 in Ashland, I told you guys that last week."

"Then maybe after the meeting we can work out a deal and all of this stuff will take care of itself. Who knows maybe we will make so much money we may not have to deal with Nancy Monroe," said Leo.

Chapter Sixty-seven

May 30, 1942 (Saturday Memorial Day)

Nancy, Gerald and Beth spent Memorial Day together. Gerald and Nancy were seeing one another on a regular basis since the middle of April, though if you asked either of them they would have said they were only good friends. If you had asked Martha, she would have said the relationship was more than that, she would have said they were in love and would not be surprised if Gerald asked Nancy to marry him.

On Saturday morning, they had breakfast together and watched the Memorial Day parade. To anyone watching, the three of them appeared to be a family. In 1942, the holiday was still celebrated on the 30th no matter what day of the week it was, not like in 2010 when the holiday was celebrated on a Monday making it a three-day weekend. After the parade, the three went on a picnic outside of town at a wayside going to Saxon. It was a marvelous sunny day and with the trees almost completely leafed out, the Penokee Range was a stunning site in the distance.

While at the picnic Gerald said to her, "the parade seemed so different this year with the country at war. It really hit home for me when I heard in December that Henry Warner was killed in the attack on Pearl Harbor. He was the first to die from this area. I wonder how many others will die from the area before this whole thing is over?"

She almost told him that over 400,000 Americans would die, but she only said, "let's pray that we win this war." Still not sure, that she might have already changed something to alter the outcome of the war.

"Nancy, I worry that if this war gets any worse, that I will be drafted even though I'm thirty-one and a single father. If that happens, I don't know who would take care of Beth. I have no close relatives."

"Gerald let's not think about that now, I'm sure you will not be drafted. If things should get worse and you had to go, I'll take care of Beth."

"You would? That makes me feel so much better."

"You know Nancy Monroe; I'm falling in love with you, in fact I am in love with you."

"Gerald, I'm very fond of you, but I think we have to take things slow. You really don't know me that well. We have only been seeing one another for the past six weeks. We have to be sure." *If you only knew.*

"How much do I have to know? I can see that you are a wonderful Christian person and I know that you care for Beth. I'm not sure I can take things slow."

In an effort to change the subject she said, "Isn't the Indianapolis 500 Race today?"

Surprised at her question he said, "No, it has been cancelled this year and I think for the duration of the war. I didn't know you were interested in race cars?"

"Yes, I used to watch the race with my father."

"You mean he took you to Indianapolis? That must have really been something."

Thinking quickly she said, "No, no silly I mean we listened to it on the radio, but just think someday in the future I'm sure we'll be watching it on television."

"You sure are such a dreamer. I don't think we'll see that for a long time. They only recently issued ten commercial TV licenses and that was for only big cities. It will take forever before it gets to Hurley."

"Why was the race cancelled?"

"I think the main reason was gasoline rationing. Come on, we better get back to town and take in the band concert at the park."

By eight that night Gerald could see that it was time to take Beth home although he was reluctant to say good night to Nancy.

When he walked her to the door, she waited for him to kiss her good night. She had been anticipating this moment all day. As he took her in his arms, she closed her eyes and tilted her face up to him. His breath was warm and sweet on her skin. Her pulse increased and she wondered, *what's taking him so long?* He seemed to be moving in slow motion. She moved her hands up around his neck and slid her fingers into his thick hair, thrilled with the opportunity to touch the man that she now knew she loved even if it had only been such a short time. Then a wave of guilt washed over her as she thought of Michael. *Is he still waiting for me? Am I being unfaithful?*

The thought quickly vanished when she felt Gerald tighten his hold on her and she realized that he wanted her as much as she wanted him. He was doing his best to control himself. Then he gently kissed her. He didn't squash her lips clumsily; instead, his mouth barely grazed hers, exploring and then possessing her lips with loving tenderness. At that moment, her heart was on fire for him. It was never this way with Michael. She thought this was the most perfect kiss ever. It was complete and rewarding. There no longer was any doubt. She loved him and wanted to marry him. It did not matter that she was a time traveler from the twenty-first century.

When they separated and after he said good-bye, she said, "Will I see you tomorrow?"

"I want to see you tomorrow and every day there after," he said. Then he hurried off to Beth who was watching from the car.

* * *

That evening after getting Beth ready for bed, he couldn't help thinking about Nancy. He knew he was in love with her and he was sure she felt the same way, but there was something holding her back and he had no idea what it was. He was aware of the fact that she was not from the area and that people said how strange it was that she just suddenly showed up one day and decided to stay. The other thing that bothered people in a small town was that she was staying with Martha Laine and no matter what Martha said people were sure that the two had never met until the day of her accident. It just did not make sense and people were suspicious.

She was so different. She was like no one he had ever met and thought of himself as a lucky man to be with her. She seemed to know the future, like today when she said she used to watch the Indianapolis 500 and then it seemed like she caught herself and said, 'I mean listened.' Granted she didn't come right out and say that they watched it on television, but Gerald was sure that was what she meant. She was so unique. She was assertive and not like any other women Gerald ever knew, not even his wife. She was forward. She did things for herself and was not dependent upon a man. She was self-sufficient. The fact was that he did not know for sure how to describe her, he only knew he never wanted to loose her and he was going to do everything in his power to marry her.

Sixty-eight

Friday June 5 & 6, 1942 (The Battle of Midway)

When June came, Nancy knew the battle of Midway Island was going to take place and she was hoping that history had not changed. In her history book, she knew this was a major turning point in the Pacific battle with the Japanese. No one knew it at the time in 1942, but from that date on the Japanese would be fighting a defensive battle. In fact, many historians went as far as to say the war was really over after the Battle of Midway. From that point on it was impossible for Japan to win. The best they could hope for was to negotiate an armistice that would allow them to keep their home islands.

Nancy knew the Japanese plan was to invade the island of Midway, 1,300 miles northwest of Hawaii and draw out what the Japanese thought were to be the only two American operational aircraft carriers. The ultimate objective, however, was the invasion of the Hawaiian Islands and the neutralization of Pearl Harbor, thus giving the Japanese complete control of the Pacific.

Nancy listened to the radio nightly during that first week of June and Martha knew something big was about to happen in the war despite the fact that Nancy told her, she was just interested in the news of the day. Even Gerald could sense the change in Nancy as she made more than one excuse not to see him and Beth.

It was not until the evening of Friday, June 5th, that Nancy heard on the radio that the battle of Midway had started. It reported that on Thursday morning a force of about 180 Japanese carrier bombers raided the island of Midway attacking airfields, docks and harbor installations on the island, but had succeeded in only inflicting minor damage.

The next day what she heard on the radio she could not believe? The remainder of the battle of Midway had turned into a stalemate with the

Japanese losing only two major aircraft carriers rather than the four that she remembered. What remained the same was that the Japanese did not occupy Midway Island. She was glad to hear that. She could only hope that this did not alter the outcome of the war. Now she was more scared than ever to think that there was a possibility that the United Sates could loss the war. *Am I the cause of this?*

Sixty-nine

Sunday June 7, 1942

In early June, two weeks before Robert arrive back in 1942, Gerald got up the courage to propose to Nancy. He could not think of a reason for delaying any longer. He loved her and he knew she loved him. He also knew that Nancy loved Beth and would be a wonderful mother. The only thing that bothered him was that Nancy seemed to have something on her mind in the past six weeks that she was not willing to share with him. If they were going to be husband and wife there could be no secrets. He was sure that they could work out any reservations as to why she could not marry him.

It was a beautiful June Sunday and Gerald was ready with his proposal. He had practiced everything he was going to say repeatedly and he had the ring that he hoped with all his heart was something she would like. It wasn't very big, but it was the best he could afford.

Beth was over at her girl friend's house so he had Nancy all to himself this afternoon. He planned a picnic lunch taking her out to Little Girls Point. He was hoping that the flies would not be too bad, because it had been cold. There was a breeze off the lake, which made for just a slight chill in the air, not cold. Then he said to her, "Nancy will you marry me?"

She knew this was coming and sort of expected it but still she was not ready when it came. She wanted to marry him and she talked all this through with Martha many times and now that time was here, she was speechless.

"Gerald, you surprised me. I really didn't see this coming."

"All you have to do is say yes and make me the happiest man in the world."

"I really want to marry you but there are some things you don't know about me."

"I don't care Nancy, I love you and I know that you are different and that's what I love about you. Don't you think that I've noticed the times you look like you're in another world thinking about things or that I haven't noticed how you seem to know the future? I know that you are different but that does not mean anything to me. I want to spend the rest of my life with you. Just say yes."

"I can't marry you until you know everything about me. I have to be fair. I can't ask you to take on all of my problems and concerns without you knowing everything about me. I'm just not sure that this is the right time and I'm not at all sure that you will even believe me."

"Of course it is the right time and why wouldn't I believe you? Tell me everything. I'm sure it will not make a difference in how I feel."

"Once you've heard what I am about I'm going to say, you may not be so sure."

"Tell me, I love you and I cannot imagine living without you."

"I'm not sure how to put all of this. What I'm going to ask you is please don't interrupt me until I finish my story. I promise that I will answer all of your questions after.

People say I came here out of the blue, well the truth is that I came here from the future."

Nancy saw the surprised look on Gerald's face as he said, "From the future!"

She placed her hand over his mouth. "You promised not to interrupt."

"I came to Hurley in November of 2009 with three of my girl friends."

Once again he could not control himself. "2009, what do you mean 2009? That's 67 years from now. That's impossible!"

"Please, don't interrupt again or I'm just going get up and leave and you'll never see me again. Is that clear?"

Yes was all he was able to say. There was no way he wanted to loose her no matter where she came from.

"Now I'll continue. My girl friends and I planned to do some skiing over the Thanksgiving weekend, but there was not enough snow. I know this is hard to believe, but please just listen to me. We were having breakfast at Sally's Café, which you know as Nuncio's. Well anyway, when I went down to use the bathroom that is when I found another room that led me into another time. The world of 2009 disappeared when I came out of the back door of the café. To my surprise I saw across the street a large hotel, what I now know is the Burton House."

She saw the astonished look on his face. "Gerald you have to believe me it was not there when we came into town that morning. That is when I later ran down the street and how I was hit by the car and taken to Doctor Frost office; I was treated and then went home with Martha Laine. Martha took me in and she is now my dearest friend—she is the only one who knows my story. I think maybe Dr. Frost and his friends are suspicious of me and they may want to take advantage of me. I got the job teaching by talking my way into it. I really like it here, but I am afraid that I might be changing history by being here; I think I really have to go back, but don't know how. I went back to Nuncio's café once, but I could not find a way back."

"Nancy, I don't know what to say. While your story explains some things it is so fantastic, I don't know what to believe."

"There's more. I had some very futuristic things with me and now they are gone. Martha and I believe that Dr. Frost and his friends broke into the house and took them. I think if these things fall into the wrong hands they could change the course of the war."

So you see Gerald I am not sure I can marry you even though I am in love with you and I adore Beth. I don't know what to do and on top of all of that, there may be someone from the future searching for me. It seems that someone was looking for me and asked about me at Nuncio's café sometime back. On top of all of that, I am afraid for my life. I think Frost and his men—the Alliance—will try to take me away and make me talk. Oh, Gerald I don't know what I'm going to do."

"What kind of things did the Alliance take from you?"

"They took things that are advanced. Technological things, that if they got into the German or Japanese hands could change the out come of the war."

"Is there anyway I can do to help you get your things back?"

"I don't think so. Going to the police would only complicate things and perhaps change the future even more."

The two of them stopped talking and just held one another not knowing what to say or what to do. Finally Gerald said, "I believe you, but you have to give me some time to let this sink in. What did you do back in Appleton? Did you have a boyfriend? What was it like? I cannot really believe that you are from the future. What is the future like? Do we win the war?"

"Gerald, see all the things that come up. I can't really tell you about the future for fear of what you might do with that information. What if I told you something and you said something to someone else and it changed the future?

There is one thing I'll say, we do win the war, but I'm worried that the longer I'm here the more likely I might be responsible for changing the out come of the war. Gerald what if we were to loose the war. Can you imagine living in a world with Nazis and the Japanese? Even if they didn't occupy the United States, just try to think about the world we'd be living in. A world of hate. I don't think we can take the risk of getting married as much as I want too."

"Nancy, I love you. You're like nobody I ever met in all my life and that includes my first wife. I want to be with you. Let's try to see if we can work things out. I need some time to come to grips with all that you told me. Maybe there is a way we can get married without me having to know the future. The only future I want is one with you."

"Gerald, maybe just the fact that we are together now has already changed the future."

"If you can't go back to your time and you have be here why not spend that time with me and we'll just have to see what happens to the future?"

"You may be right about that. I may be stuck here and I do want to spend my life with you. There is however, a chance that someone is trying to reach me from the future. He may have been here once. If that were to happen I think I'd have to go back with him and right now I'm not sure I can do that with the way I feel about you and Beth. Gerald Please take me home I just have to rest and think about everything."

"I agree, I have a lot to digest too. Let's talk in a few days and maybe we can figure something out. I might be able to help you get your things back."

* * *

After taking Nancy home, Gerald wondered why he said he might be able to get her things back. The only reason he could think of was that it might change her mind and she would marry him and stay here with him forever.

Now as he thought about it, Nancy had not said what he'd be looking for. He was not sure that he wanted to go against the Alliance. Getting her things back would not be easy. He only knew he had to try.

He knew the Alliance had an elaborate cabin back in the woods outside of town that they used for conducting personal business. He thought that this was perhaps the first place to start. There might be a chance that they were keeping Nancy's things there.

Then he thought, *I'll just take a trip out there and see what I can find. Maybe they won't be expecting anything and I can break in and retrieve Nancy's property. Is the place guarded? If someone is there, I'll just pretend that I was hunting small game.*

* * *

Monday morning was cold and misty for June and Gerald thought it had been foolish of him to say that he thought he could get Nancy's things back. The more he thought about it, he came to the conclusion that it was best to leave the Alliance alone for his own safety. Those guys did not play fair. He decided the best thing to do was to go to work.

Seventy

Tuesday June 9, 1942

On Monday afternoon, the day before the Alliance meeting with Henrik Dahl, Thomas Appleton left Duluth traveling to Ashland where he had booked a room at the Chequamegon Hotel. He was hoping to find out more about the things that the Alliance had in their possession. He thought if he could get hold of those things he would be a rich man.

* * *

Thomas Appleton was up and had breakfast early. Now he was sitting in the hotel lobby pretending to be waiting for someone when he saw the Alliance group arrive. They went to the front desk and were shown to a private room over looking Lake Superior.

A few minutes later Dahl and Lynch arrived. They too were shown to the same private room. It was exactly what Appleton feared. There was no way he was going to know what happened in that room although he got as close as he could without drawing attention to himself.

* * *

Henrik Dahl found himself looking forward to the meeting although he had to admit he knew very little about the Alliance group other than what he had learned from Leo Coppalo.

He thought of them as a bunch of small town businessmen from the Hurley area and as far as he could tell, they were nothing more than a few big fish in a very small pond. He thought for sure that there was no way they would be a match for him, but he knew from experience, never to under estimate the opposition. They had something he very much wanted and he was willing to play along and even compromise to get. If everything worked out right there would be plenty of money to be made and he himself in the end would have some self satisfaction in perhaps being able to help is own native country—Germany—win this war. He even thought, *perhaps the destiny of the world was in my hands. I might very well be responsible for changing history.*

* * *

Dr. Frost, Oscar Kosken, Ralph Winslow, Peter Cadence and Fred Banister all arrived in one car. It was a large Packard. They were early and were busy checking out the reserved private meeting room. The room overlooked the lake and it truly was a magnificent scene. Shortly there after, Leo Coppalo arrived with Ethan Lynch and Henrik Dahl. Introductions were made but it was apparent that there was no love lost between the two sides. Neither trusted the other.

Leo suggested that they order drinks. His idea was that perhaps this would take the edge off the meeting and the talks would move along a little more freely.

With drinks in hand and introductions made, they got down to business. Ethan started first. "You all know that Henrik has seen the pictures of the items you want to sell and he is very interested in working with you. He would like to see the real objects before he is willing to move any further. I'll let him tell you what he has in mind."

"Gentlemen, as an entrepreneur and a businessman, I have to say to you that just from the pictures of these items I've never seen anything like this. Let me stress, there is money to be made here for both sides. I mean more money than you can even image if the real objects are as good as the pictures."

Oscar spoke out next. "Before we move along, let me just say that if what we have to offer is so good—better than you can imagine—we have to come to an understanding of trust. Henrik how can we be sure that once you have the objects that you just won't leave us out. We'd like to know who the buyer is. You know there is a war going on and while we want to make a buck, we are Americans. You know what I mean. The other concern is that these objects have some baggage associated with them. We are looking to have some sort of contract between us."

"I understand your concerns. Why don't we proceed by letting me examine one object at a time? I can even put down some earnest money. Would that be a way to start?"

"That appears to be a way to start, but let me speak with the rest of my group."

After a short side bar meeting all agreed.

"We would like for you to start with what we call the adding machine, but actually it is much more than that. We want you to put down $5,000 in earnest money. Then after you have had time to examine the adding machine, say no more than ten days to two weeks we can meet and see where we go from there. You may even have a proposal to present."

"There is just one thing that bothers me. You want me to be up right with you, but just where did you get all of this stuff?"

"That is not your concern," said Oscar.

"Ethan said something about you getting these things from some woman and he implied that you or someone else may have stolen them. Which leads me to ask, does this mean the authorities could be investigating? Seems to me this whole thing is not so clear-cut. However, I'm still interested. I just want to know what I'm getting myself into. There is no way I want to go to prison."

"Let's just say you don't have to worry about that. We already have a contingency plan in place to take care of any legal concerns. As of right now, the authorities are not involved. You have no need to worry about going to prison," said Oscar.

"I'll take your word for that, so when can I get the first item?"

"You'll have the first item as soon as we work out a contact and get some up front money. Our lawyer took the time to work up a general contact. Look it over and if you agree we can move ahead."

"That sounds fair to me. We can work out the patent rights and ownership after the contact is in place."

* * *

Appleton could hear nothing they were saying except for a few muffled words. All the while, he made sure not to look out of place and later went to sit in the lobby. Shortly before lunch, all sides came out of the meeting. Dahl did not look happy. The Alliance, however, seemed to be pleased with the way the meeting went.

Some of the members were carrying small brief cases, however it looked like none of the participants had any of the goods.

* * *

After the meeting Henrik was now more than determine to get all of the stuff even if he had to steal it all. There was no way he was going to wait around for those little assholes to dole out one item at a time while they milked him for more earnest money. He also was interested in finding this mysterious blonde lady. There was more going on here than these Alliance guys wanted him to know. They never came right out and said so, but he was sure that they had taken the stuff from that woman and he had no idea where in the world she would have come up with these things. Ethan had already met her and he was willing to work with him to get to see her one way or another. If they had to take her by force, Henrik was not against that. He knew a number of people that for a price would be willing to do the dirty work.

In addition to that, he was worried about what the Alliance would do. These men while good at their own business in their small world were no match for what he had planned. He had to make a move and he was just waiting for the right time. Hopefully, the Alliance guys would not do anything real stupid to jeopardize the whole operation.

Seventy-one

Wednesday June 10, 1942

On Wednesday morning, Henrik Dahl was still upset with the way the meeting went, but now he was willing to accept the conditions outlined by the Alliance just to have the chance to get the other items. If he were going to have any chance of aiding the mother country, he could not wait for the Alliance. That was entirely too slow. He had to figure out a way to get all of the items at once. He still wondered where these items had come from. Who could possibly have that kind of technology? Things just did not add up and he decided to call Ethan Lynch to talk things through. They had to have a plan.

"Ethan, Henrik here. I have some questions I think you can answer for me. However, before I ask them, I want to thank you for all of your help. I thought the meeting went fine, but it did not go far enough. I have a lot of unanswered questions. "

"What do you need to know?" asked Ethan.

"The thing that bothers me the most is where did those guys get these items? You and I both know there is nothing like this around or even close to being developed?"

"The only thing I can tell you Henrik is that there has to be a connection with that blonde lady, Nancy Monroe, Leo mentioned a couple of times. I was able to locate her and I spoke to her at the Catholic School where she teaches. She really didn't say anything.

They try to cover things up, but when they thought I was not listening I know they have been keeping track of her and I am sure that is where they got everything. I even over heard them talking about how they had someone break into her house and take the items. They think that this woman is very special and one of them said that it seemed that she came out of the future.

The thing that makes me think they might be right is that I discovered that this woman appeared out of thin air back in November. Otherwise, no one knows where she came from or how she got here. As far as anyone knows she has no family here and no apparent connection with the community. The story goes that she was treated by a local doctor, Dr. Frost and is now living with his nurse Martha Laine.

The real reason I think she's involved is that after the first time I met Leo and he mentioned her name, I was able to track her down. When I asked her questions, she seemed very reluctant to answer. I think she is the link to all of these things."

"Do you think she has the knowledge to make these things or any manufacturing connections?" said Henrik.

"No, I don't think she has the technical knowledge to make them, but she is extremely intelligent and after speaking with her, I did get the impression that she knew the future. I have a hard time thinking that she is from the future. Then as ridicules as this sounds, the only thing I can think of is that she could be from the future and she brought these things with her when she came here. Just like the clothes she wore that were so different," said Ethan.

"Would there be any advantage in us talking with her again?" asked Henrik.

"I'm not sure she would give us anything and I don't think we would want to kidnap her."

"Do you think the Alliance is going to go after her or are they just going to try to keep tabs on her? I think it would be to their benefit to get rid of her. Do you think they are capable of murder?" said Ethan.

"Yes, I do. I think these guys would do just about anything to maintain their status in the community."

"I'm not sure what I am going to do next. Maybe I'll just wait for the Alliance to make the next move. If I wanted to move to get all of this stuff sooner can I count on your help?"

"Yes you can, I have no love for the Alliance boys."

* * *

That night Henrik Dahl telephoned his contact in the American German Bund and informed him that he may have some things that he felt could change the outcome of the war. He needed sometime to get all of the things and information together. While he was doing this for his mother country, he made only one stipulation, he wanted to be financially compensated.

2010

Seventy-two

Tuesday May 25, 2010

Looking left, Robert saw that the alley where he was standing led to the ATV and snowmobile trail across Fifth Avenue. Turning back, he saw the outside doors had vanished and above where the door used to be was a sign that read: Parking for Sally's Café Customers Only.

He was back in the present. *I should never have gone down in that basement. Damn it. How could I let this happen. I should have known that there might still be a time portal open there.*

Depressed and not knowing what to do he picked up his backpack and walked in the back door of Sally's kitchen. She was preparing lunch orders when she saw him. "Robert, you don't look good, are you sick? Here sit down I'll get you some water."

He did not ague. "I'll be alright, just the heat is all."

"I thought you were going out of town for a few days? Karl said he was going to look after Albert for you"

"Just a change in plans. Can I ask you a favor?"'

"Could you drive me out to my place so I could get my car?"

"Sure, I'll have Maggie my waitress drive you. We're not real busy now, but how did you get into town? You didn't walk, did you?"

"I got a ride with a friend who had to go to Wakefield, so I told him not to worry I'd get a ride home."

"Robert there is something else going on here. You walk in the back door looking like death warmed over and you're telling me that someone gave you a ride to town, I don't believe you. What's going on. Tell me."

"Perhaps I'll tell you all about it someday, but right now I want to go home so I can pick up Albert."

"Alright, but you have to promise to tell me someday when all of this is over."

"I will. I promise. Thanks for understanding and Sally, don't say anything to anybody about this. Please."

"Your secret is safe with me Robert, I'll get Maggie."

Maggie had never been out to Robert's place and was amazed at the size of the house. "Do you want to come in and see the house?"

"No, I have to get back, but wow what a house you have Mr. Rahn."

* * *

Once in the house Robert took a shower. He was relieved to see that the house was still there. Nothing had changed. Just for a passing moment, he had to ask himself if it was true that he had really gone back in time. He still blamed himself for not finding Nancy Monroe. He should have gone right up to the school when he had the chance rather than exploring that basement. He found that he was still very much in love with a woman he had never met and now felt emptiness inside at the thought of loosing her. *How silly can you get Robert? Feeling emptiness and regret over loosing someone you have never met. How ridiculous!* Tomorrow he would begin preparation for another trip back in time, however, right now it was time to head out to Karl's place and pick up Albert.

* * *

When Robert's car hit the driveway, Albert bounced off the porch to meet him. Karl met him at the bottom of the porch saying, "Didn't expect to see you for a couple of days. Albert and I were just getting acquainted."

"I had a change in plans and I guess you could say I came back before I was ready."

"Sit, I'll get us bourbon to drink. I can't wait to hear what happened to you this time."

Karl was back in a minute with two glasses of ice and a bottle of bourbon saying, "Now tell me everything? Did you manage to go back?"

"Yes! I went back to the same place I was on Sunday, I got all the way back, and this time I was not thrown back out. I stayed there, Karl you can't believe what it's like. In fact I can hardly believe I was really there. This time I got all the way back to 1942. "

"Did you find Nancy?"

"I'll get to that, but first let me finish. When I went back, I was on my land but only in 1942, the land was covered by forest and lots of alder brush everywhere. It took me some time just to get back to where the house was. From there I made my way out to the town road and I got a ride into Hurley with some insurance salesman. He let me off at the pharmacy and from there I went to Nuncio's pasty shop, which is now Sally's. I met a waitress who told me she knew of Nancy Monroe and that she was teaching at the Catholic School. That was when I made a mistake. I asked if I could use the rest room. I was in the basement looking around and that is when I found the other door to the outside. When I opened it, suddenly I was back at Sally's and it was today 2010. Looking around there was no way to go back, the portal was shut. Sally's waitress gave me a ride home and here I am. That's the long and the short of it."

"Robert I don't know what to say. If I didn't know you I'd say you were insane. Just think about what you told me."

"I know that. I can hardly believe it, but look, I've got proof. When I was at the pharmacy, I bought some aspirin. Here look." Robert handed Karl a small aspirin tin of 24 Spartan Brand aspirins. "Look at the price, 15 cents."

Karl looked it over and said, "It sure looks new, not like something I'd have in my basement for the last sixty years. However, you know someone would say that you got that from some antique dealer. "

"I know that it would be disputed, but you can see that it's new. You believe me.?"

"Of course I believe you, but others won't. Did you take any pictures?"

"Yes I did. The camera is in the car I'll go get it."

When Robert got back, Karl had refilled their glasses. "I thought you looked like you could use another drink. Now let's see those pictures."

Robert held out the camera to Karl as he flipped through the pictures. "Well what do you think? Is that proof?"

"It sure is Robert. That picture of the Burton Hotel is fabulous. It's the way I remember it. It was a fabulous building. I don't know why the city of Hurley didn't do more to preserve it. You know it was finished in 1886 and was the most modern hotel in all of Northern Wisconsin and the U.P. It was a sad day when it burned down in 1948. I've only seen old back and white pictures of it, until today. The other pictures of Silver Street are things I only have in my memory. You were really there Robert."

"I wish I would have had a chance to take more pictures, but my curiosity got the best of me. When I went down there, I abruptly came back to 2010. Karl I could kick myself for not taking my time and going up to that school to find her. I just didn't think I would find a way back that easy. In fact, I was thinking that perhaps I would never get back."

"Do you think anybody will remember you back there?"

"I suppose the pharmacist and the waitress could."

"Will they tell anyone and perhaps warn Nancy or do something worse."

"I'm not sure if they'll remember me, but do you think Nancy might be in danger because of me?"

"I was only thinking that if people were to think she knew things about the future they might want to take advantage of what she knew or perhaps they would get scared of her. You know, think she was possessed or something, like a witch. You have to remember people are leery of strangers even today and think what it must have been like in 1942 during the war. They might consider her a spy. You're much too young to remember Sacco and Vanzetti."

"Who were they?"

"They were two Italian immigrants accused of murdering a paymaster and a security guard. To make matters worse both of them were followers of some Italian anarchist who advocated revolutionary violence, including bombing and assassination. The Government did everything possible to convict them. They ended up getting the electric chair."

"Karl what does that have to do with Nancy?"

"The point I'm making is that strange things can happen during war time. People can go sort of nuts if they think their security is at risk."

"God, Karl I never thought of that. Do you suppose that I put her in jeopardy?"

"Anything is possible, but don't blame yourself Robert. You were only trying to find her and bring her back. Besides, if she's been there that long—six months—and teaching school it seems to me that she is fitting in. Who knows maybe she does not want to come back."

After Karl had said that, he wanted to take it back when he saw the dejected look on Roberts face. "You're in love with her, aren't you?"

"Yes, and you're going to say how can I be in love with someone I've never met."

"No, Robert. I think I understand what it's like to loose someone and be alone. So I can see how you could fall in love with this girl. If I were about sixty years younger I think I would be in love with her too,"

"Thanks Karl, I really appreciate your understanding and your friendship. I'm not sure what I would have done without you to talk to."

"No Robert it is you who have given me a reason to get up in the morning. I really enjoy our friendship. But what are you going to do next. Where do we go from here?"

"That is a very good question. I think I'm going to give it a little time. You know think about it. Then I'm going to try it again. I'll bring Albert out the next time I try. Now I better take Albert and go home. Thanks for listening to me."

Seventy-three

May 30 – June 3, 2010

Robert spent the rest of the week at home just trying to come to grips with what had happened. There were times when he wondered if it had really happened at all. If it had not been for the pictures he took and aspirin package, he might have been able to convince himself that none of this had ever happened. On Sunday night after much thought, he made up his mind to explore the backcountry again where he had stumbled upon the time portal and where he had seen the vision of the Sunday afternoon picnic people.

* * *

Early Monday morning, Memorial Day, he tried finding the exact spot where he had gone back in time but nothing seemed to work. He had no special feelings, no visions, no dizzy spells, no feelings of depression and noticed no changes in the weather. His only conclusion was that the time portal had closed or moved to another location. On top of all of that he still did not understand the relationship between the time portal in his backwoods and the one in Sally's café basement. Discouraged he headed back to the house.

Sitting in his study on Monday night dejected and exhausted he felt like giving up. *Perhaps all of this was pointless*, he thought. Then he noticed how full the moon was and it occurred to him that perhaps the time portals opened up only at certain times. Maybe there were certain times of the month when different time dimensions happened to come together thus allowing a person to pass from one to the other. He knew there were many people who believed that the moon influenced events here on earth. He took stock of what he knew and what he did not know.

Nancy Monroe disappeared on Friday, November 27, 2009. Looking on the inter-net he found that was five days before the full moon. *Did the time portal always open before the full moon? My first encounter with the paranormal was on May 23rd and then I went back in time on the 25th and the full moon was on May 27th. Today is the 31st four days after the full moon maybe that explains why I did not sense it. Maybe it is only open a few days before the full moon and not after. That would mean that the next opening would be sometime before the next full moon on June 26th.* With that, he took Albert out for his walk before going to bed.

* * *

On June 1st, Tuesday morning, he awoke feeling rested. He had a new idea. Perhaps he would have a better chance of finding the time portal if he were to locate the entrance to the old ancient mining site. To do this he needed some digging equipment and went to the Yellow Pages to search out an excavation and farm machinery dealers. There he saw an ad for Lowlich Implement west of Ashland.

Later that morning he and Albert headed west on U.S. 2 through Ashland and turned on Highway 63 heading to Lowlich Equipment. It was perhaps the largest implement dealer in the area and Robert was sure they would have what he wanted.

Explaining that he wanted to do some digging, the sales person showed him a Kubota M59 TLB. It was a tractor, front-end loader and a backhoe all in one, although Robert was mostly interested in the backhoe. The backhoe could dig to a depth of twelve feet and had a digger force of more than 7600 pounds. It was exactly what Robert wanted and as he wrote the check, he made sure that it could be delivered the same day.

With such an easy cash sale, the sales person had no problem with the delivery. He would have pushed it all the way there if he had had to. In all of his thirty years in sales, he had never had a sale this easy. It was not everyday that someone came in and made a purchased like this and paid list price.

As he drove away, Robert felt pleased with his purchase. Once again, he had renewed interest in his search for Nancy and the time portal.

Arriving home he had a phone message from Michael Niffin saying that he was coming up for the week and wanted to meet with Robert on Wednesday. He would be out in the afternoon.

* * *

On Tuesday, Michael Niffin drove the 240 miles north from Appleton to Hurley for the last time. He had finally made up his mind to give up the search for Nancy Monroe and move on with his life. He was tired of the weekend trips to Hurley searching for clues—that were not to be found. Besides that, he had found someone new.

He booked a room at the Days Inn in Hurley for Tuesday thru Friday. He would have liked to come up on the weekend but everything was booked because of the big ATV Rally held every year in Hurley. On Tuesday, he met with Big Doug, the Hurley Police and the Iron Country Sheriff's department and they told him that there were no new leads and the case was on the inactive list. On Wednesday, he went one more time to every place that Nancy had gone over that fateful Thanksgivings weekend. Finding nothing new, he made his final visit to Robert Rahn in the afternoon.

Michael Niffen arrived at Robert's house just after two. As Robert and Albert came out to greet him, Michael's eye caught site of the new backhoe in the front driveway delivered on Tuesday.

Robert was not sure what to make of Michael's visit, but he did admit that he felt a flare of jealousy at the prospect of having competition. Then he thought, *how silly, I'm competing for a girl I've never seen or met.* Yet the tinge of jealousy remained as he shook Michael's hand.

"Michael, how good to see you, we haven't talked since February. What brings you up here?"

"I came up here to tell the police and you that while I still care deeply for Nancy, I can't continue to let this rule my life. I have to move on."

"I understand." He said feeling relieved that Michael would be out of the picture.

"It has been over six months since she disappeared and during that time, not a shred of evidence has been uncovered to give me the least bit of encouragement that she might be alive. Robert, there are times I find myself wishing that she had just died—killed by some maniac. At least I would have had closure. All this time, part of me still believes that she might ring the doorbell and come into my apartment as if nothing had happened and yet I know this is never going to happen.

Last month I met someone new. I wasn't looking, it just happened and now it is time to move on."

"I understand Michael. You don't have to justify yourself to me."

"I know, but you gave me hope all of these months with your ideas of a time slippage as a possibility, saying that it might be possible that perhaps Nancy had unexpectedly visited another time. I didn't always believe you, but you gave me hope. Something to hang on to no matter how far out it seemed. You have to admit that much of what you said sounded like it came from the Sy Fy channel."

Robert almost thought of telling him that he had gone back and almost found her but he knew Michael would never believe him. Still part of him knew the real reason he did not say anything was that he was happy to have Michael out of the way even though he knew it was wrong of him.

"Michael, I stand by what I said. I still believe that Nancy is out there perhaps in another time or dimension." *She's alive Michael living in 1942.*

"I respect that and like I was saying I met someone. Her name is Brenda, a young ICU nurse in the hospital. It really was a chance encounter and on impulse I asked her out to see the last of the Harry Potter movies and she said yes. She was blonde and at first, I thought that perhaps she was just a substitute for Nancy. As time pasted I came to know that was not true. I really like her. Brenda made no demands on me and she knew that I was still looking for Nancy. Our friendship just continued to grow and yesterday I gave her a blue three stone diamond as a friendship ring. She said yes on one condition that I take this weekend to make sure that I was over Nancy. Robert I talked with the police and others and there is nothing new. I'm convinced I'm over her. So this is the last time I'll be seeing you."

"You know you can always stop by for a visit. As you can see I've got plenty of room."

"No, I don't think I'll ever be back. Coming here would always remind me of what happened and I want to put that all behind me."

Once again, Robert said, "I understand." Actually glad that Michael was out of his life and he could resume his search for Nancy without having to think of his involvement should he ever find her.

After shaking hands and saying good-bye, Robert and Albert stood there watching until Michael's car disappeared from view. He felt relief and was glad that Michael was out of their lives. Now he was anxious to get back to the search for the time portal and Nancy.

Seventy-four

Thursday June 3, 2010

On Thursday morning although Robert had intended to continue his search for the time portal he went into town to talk to the people at the old Museum and look to see if there were any records of a Nancy Monroe, Art Chester or an Al Hidde back in 1942.

First, he found the obituaries for Art Chester and Al Hidde. Art Chester had died in 1953 of lung cancer and Al Hidde had died in 1955 of a stroke and heart attack. Then to his surprise, he came upon an obituary notice for July 3, 1942 that listed three people; Nancy Monroe, Martha Laine and a Gerald Kershaw. All three had died on the same day. Reading Nancy's obituary, he found it unusual that the obituary did not give a date of birth. It only said date unknown. It went on to say she died under mysterious circumstances believed to be a homicide.

Martha Laine's obituary read, born in 1884. She was 58 years old, but what drew Robert's attention was the fact that cause of death was also a homicide. Reading further, he found that Gerald Kershaw's cause of death too was a homicide. This had to be more than a coincidence.

He knew that Nancy Monroe lived with Martha so there had to be the connection. He could only think that whoever had killed Martha had also killed Nancy and perhaps Gerald.

How Gerald Kershaw was connected to this entire mess, he was not sure. His only thought was that perhaps Nancy had been seeing this Gerald Kershaw and perhaps Kershaw was at the wrong place at the wrong time.

Searching for other articles, he found one that said that Nancy had been found outside of town in an old abandon warehouse where she was tied to an old bed frame and it appeared she was strangled after having been tortured. The article went on to say Leo Coppalo owned that warehouse. The police could not find any connection between Nancy Monroe's death and the death of Martha Laine. It went on to say that Martha Laine was dead from a gun shot wound to the head in her own home that might have been part of a break-in and robbery, there was no apparent connection.

The article went on further to say the death of Gerald Kershaw also appeared to be a separate incident even though his body had been found in a shallow grave not far from the warehouse.

As Robert pondered all that, he concluded that who ever this Leo Coppalo was, he must have been a very prominent person in the community with lots of influence with the local government and the police.

Now he sat there dumbfounded. He knew now it was a matter of life and death that he get back to 1942. He had at the most three weeks to save Nancy's life and perhaps the lives of Maratha Laine and Gerald Kershaw too. Next he thought, *what am I going to tell her. That I came back to save your life and if you don't go back with me to the present you will be dead in a few short weeks.*

Now despite all of his doubts there was no question about what he was going to do. He was going back to find Nancy Monroe in order to save her life and others even if that seemed impossible. He had to get back to 1942 even if it meant that he might never return.

Seventy-five

Friday June 4 – June 18, 2010

On Friday morning June 4th, Robert was up early anxious to get started. He had renewed enthusiasm from what he found about Nancy's impending death if he did not bring her back. He was also happy that Michael Niffin was out of the way. Still he knew this did not mean that Nancy was just going to fall in love with him. Yet he was still confident that he could win her over once he rescued her—that was if she wanted to be rescued. It had never occurred to him until now that she might be happy where she was or perhaps it was possible that she'd found another love. Once he got there, he would just have to convince her that her life was in danger and that she had to come back. Another thought occurred to him that she could just go some place else in 1942 to get away from those that were after her. He would just have to face that fact once he found her.

* * *

After studying the manual for the backhoe all morning, he felt confident that he had a full understanding of its operation. Just after two in the afternoon, leaving Albert in the house—which did not go over well—he drove the backhoe to an open area to practice. There he spent the remainder of the day becoming acquainted with the machine and practicing.

Convinced that he had the proper command of the backhoe he decided that on Saturday he would begin the exploratory digging in the area of the ancient mine site.

* * *

Saturday June 5th arrived with a light blanket of ground fog hanging over the low spots between the remnants of the waste rock and tailing piles giving the area an eerie look. He started to dig in the area where he had last seen the vision of the men, the boy and the girl in the pinafore dress.

The digging was slow with many large rocks that had to be pried out before the hole could be enlarged. By noon, he found progress had been much slower than anticipated even with state of the art digging equipment. Although he knew the area had an abundance of rocks, he was not prepared for the all rocks he encountered below the ground. Many of the rocks he encountered were not rocks, but boulders and required more time to remove. He had to dig a large area around the large boulder so that he could drag them out of the way. It was very time consumer. By Saturday evening, he came to a conservative estimate that it would take at least three to four weeks to clear the area. If this had been the ancient mining site, it gave no hint of having anything resembling a mining system of tunnels or levels.

* * *

After nearly two weeks of daily digging late on Friday afternoon June 18th, tired and ready to give up, he thought he spotted something at the bottom of the pit down around eight feet. Stopping the backhoe, he inspected the sides of the pit before jumping down. When working alone the last thing you wanted was to be buried alive. There at the bottom of the pit he could feel air seeping out of a small opening. The pressure in the opening must have been higher inside than outside causing the air to come out. Curious he moved closer to the opening. Taking his hands, he enlarged the opening and detected a strong flow of air coming from underneath the pile of rocks.

Climbing out and getting back on the backhoe, he feverishly began widening the opening digging out rocks and tailings until he saw rotten timber mixed with the rocks. He stopped digging and jumped back into the pit and saw a small opening about a foot in diameter. This had to be one of the laterals to the mine.

Cautiously he went about removing the debris from the opening until it was more than three feet in diameter. Taking out his flashlight he entered the opening slowly, it went straight back for fifteen feet then his flashlight shown off a rock wall. Moving closer he saw that there was an opening going down on what he thought was a 30-degree angle. He could not see how far it went and was not about to go down the hole without any safety equipment or at least a rope. He could picture himself sliding down just like "Alice in Wonderland." He also wondered if anyone had set a booby trap at the bottom.

Seeing that the sun was setting, he reluctantly gave up the exploration until tomorrow. He was disappointed that he had not had any strange feelings—no dizziness, no skin clamminess and no prickly hot skin. A since of dread came over him, perhaps this was not where the two time dimensions came together to form a time portal after all. Was all of his work for naught? Then he remembered that in the past the time portal did not open until just before the full moon, which was not until the June 26th. Perhaps all he had to do was wait. As he went home he was somewhat disappointed but never the less more determined than ever to continue the search.

* * *

When Albert heard the tractor, he was more than happy to see Robert. After Robert showered and ate, he took Albert for his walk. That evening Robert knew he needed time to think about what he had found and whether this was really the way back in time or not. If it was a way back in time he had no idea for certain what time he would enter or just how he would get back. The last time he thought he was just plain lucky to have come back through Sally's café in Hurley.

Although very tired Robert went to his study to reflect on everything that he knew and what he didn't know about the time portal. *I'm sure that there's a time portal by the ancient mine site and I know Nancy Monroe disappeared five days before the full moon. My first and second encounters were on May 23rd and 25th and that was just before the full moon on May 27th. Today is Friday, June 18th and the next full moon this month is on Saturday the 26th a week from tomorrow. That may be just enough time for me to be prepared to go back if this is the time portal. I'll have to make sure I have everything ready to go by the middle of next week. There is no way I can postpone until the next full moon on July 25th, that would be too late. Both Nancy and Martha would be dead by that time.*

I'll have to return June 28th, which was the next full moon in 1942 otherwise I'll have to wait until the next full moon on July 27, 1942 and I don't think I can keep them alive that long.

Then he thought about what Karl had told him about Marietta DeMitri. *I wonder if Karl would remember on what month and date she supposedly went forward in time. If I knew the month, date and when the full moon was, it could confirm my thinking on when the portal opens. I'll call him.*

After calling Karl, Robert was amazed at the man's memory. *There certainly was no sign of Alzheimer's in his future.* He remembered what had happened to Marietta took place a few days before the Flag Day parade and that was on June 14th. With that, Robert found out that the full moon in 1946 was on Flag Day.

That means that Marietta's slippage in time most likely took place about 3-5 days before the full moon confirming my theory. So with the full moon on the 26th the best time to see if there really is a time portal by the old mine site would be from June 21-25. That gives me almost a week to have everything ready to go back to 1942 again.

* * *

Just before going to bed and thinking of 1942, he thought of how fascinated he was as a kid with World War II history. It had all started in the third grade when one of the nuns in his New York Catholic Grade School was talking about world history. She mentioned how Germany during World War I had invaded a number of countries, but had lost the war. Then she went on to say that the Second World War would never have happened if the victorious European nations had not imposed such harsh conditions on the Germans after the First World War.

Germany was striped of its pride as a nation and so when a man by the name of Adolph Hitler came to power, promising to restore German pride they followed him as he led them into the Second World War.

That five-minute talk was enough to arouse Robert's curiosity about Germany and the world wars for a lifetime. Immediately after, he read about World War II in the school's World Book Encyclopedia. The only thing he knew about the war was that the Americans had won. He had not realized that the war had really started in September of 1939 with Germany's invasion of Poland. It read like a story and he always had wondered how Germany had lost the war by making seemingly avoidable major mistakes. Since that day, he was always interested in the war. He had collected a number of treasured rare books on the war that he had locked away.

Now he had a feeling that things in the world were changing. He had always been very intuitive to the moods of the people and of the times. That intuition was what had made him a successful banker, broker, and millions of dollars. It had also made him one to know who was going to win the elections and how the mood of the people was changing. He also could sense when major events were about to happen like 9/11. He did not know what exactly was going to happen only that it was something big.

Now his intuition told him that history, as he knew it was changing, however, impossible that seemed. That was unless someone had been able to change it by his or her presence in another time. He knew that there were always people who thought that people had traveled back in time and had been responsible for changing history. Only that the people, who were living in that time never really knew it. It was just part of the time. It was not as if people had remembered what it had been like before the change happened.

Therefore, if Nancy Monroe had gone back into the past—to a parallel world—she would find upon arrival the same history that we know in our history books. Going forward she would by her very presence there create a new parallel world.

Was it possible that she was able to change history by going back there and if she did was there a way for him to detect it here in 2010 or would it just seem to him that it had always been that way.

Trying to confirm his theory, he went to his storage vault and retrieved a number of old World War Two history books that were collector's items. Opening a book he started to page to December 1941 looking for the Japanese attack on Pearl Harbor.

There he found a well known picture showing the magazine of the U.S.S. Shaw exploding. As he read the following page, it said that two waves of Japanese bombers hit the Island. Then right before his eyes, he saw the print starting to change. He could not believe his eyes as he watched dumbstruck. Now it said that there were three waives of bombers. That was not true. He knew that there were only two waves and that the Japanese had decided against making a third attack. Did Nancy's presences have something to do with this change in history?

Quickly he went to look at several other reference books that were in his library and found that these books too confirmed that there had been three attacks on the island. He did not see the print changes in these books that were on his library shelves out in the open. It had only changed on the one locked in the vault.

Even with that, he knew that there had not been three attacks, this was not true and why did the book in the vault have the old history and then change when he brought it out. His only conclusion was that the book in the vault was protected from change as long as it stayed in the vault. Then why did he remember things differently? The only thing he could think of was that he had always been able to see things differently. Perhaps his memory was protected, because as a kid he had a form of brain Epilepsy.

What if Nancy had caused history to change? There seemed to be no other explanation. Next, he called an old college history professor friend from the University of Syracuse.

"Lloyd, this is Robert Rahn. How are you?"

"Robert, good to hear from you. Is it true that you are living in Northern Wisconsin?"

"Yes, it's true. I just had to get a way from New York City. The reason I'm calling is that a friend and I are having a history debate. He says that the Japanese launched three attacks on Pearl Harbor and I said there were only two. The Japanese wanted to launch a third strike, but decided against it. Who's right?"

"I can't believe that you are asking me such a question. You of all people know there were three attacks. The last attack hit the fuel storage and the dry-docks. Are you all right?"

"I'm fine; it just must have slipped my mind. I won't keep you, but you will have to promise me that you and your wife will come out here for a visit. You just won't believe how beautiful Northern Wisconsin is."

"I may just take you up on that offer. It was good talking to you."

Hanging up Robert still could not believe what his friend had said, but now he knew that history had changed. The only thing he did not know was how she did it or what else she might change by being back there in 1942. Just the very fact that she was living in the past had to have caused some changes. He only knew that he had to get her out of there as fast as possible before other things changed. *Was it possible that in someway she might provide information unknowingly about the outcome of the war and this could cause the U.S. to loose the war?*

Still astonished by what he had learned, he calmed himself with a glass of bourbon. He knew he had to get back to 1942, but he had to come up with a rational plan of action.

Was it possible in another dimensional world that the Germans and the Japanese won the war? Briefly thinking about the German Holocaust victims and the concentration death camps he did not even want to consider what could happen if the Allies had lost the war.

Seventy-six

Saturday/Sunday June 18-19, 2010

That weekend, Robert decided to take time off to make sure that he was ready to go back when the moon was full on June 26th. Besides, he still had the first part of next week to make any necessary changes.

After breakfast on Saturday, he sat down before his computer to work out a plan. After all, he couldn't just show up and say to Nancy Monroe, *I'm here to save you and prevent the world from falling into the hands of the Germans and the Japanese.* He had to have a well thought out plan. He had almost a week before the full moon.

He knew the Hurley area had many active iron mining operations in 1942 with all of the demands for iron and steel needed for the war and he thought he could pretend to be a miner down on his luck looking for work. His problem was that he knew very little about mining, after all he was a finance person. Then he thought that there must be a need for a bookkeeper or an accountant, both he could do with ease. He looked up several 1942 sites on the internet and became familiar with the active mines in the area.

Next, he decided that he had to have some clothing from the time period so that he would fit in. He did not want to stick out and in anyway draw attention to himself. Searching the internet for clothing styles from the 1940's he found a number of retroactive clothing sites. He had no idea why anyone would want to buy clothes from the 1940's but he was no longer amazed at what could be found on-line.

He paged through over fifty sites before finding one that suited him. The site had work clothing and men's dress clothing from the forties. He purchased a double-breasted suit made of a wool-synthetic blend yarns along with several gabardine work shirts and pants. He also found a top hat that fit the times. He punched in his credit card number, checked express shipping, and pressed place order.

Next, he searched for money that could be used in 1942. He typed in "Sliver Certificates" into the web search site. There too were a number of sites, where silver certificates could be purchase. Sliver certificates were very similar to the present day bills only that they said, "sliver certificate" and payable to the bear on demand in sliver.

Looking over the many web sites, he was able to purchase silver certificate in denominations of $1, $5 and $10 in series 1928, 1933, 1934, and 1935.

From different web sites, he purchased over $7,000 in small bills. He thought this was more than enough money, but then it occurred to him that he might have to bribe someone. Would $7,000 be enough money? Looking further on the internet, he did a search for how much things cost in 1942 and found that a new house was only $3,770 and a new car was only $920. After seeing this, he felt sure that seven thousand dollars would be more than enough money. The purchase of the cash cost him over $21,000. He too had the bills shipped by express deliver.

Just before lunch, he thought about seeking out a place to live in 1942 that would be out of the way like a boarding house. Some place where he would not be noticed. In this way, he would be able to ask questions and gather information. He was not sure if he needed to have a job or not. Getting the proper identification might be a problem. He would just have to decide those things once he got there knowing he had to have her out by July 3rd. Once established he would search out Nancy. He knew from before that she was teaching at the Catholic school. Then he would have to find a way to approach her and explain to her what he was doing there. That might be the hard part.

Later that afternoon he went gun shopping. He did not like the idea of carrying a gun, but he had no idea what he might run into and he needed a way to defend himself and perhaps Nancy. That afternoon he drove to a gun shop in Rhinelander.

He told the dealer he wanted something small but powerful for home protection. The dealer showed him a Glock G26 Compact and said, "This is a great piece for anyone looking for a compact carry piece. It's light-kicking, reliable and easy to conceal, and the clip holds ten. In fact, this gun is more accurate than I am. Try it out."

"You sold me, I'll take it. Can I get six extra spare clips and four boxes of ammunition?'

"No problem, are you planning to do some target shooting?"

"Something like that "

"That will be $735 and you can pick up the gun in three days after you pass the background check."

"I'll be back on Wednesday June 23rd if that works for you."

"That works for me. Everything should be complete by then. I'll call you if there is any delay. Thanks for your business."

* * *

In the evening after returning from the gun shop, Robert busied himself once again checking the rest of his World War Two history books to see if there had been any more changes. He knew the Battle of Midway had started on June 3rd and that it was the turning point in the Pacific war. It was where the Americans sunk four of the six Japanese battle carriers. Some historians went as far to say with that one battle the war was lost for Japan.

When he first began to read everything was exactly as he remembered. The first U.S. air attack took off at 12:30 on June 3, 1942 consisting of nine B-17 bombers operating from Midway. Three hours later, they found the Japanese transport group 650 miles to the west and came under heavy anti-aircraft fire, they dropped their bombs. None of the bombs actually landed on target and no significant damage was inflicted.

Then on June 4th the Japanese launched their initial attack on Midway itself, consisting of 180 aircraft that raided the airfields, docks and harbor installations but succeeded in inflicting only minor damage.

After that, history changed and he could not believe what he was reading. The remainder of the battle was a stalemate with the Japanese losing only two major aircraft carriers rather than the four that he had remembered.

The book went on to say that, the Japanese forces made a last second decision not to split their forces by sending ships to the Aleutians Islands like in the history book. It went on the say that canceling the attack on the Aleutians in Alaska the Japanese were able to gain some success.

Robert sat there dumbfounded unable to think straight. *How can this be happening? It has to be from something Nancy said or did. I've got to get her out of there before anything worse happens.*

Reading further into the history book it appeared that while the battle of Midway had changed the war it had not altered the outcome of the war. That August Americans landed on Guadalcanal and the war in Europe appeared to be about the same as he remembered.

Robert was not sure, how Nancy's presence in the past could change things; however, it already appeared that she had changed history. The third wave attack by the Japanese at Pearl Harbor, things were different at Moscow and now the changes in the battle for Midway Island. The good thing was that his history books still had the Allies winning the war. Nancy had not changed the final out come of the war. Thank God for that. However, what else might she possibly change just by being there before he was able to rescue her? He also considered the fact that he could change things by going back to find her. Perhaps he could even make things worse, but it was a chance he had to take.

Then he thought about the possibility that Nancy might want to stay in the past. What if she met someone? Was there such a thing as a time continuum where small changes could not affect the final out come? Say for instance, was it possible to go back and kill Hitler while he was an infant and therefore the Second World War would not have happened. Perhaps the system did allow for minor changes.

Even if he went back, got Nancy to the present things, would still be altered. He would not be able to alter the fact that Nancy had been living in the past since November 1941. Perhaps his good intensions could have disastrous consequences on history. What if by going back to make things better he only made them worse. What if his actions would be responsible for making the Germans and the Japanese win the war. There were countless times in World War Two where if things had gone even slightly different the war could have been lost. He knew from history that it only took a small thing to alter history. If Germany had not invaded Russia and had continued to bomb the British airfield and the aircraft factories, Germany may have won. What if Hitler had sent more troops to North Africa and captured the Suez Canal? What if Hitler had given a higher priority to his rocket and jet plane programs? The number of examples that could have changed the outcome of the war were endless. Could his action now be the final one that would change history?

Robert also thought that perhaps the time continuum was already in a state of ciaos and that his going back or Nancy being there might have already alter things. Was it possible that others had some how stumbled back in time just like Nancy and him. Had they already altered history? There were so many unanswered questions. After all of his thinking he knew he was going to go back and get her and perhaps time itself would straighten things out in the long run.

He put his old books back in the vault where he thought they would be safe and not change until he was ready to check them again.

Seventy-seven

Monday June 21, 2010

On Monday, Robert went back to the dig site refreshed and confident that he would find the portal. He had slept in late on both Saturday and Sunday finding that he really had needed the rest. He was sure he had all things in place. He thought he had about everything he needed; money from the time-period, retroactive clothing, a gun and ammunition and an old map of the city of Hurley and the surrounding area from the historical society. The only thing that could derail his departure was if his internet orders did not arrive on time or he was unable to get the gun although he was pretty sure that everything should be in place by Wednesday. If not, he would have to go anyway, according to Nancy's obituary she was dead on July 3rd and the next full moon was not until 26, 2010. He could not wait for the full moon in July, which would be too late. Nancy's life was in danger or she might be dead if he waited until the next full moon.

When he arrived at the dig-site later that morning, he was pleased with the way things looked, he was sure that everything was in order. He did not attempt to go too far back into the opening. He would save that for later in the week. This Monday he would only test out the site to make sure it was really a portal back to 1942. He was actually looking forward to testing out the site to see if it truly was the time portal. After all this work, he hoped he had not been working in the wrong place.

He started to have the same strange feeling as he approached the mine opening. It was the same as the last time, when he had gone back in time. The feeling grew stronger as he entered the mine. He felt the same strange tingling sensation and the surface of his skin begin to feel hot and sticky with sweat forming on his forehead. His body was warm all over and his face was flush—what his mother would have called a hot flash. Not that he ever had one. At the same time, he began to feel nauseous, dizzy and his

EMF meter reading suddenly jumped off the scale. He scrambled back not wanting to be sucked in to another time.

Now sitting on a rock pile outside of the mine trying to catch his breath he knew for sure this was the active time dimension opening. It still bothered him that he had no way to know for sure what time in history this portal would take him. He just had to hope it was set to take him back to 1942. He did wonder if he would ever be able to return back to the present. The last time he may just have just been lucky. In the end, he knew he just had to take his chances. For he if he never returned there would really be no big loss. He had no family and only a few friends. He knew that Karl and Albert would miss him.

He stood there staring at the opening not sure what to do next. The force was still at work, but he could tell it was not strong enough to pull him down. If his theory was right about the time portal, it would open about five day before the full moon on the June 26th. Today was the 21st and that meant he had only three or four days to prepare for his journey back in time. There were still a lot of things he did not know. The last time he went, he entered 1942 on the same day and time. He had no idea how long he could stay on the other side. If something went wrong and he had to wait for the next full moon, he would have to get Nancy and Martha out of the area to prevent their murders. It would all depend on how much time he needed to find Nancy and get her out of there—that was if she wanted to come back. Not wanting to spend any more time thinking about all the possibilities, he slowly backed away from the opening. He felt things returning to normal. Now away from the power of the opening he decided to stop for the day and go back to the house. He needed to reconsider his plan again before making what he hoped would be his last trip back into the past to find Nancy.

He wondered why if he came back in time to Sally's café, why couldn't he find the way to 1942 from there. It was a puzzle that perplexed him. The only thing he knew was that he had found two time portal sites, one here on his land and the other in Sally's basement. Since he came back through Sally's basement, he assumed that the two were connected. Both had taken him and Nancy back to the same time period. Why it had not taken him back to another time period he did not know. For all he knew it could have taken him back to medieval times or prehistoric time, why 1942. He just had to trust that in some mysterious way the time portal knew what it was doing. Perhaps, his mind directed the timetable. He only knew that when he went back he would be thinking of 1942.

* * *

Albert was more than happy to see him upon his return. He fed Albert than took a long hot shower even though the day was in the eighties. Next, he poured himself a glass of bourbon on the rocks in his den and placed a call to Karl. If anyone could help him sort out things, he knew it would be Karl.

Karl answered on the first ring as if he were waiting for Robert's call.

"Karl, this is Robert, how are you this afternoon?"

"Don't bullshit me! You didn't call to find out how I was. What are you up to now? Still planning to take a trip back in time and find that girlfriend of yours?"

"As a matter fact that is exactly why I'm calling. If anyone can help me it's you."

"Sure, sure, flattery will get you everywhere."

"Actually, Karl I need your help and I was wondering if you would like to come out to the house and spend several days with me. I really need your help."

There was nothing but silence on the other side of the phone. "Karl, are you still there?"

"Yes, yes I'm still here, I was just trying to imagine what sort of nonsensical thing you were up to now."

"It's not nonsensical, I have a well thought out plan and I need your help. Please Karl say you'll come. I can pick you up tomorrow and we can have breakfast at Sally's and I'll brief you what I have in mind."

"Don't suppose there is anyway to talk you out of this, is there?"

"No, Karl. I'm committed and I'll do this with or without your help. But I'd really like you there."

"Alright! Alright! I'll pack my bag tonight and will be waiting for you to come in the morning."

"Thanks Karl, you don't know how much this means to me. I'll be there at seven."

* * *

After Robert had hung up Karl stood there knowing that there was no way he would be able to talk Robert out of this. Had he had the power he would not have let Robert do this on his own. When he thought about it, it was ridiculous—time travel. He loved Robert as if he was his own son.

Chapter Seventy-eight

Tuesday June 22, 2010

Tuesday was a very warm and humid day as Robert picked up Karl exactly at seven and took him to breakfast at Sally's. The place was not very busy.

After ordering Karl said, "So what is the timing for this little travel adventure of yours?"

"I'm planning on tomorrow or I could put if off until Thursday, but what concerns me is the timing. The full moon is on Saturday the 26th and I'm not sure if I can come back on time. I don't know for sure how the full moon fits into the return. If I need a full moon in order to come back that would only leave me one or two days to get everything done. If it takes me longer, I'd most likely have to remain in 1942 until the next full moon which is July 28th. I'd have to safe guard Nancy and Martha for a month."

"Why? Do you think she is in danger?"

"I read in an old obituary that she was murdered on July 3, 1942."

"You think you can change history and keep that from happening?"

"I'm sure going to try. That's why I have to get in and out."

"What happened the last time you went back, did you go before the full moon?"

"Yes and I came back the same day. So I don't know what would have happened had I stayed longer."

"When is or was the full moon in June of 1942?"

"I looked it up and in 1942 it will be on the 28th."

"Do you think that will give you two or three more days when you're in 1942?"

"I think it does, but I'm not sure and I don't want to take the chance."

After a pause Karl asked, "You know the last time you came back it was right here at Sally's. Do you think it is possible to leave from here?"

"I thought about that and since I found 1942 the first time from the portal by my house I thought I would stick with leaving from there. Coming back, I may have to try Sally's again. I can't say where I'll be or how fast I have to get out of there."

"Do you think there is going to be a problem getting her out once you find her?"

"Not sure what I'll find, but I have to think that there may be people there who want to make sure she stays there. Let's go, we can talk more at the house."

Robert asked Sally for the check and they left to go over to the Post Office.

At the Post Office, he found that all of his on-line purchases had arrived. He had picked up the gun earlier and now he had everything he needed in order to fit into 1942.

* * *

Albert met Robert and Karl as they entered the house shortly after ten and there was no way that Albert would leave Karl alone until he went up to his room to unpack.

When Karl came down Robert said, "Let's take Albert for a walk and I'll show you the dig site from where I plan to leave."

"When are you planning to go?" said Karl.

"I plan on leaving tomorrow morning. If this only takes a few days, I could be back by the weekend or before. Remember when I get to 1942, I gain a day. Leaving on Thursday 2010 is Wednesday in 1942 and the full moon is not until June 28th in 1942."

"Do you think you'll come back here? The last time you came back to Sally's."

"I know I thought of that and that is why I think we'll go in today and park a car at Sally's. In that way I will be able to drive myself back here."

"Good idea!"

Arriving at the dig site Karl was amazed at what he saw. "I had no idea you were this busy." Pointing down into the bottom of the pit Karl asked, "Is that where you plan to leave?"

"Yes, that opening goes down on a 30 degree angle and that is where I felt the same dizzy sensations that I felt the last time. I'm sure it is the opening."

"Robert, are you sure you want to do this? Maybe you should leave well enough alone and forget about trying to find this Nancy woman. Who knows maybe she's happy in 1942."

"I though about that, but I'm sure that by her being there she is changing history and she might even be changing the outcome of the Second

World War. I can't leave this alone, what if the Japanese and the Germans win? Can you image what the world would look like?"

"There is no way I want the Japanese and the Germans to win, but how can you be so sure that Nancy is changing things?"

"My thought is that perhaps she had something with her that could change history completely. Like for instance a cell phone. That could be enough to change things. If it got into German hands, it might help them perfect their guidance system for their V-1 and V-2 rockets. Think about how that could change things. Hell, who knows what else she might have had with her? A computer of any kind might change everything."

"Do you really think if the Germans or Japanese had something like that they'd be able to turn things around that fast?"

"Just think about what the Japs did in the computer business in our own time?"

"I suppose you're right. I have to agree that it makes since for you to go back. But you know Robert you are like a son to me and I don't know what I'd do if you didn't come back."

"I know how you feel, I feel that same way about you. One thing you have to promise is that if I don't come back under no circumstances are you to come looking for me. If I'm not back in three days give me another month until the next full moon. After that, I want you to have this opening blown up. I had a power of attorney drawn up for you that gives you the rights to all of my property and capital."

"I sure appreciate all the confidence you have in me Robert."

"I really trust you. Now let's get back to the house and get everything in place for tomorrow. I still have to pack."

Chapter Seventy-nine

Wednesday June 23, 2010

The night before Karl and Robert had taken Robert's SUV and parked it in the lot just down from Sally's café. With all the cars parked at the bars, he thought no one would notice the car. It was a chance he had to take.

After leaving the car, they went back to Robert's house and Karl helped Robert pack. They put his clothes in an old suitcase that Robert had found at a rummage sale hoping that it would fit into 1942. He also took along a soft shoulder bag, which held his money, papers and his gun. He was careful not to take anything that looked like it did not belong.

* * *

Just after six in the morning, Karl and Robert headed out to the dig site. Just as Robert was walking out of the garage, he decided to take along a shovel. He thought if he had to come back through the mine opening, he might need a shovel to clear out debris.

Robert gave Karl a big hug saying, "Wish me luck. I hope that I'll be back in a couple of days with Nancy."

"Robert, I'm worried. What if you go into another time period going out or coming back. Maybe you should just forget about this. Did you ever consider how silly it sounds when you think about it?"

"Please don't worry. I know how silly this would sound to a stranger. Hey I'm going back into the past to find someone I don't even know. They'd lock me up in the loony bin. Karl, you know I've got to do this. I was there once and I can do it again. I will come back. Please take care of Albert for me." With that, Robert started down to the mine opening.

Karl called after him, "Just be careful. I'll be waiting for you every-day."

Karl stood there shivering in the cool morning air as Robert disappeared into the mine site opening.

While Karl stood there, still waving good-bye even though he could no longer see him, he heard a whoosh as if air was being compressed. Then there was a small flash of light and he knew that Robert had gone over into the past. Albert too heard the whoosh and let out a small whimper. Karl could only hope that it was the right past.

* * *

Robert entered the mine searching for the 30-degree opening and thought of Alice in Wonderland. There in the early morning light he found it. He went directly to the opening not stopping. There was no way he wanted to give himself a change to reconsider. The next think he knew as he was sliding down the opening, the smell of ether started to over whelm him and suddenly he felt a change in the air like being sucked from one pressure area to another. The air felt denser somehow as it rushed past his ears and face. When the swirling air stopped, he found himself standing at the site of the abandon mine just as it had appear the last time. Robert was sure that he was back in to 1942.

Things were familiar like before. He looked to see if the mine opening was still there but all he saw was over grown rock piles where the mine had once been. There was no sign of any tracks where he had once driven the backhoe down to the mine.

There appeared to be no obvious return route back to 2010 except for a small indentation that showed itself between the rock piles. He stood there thinking; *perhaps this is the way back, I'm glad I remembered the shovel.*

He dug into the area until he could see that indeed it did open up into the mine. He spent a half hour enlarging the opening if they had to come back this way in a hurry. The most likely escape route back to 2010 would be through Sally's café just like last time.

He stuck the shovel into the ground to mark the opening and headed for town. Just as he was ready to leave he felt light headed and sat down on a near by rock to consider his next move. *I'm really back. Now all I have to do is find Nancy.*

After about ten minutes, he headed in the direction of where his house would have been. Once on the town road he made his way to town only this time he did not want to be noticed. It was best to avoid cars. It was going to be a nice summer day in June 1942.

* * *

Karl stood by the opening of the mine waiting and hoping that Robert would reappear at any moment. After more than thirty minutes, Karl was sure Robert had passed over to the past. He still had trouble believing that time travel was possible.

For just a faction of a second Karl thought about entering the mine to follow Robert, but than he remembered that Robert told him that it was important for him to be back here watching and waiting. Robert was not sure who or what he would find on the other side. Robert also told him that it might be possible for someone to follow him back and he would need Karl's help on this side if that happened.

Now more than an hour past, Karl walked down to the opening with Albert on a leash—careful not to get too close—to make sure that Robert was not there. There was no sign of Robert. Slowly Karl started back to the house to began what he hoped would be a short wait.

1942

Chapter Eighty

Monday June 22, 1942

On Monday June 22, Ethan Lynch delivered the first item from the Alliance. It was the adding machine.

"It's been ten days since we made the deal Ethan, what took them so long?"

"Leo told me that they had a hard time deciding on what item to start with."

When Henrik saw the adding machine, he was disappointed. What he really wanted was the phone. He thought the phone could most likely change the direction of the war and assure the Germans of victory. He had no concern for what happened to the Japanese.

Despite his disappointment, Henrik found himself more than pleased with the adding machine. This certainly was not a simple adding machine. It truly was a calculator. It was three inches wide and five inches long and was about one quarter of an inch thick. On the front of the adding machine was printed Caltronic and under that was CL-887. He thought Caltronic must be a brand name and the CL-887 was a model number. Just above the screen was printed, SOLAR POWER AND BATTERY BACK UP. He knew of nothing that was solar powered in 1942. Looking at the back for the battery he saw the adding machine said made in Malaysia. He thought; *how could this be made in Malaysia? The Malaysian peninsula was part of the British Empire until it was captured by the Japanese just recently. There is no way this was made in Malaysia.*

Next, he unscrewed the back panel and found a small round battery the size of a quarter only thinner. He knew of no battery that small. The only thing he could think of was that this thing had to come from the future, but that was ridiculous. There was no such thing as time travel, but he was at a loss for any other explanation.

Next, he turned the adding machine over and pressed the "on" button and a zero showed on the small screen. Next, he hit several other numbers and they appeared on the screen as, 586. Then he pressed the square root button and the numbers on the screen changed 24.207436. Multiplying the number by itself, the screen showed, 585.99995. This was correct. How on earth, did such a small piece of equipment have the ability to perform such a calculation?

He continued to press in other numbers and watched as it multiplied, divided, added and subtracted the numbers. It was amazing. He was even able to figure out the memory functions. There was nothing like this in 1942.

There were only motor driven mechanical adding machines that had appeared in the early 1900's and were now commonplace. Every engineer had one on his desk.

The numeric input keys were arranged as a set of digits per column and were mounted on a typewriter like carriage that moved back and forth as it multiplies and divides. The machines were driven by an electric motor and were very nosy.

This adding machine he could hold in the palm of his hand and it did all calculations plus square roots. It was fantastic. It bothered him that he could not determine how it was powered or how the display screen worked.

The adding machine said Solar Powered. Meaning it was powered by light, but that too seem impossible.

He knew he really had something and was now more determined than ever to get his hands on the other things that these guys had. He was sure that if he could get these things to his country in time to investigate and apply this technology, this would assure Germany of winning the war.

He still could not understand where these things came from. If it was from that blonde woman, how did she got them? It was as if she had to come from some future world no matter how impossible that sounded.

* * *

As Ethan Lynch was leaving, a strange thought came into his head and he was not at all sure what made him think it. *Could Henrik Dahl be a spy? How bizarre that sounded. Henrik a spy? After all he and Henrik had been friends since graduating from the University of Wisconsin, back in 1924.*

While he knew that Henrik was involved with several German organizations, there was no way he thought that Henrik was not loyal to the United States? Besides, he had been here since 1914 and appeared to be very much at home here in the United States.

There was no way that he could be a spy, but he did remember once when Henrik told him that he had made a contribution to a pro-Nazi organization and at the time Ethan had thought it was just a joke. Now he made it a point to do some further investigating. If Henrik was a spy and gave this technology to the Germans there was no telling how this could affect the out come of the war.

Chapter Eighty-one

Wednesday June 24, 1942

After a ten-minute walk, Robert came to the town road that would lead to State 77 and into the city of Hurley. As he looked back, he had a hard time imagining that his house was really there in the future.

Walking along the road he heard a car coming and threw himself into the deep ditch. Covered with tall grass he waited for the car to go by before getting back on the road.

After hiding from two more cars, he decided to walk along side of the road about a hundred feet in the fields. In this way it was much easier to stay out of sight.

Finally, just before noon he was at the outskirts of Pence where Robert saw the Plummer head frame. The Plummer mine had gone out of business in 1932, but Robert recognized it from the times he had driven by it. He remembered reading that it was the only remaining iron mining head frame in the state of Wisconsin. Moving through Pence he came to the city of Montreal. Here he remembered the company-mining houses, which in 2010 were used as vacation and rental properties, now they housed real miners and their families. Next, he saw that the Carey mine was in active production. In 2010 there was only a historical marker where the mine was once located. He remembered that the mine had not closed down until some time in the 1960's. As he continued to walk up the hill into Gile he soon approached the sidewalks of the city of Hurley. He felt sure that he would blend in with the rest of the people.

The city was familiar to him from his first visit. Up ahead was the Burton House. It was as impressive as it was the first time he saw it. He still wondered why no one had bothered to save it as a historical marker. Perhaps it was like everything else, there just was not enough money. Continuing down Silver Street he saw the pharmacy were on his last visit he had purchased some aspirins. He decided to walk in to check out the date just to be sure that it was June of 1942. To his satisfaction, there on the wall was a June 1942 calendar and the only thing different was that it was Wednesday instead of Thursday. To his right was an old fashion soda fountain with six stools just like before. Al Hidde came out from the pharmacy saying, "Can I help you?"

"Yes, you can. I'd like something cold to drink?"

"Cola all right?" Before Robert could answer, the man said. "You look familiar have we met before?"

Startled, Robert took a few seconds before answering. "I don't think so I'm new in town. Do you know where I can find a room to rent?"

"Yes, there's Ellen's boarding house on Copper Street. Her rooms are real nice and clean. I'm sure she will be able to help you. Oh by the way are you looking for a job?"

"Yes, that was going to be my next question."

"Right now the mines are all hiring. It's hard work but the pay is good."

"Thanks for the tip I'll stop by the mines tomorrow."

Chapter Eighty-two

Wednesday June 24, 1942

Ellen Warner woke early that Wednesday morning expecting today to be just like all the other days since the start of the war back on December 7, 1941 when she had been notified that her husband had been killed at Pearl Harbor. She had been dating Henry for over two years on and off and when he came home on leave that November she had a weak moment and accepted his proposal—they married within the week. After a ten-day honeymoon, Henry reported back to his base in Peal Harbor and ten days after that he was dead and she was a war widow. She was not to be only one before the war ended.

She continued to run her boarding house to make ends meet. Had it not been for Henry's insurance she would most certainly have lost the place. As it was, she was just hanging on working her fingers to the bone unable to afford to hire any additional help except for her cousin who worked as a part-time cook and housekeeper.

Waking this morning, she knew she did not have the luxury of taking another small fifteen-minute nap.

After finishing the breakfast dishes, she looked down the hill and there was a man walking who looked completely out of place. He just did not belong. It was not that he was dressed so differently—in fact, he was wearing gabardine work clothes like most workers—no it was something else that made him stick out although she could not put her finger on it. He came directly to the door and knocked.

Ellen opened the door saying, "Good morning sir, can I help you."

"I'm looking for a place to stay and I was told that you might have a room."

"Yes sir I do have a room," Normally she would have asked for some identification and references, but he looked so scared and forlorn she couldn't say no. Besides, she was in desperate need of the additional money.

"I'll take it."

"Don't you want to know how much?"

Robert felt embarrassed. His only thought was that it could not cost much in 1942.

She liked the way he looked. He seemed to be very well mannered and educated, although she was not sure what he was doing here in Hurley. "I need a week's rent in advanced. That's fifteen dollars."

"That's not a problem."

His room was on the third floor although small it had a great view of the city and the surrounding Gogebic Range. Even though the room was crowded, Robert felt at home. Down in the parlor, he found a phone book and looked up Martha Laine. She lived at 221 Nichol Street. Which he thought was just up from Iron Street where the Catholic School and Church were located. Tomorrow he would go out and start asking some questions. He already knew Nancy was teaching at the Catholic School. The only problem was that school was most likely out for the summer and she would not be there. He would have to see if she was at Martha Laine's house. How he explained to her why he was here, was going to be his next dilemma.

He had a second dilemma and that was once he found Nancy how was he going to get her back to the present. He was almost sure that he was going to have to use the time portal in the basement of Nuncio's pasty shop to go back. He did not believe he would be able to get back to the old ancient mining site. He was sure that Sally's café was where he wanted to be.

He really did not know why or how these two time openings worked separated by more than ten miles. He was sure that if he had to make a quick get away it had to be through the pasty shop basement.

* * *

The next day Robert was down early for breakfast after having a surprisingly good night's sleep. Yesterday's paper was there and he read it with intense interest about how the Germans had over run the British and captured Tobruk—a British strong hold. The article went on to say that, British forces were fearful that the Germans might capture the Suez Canal. Another article said the Germans were on the move in Russia launching another summer campaign in the south. It did not say anything about the battle, which had taken place the previous winter. The last Robert knew was that the Germans had surrounded the Russian capital. He was not sure if they had occupied the capital.

After finishing his coffee, he headed out to see if he could locate the Catholic Grade School where Nancy was teaching. He easily found the school and from the looks of it, there was no activity. There did not appear to be any summer school and he was sure Nancy was not there. He thought to himself, *if someone saw me out here looking around a school in 2010, they would most likely have reported me to the police. They would have had questions as to what I was doing there. My how things have changed or had they.*

From what he had read there were people molesting children back the 1940's only nobody thought a priest or other clergy would ever do such a thing. The people had complete trust in the church and the clergy. Robert knew however, some of the recent molestation cases that had come forth had taken place back in the 1940's. There was even the possibility the parish priest here could be involved although Robert had no proof and he hoped that it was not happening in a small town like Hurley.

He paused looking at the church. It stood on the side of the hill built on Fifth Avenue out of sandstone. It had several steps to travel up before reaching the entrance door. With time to spare he tried the door and found it unlocked and then he remembered that he was back in the past when people were still trusting and churches were not locked unlike in 2010 with so much vandalism.

Entering the church, he found it cool and soothing. He knelt in one of the pews in the back and from what he could see; he was the only one there. He found it strange to see the altar against the back wall of the church and there was a communion rail. He had seen pictures of this but had never seen it in person. He took refuge in the one fact that although the appearance of the church was different it was still the same Catholic faith. Jesus Christ was present here in the Eucharist in 1942 just as He was in 2010. Praying for a few minutes, that God would let him find Nancy and that his mission would be a success he left the church feeling better.

* * *

With his faith renewed, Robert started up the hill to Martha Laine's house to finally meet the woman he had been pursuing for the last six months. The house was a large two-story gingerbread house on what looked to be an acre lot. Robert could see that this was once a prominent house. It looked over the city. The house was beginning to show some early signs of neglect with some peeling white paint.

Before walking up the sidewalk leading to the front door he had a wave of apprehension wash over him. *What am I going to say to her? Hello, I'm here to take you back to the present, because if I don't you are going to die in just two weeks. Someone is going to strangle you and some of your friends are going to die too if I don't do something about it.*

Then reluctantly he walked up to the front door and rang the bell. He waited only a few moments before the woman he had been dreaming of for such a long time opened the door. He knew immediately that this was Nancy Monroe. She was much prettier than any of her pictures. He stood there with his mouth open unable speak. Then she said, "May I help you?"

He managed to blurt out, "You must be Nancy Monroe."

Robert could visibly see her stiffen and her face turned pale as she said, "Yes, I am. What is it that you want?"

"My name is Robert Rahn and I was wondering if I could come in and talk with you?"

The name Robert Rahn slammed into her brain as the name of the man who had been looking for her back in May. Before she even knew what she was doing, she found herself saying, "Come in."

They sat in the parlor and Nancy asked him if he wanted something to drink. "I'll have coffee if you have some made."

In just a few seconds, Nancy came back with the coffee and said, "What is it that you want of me Mr. Rahn?"

"I'm going to get right to the point because I don't know any other way to say what I have to say and there isn't a lot of time. I think you know my name and I think you know why I am here. I'm from the future—your time. From what I know of my time you have been changing history unintentionally and I think you know that too. I also have to warn you that your life may be in danger and lives of those around you. That is why you have to come back with me."

She was stunned and for more than a minute, she could not speak. She already knew that if he had gotten here than it was possible for someone else to follow. The main question was how was he going to get her back. She had not found a way.

"How do you know me and how did you know I was here?"

"When you disappeared in Hurley it made the paper and I followed your disappearance daily in the paper and on the internet. I have studied paranormal phenomena as a hobby for years and your disappearance fits all of the criteria. Then on January 14th your boyfriend, Michael Niffen, called me asking for my help."

"Why would he ask you for help? Why you?"

"He called me because I have a reputation as a clairvoyant. When I first moved up here I helped the police find a missing boy and since that time, people think I can help them find missing people and runaways. You see I moved up here from New York because I had a nervous break down after my wife and daughter were killed in New York City. I'm sort of a recluse, but I do follow certain stories and when I read about your disappearance in the paper I took an interest and tried to find out everything about you. Your disappearance was so unusual that I felt it had something to do with the paranormal."

"What exactly do you mean paranormal?"

"When there is no plausible explanation for an occurrence then I have come to believe that it can only be explained by the paranormal or supernatural. An alleged paranormal disappearance could be caused by what some might consider a tear in the fabric of time where people or objects somehow pass through into another dimension—a time portal of sorts. This causes a person—like what happened to you—to become out of step with their world in terms of time and space causing them to vanish.

This is exactly what I think happened to you and I think you will agree with that?"

"Yes, I agree, that is exactly what happened to me, but how did you find me if these things are random?"

"I studied your case and was able to find that something paranormal was taking place in Sally's Café basement. The only thing I could not find was an opening or time portal to your dimension in Sally's basement. I had a real good feeling it was there, but I was unable to locate it. I started to look for alternate openings. I knew that there had been some reported missing people around the area years back and I started searching my own property. There was one lady that disappeared back in 1975 while cross country skiing and was never found. Witnesses said they saw her just plain disappeared in front of their eyes, as if she fell into a hole. Yet extensive examination and search of the area found nothing. Over the years, there were a number of Indian legends regarding tribe members disappearing. In fact the Indians went as far as to designate certain land as scared where no one was allowed.

My house is not far from that Indian land and that cross-country ski trial is close to my house and while I was out searching, that is where I found one right on my own property. When I got to this one area, I had an odd feeling. Something came over me and it took me back to another time. I had no idea what time it was, but the land was completely different. Then a strange seizure like spell came over me. The next thing I knew I was back in the present. After I did some further searching, the next time I found an area that took me back to 1942. Maybe I was back in 1942 earlier, I do not know. As far as that goes, I still do not know how the time dimensions or portals work. The only problem was that while I was here in May I went back accidentally before I got a chance to find you. Now this time I was more prepared. I was more careful and that is how I came to be here today."

"How did you go back accidentally?"

"I was in Nuncios café and asked to use the bathroom downstairs and I stumbled upon a doorway that took me back to the present. There I was back in 2010 in the back of Sally's café. I'm don't really know how it happened, but I am sure there is a time portal opening in Nuncios basement even though I could not find it when I searched in 2010."

"I don't know what to say. This is all a shock to me. I tried to find a way back in the café basement too and found nothing. Until today I was resigning myself that I was going to be here for the rest of my life and I could only hope that I wouldn't change history any more than I already have. I don't want to be responsible for us loosing the war.

Another thing is that I met someone and I am sure that I am in love him and he loves me. Now I don't think I can go back with you and yet I don't want to change history."

"Nancy, your life is in danger if you stay here and the lives of those around you. I have good reason to believe…I'm not sure how to say this, that you will be killed on Friday July 3rd along with Martha and Gerald."

She was in shock. "How can you know such a thing?'

"Nancy, I went back and read the old papers from 1942 and in there I found your obituary along with Martha's and Gerald's. It is going to happen."

"Please, don't tell Martha or Gerald. What can we do to prevent this?

What if we were to move away from here? What if we moved to California? Would that get us away from those that are out to do us harm? Do you think that would work?"

"I don't know. It might save your life in the short run, but I have no idea what that would do to history?"

"Do you think it is possible to take Gerald, Martha, Beth and me back to 2010?"

"I don't know if that is possible."

She sat there with a blank expression on her face before saying, "There is just one more disturbing complication. When I was transported here, I had my purse and in it was my cell phone, a KINDLE, a digital camera, a calculator and a number of other things. Someone took all of these things during a break-in. Martha is sure she knows who took them and why. When I came here, a car hit me and a doctor treated me. As it turned out Martha worked for that doctor and that is how I came to live here. Needless to say when I arrived at the doctor's office, I looked different. My clothes were different and so was my appearance. Martha saw my driver's license, credit cards, my money and other things and while they puzzled her she hid them from the doctor. What she could not hide was my clothing that was like nothing manufactured in the United States. That is when, I'm sure that the doctor got suspicious and started to wonder where I was from. Martha knew right away that something was wrong. There was no way that anyone here in 1942 had a photo driver's license and on top of all that it expired in 2012. She could not believe that I was from the future, because that was impossible, but there was no other way to explain things. Anyway, she took me home, but there were enough things out of the ordinary that made the doctor think. That is why we believe they broke in to get more evidence and information. The worse thing is that they now have my cell phone, KINDLE, digital camera and calculator. From what you said earlier even if I went back with you to the future these things would still be here. Think about how that could change the future of the war if they got into the wrong hands?"

"You're right, but we have got to take this slow. If whoever has the items got them into enemy hands, there is no telling how damaging that could be. We might all be speaking German or Japanese in the future.

We have to get these things back. What can you tell me about the people that you think took your stuff?"

"I would rather wait for Martha to come home before we talk about that. She can explain it better. Then too, I think we have to involve my boyfriend, Gerald, in anything that we have planned."

"I agree. Do you have any more coffee?"

Chapter Eighty-three

Wednesday June 24, 1942

Martha arrived home just after five that evening. She was surprised to see Nancy in the front sitting room with a man she had never seen before.

"Nancy, I didn't know you were having company? I'm Martha Laine."

"My name is Robert Rahn, please to meet you."

Robert could see from the reaction on Martha's face that she knew who he was.

Before Martha could say anything, Nancy blurted out. "Martha let me explain. Robert is from the future, from my future and told me that my life is in danger if I stay here. Your life could be in danger too. He wants to take me back. What am I going to do about Gerald and Beth? I love them both, I just can't go back. I belong here."

Then she started to cry.

After Nancy's out burst, Martha stood there not knowing what to say. She remained standing looking back and forth at Robert and Nancy. Then she turned and crossed the room, closed her eyes, shook her head to clear her mind. "Tell me everything. Let's all settle back and take this one thing at a time. An old lady like me could have a heart attack. I'll get us something to drink and then we can start at the beginning."

Martha returned with a bottle of brandy and three glasses with ice.

"There now let's relax a little and start from the beginning. I'm not sure how you got here Robert, but nothing surprises me now. I knew you were looking for Nancy back in May. Did Nancy tell you about the break-in and what was taken?"

"Yes, she did."

Before Robert could add anything more Martha said, "Those things that Nancy brought with her that were taken cannot be allowed to fall into the wrong hands. If the Germans were to get advanced technology like that, think about what they might be able to do."

Robert added, "During the last days of the war the Germans had advanced rocket technology and jet planes. With this technology think about what they could do. They might be able to win the war easily. We have to get those things back and take them back to the future with us or destroy them. Who has your things right now?"

"Oscar Kosken and his Alliance cronies. Is there any chance you think we can get them back?"

"You mean steal them back," said Martha.

"Yes, I think that is our only option, unless we could destroy them somehow. Perhaps we need a day or so to think about all of this. It must be a really shock having me here. I'll plan on coming back Thursday evening if that works for you and Nancy. You should invite Gerald too. He is a part of this whether he knows it or not. In the meantime I'll do some checking around and see what more I can learn about the Alliance," said Robert.

"That sounds like a great idea. We have to have a plan if we are going to beat these guys. I'll fix dinner for all of us," said Martha.

"I'll call Gerald and tell him to come over around five," said Nancy.

* * *

As Robert walked back to the boarding house he was unaware that Marvin Coppalo was following him and had been watching him at Martha's house all evening.

Robert was busy going over everything in his head. So much had happened. He could not help thinking about Nancy Monroe. She was beautiful and charming. He was disappointed to know that she had found someone here in the past that loved her although he was happy for her. The fact that she wanted to stay here surprised him and the more he thought about it, it might be good if she stayed. What would he really do if he brought her back to the present? How would he explain how he found her? He couldn't just say that she fell through a dimension in time and had gone into the past for the last six months. He thought that perhaps with enough time and money he might be able to fabricate a story that the press and the public would believe. If she stayed here, how was he going to guarantee her safety? The only thought he had was that he would have to take out the Alliance. That was not something he wanted to consider. Then to he thought about how greatly disappointed he would be not having her in his life.

* * *

When Marvin Coppalo arrived home, he went immediately to see his father. It had been well over a month that he and Henry Frost had been watching Nancy Monroe and nothing had happened until tonight. The money was good, but it was a boring job. Marvin thought that while Nancy Monroe was one beautiful woman she lived the most boring life.

"Dad, a man came to see Nancy Monroe about five in the afternoon. He stayed until around nine and then I followed him to Ellen Warner's boarding house."

"Is he staying at the boarding house?"

"Yes, from what I could tell. I waited until eleven and he did not come out."

"If he is staying there then he is not from around here. What did he look like?"

"He looked to be around thirty years old, not real big, maybe five foot eight and about a hundred forty pounds."

"Since it is summer I want you to watch what he does tomorrow. Get Henry to help. Good work."

Chapter Eighty-four

Wednesday June 24, 1942

Oscar Kosken did not have a good feeling about the way the meeting had gone with Henrik Dahl and Ethan Lynch. Actually, he was having a bad feeling about almost everything. His instincts told him not to trust Henrik. He could see that Henrik had no respect for any of them and he made no bones about showing his displeasure by telling them how superior he was to them and how lucky they were to have met up with someone of his expertise that could handle what they wanted. He clearly told them, that without him they would not make a penny on any of this stuff. He could tell that Henrik was disappointed when given only the adding machine to examine. Oscar thought the only reason Henrik agreed to the deal was that he was afraid that this opportunity might fall apart if he did not agree to the Alliance demands.

Oscar could not put his finger on it but it seemed to him that Henrik had another motive other than money for wanting to have all of the devises at once. What it was he could not be sure. That was when he decided to do a little research into his background. Just who was this Henrik Dahl?

That evening Oscar contacted, Jeff Fisher, a detective friend of his and asked him to investigate Henrik Dahl.

* * *

At the end of the week, Jeff Fisher called Oscar with what he had found.

"Oscar, I'm not sure you are going to like what I found out about your guy, Henrik. I was only able to scratch the surface, because the FBI is also interested in this guy."

"Tell me what you found, stop skirting around the edges."

"First, Henrik Dahl is not a natural born citizen. He came here with his family from Germany in 1914 just before the start of World War I when he was just a teenager. Let's just say that Henrik and his family were more loyal to Germany than the United States. Safe to say he identified with his ethnic identity. In the late 1930's he was connected to some pro-German groups that believed in Adolph Hitler and his Third Reich. Waiting for the day when Nazism would triumphant in the United States.

Henrik Dahl had a connection with one of the best-known group, German American Bund, an American Nazi organization established in 1936 to promote a favorable view of Nazi Germany. Before the group fell out of favor, Henrik Dahl was a major contributor.

It is not clear what his connected is with them now, but it is safe to say he is not working in the best interest of the United States. I'd be very careful in dealing with him."

"Thanks for the information. I have to say I never expected this. I just didn't trust the guy. Now we know where we stand."

"Just be careful and remember that the FBI has a real interest in this guy, I don't want to see you get mixed up with the FBI in the middle of this war."

* * *

That evening Oscar called an emergency Alliance meeting at his house. After everyone had arrived, Oscar told them what he had found out about Henrik Dahl.

After hearing all the facts, Oscar went on to say, "I don't mind making a buck off of this war, but I'm not about to jeopardize my country. I am an American and I won't do anything to harm this country."

"Oscar, do you think Dahl is going to use what he finds out about these gadgets to help the Germans?" said Peter Cadence.

"That's exactly what I'm saying. I'm afraid we may have harmed the United States by giving him that adding machine thing to look at and I'm saying he gets none of the other things no matter how much money he offers us. Are we in agreement?"

The rest of the Alliance all agreed.

"So how are we going to handle this from here on out. You know Dahl will want to see the rest of the things we've got. He's already has seen pictures," said Leo Coppalo.

"Here is what I am proposing. We take out Dahl and maybe we have to take out Ethan Lynch too."

"Isn't that a little drastic?" said Dr. Frost.

"In peace time I'd agree with you, but this is a time of war and I think we should do what is in the best interest of out country. If you guys have no objections I'll call my friend, Stan Offenbach, from Milwaukee and have him take care of the situation. I know he'll do anything for money and he will be discreet."

"What about Nancy Monroe, Martha Laine and that guy that has been snooping around town, Robert Rahn. What are we going to do about them?" said Fred Banister.

"I'm not sure, maybe Stan could take care of those three too. For right now let's just focus on Dahl and Lynch," said Oscar.

All agreed and the meeting adjourned.

Chapter Eighty-five

Thursday June 25, 1942

When Robert woke early on Thursday morning, he looked around his small boxlike room and still could not quite believe how he got here. *Did I really meet and talk with Nancy Monroe?*

He had a real predicament on his hands. It was no longer just about getting Nancy back to 2010. Things were more complicated than that. He knew that if nothing was done, Nancy, Martha and Gerald, her boyfriend, were going to die on July 3rd. He was not sure how to prevent that. Taking Nancy back may save everybody, but he didn't know for sure. He could stay and try to prevent their deaths from happening, but he was not sure how to do that. Did that mean killing all the members of the Alliance? He wasn't sure he could do that.

The other thing was how to make sure that all of Nancy's high tech devices did not fall into the wrong hands. Could he risk taking her back and leaving her things to fall into the wrong hands. Than on top of all of that, the full moon was on Sunday June 28th and if his theory held up he would have to have Nancy out by Sunday or lose the time portal opening. His only hope was that maybe just maybe the portal would remain open a few days after the full moon. In the end, he decided that he was just going to have to let this whole thing play out.

* * *

In the past he thought that he might be in love with Nancy from just seeing her picture, now meeting her in person, he was sure that he was in love with her. She was really the first nice girl since Debra died. Saying that she was a nice girl was an understatement if not an outright lie. She was beautiful and intelligent. He had this love for her, but from what he had observed it was not reciprocal on her part. He hoped he was not trying to make her into a new Debra. That was something that would not be fair to her or to him. Besides all of that, she already appeared to be in love with Gerald Kershaw and even if he did get her back to the present there was always a chance he'd have to deal with Michael Niffen. For now this was something that he could not worry about, there were too many other things going on.

The smell of coffee brewing down stairs brought him back to his senses. He was really in the year 1942 and today he had a lot of work to do before meeting everyone at Martha Laine's house for dinner this evening. His first job would be learning as much as he could about the Alliance members without attracting any attention.

After breakfast, he went back to his room to retrieve his Glock 26 along with one extra clip. He didn't think he would need the gun but it was better to be prepared. As he slipped the gun into the holster under his coat, he wondered what the gun laws were in 1942. Was the NRA a big factor? He wasn't even sure if the NRA existed in 1942. He just knew that on this occasion he agreed with their philosophy. He had a right to defend himself.

* * *

Walking down Silver Street, he found himself outside of the pharmacy and decided to go and talk with the owner, Al Hidde. This early in the morning Al was the only one in the store and Robert gave thanks to God for that.

"Mr. Hidde, do you remember me from yesterday?"

"Call me Al. Did you find a room at Ellen's?"

"Yes, I did. She is a very nice lady."

"Yes, she is. Lost her husband, killed at Peal Harbor. What a shame. They never really had much of a life together. What can I do for you today?"

"Well I was looking for a job and someone at the boarding house said that perhaps members of the Alliance were hiring and that was all they said. Can you tell me anything about this Alliance? Is it a company?"

"No, the Alliance is not a company. They are a group of wealthy businessmen that think they run this town and I suppose in someway they really do. They have their fingers into almost everything in town."

Although they were the only ones in the Pharmacy, Al looked around to see if they were alone before he said, "Let's just say that anyone who presents a challenge to the group's agenda does not survive in this town."

"What do you mean?"

"I mean the challengers either apologize for what they have said or they seem to fall victim to an unfortunate accident or simply disappear. You have to understand that the continued survival of the Alliance requires putting down all attacks real or perceived. The bottom line for them is all about having and maintaining power within the community. They need to be the ones in control. They think they are above the law. Let's just leave it at that."

"Do they have a place of business?"

"No, they are all separate businessmen including Doctor Frost, but they do have a place out in the country they call the club house where they have their meetings."

"Is it far out from the city?"

"You go out about ten miles west on US 2 and then turn north onto Cedar Swamp road for about two miles, there place is located in the town of Mason. I shouldn't have told you this much. You look like a real nice guy, so don't go getting involved with them?"

"Don't worry, I'll be careful. Thanks for your help."

* * *

Robert left the pharmacy and continued down the street until he came to Nuncio's Café. He paused for a minute to take in the view of the Burton House.

Upon entering the café and ordering coffee, he could tell that the place was the same as it had been on his first visit. Seeing the door to the basement, he was sure that nothing had changed and he was sure that if an escape route was needed in a hurry this might very well be his only option. He could only hope that the cellar door to the outside was still there and functioning as a time portal back to the present.

As he was finishing his coffee, looking out the window he spotted two teenage boys who were standing across the street just looking at the café. He thought it was strange to see the two of them up this early in the morning. He made a mental note to see if they followed him once he left the café.

For now, he had to see if he could find that place where the Alliance met. He thought it was too far to walk and he was not sure how he was going to get a car. It occurred to him that perhaps he could use Martha's car. He remembered that Martha worked for a doctor who had his office upstairs in one of the buildings on Silver Street. Because Silver Street was not very long he set out to find where she worked.

* * *

As he walked along looking at signs, he noticed that the two teenagers were behind him. If they were following him, they made no effort to conceal their intensions. In the next block he came across a two story building with a separate door which appeared to lead to the upstairs. The door sign said, Dr. Frost M.D.

He was sure this was where Martha worked. As he headed up the stairs, he noticed that his two young friends were still behind him.

At the top of the stairs, he saw Martha. She had a surprised look on here face. "Mr. Rahn didn't expect to see you until this evening for dinner. Are you feeling alright?"

"I'm fine Martha and please call me Robert. I was just walking around and thought I'd stop by and say hello and see where you worked."

"This is it. I've been here now for thirty years."

"Martha, I have a favor to ask. Could I use your car? I'd like to take a look at the surrounding country side."

At first, Martha was reluctant to give him her car. After all, she hardly new the man other than the fact that he said he was from the future and that he knew Nancy.

"Well I suppose it will be all right. The car is in the garage and the keys are in it. Please be careful with it."

"I'll take good care of it and will have it back when I see you for dinner this evening."

* * *

As Robert walked back up the hill to Martha's house, he noticed that his friends were still following, but now from some distance behind.

He moved up the hill and while he was out of sight of his pursuers, he ducked in between two houses and waited. As they approached he step out starling them saying, "So why are two young guys following me around? I'd think that you have better things to do on a nice summer day? What are your names?"

Their first instinct was to run, but realized that they had been found out and without thinking blurted out their names. "I'm Henry Frost and this is Marvin Coppalo."

"Is your father Dr. Frost?"

"Yes, he is."

Robert knew Dr. Frost and remembered the pharmacist, said that he was a member of the Alliance. *Could it be they are following me because they know who I am?*

"So what's it to you mister. We may be at war, but this is still a free country and we can go anywhere we want," said Henry. With that they ran off down the hill out of sight.

Robert was sure that they were going to report to their fathers, members of the Alliance. He remembered what Al Hidde said, "Don't trust the Alliance."

* * *

With his teenage spies out of the way, he went and got Martha's car out of the garage. It was a Hudson with a stick shift and Robert could not image driving such a machine.

He went out on highway 77 heading west just trying get use to the car and the roads. When he saw a sign that said County Trunk C, he slowed down remembering that this was where Karl Prosser lived. Turning on to C, he tried to remember if Karl had always lived there. *Was it the original homestead?* With time, he decided to check out where Karl was now living.

Slowing down to where Karl's driveway was in 2010, he saw the name Prosser on the mailbox. This had to be the place. Driving in he saw a young teenage boy working in a large garden. The boy looked up and started over to the car. Even from this distance, Robert could tell that this was a young Karl Prosser.

When the lad was ten feet from the car he said, "Hey Mister, can I help you. If you're looking for my folks, they are in town shopping."

Robert was astonished; he could not believe his eyes. He was really looking at a young Karl. He thought, *will Karl remember this meeting if I ever get back?*

"Actually I was looking for directions and perhaps you can help me? I'm looking for a place that a group of men have west of town and one of the men is Doctor Frost."

A scowl came over his face and then he said, "Are you sure you want to go out there?"

"I just want to drive by and see the place."

"Well mister, Doctor Frost is part of a group called the Alliance and they are really not the friendliest people. I go to school with Doctor's Frost son, Henry and believe Henry is like his father and they don't take kindly to anyone that interferes in their business. Especially a stranger and you don't look to be from around here."

"Well, thanks for the advice, but all I was going to do was drive by and take a look. Can you give me directions?"

"I'll give you direction, but I'm telling you to be careful. There was a case just this past winter where a man was snowshoeing near their place and he was beaten pretty bad. There was no way to connect it to the Alliance but everyone knew what happened. It was just another warning to people to stay away.

"So if you still want to take a look go back on C until you hit 77 again and go back into town and take U.S. 2 out about ten miles until you come to the Cedar Swamp road in the town of Mason. I think it is about a mile back and hidden in the woods. As far as I remember there is no sign, except for all of the "No Trespassing" signs warning people."

"Thanks for the directions. Their place is not far from mine. I live on Lake Forest Road about eight miles out on U.S. 2."

"Mister, I think there is a logging road out there, but as far as I know there is no Lake Forest Road. Are you sure, that is where you live?"

Robert blushed feeling foolish, it was possible the road had not been named in 1942.

"I'm sorry it was just a slip of the tongue, I must have been thinking of another town road, but I do live out that way."

As the young seventeen-year-old Karl Prosser watched Robert drive away, he could not help but think how strange the man was. It was like, he didn't belong here.

Once on Cedar Swamp road Robert knew, he had to be near the place because of all of the "No Trespassing" signs that were nailed to the trees every fifty feet. When he came to what appeared to be the main driveway he found a steel cable across the road with a sign that read, **Private Road.** Nailed to a near by tree was a smaller sign which said, **Trespassers will be shot on sight.**

Robert was sure that such a warning sign in 2010 was against the law, but perhaps in 1942 it was legal or tolerated in the rural areas. He remembered the President signing an order in February 1942 that rounded up all the Japanese American citizens. They were put in concentration camps or as they called them internment camps.

Robert felt a tinge of fear in his stomach. From what he could see, the road appeared to go deep into the woods winding its way through trees and underbrush.

After a lengthy pause, he decided not to explore any further. He would take what he had learned back to the meeting tonight at Martha's house and see what the team had to say.

Chapter Eighty-six

Thursday June 25, 1942

That evening everyone gathered at Martha's house to have dinner. When Robert arrived he found Martha, Nancy, Gerald and his daughter Beth already there. Although they were all there for dinner they all knew that dinner was secondary to what everyone had on their minds, except perhaps for Beth, but it appeared that she too knew there was something more important than dinner.

Once they had finished eating and cleared the table, they all sat down except for Beth. She had her books to read and Gerald explained that this was an adult's only conversation. She mildly protested, but understood.

Martha was first to speak. "I don't think I'll get use to the idea that someone can travel through time. Yet I know it is real, all I have to do is just look at you Nancy to know that.

I still feel like I'm living in some sort of a dream. I knew Nancy was different since the day I first met her, but in no way would I have said she was from the future other than the dates on her license, credit cards and the clothes she was wearing. My thought was that she was gifted with being able to see the future.

I was just getting use to the idea that Nancy was from the future and now you show up Robert. I'm still trying to get my arms around that. What's going to happen next?"

"I love Nancy and I haven't really got a clue as to where we go from here," said Gerald.

"Has Nancy filled you in why I'm here, Gerald," said Robert.

"Yes, she has and I'm still trying to rationalize everything. She filled me in on the fact that some things in the war have changed since she's been here and that she is concerned that she might be changing the future. I'm still not sure what we can do about it."

"First, the war has not changed so dramatically to make me think that the war could be lost. Pearl Harbor was about the same except for that third wave of bombers and the battle of Midway was a draw instead of a complete victory for the United States. That only means that now the Japanese have a better chance of winning the war. As for Germany things have not changed that much. They surrounded Moscow but were unable to take the city.

What really bothers me most is the things that were taken from Nancy when she arrived here, if the enemy were to get a hold of that stuff, they might be able to develop all kinds of that technology before we had chance to win the war?" said Robert.

"If I hear what you are saying, the first and most important thing is for us to get back all of Nancy things," said Gerald.

"Yes, think about what they could learn by having a cell phone, KINDLE book reader, a hand held calculator and a digital camera. The one thing that might stop them is that this technology is so advanced—68 years in the future—that it would take them years to develop before it would give them an advantage in the war. The question is can we afford to take that chance? I don't want to go back to 2010 and find that instead of the Russian and the Chinese as our enemies it is the Germans and Japanese. That is assuming we were not invaded and occupied. Therefore, we have to make a plan to figure out how to get that stuff back and soon," said Robert.

"What if we just let everything alone and see what happens? What If Nancy were to stay here and marry Gerald? How could that change the world? I think maybe we should just leave things the way they are. Besides Robert, if things didn't turn out right couldn't you just come back and change them?" said Martha.

"Martha, like I said earlier, I have good reason to believe that your lives are in danger. I suppose as you said we could just leave things alone and see what would happen, but if anything happen to any of you, I have no idea if I could come back and change things. There is no way that I can determine how these time dimensions and parallel worlds work for sure. I'm not sure anyone could just come and go at will. If that were the case, the Japs and the Germans could do the same thing. I think we have got to get those things back and then I believe that Nancy and I have to get back to the present," said Robert.

"When you said that we were in danger before you never elaborated? Just what kind of danger are we in," said Martha.

Nancy gave Robert a warning look asking him not to elaborate, but he had to be fair to them. They should know. He was talking about their lives.

"Back in 2010, I looked up old obituaries from 1942 and I found that you, Nancy and Gerald all died on the same date—July 3, 1942. Now can you see why this is urgent?"

Robert could see the breath come out of both Martha and Gerald. They were speechless. Then Gerald said, "Do you know if anything happened to Beth?"

"I didn't find anything on Beth as far as I know nothing happened to her other than she would be orphaned."

"How do we die? Did you find that out?" Martha said.

"Yes, all I'll say is that you all met violent deaths and I'm sure the Alliance was behind what happened," said Robert.

"That gives us seven days to prevent this from happening. What are we going to do next," said Martha.

"Martha, Robert, I love Gerald and I want to stay here and be his wife no matter what happens. Now that we know when we are going to die, I'm sure that we can devise a plan to prevent it. Furthermore I've gotten use to living in 1942 except for the war."

"That's my point Nancy. If you stayed here and we could prevent your deaths, we don't know how that would change the outcome of the war. We would still have to find a way to get your things back. Think about what could happen if the Germans got hold of your devices and it helped them win the war. What kind of a world would this be if the Germans were victorious? Nancy, you and I both know what the Germans did to the Jews in Second World War. Even if they were contained in Europe, think about how many Jews and other people would be killed. What do you think would happen to all those people in the rest of Europe and Russia, if they won the war, how long do you think it would be before they would attack the United States? Another factor is what would the Japanese be doing? We cannot afford to take the chance and do nothing?"

"Robert makes a good point. There are so many unanswered questions. I say we work on a plan to get back Nancy's things first. Like you said Robert, it would not do us any good if you and Nancy went back to the present and the Germans and Japanese were to have all of this technology," said Gerald.

"Are we certain that the Alliance has all of the gadgets?" said Robert.

"Yes, I'm positive that the Alliance has everything, unless they have contacted others," said Martha.

"So the question is, how do we go about getting them back," said Gerald.

"I think they may have your things out at their club house or what ever they call that place in the woods. Now how do we go about breaking in," said Martha.

"My plan for now would be to scout out the place, but I'll need to have a car," said Robert.

"We can use my car, but I'm coming with you," said Gerald.

"Are you sure that is a good idea?"

"Yes, I have a big stake in all of this. I'm in love with Nancy."

"Tomorrow is Friday, give me the weekend to nose around and see what I can find out about the Alliance. Then maybe next week Gerald, you and I can go there and have a look. Does that work for you?"

"Sounds like a plan."

"Before you leave there is one more thing. I discovered that the time portal in 2010 opens a few days before the full moon, but I'm not sure how it works in 1942. The full moon is on Sunday June 28th and it looks like there is no way we are going to be ready to leave here on that date. Beyond that date, I'm not sure if we can get back or if we'll have to wait until the next full moon in July. I'm resigned to letting this play out and do the best we can to prevent everyone from dying."

"I agree Robert. I will talk to you on the weekend. It's late and I have to get Beth home."

"Call me," said Nancy.

He kissed her good night and left.

* * *

After Robert and Gerald had left, Nancy and Martha sat up and had another drink.

"Martha, what are you thinking?"

"In so many ways I have a hard time thinking that any of this is real. Time travel, you have got to be kidding. Now I even know the day I'm going to die. I'd like to see you and Gerald marry and live happily ever after, but in today's world, I'm not sure that can happen. I think Robert has a point; it is up to us to stop this and make sure the war ends with us as the winner. We are going to have to think about what is right for the country and world and not just about us."

"I guess you are right Martha. I see what you mean. Robert told me when I was going to die, but I didn't want him telling you and Gerald, but I guess he was only being fair to warn you. I need to go to bed and sleep on all of this. I'm exhausted."

"So am I child, let's go to bed."

Chapter Eighty-seven

Saturday June 27, 1942

On Saturday, Nancy and Martha went to confession. Like the old saying, "confession is good for the soul," they both thought they could use some forgiveness and some assurance from Father Schuster. Nancy also wanted to warn Father Schuster about what was going to happen in the future concerning his young assistant. She wasn't at all sure that Father Schuster would take her seriously, but she had to try. She had ruled out talking to the young priest herself, because she thought he would not understand. She thought she had a better chance with Father Schuster. He mighty have more influence on the young priest.

"Bless me Father for I have sinned, my last confession was five weeks ago."

"Yes, what do you want to confess today?"

"Father I'm not exactly sure where to start. I'm not really here to confess my sins, but to warn you of some sinful things that are going to happen in the future."

"What are you talking about? This is a scared sacrament and is not for you to abuse."

"Father, please hear me out. I have to tell you this because I thought you should know and I also think God sent me here so that I could give you this warning."

"This is beginning to sound outlandish, but continue. What is it that you want to warn me about?"

"Your young assistant, Jacob Unger, will molest and abuse children in the future. I don't think that he has done anything yet, but he will. I want you to know this so that you can council him and perhaps you can prevent this from happening."

There was a long silence on the other side of the confessional screen. "How can you know that something like this is going to happen?" Before she replied, Father Schuster knew who she was—Nancy Monroe.

"I just know Father."

"You're Nancy Monroe, the school teacher. People said that you know the future, but I did not believe them. Now I'm not so sure. When does this take place?"

"He will be found out in 1975, but I think he may have started before that. We have to get him into counseling. I need your help Father."

"This is all so preposterous. You expect me to believe you. There is no way you can know the future and I'm not about to ruin a young man's future because of what you are telling me. That is all I want to hear from you. It is a good thing that we are under the seal of confession otherwise; you would be the one I'd have committed. Good Day!"

"Before you dismiss me Father there are few other things you should know."

"I don't have time for this young lady.'

"Father, just listen. In the future, the church will change in ways you can't imagine. The mass will be in English, the altar will face the front, there will be no communion rail and the people will be allowed to receive the precious blood of Christ. That is just a few of the changes coming. They will happen, Father.

What I told you about Father Unger will happen unless you can get him help and counseling. He is not an isolated case. The number of priests found abusing young people will be great. There will be cover-ups and the Church will spend millions of dollars to settle lawsuits. Some dioceses will have to declare bankruptcy. There will be a shortage of priests."

"Stop I have heard enough out of you. Get out of this confessional. You are lucky that I am not allowed to use this against you. Otherwise, I can assure you, that you would not have a job come September nor would I allow you to be a member of this parish. Now get out!"

As Nancy left the confessional, she was disappointed, but was glad that she told him these things. She knew that all of this had come as a great shock, but perhaps in time he might be able to see things in a different light. Maybe he would at least talk with Father Unger.

Chapter Eighty-eight

Sunday June 28, 1942

Henrik knew that he had to have the real things if he was going to help the German war effort. He could not wait any longer.

As far as he could see, the war was beginning to take a different course and it did not look good. The Germans had suffered several set backs. Things did not look good on the Russian front or in North Africa; he had to make a move now.

Late on Sunday morning, Henrik Dahl called Ethan Lynch.

"Ethan, I was wondering if you could go with me over to Hurley say tomorrow for a few days. There are a number of things I want to check out."

Because Ethan was thinking that Henrik might be a spy, he was apprehensive. "Just what kind of things are we talking about?"

"After examining that adding machine which is really a sophisticated calculator, I just have to know more. That calculator was the most unbelievable thing I've ever seen. It is solar powered. I've got to know more. I want to check out the Alliance and maybe see if I can figure out where they are keeping the rest of the stuff. I'd also like to meet the blonde lady, Nancy Monroe. Maybe we can get her to talk since you think she is involved."

"I'll help you, but I don't want to be involved with anything illegal, like when you say maybe we can make her talk. What are you planning to do? I'm not going to get into any kind of torture forcing her to talk."

"Now Ethan, don't go getting all honest on me. You know you've done enough things in your life that have not been on the up and up. So don't go getting righteous on me now. I'm not talking about torturing her. I just want to persuade her to open up a little bit. After all, you thought she might be the one that had all of these things in the beginning and that the Alliance stole then from her. She may be willing to confide in us."

"Yes, I hear you. I don't like messing around with the Alliance. I know those guys and they don't play by the rules. As for that blonde lady, I don't think that she is capable of making those things unless she is from the future no matter how far fetched that sounds."

"Here's the deal. You be ready Monday morning. We're going to Hurley to do a little snooping around. I'll make it worth your while and I promise you, I am not planning to get involved with the law."

"Okay, you win, I'll go with you, but no funny stuff."

* * *

After Henrik hung up the phone, he thought to himself, *No need to worry Ethan about getting into trouble with the Alliance after this little trip you will have nothing to worry about. On the way home, you'll be resting peacefully somewhere in the back woods of Wisconsin.*

Right now I need to keep you alive so that I can use you as my go between with Leo Coppalo and the Alliance. Besides, I think you have lost trust in me and are no longer loyal.

* * *

Later that night Ethan placed a call to Leo Coppalo.

"Leo, this is Ethan, I'm planning to be in Hurley later this week."

"What brings you here?"

"I'm coming with Henrik Dahl, he asked me to come along. I'm not sure just what his plans are. The only thing he told me is that he wanted to talk with you and the rest of the Alliance and that I was going to be the go between. He was so impressed with that adding machine that I know he wants to get his hands on the rest of the stuff. My concern is that he no longer wants all of the things for the money he can make; I think he wants to pass that technology and information on to the Germans. I think he has already been in touch with a U.S. Nazi group concerning these things. He even said something about stuff like this could change the course of the war. Leo I'm worried. I can't go along with that. I'm still an American. I just wanted to warn you. I think he doesn't care how he gets the things and he might even go after Nancy Monroe and try to make her talk. I'm not sure what he is going to do."

"Thanks for the heads-up. I'll get the rest of the Alliance guys together and warn them. Maybe we have to take some preemptive action. I'll see what they want to do. Ethan, if you can call me with any more information that would be helpful. Watch yourself, I don't trust Henrik either."

Chapter Eighty-nine

Monday June 29, 1942

Throughout the month of June FBI agent Thomas Appleton was not idle. He spent the majority of his time continuing to watch Henrik Dahl's every move even though his Director had cleared Dahl as a threat to the United States. Appleton thought he was still a threat and while he was disobeying a directive from up above he knew that nobody ever monitored his activates in this out of the way post. Appleton was sure that Dahl maintained a connection with a Midwestern German American organization that believed in Adolph Hitler and the Third Reich. He knew that Dahl was still fond of his German heritage and admired Adolph Hitler and the Nazis and at one time had given money to the German-American Bund.

Therefore, when Appleton discovered on one of his wiretaps that Dahl had contacted Ethan Lynch concerning a trip to Hurley to meet with Leo Coppalo and the Alliance, Appleton knew he was going to follow.

Ever since that meeting at the Spaulding Hotel in Duluth, Appleton knew the Alliance members had come into possession of some things that they termed futuristic. From the conversation at the hotel, Appleton knew that Lynch did not have the actual devices, but only pictures, but he had a good idea what they were talking about. There was a camera with no film, a reading device with a typewriter like keyboard, a very small adding machine and some sort of small telephone.

From everything he over heard he knew that the blonde woman, Nancy Monroe, was the key to everything. He had researched Nancy Monroe for the last month and was unable to find out anything about her. It was as if she had no past other than showing up in Hurley in November of 1941. Even with all of the resources he had available, he was unable to learn more. How she fit into all of this was a mystery. He did not want to believe that she was some how from the future. Things like that did not happen, there had to a logical explanation. Was it possible that she was the inventor, but who manufactured the items for her?

* * *

On Monday afternoon, Thomas Appleton made the trip to Hurley following Dahl and Lynch. His objective was to observe Dahl and see if they contacted any of the Alliance members or Nancy Monroe. If circumstances worked out, he was going to visit Nancy Monroe himself. Maybe he would be able to gain some credible information from her.

Chapter Ninety

Monday Evening June 29, 1942

Monday evening found the group meeting at Martha's house. By this time everyone had come to grips with the idea that time travel or what Robert Rahn called slipping from one time dimension to another was possible no matter how far outlandish it seemed. They all knew now, that they had to do something otherwise the future of the world was going to change dramatically. The subject of tonight's meeting was how to get back Nancy's things.

After dinner Martha, Nancy, Gerald and Robert sat around the dinning room table. Beth was coloring in the den. Robert began with a review of the situation.

"You know that Nancy and I are from the future and in our future the Germans and the Japanese loose the war. It ends in May of 1945 for the Germans. The Japanese, do not surrender until the United States drops two nuclear bombs on two Japanese cities in August. The official end to the war is September 2, 1945.

We are here to make sure that this does not change. Nancy and I know some things have already changed just by Nancy being here in 1942. The third air strike by Japan at Pearl Harbor and changes in the Battle of Midway has already taken place giving the Japanese an advantage they did not have before. We know the Germans suffered a defeat at Moscow, but not as bad as it had been. Things have changed and I'm not sure what else would change if Nancy and I just remained here.

To complicate matters Nancy came here with a cell phone, a book reader/KINDLE, calculator and digital camera. Some of these inventions will not be seen in the world until the year 2000. What we have to think about is if that technology can be deciphered by the Germans and implemented, think of what they could do with it. By 1944 the Germans will have invented and launch the V-1 and V-2 missiles at England. I worry about what they could do with a better guidance system they might be able to get from Nancy's things. We have to get those things back. Does everyone agree?"

"Robert, I'm still having a hard time trying to comprehend what these things do, much less think about what the Germans could do with them," said Gerald.

"Take the cell phone. In our world, almost every one has one. You can communicate from any place in the world. There are no wires. The book reader or the brand name KINDLE allows you to read a book on a screen that is extremely small. When you've read one book you can simply get another book or magazine sent to you for a fee. The digital camera allows you to take pictures and see them immediately. Then you can down load the pictures to your own personal computer for printing."

"You lost me Robert. What do you mean by downloading and how is it possible for you to see the pictures instantly?" said Martha.

"I'm sorry Martha, there is just too much to explain. Think about it. We are talking about 68 years of technology improvements. I do not understand everything, but I will tell you that we have very small computers that fit on a desk and can process all kinds of information. You can look at pictures and you can send all of that information to almost anyone anywhere in the world. There just isn't time to explain everything."

"I will have to admit; perhaps we might be worried about nothing. These things have what we call computer chips in them. The chips are extremely small and I don't think no matter how clever the Germans are that they are going to be able to adopt this technology over night much less put it into production. So maybe none of these things will change the world before the war ends. However given time, these things could change future history so that the world of 2010 is completely different from what Nancy and I know. Therefore, the question is can we take that chance. I think we have got to get all of Nancy's things back or some how eliminate those that now have them."

"Whoa, wait a minute when you say eliminate, what do you mean. Do you mean kill them? Because if that is what you are talking about count me out. I'll take what the world and God has in store for me rather than take someone's life no matter how bad or what kind of threat that person might be," said Martha.

"I understand how you feel Martha. The only thing I can say is that we will do our best not to take anyone's life. Let's just focus on how to get the things back or how to destroy them.

Then the next thing we have to consider is whether Nancy should go back to the present. I'm extremely concerned that by her being here things could change more and now that there are more people involved. My thought is that Nancy will always be a target if she remains here."

"Robert, I'm staying here. I love Gerald, Beth and Martha. I don't know what I'd do without the three of you. The only way I'd consider leaving is if they went back with me."

"Nancy, I love you too and I'd miss you but I'm an old woman and there is no way I want to go live in the future. I belong here, honey."

"Nancy, I'm not sure how Beth and I could go. How could we hope to fit into the world of the future? I want you to stay. I want to marry you and live with you forever," said Gerald.

"Let's just focus for the time being on how to get Nancy's thing back and then we can go from there. I'm worried that the Alliance people have already been looking for a buyer. I'm also worried that they might try to take Nancy and make her talk especially if they think she is from the future.

Then there is that person that came to see you at the school. I don't know how he fits into all of this but he could be the buyer, I get the feeling there could be a lot of money involved in all of this."

"So where does that leave us," said Gerald.

"Here's what I have in mind. Let me see what else I can find out about the Alliance and maybe get a read on where they have the stuff. Martha, see what you can get out of Dr. Frost. Maybe he will let something slip out.

Nancy you have to be very careful. I think you should stay home, now that school is out. If you have to go out be very careful.

Gerald, keep an eye on Nancy when you're not working and keep your ears open. Sometimes you can pick up on things that are said over coffee.

Today is Monday. Let's all meet back here on Wednesday night and review what we have learned."

Chapter Ninety-one

Wednesday July 1, 1942

With the dawn of Wednesday July 1, 1942 in the city of Hurley and Ironwood, things were coming to a final conclusion though at the time none of the participants had any knowledge of what was about to take place.

Nancy Monroe, Martha Laine, Robert Rahn and Gerald Kershaw had some idea of what might be going to happen, but they had no way of knowing what was about to take place next. They knew the Alliance members were responsible for stealing Nancy's things and that Ethan Lynch and Henrik Dahl were involved. They were not aware of FBI agent, Thomas Appleton.

They did not know that Henrik Dahl and Ethan Lynch were in the area staying at the American House in Ironwood. Nor did they know that Thomas Appleton was staying in Ashland at the Chequamegon Hotel and driving back and forth to Hurley. He did not want to blow his cover; it was the FBI agent in him.

* * *

Unknown to all the other parties it was the Alliance that put everything into motion by calling in Stan Offenbach, the ex-cop from Milwaukee on Tuesday June 30th after a hurriedly called meeting on Monday night after learning that Henrik Dahl was in town. Even though it was Lynch, who had told the Alliance that Henrik Dahl was in town they decided that Lynch and Dahl both had to go. Everyone felt that it was in their best interest and it was the patriotic thing to do. By taking out Lynch and Dahl, they would be eliminating a threat to the national security of the United States.

The only other problem that the Alliance had was what to do about Nancy Monroe, Martha Laine and that guy, Robert Rahn, that has been snooping around town.

* * *

On Tuesday, Oscar Kosken placed the call to Stan Offenbach. "Stan, how are you these days? Still looking for extra jobs?"

"Oscar, I'm doing find but you know I can always use a little extra money. What's on your mind?"

"We have a little situation here that needs to be cleaned up."

"How many items are we talking about?"

"Two items for sure and perhaps three more."

"You know the price goes up the more there are?"

"I know that Stan, I know. We are not sticklers when it comes to money, I know we can work something out and believe me it will be worth your while. We just want a quality job. Could you get up here by Wednesday night so we can discuss the specifics?"

"This must be important and urgent, but that should not be a problem. I'll see you on Wednesday afternoon and hey, book me a nice room."

* * *

After talking with Oscar, Stan Offenbach decided that since he had no pending business in Milwaukee it was easier for him to leave on Tuesday night, besides he needed a vacation. As he drove he thought about how jumpy, he was when he contracted out for his first murder. Now it was nothing but a job.

The 350 mile ten hour drive was miserable. He was a big man in his late fifties and had put on a few unneeded pounds and this along with the heat made the drive seem even longer. He arrived in Hurley around noon on Wednesday after spending the night in Stevens Point. He checked into the Grand Hotel a block off of Silver Street. His first call was to Oscar and they agreed to meet at the Golden Spike for dinner with the rest of the Alliance members.

* * *

When everyone was present, Oscar Kosken put forth the plan agreed upon by the Alliance members. "Stan glad you could make it up here on such short notice. We appreciate it. We want this little matter cleared up as soon as possible.

The primary mission is to take out Henrik Dahl and Ethan Lynch. They are here in town staying at the American House across the river in Ironwood, Michigan. I'm not telling you how to do your job, but I would think it would be easy to track them down and take care of things at your convenience."

"You're right Oscar. Knowing where they are makes my job easy. Since they don't know who I am it should be easy to follow them. I should be able to complete this job by the end of the week. So what is the secondary mission?"

"Well the secondary mission is really more complicated than the primary. There is this woman, Nancy Monroe that we really need to talk to first. You will know her when you see her. She is blonde and extremely attractive. She is living with Martha Laine up on Fifth Street. We are not sure how much contact she's had with Ethan Lynch and Henrik Dahl, but there is a connection. The less you know the better."

"That's fine with me. I don't have to know what you guys are up to as long as it does not interfere with me doing my job. So do you want me to take her out?"

"Yes, but first we want to talk with her. Then after that, you can take her out."

"Is that it?"

"No there is one more thing. There is this man, Robert Rahn living at Ellen's boarding house on Copper Street, he came to town out of nowhere and knows Nancy Monroe. We don't know the connection. But right now I'd say we need to have him out of the way."

"Now, is that all?"

"That should solve our problems. If there are others that get in the way we will compensate you."

"Remember, I'm not cheap. Thanks for the drinks and dinner."

Chapter Ninety-two

Thursday July 2, 1942

Stan Offenbach woke early at six on Thursday morning and was glad that he only had two drinks the night before. The older he got the harder it was to get started in the morning. Nothing was moving in Hurley as he drove over to the American House in Ironwood waiting for Lynch and Dahl to come out.

At a quarter to seven, they came out and drove across the river into Hurley. He followed as they turned onto Fifth Street making a U-turn and parked by the hardware store, just down the street from Martha Laine's house.

He parked on Silver Street and went into Nuncio's café for breakfast. He sat in the booth that looked up Fifth Street. Here he had a good look at Lynch and Dahl and at Martha Laine's house up the street. He ordered the daily breakfast special.

As he was enjoying his second cup of coffee, he knew Dahl and Lynch were waiting for someone. When he saw Martha Laine walking to work, he quickly paid his bill and left.

Once out the door and in his car he saw something else that caught his attention. There in front of the church cattycorner from the Laine house were two young kids in their teens hanging around. He could not imagine two teenagers hanging around a church this early in the morning in the summer when they could have been home sleeping. Surely, they weren't there for the morning mass. No way did they look like altar servers. *What are you two up to this early in the morning?*

* * *

Henrik Dahl and Ethan Lynch waited in their car on Silver Street where from their vantage point they could see Martha Laine's house up on the hill. They paid no attention to the two teenagers in front of the church.

At ten minutes to seven, they watched Maratha leave the house walking to work at Dr. Frost office. She was deep in thought and did not notice the two men in the car.

Now they waited for Nancy Monroe to leave the house. She usually went to the grocery store every morning just after Martha left for work. Thirty minutes later Nancy Monroe left the house. The street was empty and Dahl and Lynch had no problem in subduing Nancy and forcing her into the car. Henrik forced her onto the back seat, tied her hands and gagged her before she knew what was happening. Ethan jumped behind the wheel and they were off heading west out of town on U.S. 2.

* * *

As Stan Offenbach stood watching the teenagers at the church, what happened next came as a complete surprise. He saw Dahl and Lynch suddenly push a young woman with blonde hair into their car and drive away heading north on Fifth Street. Offenbach knew she had to be Nancy Monroe. The two teenagers also saw what had happened. Offenbach quickly got back to his car and followed at a distance. He watch as the car went onto U.S. 2 heading west. When the car turned off the highway onto a town road, he stopped not wanting to be seen. Waiting two minutes, he continued. The car was heading back into the hill country. Next, he came to a fork in the road. To the right was an abandon logging road and to the left was the continuation of the town road. He parked his car on the side of the road, grabbed his hunting rifle and proceeded on foot. After a thirty-minute walk, he came upon the car he was following parked in front of a dilapidated two-story farmhouse. He could see no activity from where he was on ground level. Then, he noticed a small bluff that overlooked the house. Climbing the bluff with his rifle, he decided to be an observer. Besides, maybe Lynch and Dahl would take care of the woman and then he would only have to deal with them. He never liked killing women.

* * *

Martha Laine was sitting at the reception desk when Marvin Coppalo and Henry Frost burst in to the office. Out of breath Marvin said, "Where's my Dad? I gotta see him right away."

"He's with a patient right now you'll have to wait."

"It can't wait, we saw a woman being forced into a car by two men."

"Do you want me to call the police?"

"No, no, we have to see my Dad."

Before Martha could stop them, they barged into the exam room. She could see that the Doctor was upset as he asked Martha to take his patient into another room.

Shutting the door he said, "This had better be good, you knew I had a patient."

"Dad we were watching Martha Laine's house and when Nancy Monroe came out we saw two men force Nancy Monroe into a car and they headed out of town going north on Fifth Street. We think they were headed out of town with her."

"How long ago did this happen."

"Not more than ten minutes ago. We came right here after it happened."

"Did you know either of the men?"

"No, never saw them before. Don't you think we should call the police?"

"No, leave everything to me. I'll take care of it. Both of you go home and don't say a word to anyone about this."

* * *

After over hearing that Nancy was abducted, Martha almost sank to her knees in front of the exam room, but before she let that happen she hurried back to her desk just as Dr. Frost came out saying, "Martha, I have an emergency and have to leave. Reschedule all of my appointments."

She was still in shock as she watched Dr. Frost leave. Willing herself back to reality, she called Robert at the boarding house.

* * *

On Thursday morning Thomas Appleton over slept. He was late getting to Hurley from Ashland. When he stopped at the American House he found that Dahl and Lynch were both gone. He cursed himself for having over slept and for having too much to drink the night before. *Where have they gone?*

His only hope now of finding Dahl and Lynch was that they might have gone to see one of the members of the Alliance. His first move was to shadow Leo Coppalo.

* * *

Dr. Frost went down the street to see Leo Coppalo. He knew Leo would know what to do. Leo knew that it had to be Dahl and Lynch, but he did not know why and where they had taken her.

After Dr. Frost told Leo Coppalo what had happened they got the rest of the Alliance together for an emergency meeting.

It was now an hour since Nancy Monroe's kidnapping. Oscar spoke first, "Does anyone have any idea where they would have taken her?"

"I was talking with Ethan some time back and he told me that he didn't trust Henrik and that he was afraid for his life. He also said that Henrik used to go hunting trips around this area in the Town of Farmington. Some place in the backcountry off Cedar Swam Road. My guess is that is where they took her."

"Everybody grab your guns and let's go out there," said Oscar.

"Where do you think Stan is?"

"I think he may already be there. My guess is that he was tailing Ethan and Henrik."

* * *

It was shortly after eight and Robert was still at the boarding house when Martha called. Martha only knew that two men had taken Nancy and that they headed west out of town. She had no idea where they were taking her. The only thing she knew for sure was that Dr. Frost had left to meet with the other Alliance members.

As Robert gathered up his gun with the extra clips, the only idea he had was to follow the Alliance and hope that they would lead him to Nancy.

He knew he needed help so he called Gerald at work and they told him that he was home that Beth was sick.

He hurried over to Gerald's house and found him there with Beth. He told him that his plan was to follow the Alliance and they in turn would lead him to Nancy.

The problem was what to do with a sick Beth. With no place to leave Beth, they had no choice but to take her with them.

* * *

Robert and Gerald watched and just after 9:30 AM they saw Oscar Kosken, Leo Coppalo, Ralph Winslow and Fred Banter get into Oscar's Buick Road Master 4-door sedan and head west on U.S. 2. Dr. Frost and Peter Cadence did not go with them. Robert and Gerald followed from a distance in Gerald's 1937 Chevrolet. What they did not notice was that Thomas Appleton was following them.

* * *

The Alliance members arrived first at the fork in the road where they saw Stan Offenbach's Ford coupe parked on the shoulder in knee high grass. There was no sign of Stan except for some muddy footprints going up the logging road.

Leo had no intention of walking and drove further up the logging road until he saw a clearing. All four got out of the car with their deer hunting rifles. They proceed up the road until they saw the house. There was a car parked up by the house and they could only think that it had to belong to Henrik and Ethan. They did not see any sign of Stan. They moved to the side of the road and hid behind a large bunch of elder brush. They heard nothing coming from the house.

* * *

Gerald and Robert with Beth asleep in the back seat of Gerald's 1937 two-door Chevrolet arrived at the fork in the road and could only see a Ford coupe parked to one side. There was no sign of the Alliance car. A further look reveled fresh tire tracks and they were sure the Alliance had driven further up the road. They decided to walk from here. Beth was asleep in the back seat wrapped in a blanket and they felt that she would be safe. They had told her on the way out that she had to stay in the car and not to open the doors for anyone no matter what she heard or saw. As they started out Gerald was reluctant to leave her, but felt he had no other choice. Nancy's life was most likely at stake. Before leaving the car, Robert put his Glock in his pocket along with six extra clips.

When Gerald saw the handgun, he was amazed. "What kind of gun is that?"

"It's a handgun from the future and these are extra clips should I have to reload. Just trust me this may come in real handy."

"I never thought that we'd have to kill somebody," said Gerald.

"I'm going to try not to kill anybody, this is just a precaution."

With that, they started up the road.

* * *

When Appleton arrived, he saw two cars parked around the fork in the road. It was beginning to look like a parking lot. Not seeing anyone, he slowly backed his car up into a hay field out of sight. Next, he cautiously pulled out his handgun and proceeded up the logging road. He had made up his mind to watch. He was reluctant to interfere. He was content to let somebody else do the dirty work. He would just clean up what was left.

Appleton knew Henrik was pro-German and because of that, he was his primary target. That was who he wanted to stop first. The Alliance was his secondary target. He found himself enjoying the adventure, it was better than being tied to a desk.

Chapter Ninety-three

Thursday Late Morning July 2, 1942

Nancy knew that Robert, Gerald and Martha had told her to be careful and not to go out of the house alone, she disregarded their warning thinking that nothing could happen in a small 1942 town.

Before she realized what was happening she was forced into a nearby car and had her mouth gagged unable to scream.

Once in the car on the back seat and she thought she was going to be sick from the smell of cigarettes and coffee. Then the feeling subsided.

She knew the one man was the man that had come to see her at school. The other she was not sure where she had seen him. She thought the car was traveling out of town going west at a high rate of speed.

Ten minutes out of town, the car turned onto a gravel road. She was still able to see outside and it made her think that if they didn't care what she saw maybe they had no intension of letting her live and now the taste of bile was in her mouth as her fear intensified.

After what seem to be another ten minutes the car made another turn onto what she thought had to an old abandon logging road that perhaps the town had favored with a small amount of pit-run gravel. The road was narrow with brush so thick on the sides that it was scraping both sides of the car. It occurred to her now, how really isolated she was. More fear entered her mind. If they buried her out here, no one would ever come across her grave. She said a few prayers asking Jesus for help and strength. Now the lost feeling inside her brought on the chills even though the temperate was in the 70's. She wondered if anyone even knew of this place. After an extremely agonizing ride, the car came to a halt and she knew that her nightmare was only going to get worse.

As they pushed her out of the car she saw an old weather beaten two-story house that looked as if it had been abandon back in the 1930's during the depression. Back when people lost everything and were forced to move off the land to try to find work in the cities.

The house was in a clearing surrounded by a mixture of waist high hay and weeds. No one had hayed these fields in years. The barns were in ruin with the roofs caved in from the winter's heavy snow.

They forced her up rickety wooded steps into what must have been the living room once upon a time. Wallpaper hung in strips showing laths and plaster beneath. Dust from time, covered the floor along with plaster. There were old newspapers and magazines strewn around the room. Only small animal paw prints disturbed the dust on the floor. Now she could smell animal urine coming up from the basement that almost made her sick again. There was clutter everywhere. The windows were boarded up, the glass long ago weathered away. Some light came in through broken slats. Whoever had lived here must have left in a hurry taking very little with them.

Now Nancy thought again, *who would ever think to look for me here?* She knew from coming up the driveway the road was seldom if ever used as she felt the car sinking into ruts and large holes. It gave her a feeling of complete helplessness. *There is no way that Robert or Gerald will ever be able to find me.* A wave of panic came sweeping over her as she tried not to think of what was going to happen next.

Dahl removed her gag saying, "Welcome to our country home. We hope your stay is a pleasant." Dahl struggled to keep a straight face.

Nancy said nothing; still too shocked to believe that she was here with these two men.

Off to one side of the living room there was what must have been the master bedroom if that term was used in 1942. In the middle of the room was an old coil spring bed frame. Henrik threw her onto the bedspring and proceeded to tie her hands and feet to the outside of the frame. Nancy hit the frame so hard she let out a yell as one of the broken springs poked her in the backside drawing blood.

"Sorry, did that hurt. I'll try to be more careful," said Henrik.

Ethan Lynch gave her a sympatric look and said, "You didn't have to do that. You said we weren't going to hurt her. "

"Get real; what difference does it make unless you were thinking of taking advantage of her. Is that what you were thinking?"

Now more scared than ever Nancy shouted out, "What do you want from me?"

"I think you know what we want? For starters, where are you from? How did you end up here in Hurley?"

Nancy paused for a minute and then decided to tell them the truth no matter how fantastic it sounded.

"I'm from Appleton, Wisconsin and I came here to live with Martha Laine my Aunt."

"You know that's not true, There's no record of you being born in Appleton or any where else for that matter. How did you come to be here?"

"If I told you, you wouldn't believe me."

"Tell us any way."

"I fell through a dimension in time. I'm from the future."

Neither Henrik nor Ethan said anything, they had both heard the talk that she was from the future, but that was impossible. If however it were true, it would explain everything. It would explain the calculator adding machine and all the other things.

"So you're from the future."

"Yes, I am. How else can you explain my presences here? You both said there is no record of my birth."

"So, from where in the future?"

"From the year 2009."

"Do the Germans win the war?"

"No the Allies win. Germany is unable to beat back the Russians and the United States and England invade Europe in June of 1944. The war ends a year later and Germany is divided into four parts with the Russians taking the eastern half. Germany is not reunified until in the 1990's."

"What happened to the Japanese? Did they win control of the Pacific?"

"No, they were bombed into submission and the war ended in September 1945."

After Nancy stopped speaking, she could see a dejected look come over Henrik Dahl's face. It was then that, she realized that he was a German sympathizer. Now she knew why he wanted her things.

"Did you want the Germans to win? Is that why you wanted all of my things, so you could help the Germans win? How can you live here the United States and want something like that to happen? You are nothing but a traitor and a coward."

Just after the words had left her mouth, she knew she had said too much. Dahl's fist slammed into her jaw causing her lip to bleed and perhaps loosened a few back teeth. For just a short time, she lost consciousness

"Just shut your mouth, bitch. This isn't over yet. I can still change history and the Germans will win. As for you, history will record you as someone without a name that died out here, that is if they ever find you. No one will remember you. On the other hand, I will change history and Germany will be victorious. Everyone in the future in the United Sates will be speaking German."

Just then, Ethan Lynch launched himself at Dahl. "You bastard, I always knew you were working for the Germans. Well I'm not going to let you get away with it."

The unexpected blow knocked Dahl to the floor and just as it seemed that Lynch was about to gain the upper hand, Dahl freed his gun and shot Ethan in the stomach. Lynch stumbled back towards the door and managed to get outside. Dahl got quickly to his feet and caught Ethan before he could get more than fifty feet away. This time he shot him point blank two times in the head. Ethan Lynch was dead instantly. Henrik stood there savoring the moment.

* * *

Nancy heard the gunshots outside and now tried desperately to untie herself from the bed frame, she sensed that one way or another this ordeal was coming to an end. She was sure that Dahl was not going to let her live.

She was here seemingly alone and could only hope that somehow Robert and Gerald would come to her rescue. She was on one side with Robert, Gerald and Martha and on the other side was the Alliance and Henrik Dahl. If her side won the world would remain the same except for perhaps some minor changes in history. If Henrik was able to get her things and provide that advanced technology to the Germans, there was a good chance that the Germans would win the war. When she thought of it, she imagined a world where freedom no longer existed. There would be no freedom of religion or speech. She saw millions of people in concentration camps and thousands more being exterminated.

She could not give up. She had to get away.

* * *

The shots fired by Henrik Dahl echoed across the entire landscape. Stan heard the shots and could see with his binoculars that one of the people he was suppose to kill was already dead. As he took aim on Dahl, he wondered if he could still submit a bill to the Alliance for both kills.

His first shot missed from his repeating rifle and sent Dahl running for cover to a nearby clump of trees. Stan did not agonize over his miss and reloaded. He was determined to keep Dahl pinned down outside the house having no concern for the girl inside.

* * *

At the edge of the woods Leo, Oscar, Ralph and Fred stood there not believing what they had just witnessed, Henrik killing that man in cold blood and from the look on his face, he seemed please.

When they heard the shot coming from up on top of the bluff they knew it had to be Stan. Cautiously they moved closer toward the house still taking cover in the thick brush.

* * *

Thomas Appleton watched Dahl shoot Lynch in cold blood, but it did not surprise him. He always felt that Dahl was a dangerous man. When he next heard the other shots from the top of the bluff, he was surprised that someone else was involved. Now he knew this was going to be war. Still he waited to see where things were going. Maybe if he was just patient someone else would kill Dahl and he might be able to get something out of this after all.

* * *

Before Robert and Gerald heard the first shots fired, Robert said to Gerald, "I think they are going to kill Nancy no matter what information she gives them. They have no reason to keep her alive. She can identify them. We have to make a move now."

Before Gerald could say anything, a gunshot rang out from inside the house and they saw Ethan Lynch stagger out followed by Henrik Dahl. Dahl fired another two shot into Ethan's head killing him.

Without hesitation, Robert and Gerald made a move to the back of the house. Next, they heard the shots coming from the bluff and saw Dahl run for cover.

* * *

Nancy in the mean time was able to free her hands and was in the process of untying her feet when she heard more gunfire coming from the bluffs.

It was then that she saw Robert and Gerald at the back bedroom window. She crawled to meet them while Dahl was still firing back at whoever was out there, she could only think that it was the Alliance.

Chapter Ninety-four

Thursday Afternoon July 2, 1942

Gerald helped Nancy though the small window opening as Robert waited with his gun ready. Nancy tumbled onto the ground outside. As they started to run from the farmhouse, Henrik still pinned down by the gunfire from the bluff saw them fleeing and fired several shots in their direction and one of them hit Gerald. The bullet entered Gerald's chest just below his sternum and he fell to the ground. Robert fired in Dahl's direction and they were able to get Gerald to cover behind a pile of fieldstones.

The look on Gerald's face was one of painful surprise as he questioned silently, *how could this be happening to me?* Robert looked at Gerald and thought, *no one really knows what it's like to be shot. This is only something we see in the movies.* Now safely behind the cover of the rock pile the blood spread rapidly on Gerald's shirt. Robert knew that the shot was fatal.

As he looked over to see Nancy, he saw the surprised expression of shock and anger that spread across her face. He knew she could not believe what had just happened. He felt her pain, knowing what it was like to see someone you loved die. This felt worse because it did not have to happen. It was not like seeing someone die with a terminal illness.

Both Nancy and Robert could hear the heavy breathing and gurgling coming from Gerald's mouth. Nancy sat there stunned and staring down at him as the life of the one she loved trickled away. She thought of Beth remembering that she told Gerald that she would take care of her.

Then Gerald raised himself up slightly on one arm and said, "I'm not going to make it Nancy. You and Robert have to go without me. Save Beth. Just leave me."

"Gerald, I love you, I can't leave you. You're going to be alright."

"Nancy, I know you love me and I love you too. But we have to think about Beth. You and Robert have to get her out of here. If either of you are shot what will become of her. Please think of Beth."

Blood ran from his mouth and with labored breathing he said, "Please Nancy, Robert take care of Beth. I love you both." With that, he was dead.

She was sorry that she had not told him that she would marry him. She had all she could to do not to black out from the dreadful images that were now forming in her mind of a future without Gerald. *What am I going to do? I'm not sure I want to go on living.* Now all of her dreams were shattered. Looking down on Gerald's lifeless body, she had no idea what she was going to do. Life without Gerald now seemed impossible.

Robert sat there looking at Nancy in her sorrow and for a brief passing moment, it seemed like time had stopped. None of this was real.

Then Robert broke the spell and said, "Nancy we have got to move. Think of Beth. If we don't get back to the car what will happen to her. I'll fire some cover rounds and when I do you get ready to make for the woods."

As they moved towards the woods, Robert saw Henrik gain the safety of the house with the others in pursuit. Looking back to his surprise, he saw that two others were in pursuit of them.

Robert fired several shot in their direction but they were out of range. He had only hoped to slow their progress.

"Nancy, you keep going, Beth is in the back seat of Gerald's car. I'll catch up with you after I slow these guys down."

There was a small bend in the road and Robert took advantage of this to hide behind a dead tree fall. He could see the two Alliance guys still running. They had not seen him slip off the road. It was almost too easy. He stood up and fired taking out the two immediately. Both fell to the ground and offered no further resistance. Robert went to check the bodies keeping his gun ready. Looking at the bodies, he recognized Ralph Winslow and Fred Banister.

For the moment, they were safe. He had no way of knowing how long it would take the others to finish off Henrik. There was no time to waste.

* * *

With superior firepower, it was not long before Stan Offenbach, Oscar Kosken and Leo Coppalo had the upper hand. Oscar had sent Winslow and Banister to cover the back.

"Come out Henrik, there's no reason to drag this out, you don't have a chance."

They waited several minutes and then they heard a single gunshot. "Do you think he killed himself?" said Stan.

"Let's be careful. Leo, you go around the back and we'll go in from the front. If he tries to get away shoot him," said Oscar.

When Leo looked in the side window, he saw Henrik with a pool of blood coming form his head. He was dead. "Hey, he's dead. He killed himself. He must have saved the last bullet for himself, like in the old westerns."

When Oscar and Stan entered the house, they found it was true; Henrik the German spy was dead. "We've done the Country a big favor. We are real patriots. Now let's get after Nancy Monroe. She is still a danger to us."

* * *

Thomas Appleton watched everything. It was as if he was a third party. Dahl and Lynch were dead and were no longer a threat to the national security of the United States. Now all he had to worry about was those Alliance assholes. As far as he was concerned, they were no better than Dahl and Lynch.

As he observed he saw two of the Alliance members in pursuit of the girl, he decided to follow. This just might be an opportunity to take out some of the Alliance members. As far as he knew Nancy and that man, Robert Rahn, had not committed any crimes.

Chapter Ninety-five

Thursday Late Afternoon July 2, 1942

Stan Offenbach, Leo Coppalo and Oscar Kosken moved down the road in pursuit of Nancy and Robert. Not far from the house, they found the bodies of Fred Banister and Ralph Winslow. Stan made a quick examination and said, "We've got to pick it up before they reach the cars and are able to drive away."

* * *

Robert caught up to Nancy just before she got to the cars. Out of breath, he said, "Get Beth out of Gerald's car. She's in the back seat."

As Nancy looked in the back seat all she saw were two blankets, but there was no sign of Beth. She screamed, **"Robert, Beth's not here!"**

"She's got to be around here somewhere. I suppose she ran into the woods when she heard the gunfire. We'll find her."

Just as they heard the Alliance men approaching, they found Beth hiding behind a large stump left over from the old logging days. She was scared but when she saw Nancy, she jumped into her arms and hugged her tightly. "Where's my Daddy?"

They were not the words Nancy had wanted to hear. She thought for a second and decided not to lie. "He was shot by the bad guys and he did not make it."

"Is he dead?"

"Yes, sweetheart, he's dead. He is with God. Robert and I are going to take care of you. You are going to be all right. You have to do everything that we tell you. The bad men are coming after us. Can you do that?

"Yes, just don't leave me."

"We'll never leave you."

"Gerald must have the car keys, they are not in the car," said Nancy.

Robert knew they were going to have to make a stand right here. He still had four clips left and he could only hope that was enough. Knowing the Buick provided the best protection, he put Nancy and Beth behind it.

With the Alliance coming, he moved quickly to the Ford coup and fired off four rounds and from the screams coming from the Alliance members he was hopeful that he had hit at least one if not two of them. If he had taken out two that meant they were down to two. In all of this, he had not seen Peter Cadence or Doctor Frost.

Then Robert fell to one knee and rolled toward the cover of the brush. There was more gunfire, a lot of it in a few seconds. Nancy could feel the bullets cutting through the air with a deadly undertone that was louder than any other sound in the world.

Then there was silence. Initially she could not hear the wind nor the low sobbing coming from Beth. Gradually those sounds impinged upon her.

She saw Robert was alive and part of her was relieved, but part of her was irrationally angry that he had survived because he was the one responsible for all of this. If he had not found his way back to 1942 none of this would have happened, she might have very well married Gerald in 1942 and lived happily every after. She gave no thought to the possibility that the war might have been lost. She never considered the fact that had it not been for Robert, the Alliance or Henrik might have killed all three of them. Right now, she didn't care; all she could think about was the fact that she would never see Gerald. She was frightened, angry, shocked, sick in her soul and badly confused.

So absorbed in her thoughts, she did not notice that Robert was bleeding. Robert was clearly in pain as he rose from his knees and hobbled towards Nancy and Beth.

"Robert, you've been shot! Let me have a look at it. I'm trained in first aid."

She could see that the bullet wound was in the upper leg and was not bleeding badly. On further examination, she determined that it had not hit the femur.

"It appears that the bullet went through and didn't hit the bone. That's good news. Wish I had something to clean out the wound. For now, we'll have to wrap it as tight as we can. Try not to use it too much. Activity will only increase the blood flow."

"I'm not sure that is possible Nancy, we have to get out of here."

He took off his T-shirt and she used it to wrap the leg. "That should hold it for a while. I wish you didn't have to move."

Looking directly down the hill, Robert stared in shock. There he could see Leo Coppalo, Oscar Kosken and another man that he did not know. All were dead. Robert was sure that he had only been responsible for taking out one or two at the most. He thought he had heard other shots, but in the heat of battle, he could not be certain. Now it was quite and he thought he heard a car driving away. He knew they all were dead except he had no idea who killed the last two men.

* * *

Appleton had observed the battle from a distance and for a while, he thought he would not have to interfere. Whoever that person was with Nancy Monroe and the girl, he sure knew how to handle himself. Appleton was also amazed at the weapon he was using. He noticed that he was quick to reload by replacing clips. After one of the three had go down he decided it was time to intervene.

The two men still living never saw Appleton approaching from behind. They had no idea that anyone was behind them. With two well-placed shots, he killed them both. Then hurried down the road to where his car was hidden and drove off.

Chapter Ninety-six

Thursday Early Evening July 2, 1942

Robert laid there resting his leg for the next ten minutes. The bleeding appeared to have stopped or perhaps that was wishful thinking. Then he hobbled back up to the car where Nancy was huddled with Beth. They were both in tears. Nancy could see that he was in pain and his face was pale. He seemed to have aged five years in the last few hours. He cleared his throat and with deep felt remorse, he said, ''I'm sorry, Nancy. I'm sorry, Beth. I'm so very sorry for all of this. But it's over now, they are all dead, and no one is going to hurt either of you ever again."

Trembling Beth looked at him and in her grief said, "I want Daddy. I want my Daddy back." *I want him too*, Nancy thought. *Oh, baby, I want him, too, I want him so bad, all I wanted was to stay here with you and your Daddy in his world.*

* * *

"I survived." Nancy said. "But Gerald didn't. I know this is silly to say but maybe if you had not come back for me, Gerald would still be alive."

"Maybe and maybe not," Robert said. "Perhaps destiny struggles to restore the time continuum pattern as best it can. Maybe Gerald would have died anyway. Besides, we can't say what more tampering would have done to the history as we know it."

Silence settled between them. He didn't say anything more. He understood her loss. They sat there, Nancy holding Beth. The wind began to increase and a light rain began to fall.

At last she said, "I appreciate everything you have done for me, but I have to tell you. I don't love you."

Even though Robert knew that she did not love him, it still came as a shock to him when she put it into words "I understand," he said.

"Right now I'm not sure I am capable of feeling anything. There is only emptiness inside of me. I cannot stop thinking of Gerald. Maybe in time I can come to love you like you already love me and than again maybe I will never love you. Only time can heal things."

"I came into your life unexpectedly and I understand that you don't even really know me. Let's just give it time. Now we have to think about getting out of here."

"Yes," she said, "I suppose we should go back to the present before history changes anymore. The only thought I have, is what will happen to my things—KINDLE, cell phone and the camera. The Alliance still has all of the items."

"If these things are locked away, I don't think anyone will find them soon and if they do they may not know what they are or what to do with them. Besides that the batteries should be dead. I think we just have to pray that nobody finds them."

* * *

In the light mist, Robert searched the bodies for car keys and was successful on the second try. The keys were to the Buick found on Oscar Kosken's body.

Getting in the car Robert could see that Beth had stopped crying. That was a good sign. He could not begin to image what was going through the mind of a ten year old. He only knew that what she had been through might get worse, before it got better. Taking her to another world could only be more devastating.

"Where are we going?" asked Beth.

"We are going to a new home where things will be better. In time I think you will really learn to love it," said Robert.

"Robert do you really know where you are going?" said Nancy.

"I'm pretty sure this is the way but things look different here in 1942. I'm trying to find the place where I will live 67 years from now, I believe that is where we will find the time dimension coming together. It was where I came through when I came here. The only thing that worries me now is the timing."

"What do you mean, timing?"

"Remember what I said before about the full moon, well it has now been four days past and from what I was able to observe the time dimension is only open a few days before the full moon and maybe a few days after. When I came here, the full moon was on June 25th and when I got here the full moon for 1942 was June 28th. The time dimension is open four days before the full moon and maybe four days after. What I am not sure of is which full moon is in control? The one in 2010 or the one in 1942. If it is 2010 than the opening is closed. If it is the full moon of 1942, the time dimension portal may still be open. That means we have today and maybe tomorrow. Let's hope the opening works from where the user is at the time."

Driving back down the town road he came upon U.S. 2 and went east. After a few miles, he saw a field that looked familiar. It was a field that one day would become a highway rest stop. Up a few miles, he saw the town road that would one day be named Lake Forest Road. Now he knew he was only a few miles from what was to be his land in 2010.

Next, he came to a hayfield opening and turned the Buick into the field. This was it. This would be his land in 67 years and there would be a very impressive house upon it.

They got out of the car and Robert saw the hay barn that was still in good shape compared to what it would be when he purchased the land in the future. Robert took them on a route that followed a fence line that led to a large old oak tree that he remembered would be split by a lightening strike some time in the future.

From the oak tree, the land went upward and then at the top they looked down at a ravine. At the bottom of the ravine was a small steam. Here were the rock piles from what was once upon a time a working mine. There was the shovel he had left. He started to dig near the shallow pit. After thirty minutes he saw protruding rocks on his right and below was the opening of a mine.

"This is the place. "

Taking Nancy and Beth, he led them limping down to the opening. Nancy and Beth held their noses and Nancy said, "What's that smell." At the same time Beth said, "I don't feel so good. I'm going to be sick."

Robert was relieved. The portal was still open and he gave thanks to God.

"Just stay with me. It will all be over shortly. This is the right spot."

Next, they all felt like they were dizzy with a feeling of tumbling hopelessly out of control and just when they thought it would never end, it stopped and all three of them were on a cement basement floor.

All just laid there motionless trying to figure out where they were. Beth was crying again and Nancy was rocking her in her arms when she said, "Where are we?"

Robert was just as confused. I think we are in the basement of Sally's café. I don't know how we got here. I was expecting us to be on my land."

Since it was late in the afternoon, he was sure that Sally had closed for the day. She only served breakfast and lunch. That was good. At least he would not have to explain Nancy and Beth. He knew that would have taken a lot of explaining.

Feeling better, he led Nancy and Beth up the stairs that came out behind the kitchen. It was how he remembered the place. The only thing different was the calendar that said it was Thursday July 1, 2010 not Wednesday.

Once up stairs, Nancy looked around and said, "I'm back, this is where I had breakfast back in November 2009. I never thought I'd see this place again."

In the meantime, Robert found Sally's first aid kit and washed out the bullet wound by the near by sink with hydrogen peroxide. With a new bandage in place he set out for the back door.

Beth never let go of Nancy's hand. It was as if she was in shock and both Nancy and Robert understood why. They both knew how scary it was for them when they went back to 1942. What a hard time they had adjusting. What must it be like for a ten-year-old?

The Buick Enclave was where Karl and Robert had left it a week ago. There was no one around. Robert found the keys under the floor mat, started the SUV and drove off.

* * *

Thomas Appleton followed behind Robert, Nancy and Beth. He was careful to stay out of sight. When they turned into the hayfield, he decided to follow on foot.

Watching them walk back into the field, he saw Robert digging at what must have been an old abandon copper mine. Then he was completely stunned. They just disappeared.

He went down to the mine opening to have a closer look. There was no way that they just could have vanished.

Looking out over the area, he confirmed that without a doubt they had vanished. There was no sign of them anywhere. While standing there he felt light headed and he had a feeling of being called closer to the opening. Once at the opening he was gone. A complete feeling of helplessness took over his body. He was helpless and no longer in control. Than as fast as it had happened, it ended and he lay sprawled out on the ground surrounded by rocks. Looking up he could see that the area looked completely different and that was when he saw the old man and heard the barking dog.

2010

Chapter Ninety-seven

Thursday July 1, 2010

It was just a week since Robert had left and Karl was more than worried. He was beginning to think that he would never see Robert—the man he thought of as a son—ever again. He came everyday with Albert and everyday there was nothing—no sign of a return. On nice days, he would bring a lunch and watch the opening for hours.

He would think about what he was going to say, if Robert never came back. Surely, people would begin to ask questions. Fortunately, it was a good thing that Robert lived such a secluded life. Robert had made out a will and if he did not come back, everything went to Karl. Karl knew that someday he was going to have to tell the authorities that Robert was missing. He could only imagine the question he would face and it was not out of the realm of possibilities that they would accuse him of murder. After all, there was the will.

* * *

He was just about to leave when a strong wind came at him from the mouth of the mine opening blowing dust in his face. He thought for sure that it had to be Robert. He wondered if Nancy would be with him.

Then he saw to his astonishment that it was a man he did not recognize dressed in a double-breasted suit. The suit reminded him of one he had in the 1940's. The man looked confused and disoriented. Karl hurried over to him and to Karl's surprise the man pulled out a gun and said, "Get back. I'm an FBI agent. Stay back."

Karl did not argue. He could not imagine that he truly was an FBI agent. "My name is Karl Prosser. I just wanted to help you."

The man had a puzzled look on his face still trying to adjust. "Where am I?"

"You are on private property owned by Robert Rahn. I'm taking care of the place while he is gone."

"What day is it?"

"It is Thursday July 1, 2010."

With that the man said, "No its not. It is Wednesday July 1, 1942."

"If you're with the FBI let me see some identification?"

The man reached into his wallet and pulled out his badge. It read: FBI Special Agent Thomas R. Appleton, Minneapolis, Minnesota District. The expiration date was August 23, 1943.

The expiration date of 1943 on the credentials explained the vintage suit. Truly the man was from 1942, but how had he come over and Robert had not?

"Please let me take you up to the house. You look like you could use something to drink. I think there is no need for the gun. At my age I'm hardly capable of overwhelming you.

Appleton holstered his gun and with that he followed Karl up to house.

"Was there anyone else with you? Like a man and a woman," asked Karl.

"No, I'm alone."

"Did you see anyone else in the area?'

"Yes, there was a man and a woman and they had a girl with them about ten years old I'd say. Then they just disappear before my eyes. When I went to investigate that is how I came to be here."

Now Karl could see the man staring in disbelief at the house and everything that was in it. Karl still had to admit that there were times when he found himself astonished by how lavish Robert's house was.

"Please sit down and I'll get you a glass of water."

Thomas Appleton took the water and asked, "What are those things that look like dark mirrors on pedestals."

"Those are television sets. Sort of like the movies only at home. Here let me turn it on."

When Thomas Appleton saw the picture, he was amazed. "Where does the picture come from?"

"It comes in by a satellite that orbits around the earth. Pretty fantastic, I don't completely believe it myself I just accept it. It's all part of today's technology."

* * *

As Karl was about to ask more questions, he heard a car drive up and saw that it was the Buick Enclave. He hoped with all of his heart that it was Robert.

He raced out to the SUV with Thomas Appleton right behind.

Hugging Robert with all of his strength he said, "My God, Robert it is so good to see you." Then in total surprise he said, "You must be Nancy."

He hugged her too and then he saw the little girl. "Who are you, what's your name?"

Shyly she said, "My name is Beth."

Now seeing the bandage on Robert's leg, he said. "What happened to your leg?"

"I got shot. It will be fine. Like in the western movies, it's only a flesh wound."

Now Robert turned his attention to Thomas Appleton, "Who are you and how did you get here?"

"I'm Thomas Appleton with the FBI, I was tracking Henrik Dahl and I am not really sure how I got here. I was following the three of you, when you disappeared. I went to investigate. The next thing I found myself tumbling out of control and I ended up here. This much I know, I want to go back."

"Are you the one that helped us in that gun battle back there?"

"Yes, that was me. I knew what Henrik Dahl was up to and I had to stop him. No way do I want the Germans to win this war. So who does win this war?"

"We do, it takes until 1945."

"What else can you tell me? Like who wins the World Series. I might be able to make few bucks by coming here."

"I don't think that is a good idea. You already know too much."

Then he took out his gun and said, "With this I think you'll tell me anything I want to know or maybe something will happen to your girlfriend or maybe to the child."

Robert stared at him in utter amazement. He was petrified. It was then that Robert noticed that Karl had slipped away. He was not sure where but he knew he had to keep Thomas talking. "Alright don't hurt anyone what do you want to know?"

"Well you must have books on sports and world events that I could take back with me that would make me a rich man. So even without the Alliance, I've hit the jackpot. Let's go into the house and you can show me those books or what other information you have. You probably have all that stuff on a computer by now this far in the future. For me, just a history book will do. In 1942 it will be worth a fortune."

As Robert, Nancy and Beth turned to go into the house, Karl was there with a Mossberg double-barreled shotgun. "Mister, I'd drop the gun right now, leave my family alone."

"Screw you old man, you're not about to shoot me. You don't have the guts."

As Thomas brought up his gun, Karl shot him with both barrels. Appleton was dead instantly.

Karl just stood there weeping. "I had to do it Robert. I'm sorry I didn't want to shoot him in from of Beth and Nancy. I'm sorry."

"It's aright Karl, you had to do it. Nancy, take Beth inside. Karl and I will clean up here."

They loaded Thomas Appleton's body on to a lawn wagon and with a garden tractor they took him down one of the paths as the sun was setting. They buried Appleton in a grave and covered it with rocks making it look like an old tailing pile. Further more no one would ever look for anyone out here.

* * *

After taking care of Appleton, Karl took Robert over to a retired friend of his who was a retired Nurse practitioner to have her look at his leg. She practiced what she called rural medicine. She had a policy of don't ask don't tell. He knew he could trust her not to report this to the authorities.

The leg had not become infected which was a small miracle with everything that had happened. She gave him some anti-biotic and pain pills, telling him to stay off the leg as much as possible or to use crutches.

* * *

Late that night Nancy managed to get Beth to bed. It was not easy with everything that happened today. She was a mature little girl and Robert, Nancy and Karl could only hope she would be able to over come what she had seen. They were thankful for Albert. The dog had taken to her and never left her side. He was now sleeping beside her bed on the floor.

They all had some bourbon to drink that night and decided that they would deal with everything else tomorrow. There were too many things going on and there was no way that they could deal with everything tonight.

Chapter Ninety-eight

Friday to Friday, July 2-9, 2010

The first thing that Karl and Robert did on the Friday morning of July 2nd was to blow up the entrance to the time portal. There was no way that Robert ever wanted to go back and they did not want any unwanted visitors coming through, like Thomas Appleton.

Robert still had no explanation for how Thomas Appleton came back on Robert's land and while he, Beth and Nancy came back to Sally's Café. He was sure it had to do with various time dimensions and how they fluctuated. As for the time portal in Sally's Café he planned to deal with that in the future for now it was not a priority.

Next, he had to figure out a way to explain the presence of Nancy and Beth. This was not as urgent because the house was so isolated. Nancy could not just show up without people like the police asking where she was for the last seven months. Explaining Beth might be even harder. What was a single man doing with a ten-year-old girl? There was no way he wanted to explain that to the authorities.

After giving it some thought, Robert came up with a plan to explain Nancy and Beth. He would place a call to dear friend, Joan Gilmore, in New York City that he knew from his investment days. She would be able to help him with new identities.

More of a concern was Beth. The ten-year-old had experienced more traumas and seen more than any ten-year-old should. He had to decided to contact his therapist from the when he had been in the sanitarium, Dr. Ruth Aspen. He felt sure that she would be willing to help and would be discreet. He might be able to fly her out here to help Beth.

* * *

The first thing he did on Friday afternoon was to call Dr. Ruth Aspen. After he explained the situation—leaving out the fact that Beth had come from 1942—she agreed to fly out and treat the girl. She also wanted to check on Robert's progress.

After that, he called Joan Gilmore in New York. She was excellent with computers and knew her way around the legal system, even if perhaps not everything was to letter of the law.

"Joan this is Robert Rahn. I need the use of your services."

"Robert, I haven't heard a word from you since you left the City for Wisconsin. I'm sorry about what happened to your wife and daughter. No one should have to go through that. What can I do for you, just name it," said Joan.

"What I want…well I guess you might say is not necessarily legal. If you don't want to hear anymore just say so and this conversation never happened."

"You have me hooked. I trust you Robert, continue."

"I want you to set up new identities for two people. One is a ten-year-old girl and let's just say for the sake of simplicity that her mother is 25 years old. Both the mother and her child are legal citizens but there are extenuating circumstances causing them to need new identifications. I'd like then to be from the state of New York or if possible from New York City. I want to keep the first names of Nancy for the mother and Elizabeth for the girl. Can you do that? I will make this well worth your while. All you have to do is name your price."

"Robert, I wasn't worried about the money. What do you want for the last name?"

"I'm not sure, pick one out for me."

"Consider this done. It will take me a few days. I'll call when I have everything complete."

"Thanks Joan, if you ever get tired of the City and need a vacation you are more than welcome to stay with me here in Wisconsin."

"I may just take you up on that offer."

* * *

On Saturday July 3rd, Nancy was starting to come to grips with what she was going to do here. She knew that she really could not go back to teaching without having to answer to authorities. How would she ever be able to explain her disappearance and the fact that she had been missing for the past seven months.

Then she had to think of what was best for Beth. She had promised Gerald that she would take care of her. Perhaps the best option for her was to stay here with Robert for the foreseeable future. While she knew, Robert was in love with her, it was not the same for her. She was however fond of him. There were just too many things to think about so for now she decided to live one day at a time.

* * *

The night of the fourth-of-July they had a cook out and Robert set off fire works in the backyard. Everyone had a good time and for a moment in time, everyone seemed to forget the past, they all forgot about their worries for one day. Beth thoroughly enjoyed herself and by ten Nancy put her to bed. She was adapting relatively well considering all that she had been through.

Karl retired to his room to read. Robert and Nancy slipped away to the third floor study balcony over looking the Lake to have a glass of wine to relax and talk about the future. The stars were out and for once there were no bugs.

Robert spoke first, “Nancy I suppose you know that I’m in love with you.”

“Yes, I know, but how can you be in love with me? You’ve only known me for the last few days.”

“That’s where you’re wrong; true that I’ve only been with you in person for a few days but I’ve known you since the day you disappeared. I followed your case everyday. I came to know everything about you and somewhere along the way I fell in love with you.”

“Robert I have to be blunt. While I am grateful to you for everything you have done, I don’t think I can love you. I’m still very much in love with Gerald. Part of me blames you for his death. If you hadn’t come to my world of 1942, perhaps Gerald and I could have escaped to some place and lived a happy life together. I may even have had children. Yes, yes, I know all about what might have changed in history and in a way I agree that being here is perhaps the best thing. Lord only knows what Henrik would have done with my things; however, I’ll always wonder what might have been. I really don’t know about all these other time dimensions and parallel world stuff.”

“I know how you feel Nancy. For now let’s just give it some time. I’m willing to give you all the time you need.”

“Thanks for understanding, maybe there will come a time when I can love you. Right now, all we are is friends.”

* * *

Two days later on Tuesday July 6th, Joan called to say she was sending Robert all the papers for both Nancy and Beth. The new last name for both was Larson—mother and daughter. She had a new social security number, birth certificate, driver's license, teaching certificate and a degree in Education from St. John's College and all other pertinent documents inserted into every database that mattered—federal, state and local, it went back retroactive to 1985 when she was born.

The same was true for Beth. Her last name was Larsen. She found the records of a child that was around Beth's age and was able to establish a birth certificate and other documents. Like baptism certificates and first communion records in the Catholic Church.

Finally, Joan erased digital footprints that she might have left in the process. In addition, she destroyed any trace that she may have left on her own computer. There were no records or printouts. They were now mother and daughter—Nancy and Beth Larsen.

* * *

On Friday July 9th, Robert picked up Dr. Ruth Aspen from the Duluth airport. Beth had been having some bad dreams and was not herself. The Doctor had the next two weeks off and planned to work with Beth. She was sure she could turn things around. She promised to keep everything confidential.

Chapter Ninety-nine

Sunday/Monday July 11/12, 2010

Robert could now explain his houseguests if anyone approached him. He knew that eventually both Nancy and Beth had to get out. He worked out a plan with Nancy that perhaps, in the future he could say that she was his fiancée and that they planned to married but did not have a definite date in mind. She agreed but reintegrated that she was still not in love with him. If she had to marry him to make this happen it would just be a marriage of convenience. She would not sleep with him. Besides, when she really got married she wanted it to be a Catholic marriage in front of a priest and in Church.

* * *

On Sunday evening while Robert and Karl were sitting out on the front porch while Nancy and Beth were making dinner, Robert said, "I have to ask you a question having to do with when you were about 17 years old."

Karl frowned at him. "Where the hell did that come from?"

"When I was back in 1942 and looking for the Alliance cabin I went out on highway 77 and saw a sign that said County Trunk C. I remembered that you lived on C. I stopped and saw you out in the yard. You were a teenager working in the garden. I asked you if you knew a place out this way run by a group of businessmen from town and one of them was Doctor Frost. You warned me that you didn't think I should be looking for them. You said they were not the friendliest of people. I thanked you and left. Do you remember that happening?"

Karl thought for the longest time. "Now that you said that, I do. I remember I thought the man was crazy to want to go out and visit those guys. I thought I gave you a fair warning."

"Do you remember the day when you heard about how all of those guys died in that shooting?"

"Yes, I remember it was a shock to the entire community. Nothing like that ever happened around here. There was perhaps a homicide once every couple of years, when a jealous husband shot his wife, but nothing like that day. Eight people shot in one place. They never caught the killer or killers. Later on there was a report that an FBI agent who may have been involved disappeared and was never found.

There is no way that I would have ever known that you were involved until you came back along with that FBI agent. It was the way things were. It was just history. The only thing I always wondered was why Doc Frost and Peter Cadence had not been part of that, both being members of the Alliance. We all thought Doc and Peter knew something, but they took whatever they knew to their graves."

"Did you know Martha Laine, Karl?"

"In a small town everybody knows everybody. I knew her from seeing Doc Frost. She felt bad after the shootings and could never really get over the death of Gerald Kershaw and the disappearance of his daughter Elizabeth or Nancy. I know she really missed them. Yet in some ways the whole town, thought she knew something about what happened. Knowing what I know now, I understand everything. I for one thought the Alliance got what they deserved. Gerald should not have died that way. He was a good man. I'm glad he lives on with us here through Beth."

"Thanks for putting up with me Karl. Please don't say anything to Nancy about how Martha felt after the shooting. I know Nancy feels bad enough that she was unable to say good-bye. She loved her so very much."

The conversation ended as Nancy called them to have dinner.

* * *

On Monday July 12th, Robert went down to the old Museum to look through the old newspapers. He searched the obituaries for 1942 and on the July 6,1942 edition, he found the following names: Oscar Kosken, Leo Coppalo, Ralph Winslow, Fred Banister, Henrik Dahl, Ethan Lynch, Gerald Kershaw and Stan Offenbach.

He only scanned the details and then went back to look for a related story of the shooting. As it turned out the article on the shooting did not appear in the paper until Friday July 3, 1942.

Hurley, Wis. – Late on Thursday evening July 2, 1942 Police discovered eight bodies in or near an abandon farm house ten miles west in the town of Farmington. All deaths were from gun shot wounds.

The following people were identified and pronounced dead at the scene:

Oscar Kosken
Leo Coppalo
Ralph Winslow
Fred Banister
Henrik Dahl
Ethan Lynch
Gerald Kershaw
Stan Offenbach

The police termed the crime scene as a gangster type shootout from the Prohibition Era. The investigation is ongoing and at this time there is not a clear motive for the killings nor do the police have any suspects in custody.

Robert read one additional editorial. It went on to say there was reasonable suspicion to believe that members of the Alliance had been involved with a Minnesota inventor entrepreneur, Henrik Dahl, who allegedly had inventions in his possession that could have changed the outcome of the Second World War. It went on to say, that Dr. Frost's son, Marvin Frost, had seen these inventions after admitting that he broke into Maratha Laine's house. He said they belonged to Nancy Monroe.

When asked, Martha Laine denied these allegations. There was no way to verify Marvin Frost's allegation since Nancy Monroe had disappeared.

Robert did not bother to read any further. He went on to do a search for information on Martha Laine, Dr. John Frost, Peter Cadence, FBI agent Thomas Appleton and for Elizabeth Kershaw.

First, he found Elizabeth Kershaw. The article dated July 8, 1942 said the police were doing everything possible to find Elizabeth Kershaw a missing ten-year-old girl. She had been missing after police discovered the shooting death of her father.

Second, he found in the 1943 edition of the paper a reference to FBI agent Thomas Appleton. The FBI Agency would only say that he disappeared in July of 1942 and was still missing.

Lastly, he found the obituaries for Martha Laine, Doctor John Frost and Peter Cadence. Martha died in 1962 at the age of 78, Dr. John Frost died in 1966 at the age of 84 and Peter Cadence died of a sucide in October of 1942.

Chapter One Hundred

August 2010

Robert had one last piece of unfinished business. He and Karl had already secured the mine opening on his property, but he was concerned about the opening in Sally's Café basement. He wanted to make sure that it was sealed.

In the middle of August, he approached Sally with an offer to buy her building and to relocate her café down the street to where Doctor Frost had his old clinic building. It had been vacant since his death in 1966. Robert had purchased the Frost clinic building in mid July.

Sally agreed to Robert's proposal without asking Robert for an explanation. She already had a good idea why he wanted her property and besides she not did really want to know any more than she already did. She was perhaps the only person besides Karl who knew who Nancy really was and she had promised Robert it would remain a secret.

* * *

In the middle of August a demolish team from Minneapolis hired by Robert Rahn arrived in town. They started on Monday and Sally's building was down by Wednesday. On Thursday, cement trucks worked all day filling up the basement with over ten feet of cement with reinforcing rods. There was no way that anyone could get down into the basement ever again.

Then on Friday, the demolition crew took down Dr. Frost old clinic building to make way for Sally's new café. Just before they started the demolition, the crew made a final inspection of the site and came upon an old safe cemented into a basement wall. The safe contained a digital camera, KINDLE and cell phone. After Robert looked at them, he knew they belong to Nancy. He took them back home and destroyed them. It was best that no one knew of these things.

Epilogue

Nancy and Beth continued to live in Robert's guest quarters. It was a complete separate living space with complete privacy.

On a late December Sunday afternoon, nearly six months after coming back to the present, Nancy approached Robert as he and Karl were watching the Green Bay Packer loose to the Patriots.

"Robert could you break away from the game, I've got something I'd like to talk to you about."

Since it seemed certain that the Packers were going to loose and with it any hope of a play-off spot, Robert was grateful for the interruption. "Sure let's talk in the den."

As Robert led her to the den, he wondered what was so important that she had to talk about it now. Then his heart started beating faster and his blood pressure was soaring with joy thinking that for sure she was going to tell him that she wanted to be with him always.

Then the second thought entered his mind, the dreadful thought of loosing her. What would he do if she said she was leaving? He knew that they were not a couple, but as long as she was here, he always thought that it might be possible. Now all that could be over. In a matter of seconds, he went from shear joy to one of desolation. He also could not face the thought of loosing her or Beth.

She could see how nervous he was and she thought. *He thinks I'm leaving him.*

Before Robert could open his mouth, she said, "Robert I want to stay here with you, I want you, me and Beth to be a family."

Robert said nothing. What she said had not registered. Then a tear came to his eye and he said, "You have no idea how happy you have made me."

"Robert, I've fallen in love with you, but I have to be honest. In some ways I'll always be in love with Gerald. I'm happy we have his daughter here with us."

"I know how much Gerald meant to you. I just want us to be a family. I love you and I want to be with you. I want us to be married."

"Yes, of course, I want to marry you. I'd like to get married as soon as possible right here in Hurley at St. Mary's Church. Father Frank can marry us. It doesn't have to be a big wedding. The question is when."

* * *

Robert and Nancy were married on Sunday January 30, 2011 with only a few close friends present. On their honeymoon, Robert took Nancy to the Super Bowl in Dallas to see his Green Bay Packers beat the Pittsburgh Steelers. It was the same Packers, that he had written off back in December.

CPSIA information can be obtained at www.ICGtesting.com
Printed in the USA
LVOW090024051011

249125LV00001B/9/P